VALERIE MARTIN

the confessions of
Edward Day

Valerie Martin is the author of three collections
of short fiction, most recently *The Unfinished
Novel and Other Stories*, and eight novels, includ-
ing *Trespass*, *Italian Fever*, *The Great Divorce*,
Mary Reilly—winner of the Janet Heidinger
Kafka prize and the subject of a film directed by
Stephen Frears—and the Orange Prize winning
Property. She is also the author of the nonfiction
work *Salvation: Scenes from the Life of St. Francis*.
She resides in upstate New York.

www.valeriemartinonline.com

the confessions of
Edward Day

Also by Valerie Martin

Trespass

The Unfinished Novel and Other Stories

Property

Salvation: Scenes from the Life of St. Francis

Italian Fever

The Great Divorce

Mary Reilly

The Consolation of Nature

A Recent Martyr

Alexandra

Set in Motion

Love

the confessions of
Edward Day

a novel

Valerie Martin

Vintage Contemporaries

Vintage Books

A Division of Random House, Inc.

New York

FIRST VINTAGE CONTEMPORARIES EDITION, JULY 2010

Vintage is a registered trademark and Vintage Contemporaries and colophon are
trademarks of Random House, Inc.

This is a work of fiction. Names, characters, places, and incidents either are the
product of the author's imagination or are used fictitiously. Any resemblance to
actual persons, living or dead, events, or locales is entirely coincidental.

The Library of Congress has cataloged the Nan A. Talese edition as follows:
Martin, Valerie, 1948–
Confessions of Edward Day : a novel / Valerie Martin.—1st ed.
p.   cm.
1. Actors—Fiction. 2. Theater—New York (State)—New York—Fiction.
3. Triangles (Interpersonal relations)—Fiction. 4. Psychological fiction.
I. Title.
PS3563.A7295C64 2009
813'.54—dc22   2008044965

Vintage ISBN: 978-0-307-38920-6

Book design by Donna Sinisgalli

www.vintagebooks.com

Printed in the United States of America
10 9 8 7 6 5 4 3 2 1

For Nan A. Talese

intrepid night swimmer

Our ordinary type of attention is not sufficiently far-reaching to carry out the process of penetrating another person's soul.

—CONSTANTIN STANISLAVSKI

An Actor Prepares

False face must hide what the false heart doth know.

—WILLIAM SHAKESPEARE

Macbeth

the confessions of
Edward Day

Part I

My mother liked to say Freud should have been strangled in his crib. Not that she had ever read one line of the eminent psychoanalyst's writing or knew anything about his life and times. She probably thought he was a German; she might have gotten his actual dates wrong by half a century. She didn't know about the Oedipus complex or the mechanics of repression, but she knew that when children turned out badly, when they were conflicted and miserable and did poorly in school, Freud blamed the mother. This was arrant nonsense, Mother declared. Children turned out the way they turned out and mothers were as surprised as anyone else. Her own child-rearing strategy had been to show no interest at all in how her children turned out, so how could she be held responsible for them?

Proof of Mother's assertions might be found in the relatively normal men her four sons grew to be, not a pervert or a criminal among us, though my oldest brother, Claude, a dentist, has always shown far too much interest in crime fiction of the most violent and degraded sort, and my profession, while honest, is doubtless, in some quarters, suspect. For the other

two, Mother got her doctor and lawyer, the only two profes-
sions her generation ever recommended. My brothers' special-
ties have the additional benefit of being banal: the doctor is a
urologist and the lawyer handles real estate closings.

My mother was a tall, beautiful woman, with dark hair,
fair skin, an elegant long neck, and excellent posture. She was
poorly educated and, as a young mother, intensely practical.
My father had various jobs in the civil service in Stamford;
his moves were sometimes lateral, occasionally up. She hardly
seemed to notice him when we were around, but there must
have been some spark between them. She had her sons in sets,
the first two a year apart, a five-year lapse, and then two more.
I was the last, her last effort—this was understood by all—to
have a girl.

Even if Freud hadn't encouraged me to, I think I would
still have to blame Mother for my craving to be someone else,
and not only because she wasn't satisfied with who I am,
though she wasn't, not from the start. My middle name is
Leslie and that's what I was called at home; I became Edward
when I went away to boarding school in Massachusetts.
Mother had "gender issues," but none of us realized how serious they were until after she died. This mournful event took
place when I was nineteen, a freshman at the University of
North Carolina, and it was preceded by a seismic upheaval that
lasted six months, during which time Mother left my father for
a woman named Helen, who was ten years her junior and bent
on destruction.

Mother wasn't naturally a warm person—I know that
now—and she must have been lonely and frustrated for years,

surrounded from dawn to dark, as she was, by the unlovely spectacle of maleness. A frequent expression upon entering a room in which her sons were engaged in some rude or rowdy masculine behavior was "Why are boys so . . ." As the youngest, I took this to heart and tried to please her, not without some success. I kept my corner of the bedroom spotless, made my bed with the strict hospital corners she used on her own, rinsed my dishes at the sink after the pot roast, meat loaf, or fried chicken dinner, and expressed an interest in being read to. I wasn't picky about the stories, either; tales of girlish heroism were fine with me, hence my acquaintance with the adventures of such heroines as Nancy Drew, the Dana Girls, and all the travails of the shrewdly observant Laura in the Little House books. I know, as few men do, my fairy tales, from Rumpelstiltskin to the Little Goose Girl, stories certainly grisly enough to terrify even a stalwart little boy and which I take to explain the surprisingly violent images that so often surface in the consciousness exercises of young actresses. Mother was a good reader; she changed her voices for the different characters. She had a cackling crone, a booming good fellow, and a frightened little girl in her repertory, and she moved from one to the other with ease. Long after I could read myself, I approached her after dinner with a book clutched to my chest and asked if she "felt like" reading to me. Many times she didn't, and she wasn't terribly nice about refusing me. But when she agreed, I was invited to lean against her on the couch, watch the pages turning beneath her bloodred fingernails, and feel her voice through her arm. She was a smoker, so there was the cloud of smoke wafting up from her lips as

Nancy cautioned her dopey boyfriend Ned not to open the suitcase they'd found in the empty house. It was all very comforting and at the same time confusing, also mysterious and sexually disturbing. But I like to remember Mother that way, and myself, her favorite, her Leslie, the good boy who hung on her words.

When I went off to school and became Edward, I had no clear idea of myself; perhaps that was why I was drawn to acting. Inside a character I knew exactly who I was, the environment was controlled, and no one was going to do anything unexpected. It seemed a way of playing it safe. Of course, real acting is the farthest thing from safe a person can get, but I didn't know that then. Perhaps in some corner of my adolescent consciousness, I understood that my mother would eventually crack under the strain of the role she herself was playing with increasing reluctance and incredulity. On school vacations she and my father were glum and irritable. One night she put a roasted chicken on the table and announced that it was the last meal she was cooking. She joined a reading group, but this quickly bored her and she decided to become a potter. This led to sculpture and ultimately ironwork. On my next vacation there was a welding torch on the kitchen table and all food was takeout. A few days before I graduated from high school my father called me to say Mother was moving out; she would be living with a "friend" named Helen, someone she had met at the artist co-op where Mother had rented a space to do her sculpture.

I saw Mother and Helen together once. They were living in an apartment in Brooklyn, two rooms above an Italian deli, strong odor of provolone and red sauce. Helen spent my visit turning over the pages of a fashion magazine at the kitchen table, occasionally fixing me with a baleful glare. She was clearly, totally nuts. Mother served me coffee and some hard cookies from the deli; she tried to make small talk, asked about my courses, disapproved of my interest in theater, recommended medicine, law, the usual. I told her I was far too squeamish for medicine; I feel faint when I see my own blood, no, seriously faint. This made Mother laugh, which provoked Helen to push back her chair and shout, "I can't stand to see you like this. I hate this part of you," after which she stormed out of the apartment.

"She's so high-strung," Mother assured me after the door stopped reverberating in the ill-fitting frame. "She's just too sensitive to live."

When I returned from this disturbing interview, I found my father meticulously washing out a coffee cup at the kitchen sink. He was stoical—civil service does that for a man—and he was mystified by Mother's abdication of her domestic reign. "So did you see this divine Helen?" he asked.

"Briefly," I said.

He turned to me, swabbing the dishcloth inside the cup. "What did you think?"

"Scary," I said.

He nodded. "I guess your mother really wanted a girl," he said.

I went back to school and after a few months Mother's sudden and bold defection seemed almost bearable. I was absorbed in experiments of my own, concocting an identity from the flimsy material of my considerable naïveté about the world in general and sex in particular. I was smitten by a senior in my theater arts class—I've repressed her name for reasons that will shortly be obvious—but I'll call her Brünnhilde, as she was a shapely Nordic princess with eyes as ice-blue as my own. To my astonishment she indulged my fawning jokes and compliments. Our classmates referred to me as her lapdog, which amused us both, and made for crude punning about laps and lapping, etc. She lived in an apartment off campus with a roommate from New Jersey who occasionally went home on weekends. It was a dumpy two rooms above a garage, but it was the height of sophistication in our set to be invited to Brünnhilde's Friday-afternoon BYOB party. One day in class our professor, doubtless sensing sparks between us, put Brünnhilde and me together for a word exercise, the results of which were so electric the class burst into applause. To my joy, my beauty leaned across her desk, pushing back her wedge of straw-colored hair and said, "Come by on Friday, after five, if you like. It's 58 Gower, in the back."

Who knows what disgusting bottle of wine I brought to this occasion; something I got a friend to purchase as I wasn't of age. Perhaps it was the ditchwater that came in the fish-shaped bottle, or the ghastly Mateus that was the coin of the realm. Or something red, to brighten the vomit that was not an uncommon occurrence late in the evening at the Gower Street gathering. My hostess only smiled and deposited my offering on the card table with the others, introducing me to the assembled guests who were all older than me, though they appeared not to notice. Soon I was ensconced on a lumpy couch, swallowing huge draughts of cheap wine and holding forth on the existential commitment required to bring truth to a theatrical performance. To be, or not to be, it wasn't just the question, it was, in fact, the method. Drivel along those lines.

The company took me up, they praised me, and I was their breathless ingenue. At some point a marijuana pipe appeared, moving steadily from hand to hand, and I had my first taste of that. It grew late, the empty bottles outnumbered the full, and couples began to drift out into the night in search of food or more licentious entertainment. I stayed on, switching to beer which was still in good supply. At last we were alone and Brünnhilde ran her hand along my thigh. "Would you like to see my bedroom?" she asked, serious as a church.

I spent the night there and most of the next day. Late in the afternoon I stumbled back to my dorm room for a change of clothes and more money, my brain grinding with amazement and apprehension. It was paradise in Brünnhilde's bedroom, but I knew I would have to be very alert, very dutiful if I wanted a key to the gates. I scarcely glanced at the message scrawled on a scrap of paper by the phone. *Your mother called, 6 p.m. Your mother again 10:30. Mother again, MIDNIGHT.* So she knew I'd been out late, but would she care? I didn't want to waste time making excuses because I was in a hurry to get to the café near the university where my darling had agreed to meet me. It would be un-loverlike to keep her waiting on what was, after all, our first real date. I would call my mother back at the earliest opportunity.

It was Sunday evening before I got the news and by that time Mother wasn't making any calls. The new message read: *Your father called. Urgent, call at once.* Even this, in my state of elation combined with sexual exhaustion, didn't make me suspicious. "Where have you been?" my father said when he heard my voice.

"Exam tomorrow," I said. "I pulled an all-nighter at the library."

"I want you to sit down, son," he said. "Something terrible has happened."

So I sat down and he told me that my mother and her girlfriend Helen had committed suicide together in the Brooklyn apartment sometime in the early hours of Saturday morning. When Helen failed to turn up at her regular Saturday appointment, her psychiatrist made repeated attempts to reach her self-destructive patient. At last on Sunday morning she called the landlord who let himself in to find his tenants in bed, naked in each other's arms, the empty bottles of Seconal lined up next to two glasses of water on the bedside table.

I wonder now what I said. I remember a torrent of incredulity; for several moments I simply didn't believe my ears. I looked around at the suddenly unfamiliar furniture of my Spartan dorm room and spotted, of course, the scrap of paper with the message that concluded: *Mother again, MIDNIGHT.* The ensuing sob that rose from very deep within me came out as an agonized groan of pain. "Son, do you want me to drive down to get you?" my father said.

"Oh Dad," I wailed. "Oh Dad . . ." But I didn't say, *She called me,* and I never did tell him, or anyone else for that matter. My roommate knew but we were hardly more than acquaintances and he, out of courtesy perhaps, never said anything about the messages. When I got home my brothers were all there and it was clear that she had not tried to call any of them, or my father, either. Just me, the baby, Leslie, who made her laugh with my horror of blood. She'd left a note, addressed to no one, two words: *I'm sorry.*

After the funeral, I returned to school. You can imagine my confusion. I was nineteen, an innocent, and my emotions were in an uproar. I wasn't so naïve as to equate sex with death, though my experience certainly suggested the connection forcefully: have sex, your mother kills herself. Rationally I knew I had nothing to do with Mother's despair, though I couldn't resist speculating about how differently things might have gone if I'd been what Mother wanted: a girl. Would a daughter have walked into the cramped apartment, taken one look at Helen, and said, "No, Mom, you're not doing this"? Worst of all was the second-guessing about the missed calls; if I had been studying in my room like a diligent student, could I have saved her? This question kept me awake at night. For months I woke to a refrain that sent me out of the dorm and into the late-night diners near the campus—*She needed me, I wasn't there.*

Of course word had gotten around that I was a motherless boy, and sympathetic female arms stretched out to me from every direction. I said Mother had died suddenly in her sleep, which satisfied everyone and wasn't entirely a lie. Brünnhilde was suitably tentative when next we met. Though I said nothing about the manner of Mother's death Brünnhilde understood that the proximity of the event to our first coupling might be disturbing to me. I declined the halfhearted invitation to the Friday gatherings and in a few weeks she had a new lapdog, a budding playwright who wrote monologues about his miserable childhood in Trenton, New Jersey.

Gradually the shock wore off and I began to take an interest in my feelings as opposed to simply feeling them nonstop. My acting classes were particularly useful for this. As Stanislavski observed, "In the language of an actor *to know* is synonymous with *to feel.*" My studies offered access to the very knowledge I most required. Many actors are called to their profession by an insatiable craving to be seen, to be admired, and to be famous, but for me acting was an egress from unbearable sorrow and guilt. My emotions at that point were the strongest thing about me; they did battle with one another and I looked on, a helpless bystander. This, I realized, mirrored the position of the audience before the stage. I wanted to find a visceral way to give an audience everything they needed to know about suffering, which is, after all, the subject of most drama, including comedies, hence the expression "I laughed until I cried." I studied my peers and attempted to assess my position among them. Many were drawn to the theater because they possessed such physical beauty that they stood out in a crowd, they looked like actors, but what, I wondered, possessed the overweight girls, the hopelessly nerdy guys who would be doomed by their physiognomy to a lifetime of character parts? One in particular fascinated me, a short, scrawny, colorless boy named Neil Nielson, who cultivated a scanty reddish mustache beneath his pudgy inelegant nose and gazed upon the world through wire-rimmed lenses that magnified his lashless, watery eyes to twice their size. Physically there was nothing appealing about him, but he had a voice that was the envy of us all, as

rich and melodious as a cello. When he laughed, a smile flickered on every face within earshot. Naturally, he was called "the
voice." A future in radio beckoned him, which was too bad because he was a gifted actor. If you saw him sitting at a bar you
wouldn't look twice, but on a stage he had a weirdly erotic
force—he would have made a great Richard III. He was interested in me because girls were, and he hoped to pick up on that
action. I liked his company because he had serious things to say
about acting. His approach was remarkably selfless; he found
his character outside himself. We once did a Pinter scene in a
workshop; I think it was from *Betrayal*. We exchanged roles after a break and did it again. I was astounded by what his interpretation did to my own, it was as if I was being subjected to a
minute and continuous analysis by someone who could see
right into the heart of me, my motivations and anxieties laid
more bare with each exchange. Later I asked him how he did
what he did and he said something I've never forgotten: "I get
myself from what I see you getting about me." It sounds like
nonsense, but I think I understood it. Neil was doomed to
bring out the best in lesser actors and to his credit, he didn't
seem to mind. He played Rosencrantz in the production of
Hamlet that was the triumph of my senior year. We did eight
performances and our brief scene together was different every
night. If there was a scintilla of suspicion in my greeting—*How
dost thou Guildenstern! Ah Rosencrantz!*—he picked it up and
proceeded with utmost caution, but if my manner expressed
pleasure and relief to discover true friends in the prison that
was Denmark, his overconfidence was his death warrant. He
made keen play of his small bit, and as our Polonius was a life-

less drone, my heart lifted when I saw Neil's pointed little beard and glinting glasses enter the pool of light that it was my sovereign right to occupy in the universe of that play.

There was nothing especially intelligent or innovative about my own performance, though everyone, including the local press, praised it as if they'd never seen my equal. My teachers gushed with enthusiasm; my director, a voluptuous graduate student, fell in love with me, and we had a brief affair. I knew I was feeling my way, that my insecurity was part of what made my prince Hamlet so appealing. I was, as he was, a youth, a student, and I had lost a parent in suspicious circumstances. It was during those rehearsals that I first allowed myself the thought that my mother's death was a crime against me, me personally. I could see Helen's angry sneer as she slapped the pages of her magazine against the table while Mother encouraged me to study medicine, and her bitter denouncement of the amity between us rang in my ears. "I hate this part of you." One night I woke from panicked dreams with the idea that I must find Helen and make her pay for what she had done to me. Then, sweating and cursing in my narrow dorm bed, I remembered that she had denied me that option. My lines came to me and I whispered them into the darkness: *That I, the son of a dear father murder'd, Prompted to my revenge by heaven and hell, Must, like a whore, unpack my heart with words, And fall a-cursing, like a very drab.* I wept, not for Hamlet, who lived just long enough to avenge his father's murder, but for myself.

Part II

I'll jump ahead to a sultry morning in July 1974. College was behind me. I was in my tiny Greenwich Village apartment packing my battered suitcase, the same suitcase I took to North Carolina when I was nineteen, the same one I carried when I arrived at Penn Station four years after that, ambitious, confident, and ignorant as a post. I experienced a pang of anxiety as I held up my swimming trunks, worn and venerable as my suitcase and woefully out of style, but there was nothing to be done about them—my ride was arriving within the hour—so I tossed them in with the rest, the T-shirts, the cut-off jeans, my Dopp kit, the gray linen jacket with the Italian label that I'd gotten secondhand, the madras shirt, the oversize belt, the black dress jeans. I snapped the top down and went into the bathroom, where I stood before the mirror, combing my hair.

Stanislavski described such a moment, a man combing his hair before a mirror, as one of perfect naturalness and ease, and therefore poetic; for him it epitomized "truth," which was the condition an actor must discover in performance. He called it "public solitude," the notion being, I supposed, that we are most "ourselves" when we don't have an audience. I smiled at my face in the mirror, recognizing that smile, the one I trusted as no other, which seems odd to me now because at the time I knew nothing about that smiling young man combing his hair; he was as opaque as a clay jug. Soon I would be on the Jersey shore in my outmoded trunks and madras shirt, and with any luck I'd have my arm around the waist of Madeleine Delavergne. Would that waist be bare? Would Madeleine sport a one-piece suit, or a bikini? Was such a thing as a bikini possible on the Jersey shore?

There would be eight of us, all acting students, though we didn't attend the same schools. Madeleine and I were students in Sanford Meisner's professional program at his studio on Fifty-sixth Street, but Teddy Winterbottom, he of the Yale degree and the large Victorian beach house, studied with the great Stella Adler. I had become acquainted with Teddy over a lot of beer at the Cedar Tavern, and though I'd never seen him act, he was a wonderful raconteur and general purveyor of bonhomie. His family was traveling abroad, and we would have the house to ourselves for the holiday weekend. There were, Teddy promised, eight beds, one for each dwarf, and one more for him.

I heard the blare of Teddy's horn from the street and crossed my narrow living room to wave out the open window. He drove an MG convertible; the top was down, so he saw me and waved back. My long legs weren't designed for a sports car; it would be a tedious, hot, uncomfortable drive, but I couldn't have cared less. I snatched my suitcase from the table and, pausing only to turn the dead bolt, rushed down the four dusty flights of stairs into the street. My poetic moment before the mirror left my mind entirely.

As it turned out, the house wasn't on the beach, but it was scarcely a block away. Like its neighbors, it was large, airy, swaddled with deep porches, shingled over, and trimmed with decorative flourishes. Red was the predominating color, the shingles a sun-faded rose, the wide-board floors gleaming cadmium, with touches of red in the furnishings, a pillow here, a slipcover there. Teddy and I spent an hour or so opening windows, plugging in appliances, distributing linens to the various bedrooms and cushions to the wicker couches on the porches. By the time he announced his intention to leave me in charge while he ran out to the grocery for provisions, I was acquainted with the house from cellar to attic. "Put Becky and James in the room with the double bed," he said. "And tell the rest it's first come, first served."

He wasn't gone long when Madeleine and her friend Mindy Banks pulled up at the curb in a rusty Dodge crammed with groceries, suitcases, and a miserable dachshund named Lawrence, who hit the ground with a grunt, trotted to a poor stripling of a tree near the curb, and peed mightily. "I'm with Lawrence," Madeleine exclaimed, bounding past me up the stairs. "Where's the john?"

We had met before, casually, in class and at Jimmy Ray's bar, always in a crowd. Aspiring actresses are often damaged, neurotic girls but Madeleine struck me as unusually stable and confident. She had masses of wavy black hair, pale skin, hazel eyes, full pouting lips, and enviable cheekbones. Her only physical flaw was her hips, which were a little wide.

"There's one just off the upstairs landing," I called after her. "On your left."

"Thanks," she said, not looking back. Lawrence left off the tree and fell to sniffing my pants leg. Mindy came up carrying a grocery bag, which she handed to me. "You're Ed, aren't you?" she said. "We met one time at Teddy's."

By dinner everyone had arrived except Peter Davis, who was bringing a friend no one knew. "Some guy who lives in a rathole in Chelsea," Teddy said. "He's only been in town a few months. He works in the bookstore with Peter, doesn't seem to have any friends or family. Peter said he felt sorry for him, so I said bring him along."

I didn't like the sound of this, especially as we had far too many males in our group already. I was making good headway in my campaign for Madeleine's attention, and I didn't want her distracted. In the afternoon, I'd persuaded her to walk with me on the beach, and I'd served as her sous-chef at dinner. The food was awful, vegetarian fare—this was before the soybean had been tamed, and good bread was only to be had in dreary co-op food stores. Salad was romaine lettuce at best, mesclun was as rare as diamonds, arugula as yet unheard of on our planet. But we had cases of beer and cheap wine, various small stashes of marijuana, and a freezer full of ice cream, so we were enjoying ourselves. As the sun went down, the breeze off the ocean cooled from torrid to sultry and we moved from the dining room to the wide screened-in porch. The talk was all of theater, who was doing what plays where, who had the best deal on head shots, the relative merits of acting teachers and schools, the catch-22 of Actors' Equity, the anxieties, perils, and hilarious adventures of those who had appeared nude on-stage. Madeleine had chosen a wicker chair near mine. On our walk she had told me of her recent breakup with a boyfriend of some duration; they had lived together in an apartment on West Forty-seventh for more than a year. She made light of the matter; the boyfriend was a slob who ate bacon-and-peanut-butter sandwiches and didn't wash the pan, left his clothes on the floor, always managed to leave a smear of toothpaste on the sink drain. The end came when she returned from a weekend visit to her parents in Cleveland to find he'd let the bathtub overflow and the downstairs neighbors had called the landlord because the water was pouring down their kitchen wall. "He was working on his play and he forgot he'd turned on the tap," she said.

"He's a playwright."

"His plays are awful," she said. "He's writing a play about Simón Bolívar, for God's sake."

Madeleine was beautiful, she made me laugh, and she was evidently available: I was rhapsodic. My quandary was how to get her away from the others. The sleeping arrangements weren't ideal, she and Mindy had chosen adjoining rooms, and I wasn't entirely clear about the etiquette of house parties. I didn't want to do anything that would offend Teddy, but fortunately he was absorbed in entertaining Mindy, who had a laugh like a braying mule. She was curvy and blowsy, crude, I thought, and given to bursts of Broadway tunes, as if she saw a producer lurking in the rhododendrons pressing against the screen. Madeleine smiled at me through the wistful refrain of "Send in the Clowns." "I want to swim," she said. "Will you come with me?"

"Of course," I said.

My feelings were mixed. It was a chance to be alone with her in a romantic setting, which was enticing to say the least. The famous still of Deborah Kerr and Burt Lancaster in a clutch on the beach in *From Here to Eternity* flashed before my eyes, but that was in Hawaii and in broad daylight (or was it what is called in film "day for night"?). The waters in Jersey were rumored to contain jellyfish—would they be worse at night? Then there was the matter of the unflattering swimming trunks, and the sad fact that my swimming skills were much inferior to Burt's. But none of this weighed more than a feather in a balance that contained Madeleine in a swimsuit at night on a beach under the moon. "I'll change," she said, leaping up from her chair. "I'll just be a minute." As she passed through the doors to the dining room I noticed a wobble in her step; she pressed her shoulder against the frame and pushed on. Was she drunk? Was I? In answer to the second question I got to my feet. No, I was exhilarated, on the up not the down side of inebriation, and a stroll in the night air might be just the thing. I hastened to my room, changed into a T-shirt and the trunks, grabbed a towel from the stack on the dresser, and went out to the hall, where I found Madeleine floating toward me in a fetching costume, a two-piece suit with a tie-dyed shawl fastened at the waist to make a loose, fluttering skirt. "This is great," she said. "I love swimming at night."

"Me too," I lied. I followed her down the stairs to the front porch where we culled our sandals from the herd along the rail and flapped out to the sidewalk. The voices of our friends drifted to us, punctuated with laughter. The house next door, blazing light from every window, gave off a mouthwatering aroma of grilling meat. Overhead the sky was clear and black; the air vibrated with the salty exhalations of the ocean. "It's nice here," Madeleine said. "I'm glad I came. The city is a furnace."

"I'm glad you came too," I said. We reached the corner, crossed the empty street, and there was the sea, black roiling under black, restless and ceaseless, combing the shore. We clattered down the wooden steps and sloughed off our sandals in the sand. Madeleine untied her skirt, dropping it over the shoes, careless in her excitement. "It's beautiful," she said. "And there's no one here." She rushed away from me to the water's edge. I tossed my towel and shirt on the pile and followed. The half-moon cast a cool light that was reflected from the sand, but the dark waves sucked it up and gave back nothing. Madeleine was already waist deep in the surf, walking steadily away from me. I pounded across the sand and into the water, which was cold against my hot skin, a startling, welcome embrace. She turned to me and, as I drew closer, batted the surface of the water gleefully. "Look," she said. "It's magic."

And it was. Strips of green light darted away from her fingertips like bright snakes, and the harder she slapped the water the more there were. "It's phosphorescence," I said.

"No, no," she protested. "It's magic." Just then the cosmic magician called up a wave, banishing the snakes and tipping Madeleine into my arms. "You're right," I said, pulling her up against my chest. We kissed.

How many kisses do you remember all your life? Four or five, I think, not many. Even at that moment I knew this was one I wouldn't forget, and I was right.

We swam and kissed and swam again, enchanted by the green light attendant on our every movement. Madeleine was at ease in the water and completely fearless, a much better swimmer than I was. She swam underneath me and came up ahead of me. We floated on our backs holding hands, letting the waves carry us to shore. We embraced in the sand, then struck back out in tandem. It was foreplay with ocean, and we extended it as long as we could bear it. We treaded water while kissing, and she wrapped her legs around my waist. At some point her suit top slipped down. To her amusement my erection strained the confines of the trunks. We spoke very little until, at last, by some visceral agreement, we scrambled onto the shore and raced back to the staircase, beneath which we laid out the towel and her skirt, stripped off our minimal coverings, and amid sighs and cries muffled by the steady rumbling of the tide, finished what we had started.

When it was over I rolled off of Madeleine, light-headed, my heart churning in my chest. She chuckled softly and rested her hand on my sandy thigh. "So, you're Edward Day," she said.

"Am I?" I replied. "Are you sure?"

"That's what I've heard," she said. She was feeling about for her suit. "I don't like to think of some of the places I've got sand in," she said. We took one last dip in the surf to rinse off. Then she shook out her wrap and tied it at her waist. I pulled on my T-shirt; we slipped on our sandals and climbed the stairs to the dimly lit street. A car passed; we could hear voices from the balconies facing the shore, but they were soft now; it was late. I took Madeleine's hand as we crossed the street, and she slipped her arm beneath mine, leaning against me. "It's as if we'd been in another world," she said.

"It is," I agreed.

"Will we go there again?"

"God, I hope so," I said.

"At any rate, we'll never forget it."

We had reached Teddy's house. Some of the lights in the upstairs bedrooms were on. A flicker of candlelight and more soft humming of voices came from the side porch, but no one was in the darkened foyer. "Should we join them?" I asked. She pressed her lips together and raised her eyebrows. We said "No" together. "I'm too tired," she added. "I know I'm going to sleep well tonight. There's no exercise like swimming, don't you agree." I laughed. She rose up on her toes to kiss me. "Good night, Edward," she said.

"You can call me Ed," I said.

"I like Edward better." With that she left me, climbing the stairs with one hand on the rail, her shoulders drooping like a weary child. I watched her go up, but, certain I wasn't going to sleep anytime soon, I didn't follow.

I know the cliché. *Post coitum omne animal triste est.* The man rolls over and falls asleep, the woman lies awake wondering why he won't marry her if he hasn't already or if he has, whether she should divorce him. Maybe it was like that for the Romans, but I've never been able to fall asleep after sex. I was elated by our adventure and restless. From the porch I could hear the idle chatter of our friends, doubtless smoking pot and gossiping about Madeleine and me. I heard Teddy's hearty guffaw, joined by a thin, mirthless laugh I didn't recognize; Peter Davis and his luckless friend must have arrived. I was in no mood to meet anyone, especially an actor with a laugh like that. I slipped back onto the front porch, careful to close the screen soundlessly, picked up my sandals and carried them with me to the sidewalk. Madeleine and I had seen a fishing pier on our walk earlier in the day, the entrance flanked by an ice-cream truck and a bike-rental concession. It had been crowded with bathers and children strolling about and shouting for the sheer joy of having escaped the city and arrived at the shore. By now, I thought, it would be quiet and empty; a good place for a late-night stroll and one last colloquy with the sea and stars before attempting sleep in the single bed down the hall from the dreaming Madeleine. Would she dream of me? How would it be in the morning when we met in the kitchen with the others; would she want too much from me by way of acknowledgment, or too little? Would our comrades have marked our absence and tease us, or would they be indifferent, distracted by their own erotic campaigns? Had I seduced Madeleine, or had she taken advantage of me because I was the most attractive, available male? Wasn't there, beneath my enthusiasm and satisfaction about what had happened on the beach, a glimmer of contempt for her? I certainly wanted to have sex with her again, but the desire I felt for her had already lost its edge. A comfortable, familiar smugness took its place. As I walked though the eerily quiet town, with its closed-up shops shedding blobs of unnatural fluorescent light onto the sidewalk, I delved into every nuance of my emotions, ambling about in search of the conjunction between the mental and the physical. An actor's emotions are his textbook. I perceived that my forehead was tight, my upper lip stretched down and pursed slightly over my lower lip. Who am I? I asked. I cast my eyes to the right and left, letting my head follow. I practiced Brando, that slow, overheated appraisal of the scene he's about to disrupt, following his prick, the wolf on the prowl for a mate.

I had reached the street ending at the pier. To my disappointment, a man and a woman lingered near the bike rental, deep in conversation. As I approached, they moved off, not touching, still talking. She walked, like royalty, ahead of him. I slowed my pace, waiting until I couldn't hear their footsteps. When I got to the corner, they were gone.

There was a lamp near the stairs to the pier, but its light didn't reach past the first few planks, and as I stepped outside its influence I had the sensation that the volume on the ocean soundtrack had been turned up. The tide was high; the water broke more forcefully against the lumber of the pier than it had against the shore, with a steady thwack and suck that sounded like slow-motion sex. I thought it might be pleasant to smoke a cigarette—get in on the sucking action. I'd left a pack on the side porch which had promptly become public property and was, by now, surely empty. I thought of my friends—I didn't know any of them well, even Teddy was something of a mystery to me, but our shared passion for the theater, for a life illuminated by floodlights, enacted for the benefit of strangers, made us not a family but a tribe. If we were successful the ordinary world would be closed to us, and if we failed, well, it would still be closed, but in a less agreeable way. So we watched one another, affably enough, to see who would make his way and who fall by the wayside. I had a good feeling about Madeleine; I thought she would succeed, and I knew it was largely this apprehension that made her attractive to me. "Madeleine," I said to the saturated air. I sniffed my fingers, but there was no trace of her; the sea had washed her scent away.

I had come to the end of the pier, high above the swirling waters. It struck me that a fisherman would need a great deal of line just to get his hook down to fish level. The sky was overcast now; the moon obscured by a moving curtain of clouds. *The inconstant moon.* Madeleine would make a stunning Juliet. *O, swear not by the moon, the inconstant moon, that monthly changes in her circled orb.* I blessed Shakespeare, ever apt to the moment, whether it be for passion or reflection, and always sensitive to the bluster the petty human summons against the capricious cruelty of nature's boundless dominion.

Dreaminess settled upon me. The muscles in my shoulders and legs were vibrating from fatigue. It had been a long and eventful day. I stretched my arms over my head—yes, I, too, would sleep well—and brought my elbows to rest on the rail before me. There was a sharp crack; for a nanosecond I believed it was a shot fired behind me and I ducked my head. My elbows were moving forward and down, following the wooden rail as it slid away beneath them. Because I am tall, the lower rail struck just below my knees, serving to shove my feet out from under me. I struggled to wrench my upper body back from the edge but it was futile; gravity had the measure of me, and the only way open was down. I knew this with the physical clarity that short-circuits reason and redirects every atom toward survival. As I fell, I arched away from the pier, seeking to enter the water as far as possible from the great mass of wood that held it aloft. It was a fall into blackness. My eyes were useless, my ears weren't even listening. The distance from the pier to the water was perhaps twenty feet, plenty of time, a lifetime, of falling. My arms stretched before me, my body straightened, approximating the proper diver's position. I tensed for the moment of entry when I would have to hold my breath. Clever calculations filled the time. I should angle in shallowly—the water might not be deep and less of it could be more dangerous than more. If it was deep I could tuck in my head and roll back up, minimizing the risk of colliding with the pier. The tide would carry me in; I need only give in to it. Was one of my sandals still dangling from my toes? At last, WHAM, there it was: an icy clutch, sudden and absolutely silent, as if a bank vault had closed over me.

The water was deep and oddly still. I executed my roll, kicked up to the surface, and took a quick swallow of air before I was clubbed back down by a crashing wave. I came up again, caught my breath, and treading furiously, tried to make out the pier or the light from shore. I couldn't see a thing. Even the green snakes had abandoned me. It was all a swirling darkness above and below. I sensed that the current was behind me and struck out before it, but I had taken only a few strokes when, abruptly, as if I had collided with a truck on some aquatic highway, I was shoved sidelong and swept in the opposite direction. I went back to treading, trying to revolve in place to get my bearings, but no sooner had my feet stretched below my knees then they were swept firmly out from under me and my body, forced to follow, slipped beneath the surface. I fought my way back up and stretched out flat, gobbling air. I was being whisked along with such dispatch I expected momentarily to be slapped into the shallows, but oddly there were no swells. Then, in the near distance, I spotted the white crest of a wave curling elegantly into its trough, a sight that filled me with such wonder and panic that a shout escaped my lips, for just as there could be no doubt that the wave was rolling into shore, it was equally irrefutable that I was being carried with overwhelming force in the opposite direction.

Out to sea. A momentary contemplation of that phrase, of what it encompassed, enormous ships afloat in it, planes flying all night and into the morning to get over it, beneath its surface whales sleeping or singing, and at the end of it, Europe. I was in a vastness in which I had no more significance than an ant, but like an ant, I was programmed to struggle against the forces arrayed against me. I knew which way I didn't want to go, and so I turned into the current and swam against it, summoning every bit of energy and skill I possessed. I didn't pause to check my progress; I just kicked and revolved my arms, turning my head from side to side to suck in air. It was like running up the down escalator, any hesitation could only set me back. The water slipped over and under me, effortlessly pushing and pushing me, but I fought against it with a dreadful, stupid persistence I hadn't known I possessed. My shoulders ached, my legs were losing propulsion, indeed I could hardly feel them. I tried to concentrate on my breathing, to keep it even—in, up, out, down—but I was missing a beat every few strokes, holding my breath in when I should have let it out, which I knew would exhaust me, but I couldn't get on top of it. Start over, I thought, as if I was on a treadmill and could step outside the belt and catch my breath. I lifted my head and my legs sank down beneath me. I could see the dark bulk of the pier jutting out into the waves. It was far away, too far, I thought, and steadily receding. I wouldn't make it, but the sight filled me with hope. Back to relentless swimming. I kicked and stroked, trying to stay as near the surface as I could because I felt less resistance there. But I was still having trouble breathing and the fatigue in my shoulders made it difficult to keep my movements organized. Grim resolve battled with increasing panic. My body was giving out on me, but my only choice was to forge on. I'd lost communication with my legs, my chest was sinking with every stroke, I was swallowing more water than air. I'm not going to make it, I thought. I'm drowning. "Help," I heard myself cry, as my head slipped under the water. I thrashed back up, cried out again, "Help!" A fierce cramp in my right calf muscle sent a shock wave to my brain. I rolled onto my back, clutching my leg with one hand, treading with the free arm and good leg, but of course I sank again. Just kick through the pain, I thought, and I got back up, took a deep breath of air and switched to frog-like pumping of arms and legs, not because I thought it might help but because that was what my body did. I had run out of thoughts; only terror and sadness inhabited me, only emotions. That's what we come down to after all.

I struggled on, but I kept going under, each time a little

longer, each breath of air more shallow than the last. It was silent below, above the only sound was my gasping and my heart pounding in my ears. "Help!" I heard myself cry as I went down and "Help!" again as I battled my way back into the air.

"Be calm," a voice commanded. Was it my own? No, it came to me from out of the air. In the next moment something big, something powerful slammed into my legs and grasped my waist. I kicked to free myself, but it held me fast, swarming up my body, pulling me down. A man's head surfaced close to mine, his arms slipped under my own, holding me close. "Don't fight me," he said.

I clutched his neck. "Save me," I pleaded, clinging to him.

"Don't push me down, you idiot," he said. "You'll drown us both." He grasped my hands and pulled them apart, pushing free of me.

"No," I cried. "Don't leave me."

He caught hold of my shoulder and pulled it, turning me away from him. "Lie on your back," he said. "Make yourself as flat as you can."

"I can't," I said, but I tried, and as my legs came up he brought his arm across my chest and pulled me in so that my head rested against his sternum.

"That's it," he said. "I'll keep your head up. Kick if you can."

"I can," I said and I tried, but my legs were numb. We were moving, however, somehow he was ferrying me through the water, not against the current but across it, so that we were still being carried away from the shore. A peculiar lassitude had taken over my senses, but I made a feeble protest. "Wrong way," I panted.

"Please shut up," he said.

I couldn't catch my breath; it was as if my lungs were frozen. Where was I? Of course, I concluded, this was a dream from which I would straightway awaken. Then I felt something swelling beneath me, lifting me so gently, and my rescuer as well, carrying us up, up, and I saw the stars, a sliver of the moon, and the twinkling of lights from the land toward which we were being forcefully conveyed on the long plume of a wave that, in the next moment, collapsed beneath us, leaving us foundering before the onslaught of the next one. I clung to my companion and held my breath.

When I opened my eyes again I was flat on my back on the sand and a man was kneeling over me, his eyes closed, his lips approaching mine like a lover. I rolled onto my side and coughed up a quantity of phlegm. He got to his feet, straddling me, without comment.

"My God," I said. "What happened?"

"You passed out," he said.

Then I remembered the rail slipping away, my plunge into the waves, the current carrying me against my will. I turned onto my back and gazed up at him. "I was drowning," I said. "You saved my life."

In the dim moonlight I could just make out his face. His dripping hair was dark and long, like mine, his eyes were deep set, heavy lidded, his jaw was strong. He was tall, like me, and handsome, like me. He considered me, still wheezing pitiably at his feet, while the waves pounded in and the moon, obscured by a passing cloud, cast us into darkness. I was conscious of how cold and wet the sand was, and how it gave beneath me, sucking at me, ready to cover me over like the rest of the debris disgorged and deposited on the shore by the ceaseless scouring of the tides. I was sick, weak, and grateful to be alive. My rescuer stepped away from me, addressing the air. "That was quite a performance, Ed," he said.

A deeper chill invaded my spine. Had I heard him correctly? "How do you know my name?" I asked.

"Why shouldn't I?"

I pried myself out of the sand; just sitting required an exertion of energy that alarmed me. Where was my strength? "Because I don't know you," I said.

He smiled at this, a mocking smile that took offense. "You know me, Ed," he said. "I'm Guy Margate."

The name meant nothing to me but there was something familiar about him. I must have met him at some party, or in a bar. "Sorry," I lied. "I didn't recognize you. I'm not myself."

"Are you ever?"

"What?"

"I came out to have a smoke on the pier," he said, "and I heard you screaming."

I staggered to my feet. "You saved my life," I said again. "How can I repay you?"

"Oh," he said. "We'll think of a way."

I dusted the sand off my legs, looking up and down the beach. We weren't far from the pier. A car, creeping along the road, turned in toward the town.

"Can you walk back to Teddy's house?" he asked. "Or should I go get a car and drive you?"

Teddy's house. Of course. "You're Peter Davis's friend," I said. "You came with him."

"That's right. We just got in. You were out with Madeleine."

Madeleine. How long ago, that torrid, sandy coupling with Madeleine beneath the stars? It was all coming back to me now, my life. "I can walk," I said.

There wasn't much in the way of conversation between us on the brief stroll back through the somnolent town. I was too exhausted to make small talk. I took Guy's silence as a form of courtesy, allowing me to recover my bearings as well as my breath. As we turned the last corner, he said, "You don't have any cigarettes, do you? I never did get my smoke."

"I had a pack on the porch, I left them there. They may be gone by now."

"I'll check that out," he said. The house was dark, and for a moment I feared we would have to rouse someone to let us in. I wasn't up to talking about my misadventure. "It's here," Guy said, lifting a potted geranium and extracting a key.

"How did you know it was there?" I asked.

"Teddy told me. How else?" He slipped the key into the lock and pushed the door open, glancing back at me with a look I couldn't read, though it wasn't in any characterization friendly. Without another word, he switched on the hall light and went out to the porch. I dropped the key back under the pot, closed the door, trudged up the stairs to my room, where I peeled off my damp clothes and left them on the floor. Scarcely a minute after I stretched out on the bed, my head cradled in the luxurious down pillow, I was asleep.

When I woke, the sun was blasting through my window and the sound of laughter floated in from the street. As there was no clock in my room, I had no idea what time it was. I indulged myself in the luxury of not having to care. The laughter drifted away; was it our group or another? At length, I sat up and looked around for my suitcase, which gaped open on an old-fashioned ribbon luggage rack near the door. My wadded swim trunks and T-shirt, still damp, gave off a faint scent of brine. The night came back to me, all of it. Madeleine and the magic green snakes, the fall from the pier and the irresistible current, the baffling appearance of Guy Margate, who seemed to know me though I felt more and more certain I'd never seen him before; who claimed he heard me screaming—was I screaming?—and plunged into the ocean to save my life.

I pulled on a clean shirt and shorts and went down the hall to brush my teeth. The house was quiet; most of the bedroom doors stood open. I peeked in at Madeleine's; the bed was neatly made, the suitcase closed, a bottle of water, half empty, and a glass occupied the bedside table. In the bathroom I confronted my reflection. I didn't look good. Nearly drowning had left me pale and drawn. I remembered swimming and then the awful, constant pull of the water, dragging me along until I was too exhausted to resist. I slapped my face with cold water, ran a comb through my hair, and went down the back staircase to the kitchen. Teddy, sitting at the long wooden table perusing the pages of a newspaper, a half-full mug of coffee near to hand, looked up. "Here he is," he said. "The drowned man."

So Guy had told the story. Well, why wouldn't he? "What time is it?" I asked.

"A little after noon."

"Is there any coffee?"

"It's in the carafe by the stove. Mugs on the hooks there. How are you feeling?"

"I've been better."

"Bread by the toaster. Help yourself."

"Thanks," I said. "Where is everyone?"

"They're all at the beach burning themselves to crisps."

"But you didn't go."

"Truth to tell, Edward, I loathe the beach. I never go out there if I can help it, even to chase women, which is the only conceivable reason a person in his right mind would go."

I pulled out a chair and sat across from him. "I think I agree with you."

He folded his paper. "You look like hell."

"Do I?"

"Guy said you were nearly done for."

"Did he tell everyone, or just you?"

"Everyone. At breakfast. The ladies were filled with admiration."

"He's a powerful swimmer," I said.

"Turns out he was a lifeguard, several summers, all through high school. Rescue is one of his fortes."

"Lucky for me."

"Well, if it had been me on the pier you wouldn't be feeling too lucky right now. You wouldn't be feeling anything."

I detected an undertone of accusation in this remark, and it stung me. "No, I know it. I'm grateful, believe me. I'll be in his debt forever."

Teddy got up to refill his cup. "When I think I might have invited you out here and on your first night you drowned. Jesus."

"I don't know what happened. I got caught in some kind of undertow."

"A rip current," Teddy corrected me. "Guy told us all about it. Some people call them riptides, but that's incorrect. They run against the tide and open out in a mushroom shape. If you don't fight them, eventually they thin out and dump you back into the tide. If you get caught in one all you have to do is swim parallel to the shore and you'll get free."

"I didn't know that. All I knew was I couldn't get back."

"The girls were much edified. They all know what to do now, thanks to you."

"Are you mad at me, Teddy?" I said.

"Good God, no." He opened the refrigerator and peered at the contents. "I'm going to scramble eggs. Do you want some eggs?"

"I do," I said. "I'm starving."

"Bless those girls; they don't eat it but they have brought home the bacon."

"I could go for bacon."

Cradling packages of eggs and bacon in one arm, he pulled

down a skillet the size of a garbage-can lid from the constellation of cookware dangling over the stove.

"So what do you think of this—"

"Guy," he said. "It's a problem, the name."

"This guy, Guy," I said.

"I think he bears watching."

"Doesn't immediately bowl you over with confidence?"

"Yet, evidently, he's a lifesaver."

"A lifeguard, at least."

"He looks a lot like you."

"Does he? I thought he did."

"He says he knows you."

"Maybe he does. I mean, obviously he does. But just between you and me, Teddy, I don't remember the guy."

"Guy."

"Right."

Teddy had the burner up and was marshaling his forces in the skillet. "Peter likes him, at least he's sympathetic to him, but not simpatico sympathetic; the other kind."

"What did the girls think of him?"

"That's one of the things that bear watching." We heard voices from the porch, female laughter, high and bright and the screen door creaking on its hinges. "As you're about to find out," Teddy concluded.

Peter Davis came in first, resplendent in paisley swimming trunks, a bright-yellow towel draped around his neck. He greeted me, holding out his hand for a manly shake. "Ed," he said, "really glad you're still with us." Becky and Mindy followed, interrupting their conversation to gush over me. They amused themselves with an exaggerated display of hugs and kisses. "I'm fine," I assured them. "I'm fine." Over their sun-burnished, brine-scented shoulders I saw Madeleine and Guy pause in the doorway to take in the spectacle. Their bodies inclined toward each other. Madeleine's droll expression suggested that Guy had just said something entertaining and he had the smug look of a man relishing his own wit. Was there a joke between them? Was it at my expense? My tongue probed my teeth in a hopeless quest for words. The dithering girls released me and alighted on Teddy, who announced that he was taking orders at the stove. Madeleine approached without speaking. Tenderly, she laid her palm along my check and dropped a chaste kiss on my forehead. "You should have gone to bed when I did," she said softly.

I turned my face into her hand, closing my eyes against the humid web of her fingers and kissing the soft pad at the base of her thumb. It came over me that, along with everything else, I had come close to losing her, and losing her before I could say with any confidence that I had found her. We'd had an intimate yet brief encounter, but now the benignity of her touch, the gentleness of her reproach called up in me an emotion so pure and deep it shook me to my core. As an actor, it is my vocation to reproduce such feelings at will, and in fact that moment has stayed with me all these years, and when I am called upon to find, for the benefit of an audience, the outward expression of inconsolable sadness and loss, I feel my eyes closing and my face turning into the warmth of Madeleine's hand.

It was a public caress, noted without comment by a lively

group intent on pleasure. My desolation was off-key, out of tune, too intense for the company, and I let it go as quickly as it had come. So did Madeleine. Briefly she pressed her palm against my lips, a subtle pressure no one else could see, and then she withdrew her hand and offered her services to the chef, who, having insufficiently separated the bacon strips, was dodging and cursing over a viciously sputtering lump of fat. Wistfully I regarded her back; when would we be alone again, how would we manage it? I sensed a movement behind me, a shadow flickered across Teddy's folded newspaper, the chair across from me gave a muffled shriek as it was dragged back from the table, and Guy Margate dropped into place before me.

I don't deny that, superficially at least, Guy looked a lot like me. We were both tall and lean, our eyes deep set, and our beakish noses jutted from the eyebrow line. We were a type; in a casting call, we were the handsome white guys. But Guy was darker than I, his hair black and straight, his eyes a deep chocolate brown. He could do an Italian, or a Latino, even an Indian at a stretch. My looks are more startling because my hair is wavy and I have light eyes. I can turn the atmosphere on a stage to ice with a sudden glance.

Guy must have envied me my eyes. He had to withhold something to cool things down, something overheated and demonic. Personally I think it's difficult for anyone with brown eyes to do a real chill. Brando could scare the life out of you, but if he turned a cold shoulder it wasn't distance, it was a death warrant, it was violence. His cold shoulder was hot. Pacino does restraint well—same effect—he's just decided not to tear your head off right this second. Jeremy Irons is an exception;

he has brown eyes, but he can do a prodigious chill. That's because he's got Britishness, which is the definition of cool on a stage; also he's slight of build, and he has a quality of longing combined with deep boredom—that's the Britishness again. You know he'd give anything to be human, to have a real feeling, but he's just not going to get there because he's dead, actually, and you forgive him for that. For me, Irons epitomizes what I call "the remove."

So, although Guy was giving me what anybody else would have characterized as a cold look over the kitchen table, my perception was that he didn't do it very well. I could do it better and for a moment I did. I smiled slightly, I allowed my eyes to rest on his face, not meeting his eyes, and I waited for him to speak.

I know what you're thinking—what kind of ingrate is this? Here he's reencountering the man who saved his life not ten hours earlier and all he's thinking about is who's the better actor. Well, perhaps you're right, but remember, Guy Margate had seen me at my most desperate. I had clung to him in panic, lost consciousness from exhaustion and fear; on the shore I had retched into the sand at his feet. Thanks to him it was understood by my friends, and especially by the woman I most desired, that my plight had been largely the result of my ignorance. Any competent swimmer could have saved himself. As every actor knows, emotions succeed each other in sequences that are often inappropriate and counterintuitive—this is what polite society was created to conceal—but one sequence that rarely, if ever, obtains is for humiliation to be followed by gratitude. If politicians could only grasp this simple precept, the world would be a much more peaceful place. I knew by all rights that I should feel grateful to Guy Margate for saving my life, but what I felt was not gratitude. I felt wary of him, but I was prepared to present him with a reasonable facsimile of the proper emotion.

"How are you?" he said at last.

Now how did he say it? That's important. Did warmth and solicitude pour from his eye, did his tone betray more than ordinary interest in the answer to his question? No and no. His interest was distant, his voice flat.

"I'm fine," I said.

"You don't look fine," he observed.

Oh, all right, I thought, all right. "I'm glad to be alive," I said. "Thanks to you."

He smiled. He had long canines and a wolfish grin, very sudden and over before you knew it. "My pleasure," he said.

Then an unpleasant thing happened. Madeleine approached with a mug. As she leaned over his back, the top of her chest pressed into his shoulder. "Here's your coffee," she said, setting the mug before him. He brought his hand up and touched the inside of her elbow. "Thanks, dear," he said.

"You're welcome," Madeleine sweetly replied, turning back to the stove. Guy lifted his eyes to mine, as my heart sank. "She's lovely, isn't she?" he said.

The rest of the weekend was torture to me, though it ended well enough. After lunch everyone but Teddy went back to the beach and I tagged along. It was agreed that I must get back in the water, just as a fallen rider is advised to get back on a horse, no matter how damaged or reluctant he feels or how blatantly vicious and unruly the animal might actually be. I wasn't unwilling; I even felt some crude masculine urge to prove myself, especially to Madeleine, but when I stood on the sand looking out at the fathomless depths, I felt my throat closing around a solid lump of panic. The beach was crowded; all manner of people were thrashing about in the water: oldsters, pubescent girls, pregnant women, children were in it, babies were being dunked in it or toddling about in the shallows. I wanted to cry out, Run for your lives! Swimming struck me as a species of madness; one might as well try to ride a tiger or leap into a vat of poisonous snakes. My friends, unaware of my stark terror, encouraged me, all but Guy Margate, who strode out into the shallows, dived into an incoming wave, and beelined at motorboat speed out past the breakers, where he bobbed like a cork gazing back at the shore. Madeleine and Mindy chortled over his prowess, reminding me, as if I needed reminding, what a bit of luck it was for me that I had managed to nearly drown within range of such a man. Drowning began to look good. I swallowed my fear and walked into the swirling waters, noting that even close to shore you can feel the pull of the tide, its willingness to take you down. Peter Davis caught up with me and we chatted as the sand declined beneath my feet and the water gripped my waist. "How long have you known Guy?" I asked him.

"A few months. He's only been in town since February."

"Where's he from?"

"I don't know. One of those states in the middle. Iowa, Ohio, something like that. Kansas, maybe."

"He didn't learn to swim in Kansas," I said.

"No? Don't they have lakes?"

I shoved off into a wave and Peter followed. It was OK, I could stand it. I wasn't going to drown with this many people around and the ocean was doing a gently pulsing, I'm-not-scary routine, which I now understood to be the equivalent of entrapment. We swam along, parallel to the shore, stopping to tread a bit and look for our crowd. I saw Madeleine swimming out strongly, rising upon a billow and disappearing briefly behind it. She was heading for Guy, who watched her approach, treading so effortlessly that he appeared to be sitting on a chair just beneath the surface of the water. In another moment Madeleine was next to him. They looked like two seals in their element, barking cheerfully at each other.

What if Madeleine had saved me, I thought. She was certainly a strong enough swimmer. Then I would owe my life to her: Would that really be desirable? I could deny her nothing and she might look upon me with pity. At best her feelings would be maternal. No, I wouldn't like that at all. "I'm going in," Peter said.

"I'm with you," I said. It was an easy return; we hadn't gone out very far. My feet found the bottom and I stood up feeling I'd vindicated myself somewhat, at least in my own estimation. Mindy was on a blanket rubbing lotion into her thighs, squinting at the sea. She spotted Peter and me and waved encouragingly.

"Teddy's sick for her," Peter observed. "I don't see it myself."

"She's sweet," I said. We arrived at the blanket and threw

ourselves down on the sand. When we were dry and broiling in the sun, Guy and Madeleine emerged from the sea and ran up the beach to accost us, shaking off water and wringing their hair over us, playful as puppies. Pretending to be excited by the madcap jollity of it all, I caught Madeleine's ankle and pulled her down on the sand. She shouted as I play-bit her calf, but she wouldn't tussle; she was on her feet in an instant, kicking sand in my face. Mindy caught some of it and complained. "It's too hot for that," she said. "Let's get ice cream." Madeleine, playing the petulant child, whined, "Yes, yes, I want ice cream," so there was nothing for it but to pull up the blanket and set off for the ice-cream emporium. Madeleine and Mindy led the way, chattering nonstop while Peter, Guy, and I crowded along behind on the sidewalk. The rest of the day went like that, Mindy and Madeleine were inseparable, as if they'd made a pact, and I wondered if, in fact, they had. At the house Teddy was loading a cooler with beer. We started drinking by four. Becky and James, our resident lovers, smooched in the shadows on a big chaise lounge while the rest of us milled about aimlessly, smoking, drinking, doing shower rotations to cool down. Even on the porch with the ceiling fan running, it was hot. I switched from beer to vodka and cranberry which only made me more irritable. Mindy put on some mix tapes she'd brought with her, one dreadful Broadway show tune after another. No one seemed to mind, even when she joined in on the chorus. Teddy, desperate to separate her from Madeleine, engaged her in a teasing version of "Cabaret," followed by a faux-tango to "Hernando's Hideaway." I took the opportunity to steal Mindy's seat next to Madeleine. Teddy whirled Mindy this way and that, a suave and confident dancer. "Teddy's a revelation," I said to Madeleine. She gave me the blandest of smiles. Guy, watching the show from the dining-room doorway called out "Olé!," his eyebrows lifted and his lips pursed, thwacking his palms together in the approved flamenco style, a parody of the excitable Latino male. Madeleine laughed. Their eyes met across the room; something sly and charged in the exchange put me over the top. "Come dance with me," I commanded Madeleine, grasping her wrist. I lurched to my feet but she resisted, throwing me off balance. I still had my drink in hand and I stumbled a few steps, trying to keep it from spilling over. I heard Guy say, "Oh, señor, be careful." Teddy was twirling Mindy in my direction as she sang the required knock code and password to give at the door of the hideaway. We collided. I poured my drink neatly down the front of her blouse. "Joe!" Mindy exclaimed. The music stopped.

"Well done, Ed," Guy said.

I looked back to see Madeleine frowning at me in a way I didn't like. Mindy, ever good-natured, only laughed. She plucked an ice cube from her bodice. "Very cooling," she observed.

"I'm so sorry, Mindy," I said. "Please forgive me."

"Don't be silly," she said.

I put my arm around her waist and led her toward the kitchen. "Let's clean you up," I said. "Let me help you out of that top."

"Teddy," she cried joyfully. "Ed wants to take off my top."

"That's a job for two men," Teddy said, enfolding her from the other side and we propelled her to the kitchen where we did get her blouse off and made a show of washing it in the sink while she poured herself a glass of wine and stood watching us in her black lace bra. Cleverly Teddy sent me to the basement for some detergent. When I came back, he and Mindy were in a clutch against the refrigerator. I ducked back onto the porch to find only the lovers and Peter Davis, who was playing solitaire at a low table he'd pulled up between his knees.

"Where'd they go?" I asked.

"They went for a walk."

"Damn," I said and Peter chuckled over his cards.

"I'm losing too," he said, "against myself."

I sat on the porch steps looking up and down the sidewalk but there was no one in sight. I was thinking about Guy's Latino impression, which had been so successful with Madeleine, and of how disarming is the ability to make people laugh. It's a gift, mimicry, but it's not acting; in a way it's the opposite of acting, which is why comedians are seldom good actors. There's an element of exaggeration in the imposture; the copy is the original painted with a broad brush and it can be grotesque, even cruel. But no one is offended. People are drawn to the funnyman who can imitate a politician or a famous actor or an ethnic type, especially his own ethnic type.

Guy was an excellent mimic. He could pick up the voice, accent, posture, inflection, facial tics, laugh, walk, and conversational manner of anyone he studied for a few minutes. He had the requisite deadpan, the refusal to enter the joke, but it wasn't willful. He was not one of the clowns derided by Hamlet *that will themselves laugh, to set on some quantity of barren spectators to laugh too.* Though he could mock those who did, Guy simply had no sense of humor. "Barren spectators," I thought. That was good.

So by disdaining a skill I don't possess, I got my mind off my present predicament and made myself feel superior to the competition, a serviceable gambit rendered worthless when at last Guy and Madeleine came into view. They didn't see me and I was free to study their approach. They weren't touching, which was a relief, but they were talking, or rather Madeleine was talking and Guy was listening closely, nodding his head as if he was taking instruction. At last he spoke and Madeleine, glancing ahead, noticed me on the steps. I raised my hand in humble, hopeful greeting. To my relief, she smiled. As they turned up the walk, they fell silent. When she was very close, Madeleine said, "Did you get Mindy's blouse off, Ed?"

"That was just a joke," I said.

"Was it?" she replied. "I wonder why it wasn't funny." She passed me, her flip-flops snapping out a brisk staccato of dismissal, concluding in a sharp rap from the closing screen door. Guy came up the steps and sat down beside me.

"Things aren't going very well for you, are they?" he observed.

"I wouldn't say that," I said. "She's obviously jealous; how bad could that be."

"That's a very positive way of looking at it," he said.

"You'll find I'm a very positive sort of guy, Guy."

"Unfortunately that's not always enough."

I took this cryptic observation as my exit cue and got to my feet, looking down at Guy's bowed head. As if addressing his knees he said, "I find myself in financial straits."

The sagacity of hindsight makes me think I apprehended something ominous in this remark, that it contained an element of moral challenge, one I sensed I might fail to meet. Perhaps I had no such trepidations, but I didn't move away and the air was oddly still, as if listening for my response.

"It's the actor's chronic condition," I offered.

"I thought you might want to help me out." He didn't say the rest of it, but I heard it loud and clear—*because I saved your life.* I heard it and I knew it was true. My life, the air moving in and out of my lungs, the blood coursing through my veins, the thoughts hurtling like traffic in the precincts of my skull, the emotions which at that moment were a rush of contradictory impulses, one of which was resentment, another, the consciousness of boundless obligation, everything I knew and cherished about myself was standing on that porch looking down on the person who, by a selfless effort, had made my standing there, breathing, feeling trapped and resentful, possible. If he had not jumped in to save me, I would have drowned. I couldn't deny it; I owed him my life and my obligation was a bond that must endure between us forever.

But it didn't make me like him. "How much do you need?" I said.

"Fifty bucks would do it for now."

Fifty dollars, at that time, was a fair amount of money. It was half my rent. I had that much in my bank account, but not a lot more.

"I didn't bring my checkbook," I said. "Can you wait until we get back to town?"

"Sure," he said. "Monday?"

"After work. I could meet you at Phebe's. Bowery and Third, you know it?"

"I can find it. What time?"

"Make it seven."

"I'll be there," he said.

Immediately I was annoyed with myself for inviting him to my favorite dive instead of choosing some impersonal, public place like Washington Square. If I just handed him the money and walked away, there could be no assumption of friendly feeling, which it seemed important to keep at a minimum. The hostility between us was not, I was convinced, all coming from me; Guy had been contemptuous of me even when I was drowning. He had called my struggle with death a "performance." Obviously shame was a large component of my feeling about the entire episode; if I could have arranged never to see his face again—with no harm to either of us—I would have done it. At the moment, all I could do was continue on my course back into Teddy's house. I went up the stairs, closed the door of my bedroom, and stretched out on the bed. I didn't want to talk to anyone.

However, as there's no such thing as a reclusive actor, after a brief nap, I rejoined the party on the porch. The men were playing cards and the women were in the kitchen torturing vegetables and the dreaded tofu into a casserole. There was no pairing off and no music, just general bonhomie until after dinner when we heard the band strike up "The Star-Spangled Banner" in the bandstand at the nearby park where, Teddy told us, there would soon be an impressive fireworks display, well worth "toddling over" to see. Off we went.

It was too American for words, this Jersey shore. The grilling hot dogs, the ice-cream cart, the stand purveying that strangest of all confections, cotton candy; gossiping oldsters, darting children, a bevy of sweating young parents dancing under the cover of an open tent near the bandstand—the scene was so innocent and good-natured it warmed my anxious heart. I sidled up to Madeleine, who, with Peter Davis, was admiring the singer, a middle-aged Mafioso with a voice as smooth as olive oil. With mock politesse, I asked if she would give me the honor of a dance.

It worked; she smiled, held out her hand, and in a few moments she was in my arms under the tent. I swelled with confidence. I'm an excellent dancer and, it turned out, so was she. We whipped through a brisk number and then I held her close as the band segued into a surprisingly soulful, languid arrangement of "Blue Moon." She rested her cheek against my chest, her hips brushed my own, but I was careful not to introduce into this public embrace anything resembling erotic play. She'd surprised me with her reaction to the admittedly poor joke I'd made at Mindy's expense, showing me a prudishness and respect for the proprieties that was unusual in young women of my acquaintance and completely at odds with her frankly provocative behavior on the beach the night before. She was complicated, and I liked her better for that. When the crooner hit the line "Please adore me," I whispered the words into her ear. She chuckled, looking up at me. "This is nice," she said.

"It is," I agreed. "Let's dance all night."

And we did. When the music stopped and the dancers abandoned the tent for the lawn where the fireworks were about to begin, we ambled over to our group arm in arm. Teddy and Mindy, kneeling on a blanket, handed out beers from the cooler. It was a clear, hot night, the sky a perfect blue-black canvas for a pyrotechnic display. Without warning the first volley sent a white streak heavenward and all were riveted by a fountain of sparkling diamonds raining harmlessly down upon us. Madeleine stood in front of me, her head resting against my chest. "Oh look," she said as a diaphanous red flower blossomed overhead. The booms of the rockets crackled in the air and the displays grew more complex. I slipped my arms around her waist and joined in the soft exclamations of the crowd. A collective "Aaaah!" greeted a spectacular burst made of bright ribbons, red, white, and blue, of course, which exploded into half a dozen concentric rings inside of which more ribbons shot up to another level of shimmering rings. Everyone knew the end was near. The pauses between explosions extended, giving the designers time to coordinate their missiles. It's like sex, I thought, glancing about me at the raised faces, all bright with expectancy. The air over the firing station was flushed with hellish red smoke. I could hear the ratcheting of the machinery and the boom and hiss of multiple shots as a dozen streamers rippled past. Not far off, literally by the light of the rocket's red glare, I spotted the only spectator besides myself who wasn't closely attending the grand finale. He was standing apart from the crowd, his gaze fixed purposefully on me, and I had the sense that he had been watching me for some time. Our eyes met and I lifted my hand in a diffident salute, but Guy made no gesture in response. Then, just to unsettle him, I nuzzled Madeleine's neck with my lips, tightening my grip on her waist. "Oh, look," she said again, softly. The sky seemed to be raining stars into a tide of blood steadily rising to meet it. I looked back at Guy, who hadn't moved a muscle. There's something wrong with him, I thought, but I got no further than that, for the show was over, and Madeleine, who had turned in my arms, brought her lips to mine.

Phebe's is spiffed up these days, and surrounded by other buildings, but in the '70s it was a glittering oasis in the desert of the Bowery, the haunt of panhandlers, drug dealers, and actors. At Phebe's the beer was cheap, the food wouldn't kill you, and the proprietor was actor-friendly. I went there two or three nights a week. Sometimes Teddy came with me, but he preferred the more literary scene at the Cedar which was closer to Fifth Avenue and the world of his heritage.

I'd never seen Madeleine at Phebe's, but that Monday night when I went to meet Guy and give him the fifty dollars in exchange for my life, there she was at a corner table, dragging fried potatoes through a pool of ketchup and biting off the bloody-looking ends, while Mindy rattled on across from her. They spotted me and beckoned me to join them, but their table was a two-top and pulling up a chair would have put me in the aisle to the peril of the waitress. "Thanks," I said. "Thanks, but I'm meeting someone." Madeleine swallowed more potato, somehow managing to smile around it.

We had returned to the city separately with no particular understanding, but I had her phone number and had promised to call, which I had every intention of doing. I wanted to get the Guy matter over with first. I could tell by her smile that she assumed the someone I was meeting was another woman and that, should this prove the case, she would affect indifference. Mindy had some gossip about an actor who'd been sacked at the behest of the leading lady, who said she couldn't stand kissing him, and we laughed over that, though actually it wasn't funny. The power struggles that go on backstage can be brutal and destructive, and I couldn't help imagining how I would feel if something like this happened to me, which naturally led to some thoughts about the quality of my kissing. "Couldn't they just get the poor guy a kissing coach?" I suggested and got not only the laugh I was after but an unexpected and deeply reassuring compliment from Madeleine, who said, "You could hire yourself out for that."

"Do you think so?" I said lightly, disguising the deep seriousness I felt about her answer. Mindy was silent, looking from one of us to the other, her eyes dancing with amusement.

"Oh yes," Madeleine said. "And I'm a good judge of that. I've had a wide experience."

"I'll bet you have," I said.

She took up another potato and wagged it at me. "On the stage of course," she said.

"That's the only place it really matters," Mindy added.

We all laughed at this and then Madeleine announced much too cheerfully, "Look, it's Guy Margate."

"He's coming to meet me," I said.

He passed inside and stood near the door, surveying the room critically.

"Excuse me," I said to the girls, leaving them to cut him off at the bar. The last thing I wanted was witnesses to the money exchange. When he saw me, his expression changed only slightly. Fortunately the room was crowded and we were forced to take a seat at the bar.

"So how are you?" I said after we'd ordered our beers.

"Pretty good," he said. "I have a callback. I just found out."

"That's fantastic," I said. "That's something to celebrate. Where is it?"

"Playwrights Horizons."

Playwrights Horizons was an impressive venue for a callback. It was an Equity house, they did new edgy plays, the directors were generally up and coming, and they got reviews. But, I reminded myself, a callback wasn't a part. "That's great," I said. "Good luck."

"I think I've got the job," he said. "The director really liked me."

This was an incredibly foolhardy and naïve thing for an actor to say, a certain jinx on his chances, and I marveled that he didn't seem to know it. But I wasn't going to set him straight. "That's great," I said again. He was looking around, ready to change the subject. "This is a nice place," he said.

"It is. I come here a lot."

He studied the brick wall behind the bar. "Do you have the money?" he asked.

I dug the carefully folded bills from my back pocket.

"Sure," I said, handing them over. He took the money, counted the bills, and stuffed them into his jeans pocket. "This is an actors' hangout," he observed.

No word of thanks, no acknowledgment of any kind, surely the proper reception of repayment by the debtor. Why would you thank someone for that which is owed? It wouldn't make sense. Do bankers thank you when you pay exorbitant interest on a loan? Does city hall send a thank-you note when you pay a parking fine? "Where do you live, Guy?" I said, hunkering down over my beer.

"Chelsea," he said. "Great, Madeleine and Mindy are here." I looked up and there they were, moving through the tables to the bar.

"What a surprise," I said.

"Hey, Guy," Madeleine said as she sidled between us. "I've never seen you here before."

"That's because I didn't know you came here," he said.

Not bad. Not exactly wit, but quick. Madeleine's eyes softened as they do when she receives compliments. It's hard to tell if she's taken in or just letting the moment pass. "Have a drink with us," I said. Guy was already pulling up a stray barstool and in a moment the girls were perched between us. Madeleine chose the seat next to Guy, which I took to be bad news. The bartender plunked down the glasses of red wine they requested. Guy announced that he had a callback, which focused the attention of the women nicely. They wanted to know all about it. This time, playing to his audience, he was self-deprecating—it was a small part, he probably wouldn't get it. The women affirmed that auditions were hell, rejection was more likely than not, and a callback meant you were doing something right. Mindy had heard of the playwright, an Italian from Brooklyn, he'd had a play at Yale Rep a year ago that did pretty well; she couldn't remember the title. The talk turned to other plays; who was casting what and where. We were all non-Equity at that point, so we had the option to work for little or no money. If Guy got this job he would be able to join the union and be guaranteed a minimum wage. The old chestnut "Get your Equity card and never work again" was passed around, though we all knew it was just a variety of sour grapes. Madeleine had already applied for the group auditions in April, a cattle call for summer stock companies. It was a good way to get into the union as well as spend the hot months out of town. Guy hadn't heard of this and vowed to do the same. I had a vision of Guy and Madeleine sporting on a green lawn in Vermont or the Berkshires next summer, which sickened me. "You're quiet, Ed," Madeleine said. "Are you OK?"

"I'm depressed," I said. "I'm working double shifts three days this week." This was true. I'd agreed to work overtime because I needed money to pay Guy and my rent. The worst part was, by Friday I would be exhausted and broke, so I couldn't invite Madeleine to dinner or a movie. Guy shot me a chilly look and said something to her I couldn't hear. She turned away to answer him, effectively closing me out. Mindy finished her wine and set the glass on the bar, slipping two one-dollar bills under the base. "I've got to meet Teddy at La MaMa," she said. "He's got tickets for a new show." As she kissed my cheek and slid from her barstool, a flush of fragrance rose from her bosom, baby powder mixed with sweat, not unpleasant but not enticing, either. I pictured Mindy après shower, dowsing her breasts with baby powder while she sang "Don't Rain on My Parade" at full blast. "Take it easy," she said kindly. "Don't work so hard."

"Right," I said. "Tell Teddy I'll call him." I watched as Madeleine and Mindy hugged and cooed. Guy accepted the same cheek busses I'd received. As Mindy flounced out the door, Madeleine and Guy went back to their conversation. For what seemed like a long time I sat drinking my beer and admiring Madeleine's back. What were they talking about? I found Guy's conversational mode peculiarly deadening, but Madeleine seemed both engaged and amused; her soft laughter rustled her shoulders and she nodded her head now and then in agreement or approval. I could see Guy's lips moving, his dark eyes fixed on her face with a sinister, distant interest. Now and then his sudden grin flashed; something unnerving about it, I thought, something menacing. Christopher Walken had a similar death's-head grin. I'd seen him in *Caligula* at Yale. It was amusement provoked by the apprehension of weakness, and I didn't like to see it leveled at the unsuspecting Madeleine. I shifted to Mindy's stool and leaned into the bar. "That's hysterical," Madeleine was saying.

"What is?" I asked.

She turned her bright eyes upon me. "Have you heard this? They're rehearsing a musical of *Gone With the Wind* in Los Angeles. Guess who's playing Scarlett?"

"Julie Andrews," I suggested.

"Lesley Ann Warren!" she exclaimed.

"Not far off," I said.

"And guess who's playing Rhett?"

Because I had been thinking of him, I said, "Christopher Walken."

"No, he would be good, actually. It's Pernell Roberts."

"Who's he?"

"Bonanza," Guy said. "Adam."

"The strong, silent one," Madeleine added.

"Good God," I said.

"Tell him about the songs," Madeleine insisted.

Guy nodded. "There's one called 'Tomorrow's Another Day,' and 'Why Did They Die,' and 'Atlanta Burning.' " This really did make me laugh.

"It's a huge cast," Madeleine said. "More than fifty parts."

"How do you know about this?" I asked Guy.

"I have a cousin who's in it. He plays one of the Tarleton twins."

"Is that where you're from?" I asked, though I knew he wasn't.

"No," Guy said. "I've never been to L.A. Have you?"

"No," I said.

"Do you want to go?"

"No," I said. And then we talked about L.A. and how different film acting was from stage acting and how little work there was in New York, unless you happened to be British or Italian. It was banal conversation and Guy held up his end well enough, though, as we were both entirely focused on Madeleine, there was a competitive edge to it. Then, abruptly, Guy stretched his wrist out to check his watch and pretended surprise. "Gotta run," he said, kissing Madeleine on the cheek. "Friday, six thirty."

"See you there," she replied.

He turned to me extending his hand for a gentleman's parting. "Ed," he said. "Good seeing you. Get my beer for me, would you?"

"Sure," I said. "Why not?" Madeleine smiled upon us, pleased to see this amiable exchange between friends. When he was gone I pulled my stool closer to Madeleine and said, "Friday? Six thirty?"

"He's got tickets to *Jacques Brel.*"

I snorted. "That old rag?"

She regarded me coldly. "Don't be ridiculous. Jacques Brel is great. I've been wanting to see it." She finished her wine while I pictured the inside of my wallet. What a jerk Guy was to take my hard-earned money and then stick me for the price of a beer, especially since he was flush enough to buy tickets to a popular musical revue. My chance with Madeleine was at hand and I determined to take it. I signaled the bartender to refill her glass and when she demurred I insisted. "On me, please. I haven't had a minute alone with you since—"

"We went night swimming," she finished.

"Yes," I said. "You were right. That night was definitely magic."

"It was," she agreed. The bartender set a full glass before her.

Two hours later we were hand in hand, climbing the narrow stairs to my apartment, pausing on each landing for long embraces. The next morning when I opened my eyes to find her arm draped around my waist, her soft breath oscillating against the nape of my neck, I sighed with satisfaction. Guy could have the money. I'd beat him to Madeleine a second time.

Like most actors I worked for tips in restaurants that I couldn't afford to eat in. Three days a week I did the lunch shift at Bloomingdale's, where stylish ladies who had just maxed out their husbands' credit cards picked at cold chicken salad and vowed to economize, beginning with the tip. On Thursday and Friday nights I served dinners to artists and gallery owners at a trendy bar and restaurant in SoHo, which was a good gig because artists have often worked as waiters themselves, so they're sympathetic; also, not being good at math, they tend to round up the percentage. This gave me Monday and Wednesday nights free for my classes with Sandy, Thursday and Friday all day to pursue auditions. Doubling up meant losing audition time as well as Saturday night. So I spent the week resenting Guy Margate, though I was perfectly conscious that if not for him I wouldn't be working at all, I would be a waterlogged corpse tossed up after a thorough pounding on some rocky beach in New Jersey. Friday night I had the additional pleasure of imagining Guy and Madeleine out on the town on the money I was working my ass off to replace. It was midnight on Saturday when I hung up my apron and counted my take, which was unusually good. I decided a nightcap at Phebe's was in order and set out across the cultural divide of Houston Street with a firm resolution: no beer, straight whiskey.

The traffic was light, only the occasional yellow flurry of cabs and a few delivery trucks. The streetlamps hissed and buzzed overhead, shedding a blue metallic light. Phebe's glowed like a golden spaceship dropped down in a grim future world; the sound of voices and music ebbing and flowing as the doors opened to exiting aliens. As I crossed Third Avenue, a panhandler appeared from the shadows and planted himself on the sidewalk so that I couldn't pass without getting his pitch. He was a gray, wizened fellow, with hair like a mudpack, wrapped in a combination of blanket and plastic sheeting that served as both his attire and his lodging. "Jesus," I said, as he stuck out his grimy hand. "Aren't you hot?"

"Any spare change?" he said. His voice was lifeless, but his eyes were black and keen. I dug into my pants pocket; I actually had a lot of change, and extracted a couple of quarters and a dime. "You need to work on your patter," I advised him.

"Fuck you," he said. I dropped the coins into his palm and pressed past him. Actors are superstitious about beggars, perhaps because we're largely in the same line. They know this and make a point of hanging around stage doors, particularly on Broadway. Long-running shows have regulars, who call the stars by their first names. "Dick, the reviewers are in tonight." "Shirley, look at you, you're drop-dead gorgeous as always." So I didn't relish being cursed by a panhandler. He stepped back into the darkness from whence he came and I pushed on to Phebe's, feeling tentative and anxious. The bar was packed, with some overflow to the tables, and the two bartenders were constantly moving with the speed and agility of jugglers. I spotted Teddy at the far end, looking glum, his chin resting in his hand, his eyes fixed on the glass in front of him as if he saw something alive inside it. I squeezed in beside him and said, "What's wrong with that drink?"

He looked up, smiling wistfully. "I fear it is empty."

"We'll take care of that," I said. "Let's go sit at a table." I signaled the bartender, pointing at Teddy's glass, raised two fingers, and received a terse nod; he was on the case.

"Are you drunk, Teddy?" I asked.

"I have no way of knowing."

"Well, how many drinks have you had?"

He glanced at the wall clock. "About two hours' worth."

Two full glasses appeared and I lifted them carefully. Teddy got down from the stool and followed me to the table. "Well done," he said. "I'm glad to see you. Where have you been all week?"

"Working," I said. "I've been killing myself working."

"Why would you do that?"

"I need the money."

"Oh yes, they pay you." Teddy sipped his drink, opening his eyes wide. He had an actor's face, full of expression, long, pale, freckled, a weary drooping mouth, an aristocratic nose, pinched at the nostrils, hazel eyes rather round and flat, and a nimbus of curly red hair. He was slender, lithe, and quick on his feet, not handsome but appealing and wry. I knew a bit about his family—his banker father who wasn't pleased about the acting ambition; his dramatic alcoholic mother (at the beach house there was a painting of her, an English beauty with skin like a blushing rose); his ne'er-do-well older brother, Robert, who befriended thugs and gambled on anything that moved; and his talented younger sister, Moira, who was studying painting in London. He'd been to prep schools and then Yale Drama, his path strewn with privilege at every turning, but he was no dilettante. Money got him to the stage door, but only talent and dedication could get him onstage and he knew it. I sipped my whiskey, which was both smooth and potent, some brand known to the Ivy League and doubtless twice the price of the bar brand, but I didn't care. I was in a funk about the whole business with Guy and I weighed the option of consulting with Teddy. As if he read my mind he announced, "Guy Margate got a job."

This news hit me like a blow and I dropped back in my chair, struggling to accommodate it and to take account of my emotions. There was a strong element of surprise—I hadn't thought he would get the part—and a fair component of jealousy, mixed with deep resentment. Teddy watched me attentively, his chin resting in his hand, his eyebrows lifted. "How do you know this?" I said.

"Mindy had it from Madeleine. Big celebration last night."

"Mindy was there?"

"No, Madeleine called her and she called me. The celebration was just Madeleine and Guy; they had a date."

"Right," I said.

"It's Playwrights Horizons."

"Right," I said again. "Equity. What's the play?"

"*Sunburn* I think it's called. Or maybe *Sunstroke. Sunburst.*

It takes place on a beach. It's written by an Italian I never heard of."

"Guy plays an Italian."

"Presumably."

I reached for the whiskey and swallowed a big gulp.

"It will keep him busy," Teddy observed.

"That's true. And I won't have to give him more money."

"You gave him money?"

"Fifty bucks. He pretty much demanded it. That's why I had to work so much this week, but I've made it up and first thing tomorrow I'm calling Madeleine."

"That's the spirit," Teddy said. We drank in silence for a few moments. The bar was emptying out. "It'll probably flop," Teddy added.

"That's true. And it will keep him off the streets for a couple of weeks at least."

"Also true." We snickered companionably, but the likelihood that the play would fail was cold comfort against the dismal fact that stood before us: Guy Margate had a part and we did not.

When an actor has a part, he has a life, and a full one. When he doesn't have a part, his life is looking for one. Parts are few, the competition is stiff, and even if one succeeds in being hired there are still a variety of avenues that lead directly to failure. The backers can go broke before a play goes into rehearsal; the play can close after a tryout; the director may be incompetent, lack nerve, or just lose control (as evidently happened in the profitable but unnerving production of *Hamlet* in which Richard Burton, directed by John Gielgud, delivered a mind-numbing impersonation of Burton saying Shakespeare's lines very fast); the play can be difficult, unwieldy, or just banal; the actors may be miscast; illness, divorce, or lawsuits may hamstring the production; critics may hate the play and say so; audiences may fail to show up.

Or the leading lady may go mad onstage.

But without a part, an actor can't even fail, so when a play is cast the thespian community recoils and regroups, simultaneously discouraged and reinvigorated, for if that miserable actor Joe Blow can land a juicy part, anything is possible.

I'd been in the city a year and had appeared in two productions, one an Equity-waiver workshop at the Wooster Open Space and one a two-week run of one acts at a tiny theater in the West Village. The plays were new and forgettable and my parts were negligible, though I did have a nice bit of comic business in the one act, in which I got tangled up in my trousers while trying to seduce my female employer. I went to my classes, gossiped at the right bars, circled the roles I thought might be suitable in the casting-call pages of *Back Stage* and *Show Business,* and lined up at the doors with the rest of the cattle, but I wasn't getting anywhere and I knew it. The news that Guy, an obscure bookstore clerk, new to the scene and not connected to any school that I knew of, had a part in an Equity production was like an injection of iron into my resolve.

On Monday, I went to class with an edge of self-loathing that felt new and dangerous to me. Madeleine was eager to tell me about Guy's success, but I shut her down with a grimace.

"Teddy told me," I said. She studied me a moment, her head cocked to one side, thoughtful, interested, the way adults look at a child who has revealed in some completely transparent and inappropriate fashion that he is in pain.

"Look," I said, "I'm wondering if I'm just lazy, if I'm not hungry enough, if I'm just kidding myself."

"This amazes me," she said.

"I don't lack confidence; I know I'm good, but maybe I'm too comfortable hanging out at Phebe's pretending to be an actor."

She nodded. "I've been having the same thoughts all day. It's eerie." Our eyes met and held. I think some elemental bond was struck in that look, a passion to further each other's interests.

"What should we do?" I asked.

"After class, we'll talk," she said, for the inimitable Sandy Meisner had arrived, his ogling eyes behind the thick spectacles that allowed him to see, to which was attached the microphone that allowed him to speak, sweeping the room for the girl with the most revealing top.

We went to the Cedar because it was quiet, and over beers and fries worked out our plan. We would take time off work as much as possible for three weeks and concentrate on nothing but the pursuit of parts. We would try out for everything, suitable or not, wild stretches and stuff we thought beneath us, even musical revues. We would drop our head shots off at agencies, take our meals at diners, prepare our pieces at night in my apartment. We would be relentless, we would urge each other to the limit, we would succeed.

And we did. In two weeks I had two callbacks and Madeleine had three. We stayed up late refining our readings, drinking coffee until we were revved past endurance. Then we got into my bed and blasted ourselves into oblivion with athletic sex. It was great. I felt sleek, powerful, cagey; in the mirror I detected yon Cassius's lean and hungry look. Madeleine was glowing from all the sex and edgy from lack of sleep. She was living on fruit and coffee. One of her callbacks, an enormous long shot we'd chosen because she was so definitely right for it, was for the role of Maggie in a revival of *Cat on a Hot Tin Roof*. She wanted it almost beyond endurance. The call had sent her dancing around the apartment, over the couch, knocking down chairs. "I'm Maggie," she crooned. "They know it, they know it, I'm Maggie." But they didn't know it and she didn't get the part. When the call came, she broke down and wept. She was hysterical actually; I couldn't get near her. She lay on the bathroom floor kicking her feet and pounding her fists against the tiles. Then she got up and vomited into the toilet. It was pure nerves and rage. I got her cleaned up and tucked into bed where she cried herself to sleep. In the morning she was pale and haggard, but she took a shower, disguised the dark circles under her eyes with makeup, drank two cups of black coffee, and set out for another day of rejection. She came back with a callback for a new play at the Bijou and a week later she got the part.

I'd been striking out all over town and my last shot was a new play about criminal activity in a bakery. I had a scene for the callback and Madeleine and I worked it over so scrupulously that I didn't need the book. When the audition was over the stage manager reading with me looked like he'd run into a train. The director stood up and shouted, "That does it." I had the part.

Naturally Madeleine and I wanted to celebrate. I called Teddy, got his machine, and we shouted "WE HAVE JOBS!" into the receiver. Within the hour Teddy called back, as excited as we were. "No burgers tonight," he said. "Meet me at Broome Street. Dinner's on the pater."

Teddy had an evolving theory about the importance of actors in the survival of the human species. At Yale he'd been in a play about Charles Darwin, with the result that he had actually read *On the Origin of the Species,* which inspired in him an informed but idiosyncratic respect for the theory of evolution. Actors, he maintained, are imposters and imposture is an evolutionary strategy for survival. He described the butterfly whose wings so resemble a leaf that even water spots and fungal dots are mimicked, a perfect imitation of random imperfection. All manner of camouflage delighted him, the lizard who turns from bright green to dull brown as he wanders his varied terrain, the deer on his father's land in Connecticut, coppery red in the coppery fall and drab gray in the winter, when the world is monotone and dull. The actor, Teddy concluded, is selected for survival, like the white moths in a British mining town which, as the coal dust blackened the local birches, mutated to black. Predatory birds couldn't see the black mutants so only blackened moths survived to reproduce themselves.

Because humans have only other humans as natural predators, and are, by nature, tribal and territorial, what could be more essential to the flourishing of one's genetic material than the ability to pass for the prevailing type, to play before the fascist, another fascist; to offer the drug-crazed, gun-wielding holdup artist a fellow in addiction. In their predilection for imposture, their insistence upon the necessity of a counterworld in which they play all parts, banker and pauper, murderer and victim, man and beast, actors are equipped for survival. They are human chameleons, born with a natural ability to take on the coloration of the psychological and physical environment. And, according to Teddy, it is this evolutionary edge that accounts for the paradox of the actor's social condition. He is both lavishly admired and eternally suspect. Actors make ordinary people uncomfortable, yet they inspire reverence and awe.

It was nonsense, but entertaining, and Madeleine hadn't heard it before, so we encouraged Teddy, over glasses of white wine and plates of grilled fish, to expand upon the struggle for existence and our part in it.

"So according to your theory," Madeleine observed, "actors are born not made."

"Exactly," Teddy agreed. "There's got to be something genetic going on. I mean, what is the attraction of a life in the theater? It's certainly not the money. Yet look how many there are in every generation who are drawn to it."

"I thought it was something to do with exhibitionism," I put in.

"The common error," Teddy said.

"But I don't want to blend in," Madeleine protested. "I want to stand out."

"Of course," Teddy said. "You want to be recognized as Madeleine Delavergne, the actress who can play all parts, from ten to ninety, male or female, aristocrat, cutthroat or tramp."

As Teddy ticked off this list, Madeleine made small adjustments in her expression and posture, her spine straightening at "aristocrat," her eyes and lips narrow at "cutthroat," her mouth ajar and eyes sultry at "tramp."

"She's good," I said and we laughed.

"Now if you want to see an actor who only wants to be seen," Teddy said, "check out Guy Margate in that Italian thing. I saw it last night."

I hadn't thought of Guy in weeks and I found I didn't want to think about him. "Has that opened already?" I said. "I've lost track of time."

"Is it any good?" Madeleine asked.

"It opened last night and no, the play's not good, though I've seen worse. Guy has a lot of lines and he's in the altogether for the whole last scene, so it feels like there's more of him than anyone else."

"He's naked?" Madeleine's eyes were wide.

"Starkers," Teddy said. "He has a towel around his neck and I kept thinking he was going to wrap it around, you know, but he never did."

"This I've got to see," Madeleine was giggling like a teenager.

"Haven't you already seen it?" I snapped.

"Darling, you don't have to answer that question," Teddy said, and Madeleine, frowning, replied, "Believe me, I'm not going to touch it."

"See that you don't," I said.

"Children, children," Teddy chuckled. "Play nicely."

I had no intention of going to see Guy's play, but the next day he called Madeleine's machine to tell us he had left two comp tickets in her name at the box office and Madeleine insisted it would be rude not to go. "Why us," I complained. "Are we the closest thing he has to friends?" To which she replied, "I don't understand this antipathy you have for Guy. After all—"

"He saved my life," I finished for her.

"Well, yes, Edward," she said. "He did."

I can hardly remember what the play was about. An Italian family, all staying at a beach house. Two brothers, one girl. Something like that. Or maybe it was a brother and sister, and the brother's friend. The older generation included a doddering grandfather. Generational conflict, the changing world, expectations too high or not high enough.

As Teddy promised, Guy had a lot of lines and in the last scene he appeared naked, save a thin towel across his shoulders which he used to pop someone, his brother or his friend, or maybe it was his father, someone who was shocked to find his friend/brother/son naked in the kitchen at nine o'clock on a Sunday morning. Guy had a nice monologue near the end, to the effect that his family was smothering him and he didn't know what to do with his life, which he delivered while holding a glass of milk.

I watched halfheartedly, one eye on the stage, the other on Madeleine, who appeared to be enjoying it much more than I was. She laughed at all the lame jokes and she followed the actors closely as they moved about. Her eyes never left the stage. When the lights came up on Guy's bare back at the open refrigerator pouring out milk, I gave her a close look, noting something, amusement, admiration, maybe just intense interest, that irritated me. Guy turned around and the audience gave the requisite inhale attendant upon full frontal nudity. There was a lot of it on the stage in the '70s, more than there is now. *Let My People Come* was just around the corner, a cast of fifteen without a stitch on for two hours, they even had an orgy onstage, so people were getting jaded about all that, still, a naked man or woman in a social setting where everyone else is clothed always creates a frisson. I looked at Guy, who was drinking his milk, staring out over the footlights, a self-satisfied smirk on his face. He was loving it; he was in heaven. His sister or girlfriend, or his brother's girlfriend, whoever she was, sitting at the kitchen table, spoke to him. He turned to her, jutting his hips forward, and praised the virtues of milk. The audience, save one, laughed. Madeleine's mouth was open, the corners lifted, her expression engaged and titillated. I studied my knees. Disgruntlement and disgust were churning into something solid in my gut. I wanted to get up and walk out, but I knew Madeleine wouldn't forgive me and I didn't want to risk that. Also, if I left, I was in effect leaving her alone with Guy, who was strutting about the stage, spewing his lines like a sick baby, while his fellow actors stood by attending their cues. What else could they do? He was a hog of an actor, over the top and out of control; he even managed to upstage the girlfriend/sister's weepy confession of her long-repressed, undying love. I recall one line—"You were a fling for me"—at the conclusion of a longish tirade about his inability to love. He tossed it at her like a brick, blindsiding her, so that she appeared to be struck dumb. It was one of those perfectly dead moments when everything comes together, the banality of the script, the ineptitude of the direction, the stereotyped superficial performances of the actors, the moment when the complete falsity of the enterprise is manifest and you know a play really stinks. If, instead of yelling the idiotic line, Guy had whispered it, there might have been hope; the actress would have had something to do, she wasn't bad, she might have made something out of it. But Guy made the scene all about his character, a big, stupid, naked, self-absorbed, unfeeling ape.

"He's got no subtlety," I said to Madeleine after the show. We were drinking beer at Jimmy Ray's on Eighth Street. "There's nothing going on underneath. If the guy's a dick, that's fine, but there's got to be something behind that, I mean, there's a reason he's a dick. It didn't just happen; he wasn't fucking born a dick."

"What did you think of his dick?" Madeleine asked.

"That's an incredibly crude thing to say," I snapped.

She laughed. "It just seems to be on your mind."

"Frankly, I was too aggravated by his acting to notice, but I'm sure you have an informed opinion."

"I didn't think his acting was that bad. It's not a great part, but he made the best of it."

"Oh please," I begged.

The play got two reviews and the critics agreed with Madeleine. One called Guy's performance "stalwart," the other said he'd attacked a difficult role with "brio."

"If the audience is conscious that the actor is attacking his character," I told Madeleine, "it's all over, it's a failed performance."

"You need to get over your envy of Guy," she replied. "It's not very attractive."

Of course everyone was talking about Guy's success; you couldn't go out for a burger without hearing about his latest coup. The reviews resulted in the acquisition of an enthusiastic agent and a callback for a play at the Public and another at St. Mark's Theater. Christopher Walken beat him out for the part at the Public, but who could complain about being bested by Christopher Walken, etc. The Italian thing ran for its allotted stretch during which time Madeleine and I began our own rehearsals, so I didn't actually see Guy for several weeks. Then, one night, Teddy invited a few friends to his apartment for drinks and there he was, the new, improved, Equityed and agented Guy Margate, lounging in an armchair before a non-functional fireplace with a glass of Teddy's good Scotch and a pretty, rabbity blonde leaning over him to give him the benefit of her cleavage. Madeleine and Mindy went into a giggling clutch at the door. "Who's the blonde?" I asked Teddy.

"She was in the play, the sister. Or was it the girlfriend?" Teddy said. "Her name is Sandy. Sandy something."

Sandy was laughing and Guy watched her with that peculiar avidity he had, the dead gazing upon the living. His shoulders were bigger than I recalled; he must have been lifting weights. He was unshaven, his hair unkempt. Was he going for an Italian-stallion look? He lifted the Scotch to his lips and his gaze, surveying the room, settled on me. I nodded—yes, I recognize you—nothing more personal than that. Then he spotted Madeleine behind me, she was still buzzing with Mindy, and his focus narrowed to a fine point. If he had used his eyes that well onstage he might have made something of that character.

Which was Guy's problem in a nutshell. He could never see himself from himself. He created character from the outside looking in, he constructed a persona. Basically anyone can do it, politicians do it nonstop. It's not, perhaps, a bad way to start. But Guy could never inhabit a character because he was himself so uninhabited. Nobody home, yet he wasn't without strong emotions. I didn't know that last part then.

Madeleine released Mindy and threaded her arm through mine, rubbing my shoulder with her chin. Guy took this in with only a compression of his lips, but I knew he wasn't pleased. I bent my neck to brush Madeleine's hair with my lips, my eyes on Guy, and I smiled at him pleasantly, complacently, as a poker player smiles when he lays a straight flush upon the table.

This brought him to his feet, narrowly missing the cleavage with his nose as he stood up. Madeleine noticed him and released my arm. "Guy's here," she said and in the next moment she was stretching up to plant a kiss on his rough cheek. His hand rested on her waist, his eyes closed as he bent down to receive her greeting, then he straightened up and held his hand out to me. "Teddy tells me you two are working," he said. "That's great."

"It is," Madeleine agreed.

I offered my hand and he grasped it heartily, tightly, and for just that moment too long that bespeaks the will to domination. "Give me the details," he said. "I'll make sure my agent shows up. She should see you two."

"That would be fantastic," Madeleine gushed.

"She's terrific," Guy assured us. "She's opening doors all over town for me. I'm up for the new McNally next week."

While Madeleine expressed her delight at this prospect, I eased past Guy and made an excuse about my urgent need for a drink. Peter Davis was talking up the now neglected Sandy near the bar, so I pressed myself on them, keeping my back to the room. My emotions were in such a tangle I felt it would take a soliloquy of some duration to sort them out, but this wasn't the time or place. Peter's gossip was about Stella Adler, who had stripped down to some disheartening underwear in her effort to break an obdurate student's performance. "No," she shouted, lurching about the stage in her high heels, bra, and girdle. "This is boring, you've got to open up, you can't be afraid, you can't be timid and afraid, you must be naked in the theater, take your clothes off, you must be absolutely fearless and naked in the theater."

"She's a genius," Sandy said.

I could hear Guy talking behind me; his voice had grown since he'd been absolutely naked on the stage and after every fifth word he said, "my agent." At some point he exclaimed, "Oh, who reads reviews!"

Teddy came up, rolling his eyes in disbelief at this remark and I put my arm around him, desperate for an ally. "Success spoils Rock Hunter," he chortled and I said, "What was there to spoil?"

Sandy, offended for her hero, said, "You two are like catty teenagers." Then the room exploded with the primate roar of Guy Margate's laughter.

Later, as we undressed in my bedroom, I remarked to Madeleine that Guy was an intolerable blowhard.

"You won't think so if his agent takes you on," she said.

"His agent isn't going to take me on," I replied. "His agent thinks Guy is a good actor."

"So if she's interested in you, you'll turn her down."

"She isn't going to be interested in me," I said.

And I was right, she wasn't. She was interested in Madeleine.

The criminal-bakery play received the mildest notices. Everything was "adequate" and "not without interest," a few of us were "promising" and the playwright bore "watching." Only "newcomer Edward Day" was signaled out for abuse. One reviewer described his performance as "erratic," the other called him "a mincing, predatory fop." Madeleine maintained that the latter designation might be a compliment but I knew better. The play was a flop but it ran its scheduled six weeks, each night to a smaller audience.

One Saturday night as I was cleaning my face in the dressing room, Guy appeared at the doorway. The dressing room was a converted storage closet, scarcely wide enough for two to pass abreast, with a long counter, wooden stools, and a hazy mirror lit by a row of bare lightbulbs. As they finished their ablutions, laying aside their characters for another night, my fellow actors filed out in a gloomy procession. We had less than a week to go and we were all bracing for the plunge back into merciless reality where none of us had jobs. Guy spotted me and stepped inside. He looked big in that room and the garish light gave his skin a greenish cast. I was in no mood to accept the obligatory compliments he had doubtless come to offer, nor did I imagine he had any sympathy with my performance. He pressed against the wall, allowing one of my departing colleagues to pass, then claimed the vacated stool next to mine. "I've been arguing with my agent all evening," he confided loudly. "She came to the matinee and she just didn't get the play. I said, 'Forget the play, what about the Day,' but she said she thought you were muddled. What a stupid thing to say."

"Good night, Ed," another colleague called to me as he went out.

Before I could answer, Guy butted in. "Hey, good night. You were terrific."

The poor fellow perked up at this praise. "Thanks," he said, "thanks a lot."

I watched Guy in the mirror, wearily noting the resemblance between us, especially marked in profile. He was wearing a black turtleneck sweater which might have been chic were it not for the specks of dandruff scattered across the shoulders. As the voices of the actors in the hall were silenced by the slam of the heavy backstage door, Guy ran his fingers through the lank hair straying over one ear, tossing his head as he raked it back like an anxious ingenue. Was Guy anxious?

I found I didn't care. Lethargy settled over me, not unexpected, as I'd done the damned play twice in a day on very little sleep. I resented Guy shouting out his agent's appraisal of me for all to hear. Surely my fellow actors were talking about it now as they rambled through the chilly night in search of a drink, agreeing with the criticism—Day is muddled; he's dragging down the whole show—each inwardly wondering if the agent might have been impressed by his own performance. Better check the phone service before bed.

I recalled, with grim specificity, the matinee. Matinees were never strong, everyone knows this. Old people with hearing aids come to matinees. Even if there was something to *get* in a play, which, sadly, in the thing about the bakery there was not, they wouldn't get it, so why waste the energy. I routinely saved what I could for the evening performance. Why in hell had Guy's vaunted agent chosen a matinee to check out my potential? I dabbed a tissue at the last of the cold cream near my mouth. Guy turned back to me. "I tried, Ed," he said. "But she wouldn't listen to me."

"Why did she come to a matinee?" I asked testily.

He was distracted by his own reflection in the mirror. He frowned, first at himself, then at me. "She's a busy woman," he said. "She had to fit you into her schedule. I didn't know when she would come. She only did it as a favor to me."

I chucked the tissue into the trash can. "Do me a favor, Guy," I said. "Don't do me any more favors." Our eyes met in the mirror, mine a glaring hound, his a wounded doe. The favor he had already done me wafted between us like stage fog and I was back in the ponderous deep, gasping and thrashing for life. I seldom thought of that night, though occasionally it recurred in a dream from which I woke with a shout. In an uninteresting twist sometimes it was my mother who was drowning and I who was trying to save her. Guy's gaze shifted back to his own reflection, which clearly soothed and pleased him, leaving me to glower at the unedifying spectacle of an actor admiring himself. He turned his cheek, raising his chin to take in the strong line of his jaw, giving himself a sly smile.

"Who are you?" I asked. "Narcissus?"

"The sad part," he said, "is that my agent is right, your performance really is a muddle. You just don't have a grip on that character, Ed, you're all over the place with him and it's not such a bad part. You throw that whole scene with the Mafia don away and he's an excellent actor. He must want to murder you."

I snorted. "You're killing me," I said. Guy assessed the other side of his face. The stillness of the theater weighed down on me. All those seats, all those empty seats.

"I was surprised, frankly," he continued. "Madeleine has a high opinion of your work. I expected something better."

"God, I hate to disappoint you," I said.

"Has Maddie seen this show?"

"She hates being called Maddie."

"Thanks for the tip. What does she think?"

"You tell me."

"Would you like me to sound her out for you?"

"Not much."

"I just don't think this teacher you've got, what's his name?"

"Meisner. Sandy Meisner."

"Right. I don't think he's doing you any good. He's got you all tied up in knots. I mean, you don't look comfortable on that stage, Ed."

"You mean I'm not upstaging everybody with my cheap theatrics. I'm not waving my arms and bobbing my head around like a puppet; I'm not wagging my limp dick at the audience?"

Guy thrust his face closer to the mirror and commenced probing the skin over his cheekbone. "Damn," he said. "There's a zit starting."

I stood up and pulled my jacket from the hook on the wall. I was uneasy about the next part. I couldn't very well leave him in the theater—he had no business there—but I didn't relish walking out with him. I had to turn off the dressing-room lights and walk about twenty feet in total darkness to get to the door. I paused with my hand on the light switch, looking back at him. "Go ahead," he said. "I'll follow you." I flipped the switch and stepped into the black hole of the hall, expecting to hear his footsteps behind me but there was nothing. Instead his voice rang out, low and serious: "We've got to stop meeting like this, Ed." It was ridiculous, it was actually funny, but there was something eerie and threatening about it that made me scoot for the door and fling it open with more than necessary force. Outside a lamp illuminated the shabby entryway. I leaned against the bar that opened the lock from the inside, gazing back into the gloom from which, all at once, Guy appeared, striding confidently toward me.

"Let's go to Phebe's," he said. "I'll buy you a beer."

Madeleine's play ran six weeks and got extended for an extra two. One reviewer found her "fresh" and "appealing," another described her as "a young actress with talent to burn." Guy's agent, Bev Arbuckle, a deeply frightening redhead from Long Island, went to the show one night, liked what she saw, called Madeleine to her office, and took her on. Bev was certain Madeleine would do well in commercials and we had a long, difficult weekend of tears and protests before she agreed to try out for a few, which she didn't get. We were back to the audition trials and it was clear that Madeleine was getting more tryouts and more callbacks than I was, but she was not gratified by this. If anything she was more apprehensive and desperate. This surprised me and it irked me: I was spending far too much energy trying to keep Madeleine's ego properly inflated when my own was sagging well below the recommended pressure level. I listened to Madeleine's side of panicked consultations with Bev on the phone and chewed my casserole to a monologue on the subject of Bev's failure to understand the full dramatic range of her new client. Sex was still good and we resorted to it for distraction, which certainly beat television, but I found myself forestalling the orgasm because it meant we would have to go back to talking about Madeleine's career. If I turned the subject to my own daily confrontation with oblivion, she reminded me that the theater was a notoriously hard taskmistress and that success was the exception to a whole universe of rules.

We didn't actually live together. Madeleine still paid rent on a two-room apartment she shared with a college friend where she dropped in once or twice a week, mostly to do laundry for us both, as I didn't have a washer. She was reluctant to give the place up because the friend needed the rent and would be forced to find someone to replace her. So though she spent most of her nights with me, she wasn't helping with my rent and it didn't occur to her that she should. She bought and cooked most of the food we ate. Her repertoire was limited, pasta with sauce, vegetable soup, and macaroni and cheese. She was no longer a vegetarian, so once in a while she roasted a whole chicken and we ate that for a few days.

Gradually we began to have arguments about small matters: the tea bags she left in saucers all over the place, the way I broke the spines of books by laying them open to mark my place. Sometimes when we went out for a beer, we sat at a table without speaking. Teddy came across us like this one evening at Phebe's. He pulled up a chair and sat in the empty, silent space between us. "Trouble in Paradise," he said.

"What do you mean?" Madeleine asked.

"Our lovebirds are not cooing," he said.

She looked at me quizzically; I raised my eyebrows and shrugged. "I'm just anxious about an audition I have tomorrow," she said. "It's a small part, but Bev thinks it could be important."

Teddy patted her hand, all fake sympathy. "That is nervous-making," he said.

"Bev is nervous-making," I said.

Madeleine gave me a sharp look. "And what am I supposed to do about that according to you?"

I let it pass and Teddy changed the subject. He'd just seen an amusing farce by Alan Ayckbourn in which a British actress spent the second act quietly attempting suicide while her friends, bent on kitchen repair, worked around her. Teddy described Stella Adler's hostility toward British actors; in her view they were inferior and she mocked students she suspected of succumbing to their influence. When someone pleased her she said, "Yes, we will have great *American* actors." Teddy did an impression of his teacher's un-American pronunciation of the word "American."

"How old is she?" Madeleine asked.

"Who knows?" Teddy said. "As old as God."

"No," I said. "She's older than Sandy and he's as old as God."

"I hope I don't wind up like that," Madeleine said.

"Like what?" I asked. "Old? It may be hard to avoid."

"No," she said. "Old and teaching."

We nodded over our beers. Madeleine had summoned a specter no actor contemplates tranquilly. The personal lives of our teachers didn't interest us; they existed, as far as we were concerned, only for what they had to give us. We treated them with respect. They could reduce us to quivering jelly with a harsh word. They had power; some were rumored to use it maliciously to elicit unhealthy dependency, as Strasberg was said to have done with the phenomenally talented Marilyn

Monroe, but ultimately we believed our fate must be to leave them behind.

"Somebody's got to teach," Teddy said ruefully. "Acting is an art, after all."

Madeleine's eyes drifted toward the windows. Outside a couple clutching their coats against a gust of wind struggled by. The temperature was dropping steadily; the first hard freeze was predicted. "I really want that part," Madeleine said.

What strikes me when I look back over these pages is not only my ignorance, which was prodigious, but my myopia. This is always the case with hindsight, when the inevitability of choices that seemed difficult and complex is revealed to have been obvious. I wanted to be an actor; I needed to act, to play a part; and I was driven by an ambition I scarcely understood. I knew that great acting is an art, one which requires dedication, study, and patience. I was open to learning everything I could in any way possible, that was my strength and this openness drew the best teachers to me. It was this and not my talent that excited them. At that time I had not found the teacher who, as the Buddhists remind us, appears only when the student is ready. She was waiting for me.

I was frustrated by auditions and my classes bored me; the relentless exercises that led to small moments when, egged on by the relentlessly nagging Meisner, I had a momentary revelation of the depths I would have to mine in myself if I was ever to act fully. I wasn't afraid; it was just such hard work and I was often physically tired from my jobs, and from keeping Madeleine on an even keel. Sandy said things like "Edward, I don't know why you can't just look at that table. Is there something that's keeping you from looking at the table?" or "Mary, that was good, you were urgent, it was good. Ed, try joining her there."

"I don't think Sandy's the right teacher for me," I told Teddy, but he only smiled and said, "He's as good as any."

Meisner was well loved by his students and occasionally successful actors returned for a tune-up with him, especially those who had been working in television and wanted to recover their energy because the daily grind of TV was so deadening. One chilly December morning the news was that Marlene Webern, a fine stage actress who had been appearing in a popular television drama about a hospital, was among us. She enjoyed directing improvisation exercises and, after consultation with Sandy, posted a list of students invited to participate. To my surprise, my name was on it.

Marlene was in her early forties then, though of course she didn't look it, and she had a long career both behind and before her. The first time I saw her she was seated at a table in the wings of a makeshift stage, turning over the pages of a script. Her heavy red hair was pulled back in a ponytail; she wore a white men's-style shirt, jeans, and a pair of short red boots, the exact shade of which was matched by the polish on her fingernails. There was a pitiful low-wattage lamp to read by so she was hunched over the page, her brow furrowed above a pair of bifocal glasses. As I approached, she whisked off the glasses and her face came to life, though her eyes were still unfocused. Her smile had about it, always, I was to learn, a trace of sadness. "Who are you?" she asked.

"I'm Edward Day," I said. "Is this where the improv session will be?"

"Is that your real name?" she asked.

"It is," I said. This meant Marlene Webern was not her real name but I didn't pursue it. Later I learned her name was Cindy Webewitz and that she came from the Bronx. Another student arrived and another until we had a troupe of eleven. Marlene herded us onto the stage, announcing that we would do a warm-up called "catch." This was a silly business in which the actors stand in a circle while one among them assumes a peculiar posture and movement. "Mark," Marlene instructed, "start with a chicken." Mark stretched his neck up, thrust out his butt, flapped his arms, and turned his legs into strutting sticks. He bobbed his head, making chicken clucks, and bopped into the center of the circle. After a bit of preening he approached a pretty young woman named Becka, who responded with a quick peck and screech, took on the chicken, entered the circle, and modified the movement into something slithery and reptilian, which she then passed on to me. I turned the snake into something, I don't remember what, passed it on, and so on. Actors love this sort of thing; it limbers the instrument and allows for fierce grimacing and eye flashing. Marlene got something piggish, transformed it into an insect walking on water, then snapped abruptly back into Marlene and said, "That's good." She went to a table and took up a folder of pages which she handed out to each of us. "These are the improvs," she said. "There are six of them. They're all two-person scenes, so pair up. I'll have to do one too; Ed you be with me. We'll do number four."

All eyes shifted to me momentarily, and then there was a brief hum as we read over the pages and couples gravitated together. Marlene assigned random numbers and sent all but the students assigned to the first exercise into the audience.

They were clever scenes. I don't remember much about the others, one was an argument in a bar, and in another a man didn't want his wife to know what (or who) was behind a curtain. But I recall every detail of my own. It was the improv that changed my life.

The scenario was elaborate. I was a young man named David who wanted to go to Japan and become a monk, but I didn't have the money for a plane ticket. I sneaked into the kitchen of my mother's house and there on the table was her purse. I decided to steal her credit card; she came in and surprised me in the act. Marlene would be my mother.

As the others created conflict and comedy and pathos from thin air on the stage, I tried to work my way into a condition of such desperate urgency that I would steal from my mother. I kept my real mother in a safe place; I seldom took her out to look at her and this bit of fluff with Marlene Webern was clearly not an appropriate venue for delving into that dark and painful cache of emotion memory. I understood that I would never have stolen a dime from my mother, no matter what my condition, so there was, in addition, no point in dredging about in my own past. I queried my character, who was my own age and determined to make a complete break from the world as he knew it. He wanted to be in Japan, and he wanted to be there right now. Why? Because he had failed somehow, because he regretted actions he couldn't repair. What sort of actions? What would make me desperate to enter a monastery in Japan? I must have betrayed someone, or someone had cruelly betrayed me, but who and how?

I was getting nowhere and the scenes were ticking by. There was a round of bright applause. "All right, Ed," Marlene called to me as she dashed up the steps lugging a large red purse. "You've got to get to Japan. Chop, chop."

Everyone laughed. I followed, stumbling behind her. I'd done this sort of thing before, we all had; exercises of this kind were our daily bread, but I felt unprepared and anxious. I've got to get to Japan, I told myself. I must get to Japan, today. If I can get the money now, I'll make the plane. I have a reservation; my bag is packed.

Marlene put her purse on the table and pulled it open, producing a leather wallet from inside. "This is my wallet," she said. "The credit card is inside." She dropped the wallet into the capacious purse. It had a satchel-style opening which she snapped closed. "You'll have to open the wallet to get the card," she added needlessly. "You come from there"—she pointed to the wings offstage right—"and I'll come from this side."

I went into the wings where I stood for a moment pulling my cheeks down with the palms of my hands. I'm desperate, I thought. I've got to get to Japan. I know Mother won't want me to go, she won't help me, but if I could get her credit card somehow without her knowing, I could pay for the ticket. I'll pay her back later, once I'm settled in Japan. I stepped onto the stage and there was the table with the purse. All I had to do was open the wallet and get the card. I paused, listening—was she nearby? Was she even in the house? But there was nothing. Now's your chance, I advised myself. Do it quickly. I rushed to the table and snapped open the purse. It was crammed with stuff, makeup, a checkbook, pens, wadded tissues, a tin of mints, but the wallet was riding on top of it all and I snatched it, glancing behind me, though I knew very well that Mother wouldn't surprise me from that direction. That backward glance stymied me—it was forced, something from vaudeville, the anxious thief fearing apprehension. I imagined Meisner chortling at my ineptitude, my loss of focus. The wallet, I thought, just get the card before she comes in. I lifted the snap and the wallet flopped open like a book. There were three credit cards on one side, the shiny edges visible above the thin leather sheaths, like toast in a toaster. On the other side was a plasticized pocket designed for a driver's license. My eye was drawn to this because it displayed not a license but a photograph of a naked woman. She reclined upon a couch, odalisquely, her red hair loose and waving along her shoulders, her chin lifted and her eyes gazing into the camera. Lovely full breasts with unusually pale nipples. My God, I thought, this is Marlene.

Should I be seeing this? What was I to do? Get the credit card, I reminded myself. This is a trick; she's playing with you. Get to Japan, that's all that matters. Take a card, any card; take the green one, that's American Express, good round the world. I extracted the card and dropped the wallet back into the purse as if it was burning my fingers, which it was. A titter of laughter from the audience exasperated me. What were they laughing at?

Though I didn't register the roar from the wings as human, much less female, I heard Marlene before I saw her. She burst upon the stage brandishing a board as long as she was tall and she came straight at me in a fury that no one would mistake for an act. My brain, confused beyond endurance, concluded that she was angry about the photo. But how could that be, she'd put it there, she knew I would find it. "Get out of my house," she bellowed. I backed away as she lowered the board, leveling it at my head for what promised to be a mighty blow. "Mother," I cried, staggering, but she kept coming. My knees buckled and I sprawled to the floor, covering my eyes with my hands. "Don't hit me," I whimpered.

"David?" she asked incredulously. The board, inches from my face, shifted to the right and came down with a crash on the chalky stage planks. "Oh my God, David," she said. "It's you. What are you doing here?"

Tears burst from my eyes; my heart hammered in my ears. I tried to sit up but an emotion of such helplessness and guilt overcame me that I rolled onto my side, clutching my knees to my chest, my head to my knees. The sharp edge of the credit card—I was still clutching the credit card—pressed into my cheek. "I've got to get to Japan," I wailed.

"What are you doing?" she cried. "Are you stealing from me? David, are you stealing from me?"

Then it was over. I got to my feet and tried to defend myself for my action. Marlene demanded the card; I refused to give it to her. We had a brief tussle over it, but it was all acting.

I was even conscious of the audience, my fellow students, and I knew they knew we were just winding down, cleverly, skillfully, but that for that one moment when I fell to the floor in terror and shame, I'd found that for which we all strove, a pure emotion expressed in my own person. There had been no space between my character and myself. I hadn't considered what David might do, or what I might do in David's place, I had simply cried out in David's voice, David's desperation, which was my own. Anyone watching understood that something real had happened in the last place one might expect to find it, inside an actor, on a stage.

Marlene stopped the scene with a raised hand and a sharp "That's it." My fellow actors burst into wild applause. I realized that I was sweating, that my knees were still weak, my heart racing. The whole business had taken about four minutes. I bowed stiffly and Marlene said, "Well done, Ed." I took her hand and kissed it, gratitude flooding up from the bottom of my soul. "Thank you," I said.

"My pleasure," she replied. I raised my eyes to her bemused, almost tender smile. She was pleased with herself and with me. It had been no accident. She had taken my measure and contrived how best to get me to the place I needed to be. The photo, so startling and confusing, the furious board-wielding territorial mother, it was all of a piece. And of course, because of what she had put me through and because of what I now knew about myself as well as about her, I was in love with her.

———

Winter dragged on. I had a small part in a play about García Lorca which got no reviews. In the spring, desperate for an Equity card, I did the group auditions for summer stock. To my surprise I secured a place at a playhouse in Connecticut.

In my first summer at college I had worked as a technical intern at a summer theater in upstate New York, so I had some notion of what to expect. We interns were the equivalent of a Suzuki orchestra of ten-year-olds, grinding out Bach on tiny violins with no idea of theory or art, running on the enthusiasm of being young and attached to a real stage. We were turned loose in an old, run-down hotel a long walk from the theater. The walls were peeling, the water was rusty, and the kitchen was inside a cage constructed of chicken wire to keep out the raccoons which patrolled the place so stealthily and determinedly that if one of us failed to secure the latch at night, in the morning it looked like a band of crazed drug addicts had staged a break-in. The clever creatures opened every door, including the refrigerator, as well as every box, jar, and carton. What they didn't eat, they scattered, and what they scattered, they pissed and shat upon. Hostilities broke out between those of us who carefully secured the latch, hoping to preserve our little stashes of comestibles—a process that required threading a length of wire through two holes—and those who couldn't be bothered. Signs were posted—FASTEN THIS GATE YOU JERK—and scrawled over with tart graffiti. Those determined to prepare decent meals (coffee and sandwiches was the platonic ideal, though one sad, anorexic girl, the child of divorcing parents who didn't care to know exactly where she was, lived on nothing but cereal for two months), tried securing cabinets with metal ties and clamps. One boy bought a steel box with a padlock in which he successfully stored a loaf of bread, but it was a pitched battle and for the most part the raccoons were the victors. My roommate opened the refrigerator one morning to find a raccoon inside, leisurely finishing up a package of sliced ham before making an escape. A sweet high-school student from Ohio was reduced to tears when she found the contents of a tea tin scattered across the linoleum in partially masticated clumps. "My aunt brought me that tea from England," she whimpered. "I only got to have one cup."

The actors were lodged in small apartments in town or in cabins in the woods. Being New Yorkers they were made anxious by the proximity of so many trees, terrified of the deer and the occasional bear, and paralyzed by the swift descent of the deep, black, unilluminated nights. Our leading lady had to be escorted, shrieking at every rustling bird or cavorting rabbit, by a phalange of techies from stage door to cabin.

Three days after we arrived it started to rain and it didn't let up for the rest of the summer. The theater was a well-designed, decently equipped proscenium that seated upward of three hundred, and our actors, if they found their way to rehearsals, were serious professionals. But the weather took a toll and when we were finally up and running we played, night after night, to audiences of forty or fifty who looked on like lost children in the wilderness of empty seats. Their applause sounded like dried peas rattling in a tin can.

This time it would be different. The playhouse in Connecticut was an old and respectable one, and I wouldn't be there to carry coffee, drive nails into frames, or escort nervous drama queens. I would be one of a company of actors. We would do four plays in three months and I would have a part in every one of them.

It meant being apart from Madeleine, a prospect I viewed with equanimity. We were having constant squabbles, some of which escalated into storms so furious even sex couldn't calm the water. In April she got a small part in a comedy she and Bev thought was poor, but it paid union wages so she couldn't turn it down. She spent hours waiting around for the five minutes a night (ten on Saturday) when she was onstage. I was looking for someone to sublet my apartment and she didn't like that. She felt our space would be invaded and violated by a stranger and would thereby be unrecoverable, but she didn't want to give up her shared place and couldn't afford to pay two rents. I put the word out at school and of course a beautiful neophyte actress from Georgia snapped it up, which put Madeleine in a state. "What am I supposed to do?" I reasoned. "Pay rent on an empty apartment in New York? No one does that, Madeleine. I can't afford it even if I wanted to do it, which I don't. Be reasonable."

"It's not about reason, Edward," she snapped. "It's about feeling."

"Feelings don't pay rent," I replied.

One evening, just a few days before I was to leave for Connecticut, I went out with Teddy for Chinese food. He was on the outs with Mindy and his father was bearing down on him to give up acting and pursue a "real" career. "Mindy takes his side," he explained over his mo shu pork. "She thinks I should go to law school. Then we could get married and she could be an actress and I could sue the producers who try to screw her."

"She wants to get married?"

"To Teddy the lawyer, not to Teddy the actor."

"Is she that blunt about it?"

"Pretty much. Yes. You know Mindy, she doesn't mince words."

"Are you seriously considering this?"

The waitress, an adorable Chinese with a long braid and quick, furtive eyes, brought another round of Tsingtao. "I'm seriously considering asking this lovely young lady what time she gets off," he said.

"You are an actor," she said in unaccented English.

"How can you tell?" Teddy asked.

"I saw you at an audition. Last month. It was at La MaMa."

Her name was Jasmine and she got off at ten. We drank beer and ate almond cookies until she was free and then headed over to Phebe's, where I was to meet Madeleine after her show. Before we left Jasmine introduced us to her aunt, Mrs. Lee, who owned the place and insisted on mixing up a round of Chinese cocktails for us in the kitchen. "Lychinis" Jasmine explained. "A lychee martini."

"Jasmine is great actress," Mrs. Lee informed us as we sipped the strange concoction. "But theater very hard for Chinese. No parts."

It was a gorgeous night; the trees, such as they were, had unfurled their delicate sap-green leaves and exhaled chlorophyll-scented oxygen into the atmosphere. We agreed to walk uptown rather than descend into the underground where breathing was a necessarily shallow affair. I expanded my chest, opened my arms to the invigorating air, and declared the lychini the liquor of the gods. Teddy observed that on this fair night in this part of town one could actually see the stars, and we paused on the curb to gape at the heavens. " 'Twere all one," Jasmine recited, "that I should love a bright particular star and think to wed it, he is so far above me."

"Are you in love?" Teddy asked.

She smiled. "On a night like this I could be. Don't you think I could be?"

We marched on, combing our brains for tributes to the stars. Teddy, overexposed to show tunes by his connection to Mindy, crooned, "Today, all day I had the feeling, a miracle would happen," which put us on the track of the most mawkish song we could find. By the time we got to Phebe's we were on "Some Enchanted Evening," and we burst into the nearly empty bar proclaiming, "Fools give you reasons, wise men never try." A few diehards nodding over their drinks ignored us, the bartender rolled his eyes. Madeleine, alone at a table with an empty glass before her, regarded us so sourly that Teddy muttered "Good luck" and steered Jasmine to the far end of the bar, leaving me to my fate. I leaned over the table, my eyes moistened by the smoky pall that hung upon the air. "Hey lady," I said, in a low-life pitch somewhere between Brando and De Niro, "can a fella buy you a drink?"

My queen was not amused. "Where have you been?" she asked. "I've been waiting for over an hour."

"We walked from Chinatown," I said. "It's a beautiful night, didn't you notice?"

"I'm tired," she said. "My stomach hurts."

"Well, have a drink with me and we'll walk home and you can go straight to bed."

She glanced at Teddy and Jasmine, who were perched on stools, chatting up the bartender. "Does Mindy know about that?"

"That's Jasmine," I said. "We just met her at the Chinese restaurant. She's an actress. What do you want, sweetheart? Have a liqueur; it will settle your stomach. Have a Sambuca."

"OK," she said. I went to the bar and answered Teddy's inquiring look with a thumbs-up all clear. When my drinks came, he and Jasmine followed me to the table where the introductions quickly yielded to the important info that Madeleine was tired because she had a job and had come straight from the theater.

"I've heard about that play," Jasmine exclaimed. "You're in that play? That's so cool. I really want to see it."

"It's a small part," Madeleine demurred.

"I really want to see it," Jasmine repeated.

"Our Madeleine plays a maid of easy virtue," Teddy said, keeping the subject where we both understood it needed to be.

"Typecasting," I joked.

Madeleine flashed me a look that made my stomach tighten. "What are you talking about?" she said.

"Mitt Borden is the lead, isn't he?" Jasmine said. "He's fantastic."

"What are you talking about?" Madeleine persisted, glaring at me.

"Just teasing, love," I said.

"What's he like?" Jasmine asked, but Madeleine ignored her. "Did you see him in that Wilson play? I thought he was hot."

"He's a good actor," Teddy agreed. "He's got a lot of presence."

"He stinks," Madeleine said, releasing me from her cold inspection.

"You don't think he's good?" Jasmine asked.

"He's an OK actor," she said. "I mean he smells bad. He doesn't wash enough."

"Oh. He stinks stinks!" Jasmine cried, collapsing into charming, girlish giggles.

When was the last time I'd seen Madeleine laugh with such simple openhearted glee, I thought. She watched Jasmine's amusement with a chilly, distant smile. She was angry at me for my remark; she had passed over it for now but I knew I'd hear about it later and I was right. On the walk home she was silent, loading up her argument, and when she got to the apartment she opened fire. I had as good as called her a slut in front of someone she had just met. It was clear I would only make such a remark to let Jasmine know that I was not in any way attached to Madeleine, that everyone knew she was sluttish, which simply wasn't true. I had no reason to make such a charge, it was outrageous and uncalled for and she wasn't going to forgive me for it. I defended myself indifferently, apologized insincerely in the hopes of toning down the scene, but she was having none of it. It was clear to her that I wanted to go to Connecticut just to get away from her and prove to myself that I didn't need her. Well good, that was good. I should go ahead.

That was fine with her. She was too busy anyway; her career was the most important thing and it was obvious that I was jealous of her because she was talented and ambitious. By this time she was weeping and trembling, genuinely exhausted, so I got her to bed, protesting my affection for her, cradling her in my arms until, in the midst of snuffling tears, she fell asleep.

I got up and fixed myself a drink. She was right, of course. I was tired of the relationship. I had been for some time, and all I really wanted to do was get through the next few days without more hysterics, get on the bus, and head for Connecticut.

On the morning I left, Madeleine was subdued and remained so until I packed my old suitcase, kissed her goodbye, and hopped on the bus. I was in a cheerful frame of mind. I didn't know who the other actors would be, but there was always a star or two, older stage actors or television actors desperate to play a scene without someone yelling cut and eager to be nearer the city where real theater still more or less thrived. Agents routinely toured the summer productions and there was occasionally a new play, which meant spending time with an ambitious playwright, always an interesting opportunity for an actor.

A theater functionary met me at the station and drove me to a rambling Victorian rooming house with a long porch across the front straight out of Thomas Wolfe. "Here we are," the driver informed me.

"Very Thomas Wolfe," I remarked.

"The actors all seem to like it," he assured me. "Most of

them are here." The porch screen drifted open revealing a stunning young woman, all golden curls, honey skin, and startling green eyes, dressed in a white halter-top dress that reminded me of the bubbling skirt Marilyn Monroe famously battled down against the subway draft in *The Seven Year Itch*. She flashed me a camera-ready smile and stepped out into the light. "I'm Eve," she said.

"I think I'll like it just fine," I told the driver.

From there things got better. Eve escorted me to my narrow room just three doors from hers, and left me to "get settled in." On the pine desk I found a folder packed with useful information, including a list of all the actors in our company. Here I learned that Eve's full name was Eve Vendler and that she had studied at Yale. I didn't recognize any of the other names, save two. One was Gary Santos, an actor I'd seen in a good production of Joe Orton's play *Loot* in some miserable little theater downtown. The other was our star, the talented stage, film, and television actress who, it turned out, had a long association with this festival playhouse and was returning for her sixth season, the immensely talented and widely acclaimed Marlene Webern.

The first cast meeting was the following morning. As the dress code was casual, I pulled on a T-shirt, my most faded madras shorts, sandals, and in case of overactive air-conditioning, the linen jacket, and went forth confidently to join my company. The rehearsal shed was a short walk from the boardinghouse and we actors went over in a troop, chattering away with introductions and gossip. Gary Santos, who was there for a second season, enthused about the venue and praised the talent and temperament of our star. "Marlene is great," he declared. "Nothing pretentious about her and she's brilliant."

I said nothing, as I doubted that Marlene would remember me—though she had, in the brief encounter we had shared, changed my life—and I didn't want to embarrass myself by suggesting a connection where there was none. But when the time came and I stood diffidently before her, protesting that it would be unlikely if she recalled our little scene together, to my delight, she claimed me. "Of course I remember you, Ed," she said. "That's why you're here."

That's why you're here.

Close your eyes and imagine you are standing before a strange door in a whirling snowstorm. Your fingers are numb; you're frozen to your bones and hungry as well. The door swings open upon a sunny, tropical isle, birds are singing, exotic flowers nod in the soft breeze beckoning you, a table is spread with a magnificent feast. Bathing beauties, if you like bathing beauties, emerge from the calm waters calling your name. Ed, you're here, at last, you're here, we've been waiting for you, that's why you're here. In just that way Marlene's greeting caught me by surprise and I blurted out, "That's great," much to the amusement of my fellow actors who took me for an innocent. And so I was, so I was. But not for long.

We did four plays that summer; one was a musical, *Dames at Sea;* two were insipid pieces in which I had negligible parts; and the fourth was Tennessee Williams's *Sweet Bird of Youth*. I was cast as Chance Wayne, chauffeur and paid gigolo of the drug-addicted, over-the-hill screen star Alexandra del Lago, also known as Princess Kosmonopolis, played by Marlene Webern. Eve, the delicious Eve, was my long-lost sweetheart Heavenly Finley. Mine was a plum part albeit one in which I was castrated onstage every night. The play felt seriously dated even then; now it seems like some embarrassing relic. The shock value of drugs and venereal disease had faded through the '60s, but Connecticut audiences were perfectly content to have their prejudices about the Deep South confirmed and chalked the strangeness of the play up to its author, that gay blade who doubtless knew everything there was to know about VD and drug addiction.

Marlene was perfect for her part and she knew it, but I was miscast in every way, including the color of my hair. Chance Wayne is so golden the ladies talk about it; it's one of his great charms. I assumed I'd wear a wig, which worried me. A wig is a big deal, a serious distraction. I'd need to wear a wig night and day for a week at least just to get past it, or get even with it. So I was relieved, early in the rehearsal period, when the director took me aside and said, "I've made an appointment for you at the salon in town. It's the Wee-Hair-Nook on Main Street. Just show up at two o'clock and ask for Beatrice. She knows what to do."

One really must admire the persistence and imagination of women when it comes to approximating their ideal self-image. Beatrice was an artist and the challenge I presented excited her. She laid swatch after swatch of fake hair against my cheek, from champagne blond through honey to strawberry, with variations in between so numerous and slight I couldn't detect a difference. "This one's a little cooler," she said, or "This is pushing toward red." She kept returning to a panel of haystack yellow. "With your eyes and skin, I'm thinking we can go Scandinavian and get a real natural look."

The process was horrific, toxic, vile smelling, with a long stint under a dryer so hot I thought my scalp would fry. But when it was over and Beatrice pulled the towel away with a flourish, I gasped at the rakish fellow in the mirror. "I'll be damned," I said. "It's fantastic."

Beatrice beamed at me, drawing a few damp curls over my forehead. "There's a blond in all of us," she said. "We just let him out."

Back at the theater my colleagues were agog. "I didn't recognize you," Eve exclaimed. "It makes your face look bigger."

"You're standing different," Gary Santos observed. "Are you conscious of that?"

Then a rich, theatrical voice called from the stage. "Is that Chance? Is that my driver, Chance Wayne?"

"At your service, Princess," I said, turning to Marlene who looked me up and down so ravenously I felt a blush rising to my cheeks. "I have such a weakness for blonds," she said. "I fear it will be the death of me."

I pressed my fingertips to my lips, regarding her coolly. "You could be right about that, Princess." She shook her hair over her shoulders, reminding me of the photo she'd tantalized me with at our first meeting. It was then I decided I would have sex with her and soon. Chance Wayne wasn't a guy who would wait around for the prize to fall from the tree and I was, at that moment, feeling just as useless, hungry, stupid, hot, and blond as Chance Wayne.

As everyone knows, in my profession we go around screwing each other as much as possible, mostly to see ourselves do it. Narcissists are always making love to number one. Eve was a perfect example. I asked her to my room to share a bottle of wine and she was in the bed and down to her lacy underwear before she finished the first glass. She disported herself charmingly, wiggling around to present her various assets as if there was a paying audience seated on the dresser. She made interesting noises and urged me on with cries of "Oh my God" and "Do it." Afterward she wanted a cigarette, but I didn't have one. She pouted her pouty lips. "Eddie, I really need a cigarette," she said. So I got up, put my clothes on, and walked down to the general store to buy a pack. On the walk back, I found myself thinking of sex in general and Madeleine in particular, definitely a different ball game from Eve. More inhibited but, oddly, more intense. Eve had no shame, which wasn't as much fun as it should have been. It struck me that she might wind up in porno films, and in fact, this turned out to be an accurate prediction.

Eve was entertaining, but my real goal in the sexual stakes game was Marlene Webern. Marlene wasn't just a different ball game, she was a different planet, and one not easy of access. In public she flirted and teased, it was part of her role as Alexandra del Lago, and we enjoyed bantering in a familiar way, as if we had actually driven into town from the Gulf Coast, stopping over at chic hotels where we took drugs and she was serviced by me at considerable expense to her pocketbook and my self-esteem. It was tantalizing, but we were never alone. After a week of rehearsals I noticed that she contrived to keep it that way and I resolved to break her will.

This wasn't easy. As the star she received special perks and was much in demand. She was lodged in a private guesthouse tucked into a garden behind a mansion on the green in town. The owner, a patron of our theater, occasionally sent a chauffeured car to pick her up after rehearsal and whisk her off to private dinner parties with the local elite. When she was reduced to dining with the rest of us, she was seated next to the producer or the director, both of whom were clearly in love with her. I couldn't get next to her, except onstage, where we were very close indeed. We spent the whole first scene sparring in a hotel room. I held her in my arms, she examined my bare torso, I picked her up when she fell on the floor, and at the end, after we agreed that we were both ashamed of our degraded connection, I got in the bed with her and tried to make her believe, as she put it, "that we're a pair of young lovers without any shame."

In the Broadway production Chance closes the hotel shutter on this line and the stage goes dark, but that was in the '50s and this was the '70s. Audiences wanted to see actors making out. It was fine with me. All I had to do was call up the photo I'd seen in her wallet and I was eager to clamber on top of her and try to remove her blouse. The look she gave me as she held her arms out to me was such a combination of fragility and appetite that it touched my heart and my groin at the same time; who wouldn't want to make love to such a look as that.

We weren't exactly the people we were playing, a washed-up star and a boastful neophyte, but we could certainly imagine the desperation that would drive these two together. Marlene opened her lips beneath mine and arched her spine as I slipped one hand around her back and pressed her thighs apart with the other. She was wearing a cotton T-shirt and jeans, so it wasn't as if I could really get anywhere, and the director always interrupted too soon with his "Good, that's it, that's hot." We sat up on the bed, side by side, disheveled and overstimulated. Marlene came back to herself in an instant, patting down her hair, blowing out a puff of air as she lifted and lowered her shoulders. It wasn't so easy for me. I tried not to listen to the riot in my senses as the director droned his notes for the scene.

Scene 1 was fine, it's well written, lots for the actors to do, but after that the play is pretty much downhill. Nothing fazed Marlene; her character was entirely in place and she was convincing no matter how bizarre or nonsensical the requirements of the role. She made it easy for me; she let me act around her solid interpretation and if I came up with anything new, some little insight into my character, she followed me like a willing dance partner. We searched for Chance Wayne together. I couldn't decide how dishonest he actually was. When he said he'd slept "in the social register" in New York, was that true? Was he in the chorus of *Oklahoma!* as he bragged he had been, or was even that small distinction beyond him? Did he have an Equity card? One day when the director told me my "YIPEEEE" sounded like a death knell I spoke up. "I don't get it," I said. "Why would I brag to this famous film star that I was in the chorus of *Oklahoma!*? Am I so stupid I think that's a big deal? Did I actually do it, or did I just try out for the chorus and didn't even do that? I know I'm a loser, I've got that, but just how big a loser am I?"

Marlene, lounging on the divan, her arms stretched out over her head, flipped one of her red sandals to the floor. "Big," she said.

I turned on her. "That's what you think, Miss Has-been," I said.

She narrowed her eyes at me as if she was looking into my brain. "It's what I know, Chance darling," she said.

That's it, I thought. It's all a lie. From start to finish. I'm a complete fraud. I was never on the stage in New York. I never made it out of Florida. *I sang in the chorus of the biggest show in New York,* I proclaimed to her and to the world. *In* Oklahoma!, *and had pictures in* Life *in a cowboy outfit, tossin' a ten-gallon hat in the air! YIPEEEE.*

"That's more like it," the director said.

The rest of the rehearsal went well. I hardly thought about who I was, I just concentrated on being a liar. Everything I said could be proved false; therefore I was always in danger of being unmasked. This gave me an edge I hadn't been able to find. I appreciated the peril of my situation. At the end of the day the director's notes were distinctly upbeat. "Ed," he said, "you're getting there." I glanced at Marlene for confirmation, but she was fully concentrated on every word issuing from the lips of our director.

That night we had a cookout on the plush green lawn behind the boardinghouse. Tubs of ice sprouting beer and wine bottlenecks dotted a multicolored carpet of blankets and towels upon which we actors preened ourselves in mocking rivalry. Near the house a smoldering charcoal grill, lovingly tended by our prop man turned grill master, pumped into the warm night air the tantalizing fragrance of burning flesh. I was poking a wiener mischievously at the appreciative Eve when I spotted Marlene strolling across the lawn. She was relaxed and oblivious to the palpable alteration in the atmosphere occasioned by her presence among us. She's like the queen stopping in at the local pub, I thought. She will never know what it's like when she's not there.

"It's Marlene," Eve sighed beside me. "She's so fantastic." I got to my feet and weaved my way among the blankets. Gary Santos was pouring wine into a plastic cup while the prop man pointed out to our unexpected guest the choicest bits sizzling above the coals. I popped into the space beside her. "Princess," I said. "What are you doing out among the hoi polloi?"

She was wearing dark sunglasses, her hair was loose, and her smile was at its most enigmatic. "Oh Ed," she said, dismissing the charade of our characters. "Here you are. Advise me. What is a tofu pup?"

"It's a perfectly tasteless wad of soy cheese."

"Oh," she said. "That sounds appetizing. I'll have one of those."

"Are you a vegetarian?"

"No. I don't think so. Are you?"

"No," I said. "At least put some mustard on it." I led her away to the condiments table, snatching a beer from a tub as I passed, acutely conscious of all eyes upon us. I had her, I had her, and I didn't want to share her. I particularly didn't want to share her with Eve, who looked on with slack-jawed amazement, but no sooner had Marlene buried her pup beneath a blanket of relish and mustard than she looked out over the field of players and said, "Let's sit with Eve."

"Sure," I said. "Of course." As we settled on the blanket, Eve gushed like an overflowing bathtub. "Miss Webern," she said. "I can't tell you what an honor it is to be on the stage with you. I've admired your work for so long. I saw you in *Tiny Alice* when I was in high school and that's when I decided I wanted to be an actress."

"Was that a long time ago?" Marlene said, fiddling with her tofu pup, which had slipped out of its bun.

"Well, I was fifteen."

"Best not to tell me how old you are now. Ed, darling, how am I to eat this?"

Eve closed her mouth and sent me a troubled look.

"It's a disgusting thing," I said.

"No, no," she laughed, pressing it back into the limp folder of bread with her bloodred fingernail. "I'm sure it's delicious." As she lifted one end, mustard and relish poured out the other.

"Let me have it," I said, taking the plate from her. "It's going to squirt all over you."

"That would be discouraging," she said.

"Hold a napkin under your chin."

"I had no idea you would take such command," she said, unfolding a napkin and cupping it beneath her chin. I grasped the sandwich gingerly and brought it to her lips. "Just bite it," I said.

She obeyed, baring her teeth and taking a sharp bite, neatly catching the dripping condiments in her napkin.

"Ed," Eve whispered anxiously.

"Be quiet," I snapped. "Let this woman eat her pup."

Marlene was convulsed with laughter, but she managed to swallow what she'd taken and opened her mouth for another go.

"It's awful, isn't it?" I said.

"Completely," she agreed, chewing thoughtfully.

"Let me throw it away."

"Definitely," she said.

I got to my feet folding the plate over the soggy mess. "Do you want some corn? Or a burger?" I asked.

"No, thank you."

"More wine?"

"Yes," she said. "That would be nice. Tell me, Eve, are you a vegetarian."

"No ma'am," Eve replied as I ambled off to the nearest trash can. I was working out a plan. If Marlene wouldn't eat what we ate, I might persuade her to go somewhere alone with me. I had very little money; I certainly couldn't afford any of the chic restaurants in the town center. The only place I'd been inside was the pub and I couldn't picture Marlene tucked into a leather booth with a plate of fries and a beer in front of her. I filled a plastic cup with wine and turned back to our blanket. Eve was blathering about something while Marlene bent upon her a look of fascinated concentration, such as you might give an overturned beetle struggling to right itself next to your bare foot on the bathroom floor.

"Yale is an excellent program," Marlene was saying as I rejoined the conversation.

"Yes," Eve said. "I'm so lucky to be there."

"I'm sure luck had nothing to do with it."

I agreed. I thought Eve had probably gotten into Yale by fucking someone on the admissions committee. Perhaps the whole committee. She was a wretched actress, empty as a kettledrum.

"Now what will you do?" I said to Marlene. "You've had no dinner."

"I have plenty of food in my little cottage," she said. "It's a lovely evening. I'll just sit here a bit and then go back and fix myself something. Frankly it will be nice to be on my own."

"I can understand that," I sympathized, my spirits rebuffed. She was slumming, we were a distraction, but what she really wanted to be was alone. After a few more exchanges she got up and wandered over to the grill where she chatted with the prop man and the lighting designer. I looked on woefully, sucking at my beer while Eve told me Marlene had pronounced her horrible fake Southern accent "charming."

"You know," I said, "I think I'll get a burger while they still have some left." I got back to my feet and slunk along the edge of the blanket patch until I came up behind Marlene.

"I'm using a blue filter for that whole scene," the lighting designer was saying. "It makes the palm trees black, very spooky." Marlene drained her cup and turned to me as if I'd arrived on cue. "Perfect," she said. "Here's my driver. I think I'm ready to leave now. Ed, will you walk with me?"

"At your service," I said, spirits surging back up like champagne behind the cork. Her cottage was a good ten-minute walk. How much could be accomplished by a youthful suitor in a ten-minute stroll through a sleepy summer evening? Marlene had a way of opening and closing the distance between herself and an admirer that was something to see, like watching a skilled angler with a bright fish on the line. She always knew exactly where you were because she controlled the line and understood the play of the currents. This analogy presumes the fish, once hooked, longs to be hauled in, which is the opposite of the truth, but I was eager to leap from the shallows into her lap, and she knew it. I calmed myself as we left the party grounds and set off along the sidewalk. Several conversational openers flitted across my imagination: *Say, I love kissing you in that opening scene* or *You know that photo you have in your wallet, could I see it again* or *I'm in awe of you, you are my ideal* or *When we get to the cottage, what say we hit the sack*. Playing them out while I waited for her to speak—for I was determined that she must set the tone, even if we had to walk the whole way in silence—entertained me. I allowed expressions of pleasure, wonder, yearning, bold aggression to flit across my features. A block went by and another. The front lawns deepened and the houses accumulated grandeur.

"Ed," she said at last. "What are you doing with your face?"

I laughed. "I'm going over the things I'd like to say to you."

"Why not just say them?"

"That's a good question."

"Do you feel intimidated by me?"

"No. But I wouldn't want to bore you."

"I'm not easily bored," she assured me.

"You weren't bored by Eve?"

"Not at all," she said. "But you are."

"I wasn't thinking of talking about Eve."

"No? You'd rather not?"

"Definitely not."

"But you brought her up. You see, I find that interesting."

I chuckled. "You're good," I said.

We paused at a corner to allow a Mercedes convertible to roll by; the town was full of them. I watched Marlene watch the Mercedes, or so I thought, because her sunglasses made it impossible to tell what she was doing with her eyes; they could have been closed. She wasn't old enough to be my mother, but she was older than any woman I'd kissed before, and she had the aura of confidence and ease only actors who work a lot possess that flooded my veins with envy and desire. Her mouth was set in the cheerful lines that seemed to be their natural inclination and it occurred to me that she seldom actually frowned. She had a great line in the play—*When monster meets monster, one monster has got to give way and IT WILL NEVER BE*

ME!—which she delivered with verve and conviction, her eyes flashing at full star power, but there was still this quality of mild self-mocking about the mouth, this detachment behind which, I surmised, the real Marlene, the Marlene who could suffer, resided.

"It's getting dark," I said. "Don't you think you should take off the shades?"

As we stepped into the street she whisked off the sunglasses. "Shades?" she said.

"I want to see your eyes."

"You're a very bossy young man," she observed.

"Bossy?" I said.

She laughed and to my delight took my arm. "We turn here," she said. We went along another block at the end of which was a wide drive leading to a mansion. "I want to show you my cottage," she said. "It's like something from a storybook." The drive forked and we took the narrow path that curved around the house and through a garden riotous with flowers. An arbor laden with deep purple blossoms framed the doorway of a pink stucco cottage. "These are clematis," Marlene said as we passed beneath the arbor. "And here it is. Isn't it charming?"

It was certainly charming and I was on tenterhooks to know whether "showing" it to me meant I would be invited inside. Marlene released me and opened the door which wasn't locked, glancing back as she entered. "Come in and have a glass of wine," she said, "and let's see if I have something we can eat."

I stepped cautiously inside; carefully I closed the door behind me, resting my hand against the panel, advising myself with a maturity beyond my years, *This is your chance. Don't blow it.* The furnishings were summery, rattan and floral cushions, lacy curtains at the windows. There was one big room with chairs, couches, a table, a desk, and beyond that a wide arch through which Marlene passed. A painted screen partially obscured another arch which led, I presumed, to the bedroom. I followed Marlene and found her standing before a wooden tray in the gleaming kitchen, twisting a corkscrew into a bottle of white wine. "May I do that for you," I offered.

"No, you may not," she replied. "Look in the fridge and take out some cheese and there's a bit of a sausage I think."

"You're right," I said, choosing among the colorful packages of cheese with French names on their wrappers, "this is quite a fine place."

"Beats that boardinghouse?" she said. "Put that on the tray."

"Oh yes. By a lot."

"Well, they couldn't expect me to stay in a boardinghouse." Expertly she pulled the cork free and poured out two glasses. I spotted a plate for the cheese in the dish rack.

"No," I agreed.

"So you think it's fair. The whole star-system thing?"

"No question about it," I said.

She slapped a baguette across the tray and held it out to me. "Take this to the table," she said. I went out, perplexed by her line of inquiry. She was the star, why would she be lodged with the underlings?

I set the tray on the table and looked about me. There were

signs of her, a paisley shawl thrown across the back of a chair, a few magazines on the coffee table, *Vogue* and *Ms.,* papers, a book, and what looked like an oversize deck of cards on the desk. I leaned over the desk to check out the book title. It was *World of Wonders.* I'll say, I thought. I turned up the top card on the deck: a happy baby riding a horse, a smiling sun beaming down upon him. Marlene came in carrying plates, an apple, and the bottle of wine. "Do you read tarot cards?" I asked.

"I do. Does that surprise you?"

"Not really," I said, which was true. Actors are a superstitious tribe, always looking for luck and a glimpse of the future. They read their horoscopes, practice strange ritual behaviors before performances, carry totem objects with them for special occasions. Madeleine had a silver bracelet she'd worn when she won a state competition in high school that she kept in a velvet bag and wore only to auditions. Teddy had a lucky belt.

"Let's sit down," Marlene suggested. "We'll eat and talk, and then I'll read your cards."

"Great," I said.

We talked. What did we talk about? I believe we talked about me. Marlene asked me questions about what I'd read, my training, what plays I'd seen, what I thought of them, what I thought of the actors in them. She made me feel more interesting than I knew I was.

At one point she asked me what I knew about her. The photo in the wallet sprang into my brain, but even after a few glasses of wine I was cautious with her. "They say you are married and have a son tucked away in California and that you don't answer personal questions in interviews."

"Is that all they say?"

"And that you are a great actress."

"Oh, well, of course," she said. "They would say that."

"I believe it."

"You flatter me," she said, creating the sudden distance that kept me so off balance. "Now bring me my cards and let's see what they have to say about you."

When I stood up I found myself sure on my feet but light-headed from the wine. Outside it was dark and humid; a sultry breeze lifted the curtains, rustling the papers on the desk. Marlene switched on a lamp. I handed her the cards and took my seat, oddly excited by the prospect of mumbo-jumbo in a summer cottage with Marlene Webern. One could make a play of it, I thought. The ingenue and the actress. "This is fun," I said.

"No," she said. "It's serious." She fanned the deck open and extracted a card. "First we choose your signifier," she said, laying down a picture of a dark youth on a horse. "You're a blond now, so ordinarily I would choose a cup or wand, but I know your true color is dark. And this boy suits you. He stands for vigilance."

"I'm sure you can't fool the cards with a dye job," I said.

"No," she said. "You can't." She shuffled the cards and laid the pack facedown in front of me. "Now we're going to get to the bottom of Edward Day."

"I don't like the sound of that," I said.

"Cut to the left three times, three times."

"Three times, three times," I said, breaking the deck into stacks and reassembling them.

"And ask a question in your mind."

"What sort of question?"

"It should be a general question."

So I couldn't ask if Marlene would go to bed with me, though that was uppermost in my thoughts. I settled on "What will become of me?" One couldn't get more general than that.

"I hope I get the baby on the horse," I said.

She smiled. "That's a very good card," she agreed. She turned the top card up and laid it across my signifier. "Oh dear," she said.

It was the horned devil, all goat legs and bat wings perched on a block; at his clawed feet a naked man and woman, sporting horns and flaming tails, were chained by their necks to a ring on the block.

"That doesn't look promising," I observed.

"It's not so bad. It covers the general atmosphere of the question. It suggests you're in bondage to the material world."

"Oh, is that all," I said.

"Well, it could be something more extreme. It could be black magic."

"Heaven forbid," I said, refilling my wineglass.

"You're not interested in spiritual matters then."

"No. That's right. I'm not."

"Well, you should be."

"Do you think so?"

"The cards think so." She turned up the next one and placed it crosswise on the other two. "This crosses you," she said. It was a man standing before a series of silver chalices from which snakes, castles, laurel wreaths, and precious jewels overflowed. It was a dreamy picture; the cups floated on clouds.

"Scattered forces," Marlene said. "You waste your energy on fantasies."

"That can't be denied," I said.

"Well, you're young. It's natural. How old are you?"

"Twenty-five."

Turning up the next card she said, "This card refers to something that has happened in the past." She placed it carefully below the first three. For a moment we sat staring silently at my past.

The image was brutal. A man lay facedown on the ground with ten swords thrust into his back. The background was black. A liquid that was probably blood pooled near his head. "I'm really not enjoying this very much," I said.

"It's not death," she reassured me again. "Obviously in this position it can't be. It's a card of sudden loss, of betrayal."

Something about the card made me queasy, yet I couldn't look away. *I want you to sit down, son*, I heard my father say. And then, very clearly, a voice I'd heard only once in my life: *I hate this part of you*. Tears sprang to my eyes. "I'd like to stop here, if you don't mind," I said.

"Ed?" Marlene looked into my eyes with an expression of sympathy I found too bold, too easy. "Are you all right?" she asked.

I cleared my throat, clearing out my mother and her cracked girlfriend and the notes fluttering on the desk in my dormitory room: *Your mother called. Your mother again*. "Do your son a favor," I said coldly to Marlene. "Don't kill yourself."

She drew in a breath, leaning away from me. "I'm so sorry," she said.

"There's no reason you should be sorry."

"I mean, I'm sorry for you. I'm sorry for your loss. When did it happen?"

"When I was a freshman in college."

She was quiet for a moment. "It does explain something about you, as an actor."

"I don't much care what it explains," I said.

She picked up the card and examined it closely. "I don't believe in fate," she said. "And I don't think cards can predict the future. Only stupid people believe that. But the symbols on these cards are very old and they speak in a language we apprehend without having to think about it, without words. They speak to the unconscious, in effect, they speak to our emotions. That's why I like them."

"Good for you," I said.

Oblivious to the wave of ice I was sending her way, she went on. "What a strange set of circumstances," she said. "That you should come here to do this particular play with me at this point in your career. It's truly fortuitous."

"But you don't believe in fate," I said. "And you wanted me to come here, you said so yourself."

"Who are you angry with? Is it me?"

"I'm just saying it isn't fortuitous."

"You're a talented actor, Ed. You have a gift, and you have ambition. And you're not envious and competitive, that's something, that's good. Envy can be killing to an actor. Well, it's ruinous in all the arts."

"Are you getting at something, Marlene?"

"I am. Be patient. You're a good actor and you could be a

great actor, but only if you understand that your life must be given up to your art. You can have no other life. There can't be Ed having an emotion on the stage and Ed having an emotion, a strong, pure, deep emotion here in this room and a curtain drawn between. You mustn't sit here and try to push away a powerful emotion because it's painful. As an actor you have no right to do that."

"I'm not going to bawl about my dead mother, if that's what you want."

"I don't want anything. It's what you want. And what you need, from yourself, as an actor. Let go of your response to the emotion and study it. Study what it did to you, how it evolved in you, how it came about, Ed, dear, that *I* could see it and know it was real. Not faked. That it was real. You have to make use of yourself, of who you are."

"Sandy is always on about that in class," I said.

"Yes, well, he's right. Listen, you know that moment in the first scene when Scudder tells Chance Wayne his mother is dead and Chance says, 'Why wasn't I notified?' "

I'd been listening to her halfheartedly but now she had my complete attention. Incredible as it may seem, I had not until that moment connected the death of my character's mother with my feelings about the death of my own. His mother had been sick, she sounded old and petulant. That's why he'd come back to town. He hadn't been notified of her death because he'd left no reliable address. He was out starfucking, trying to get into the right crowd, sleeping "in the social registry," when his mother needed him. She had died a few weeks before he got around to caring about her.

"You always make yourself go cold when you deliver that line," Marlene continued. "You clench your jaw as if someone had just trod on your foot and you didn't want to let on. It's a dead line when you deliver it, nothing is revealed. Now I know why."

"I never feel comfortable with that line."

She handed the card to me. "Take it, look at it. Memorize it, not in words, don't say, 'It's a man with swords in his back,' just visualize it."

I took the card and did as she instructed, but words rose up in spite of me, and those words were, *It was my fault.*

"Now say the line."

I studied the card. It was myself I recognized, slain there.

Marlene gave me my cue. "Your mother died a couple of weeks ago."

I looked just past her at the curtain rustling in the breeze. A shiver, like spidery pinpricks ran up my spine. "Why wasn't I notified," I asked her. It wasn't a question, I wasn't seeking information. It was an admission of guilt.

"There you are," Marlene said. "There you are."

I held the card out to her. "Thank you," I said.

"Keep it," she said. "It's yours now."

I did keep it; I still have it somewhere, I'm not sure where, but I know I never threw it away. I didn't keep it for luck or out of superstition, but as a souvenir of that strange night when I was in love with Marlene Webern and she was generous to a young actor who had no idea what he was doing. I wanted to have sex with her, she wanted me to commit to my art. She sent me back to the boardinghouse that night with a kiss as chaste as Thisbe gave Pyramus through the chink in the wall and the next morning at rehearsal, she held her arms out to me again and I snuggled down into her warm, fragrant bosom and kissed her parted lips, sick with desire. What an actress that woman was! I never did get her into bed, but perhaps that was just as well. Best not to sully the ideal: I think she knew that.

Our play opened a week later and was, in the insular, hot-house world of summer stock, reckoned a success. The local press gushed over Marlene's performance as well they might, and I was singled out for hyperbolic praise: "A young actor of startling prowess." "Newcomer Edward Day commands the stage." Stuff like that. I was fucking the luscious Eve at night and worshipping at the altar of my goddess by day; my fellow thespians were a spirited, pleasure-loving lot; I was working hard and playing hard; and I had, at long last, an Equity card. The future was dazzling, and I gazed upon it from the evanescent interior of a bubble.

We had only one phone in the front hall of the boarding-house, so making and receiving calls wasn't easy. At the end of the first week I had left a message at Madeleine's service, giving her the number, with the frustrating addendum that there was rarely anyone in the house to answer it. A few days later I found a written message under my door: *Madeleine called; please call her at eight a.m. on Friday.* Dutifully I made the call but got the service again. "She had an appointment," the sleepy employee explained. "She said to tell you she's fine, very busy. She'll try to give you a call on Sunday."

"That's not good," I said. "We're in rehearsal all day."

"I'll tell her," he said. "How is it up there?"

"It's great," I said. "Are you an actor?"

"Why else would I be doing this job?"

"Right," I said. "Tell her I'll send her a card."

And that was the end of that. These days everyone has a cell phone stuck to his head and the idea of being out of touch is unthinkable, but at that time an exchange passed through a stranger was sometimes the best you could do. The next day I sent Madeleine a postcard with a photo of the picturesque town green.

Dear Madeleine, I wrote. *I'm working hard and loving it. I have the lead in Williams's* Sweet Bird. *It's a good group. The director's no genius, but he's not vicious and the theater is charming. Sorry about the phone situation. It's basically impossible. Glad to hear you're busy too. Love, Edward*

I didn't want to lose her, I thought, as I dropped the card into the postbox. I just didn't want to deal with her until we were face-to-face again.

A week later I got a card from her; the Statue of Liberty, which I took to be a good sign. *Dear Edward, Your card sounds like you're writing to someone you've recently met—or to your maiden aunt. Everything dead and hot here. I've got an audition at the Circle—wish me luck. I miss you. (You forgot to say that.) Love, Madeleine*

That last bit made me smile. Sufficiently tart, put me right in my place; that was Madeleine. I missed her too.

One evening toward the end of July, Gary Santos stopped in at the dressing room—he played the thuggish Tom Junior and took his part in my onstage castration with what I considered excessive glee—to say a friend had stopped by the boarding-house asking for me.

"What's his name?"

"He didn't say. Tall guy, long hair, beard, looks like a hip-pie. Said he'd see you after the play."

I could think of no friend who matched this description and straightway forgot about it, being absorbed by the cruel fate of Chance Wayne. The performance went well; the audience chuckled at all the jokes and took in breath during the brutal bits, applauded strongly for the full duration of our bows at the end. Marlene squeezed my hand as she smiled into the lights and I lifted her fingers to my lips, gazing longingly into her eyes. I was still in hot pursuit which amused her, but I hadn't been in-vited back into the sanctity of the cottage. In the dressing room I cleaned off my makeup, pulled on a T-shirt, and went out with a group who were heading for the local pub. We arrived in high spirits and occupied our customary booth near the back. The waitress, who knew our preferred brews, at once began ferrying icy mugs from the bar. Eve was next to me bending Gary's ear about the high professional standards at Yale, but her eyes kept drifting to the mirror behind him. "Stop admiring yourself," Gary demanded. "It's disgusting."

"I'm not," she protested.

"Right," Gary and I said in unison.

Eve giggled theatrically. "No, you sillies, I'm not. There's a cool-looking guy at the bar watching us. He looks like Warren Beatty in that movie, you know, with Julie Christie. I think I've seen him in something."

Gary and I both craned our necks for a celeb sighting. He was standing with his back to the bar, propped on one elbow, drinking beer from a bottle in a studly pose and, Eve was right, he was watching us. His black hair was long, past his chin, and he had a short, neatly trimmed beard. He raised his bottle to us in a friendly salute and flashed a disturbing smile like a coconut cracking open. With his free hand he pulled up a leather satchel resting on the barstool. "That's the guy who was looking for you," Gary said and Eve whispered, "Look, he's coming over."

"God, Ed," Guy announced as he arrived at our table. "When you came out on that stage, I didn't recognize you. I thought I was in the wrong theater. You make a fantastic blond. I think you should stick with it."

"I didn't recognize you, either," I said, which was true.

He patted the beard tentatively with his fingertips. "Oh, yes," he said. "I've changed too." His quick eyes raked the company and settled on Eve. "You were just great," he said.

"Thanks," Eve said.

"This is Guy Margate," I said. "This is Eve."

"Guy," Eve said, rising up in her place to shake hands. "Nice to meet you."

Guy fumbled in the bag and pulled out a Polaroid camera. "Can I get a picture of you guys?" he said, popping off the cap and stepping back to frame his shot. Eve grinned and leaned across the table, resting her hand on my arm. Gary and I laughed at her eagerness. "She's always ready for her close-up," Gary said. There was a flash and the zip of the magical square sliding out like a white tongue. Guy pulled it free and fanned it languidly, smiling at us.

"What brings you to Connecticut?" I asked.

"Well, I wanted to see your show."

"That's really nice," Eve said.

I didn't think it was nice; in fact I was sure it wasn't. He was up to something; he wanted something. Fortunately there was no room in our booth so I had a good excuse to separate from the group and join my old friend Guy at the bar. He passed the photo around, discharging a few fulsome compliments upon the players until the picture came back and he followed me.

"Jack Daniels," I said to the bartender. "Straight up, water back."

Guy drained his beer. "I'll have the same."

I watched the bartender pouring the drinks, unable to think of anything I wanted to say to Guy. "Man," he said at last. "I can't get over you as a blond. It almost looks natural." He pulled thoughtfully at a thick strand grazing his cheek. "Maybe I should try it."

"It wouldn't look natural," I said.

"I don't see why not."

"You're actually darker than I am," I said. "Your coloring is all wrong."

"There are lots of blond Italians."

"Is that what you are?"

"It probably wouldn't be worth the trouble." Our drinks arrived and he sipped his.

"Why the beard?" I asked.

"It's an experiment. There's a Chekhov play coming up,

well it's actually a play about Chekhov. Bev knows the casting director and she thinks she can get me an audition."

"You see yourself as Chekhov?"

"Or just generic nineteenth-century Russian; they all had beards. Sure, I could do that."

"You have a lot of confidence in yourself," I said.

"Why shouldn't I?"

I swallowed half my bourbon glancing back at my friends in the booth. I could hear their sudden bursts of laughter, but I couldn't make out what they were saying. The room was dimly lit and smoky; they seemed far away. A green shaded lamp over the mirror cast threads of light on the reflection of Eve's golden curls, her rosy cheeks, as she reached across the table to snatch a cigarette from the communal pack. "That girl finds you very attractive," I said to Guy.

His eyes followed mine, but listlessly. "You're having a fine time here," he said.

"I am," I agreed.

"Are you fucking that TV actress?"

"Marlene? I wouldn't say if I were." Eve, feeling our eyes upon her, sent me a provocative smile, a wave, a wink.

"You're fucking that girl," Guy observed.

"Why are you interested?"

"I'm not interested," he said.

"What is it you want here?"

He smiled, but not at me. "You're not bad in that role," he said. "The hustler who thinks he could be a star. It suits you, eh?"

"Actually no. I'm acting."

This made him laugh which was never a pleasant sight. "Is that what you call it?"

"You're always ready with the critique," I said. "Who asked you to come here anyway?"

He took a beat, drawing down his eyebrows and upper lip in a mockery of serious consideration. "Madeleine," he said.

I didn't believe him, but I was curious. "Did she send you to check up on me?"

"It's too late for that, isn't it?"

"What is it about being asked a question that you don't get?"

"She's pregnant," he said.

This was a conversation-stopper. I took the opportunity to signal the bartender for another drink. Guy looked back at the table where the waitress was setting down two large pizzas. "That girl is pretty enough," he said, "but she's a terrible actress."

"Madeleine sent you to tell me this?"

"It's not as if she can reach you on the phone," he said. "And it's not the sort of news one puts on a postcard, is it?"

This was true enough, but still I didn't believe him. "Why didn't she come herself?"

"She doesn't have time."

"So you're the wicked messenger."

"I take it this is unwelcome news."

"When did you and Madeleine get so close?"

"We've been friends a long time; we have the same agent."

"And I've been away for two months."

He looked back at Eve. "You know, I think it's really a bad idea to have sex with an actress whose work you have contempt for. It coarsens you."

"So who's the lucky father?" I said.

"That's just what one can never be sure of, isn't it," Guy said. "Much has been made of that very problem in the theater."

"What's she going to do?"

He lifted his chin and tapped around the edge of his beard as if he was securing it to his face. "I think the question is: What are you going to do?"

"Is the beard real?"

"Sure it is," he said.

"I just can't believe Madeleine would send you to tell me this news." It was so unfair, I thought. Everything was going so well. "I'm going to have to think about this," I said.

"You wouldn't want to do anything impulsive."

"Exactly," I agreed, but then I realized he was attempting irony, which was a stretch for Guy. He couldn't get the inclusive fellow-feeling element that tempers the blade of wit. Instead of humorous prodding, his method was the full frontal sneer. My jaw and throat felt tight; I narrowed my eyes. I was angry with Madeleine. How could she put me in this intolerable position? She knew how I felt about Guy. And what if she was sleeping with him? I didn't trust either of them.

The group confined in the booth broke ranks and drifted toward the bar. Eve made a beeline for the stool next to Guy, engaging him at once on the question of what she should drink. This suited me; it gave me time to figure out what to say. My assumption was that Madeleine would want an abortion. She was far too ambitious and obsessed with her career to put it on hold to have a child no one really wanted. I figured she would know how to do whatever she wanted to do, but what she would need would be money. I had a little, not much. How should I send it to her? Should I give it to Guy or send a check in a letter? I wanted to help her without making any kind of commitment.

Guy was flirting energetically with Eve and she was eating it up. I heard the golden phrase "my agent" more than once and some disparagement of the reviewers who had courteously withheld comment about Eve's performance in our production. It was a rerun of the scene at Phebe's a year ago, when Guy had made a play for Madeleine, but this time I was wishing him success. If he spent the night with Eve it would prove something I wanted proved, though I wasn't sure exactly what that was. That Guy was a hypocrite? That he was heterosexual? Something along those lines.

But in spite of Eve's best efforts, Guy wasn't tempted. At length he turned to me and announced that he had to catch the last bus back to the city. "Walk over with me," he said. "And we can finish our conversation."

I followed him out into the street; my shoulders drooped, my feet shuffling like a reluctant child. The walk he proposed, which wasn't half a mile, stretched out interminably. I felt I'd been sentenced to a term at hard labor. After a block of this he looked back sharply. "Good grief," he said. "Can't you keep up?" I hustled along, allowing hostility to double for energy. Why did Guy always make me feel so tired and so shamed? I'd done nothing wrong. "So what do you want me to tell Madeleine?" he asked.

"I don't want you to tell her anything."

Again the close, deprecating look. "So I'll tell her you have nothing to say to her."

"Does she need money?"

"I should think so."

"Tell her I'll send her some money."

"You could just give it to me."

"No, I'll mail it."

"I'd rather you didn't do that."

"I don't get why you're in the middle of this," I said. "Why should I care what you'd rather I did or didn't do about Madeleine?"

"Because Madeleine doesn't know I'm here."

I stopped short. "So you lied?" I said.

"For a good cause."

I pressed the heels of my hands into my temples. "Who do you think you are?" I exclaimed.

"Would you come on," he said. "If I miss this bus I'll have to sleep on your floor."

This was a persuasive argument. I matched him stride for stride while he explained his mission. "I told her I would come talk to you, but she didn't want me to. She said you'd only sent her one postcard and it was hardly even friendly. You really hurt her with that. She figured you didn't care what happened to her and knowing she was pregnant would only make everything worse. But I thought you had a right to know."

"Did it occur to you that she doesn't want me to know because I'm not the father?"

"She's more than two months pregnant, Ed."

"That doesn't prove anything."

He grasped his beard in both hands and, without missing a step, tore it loose from his chin. "This thing is driving me nuts," he said.

"Does it itch?"

"Like fire ants," he said. "It's like having fire ants on your face."

The bus station was a bench and a sign in front of a news-agent's store and as we turned the last corner we could see a few people milling about in the bug-saturated light of the streetlamp. I wanted to close the conversation on a clear and final point. "The way I see it," I said, "is that it's up to Madeleine to decide who to tell and what to do. If she doesn't want me to know, so be it."

Guy stuffed the beard into his satchel. "The way I see it," he said, "is that Madeleine is a girl in trouble and you can't be bothered. Which is fine, Ed. I should have known. I should have known."

I reached into my pocket and pulled out all the cash I had, about fifty dollars. "Look, this isn't much, but give it to her. And I'll send you a hundred more tomorrow. Just say you're giving it to her; she doesn't need to know it's from me."

He took the cash and held it for a moment, as if trying to

make up his mind whether to keep it or throw it in my face. We were close to the stop and we heard the huffing of the bus before it lumbered into view. The waiting passengers formed themselves into a civilized line. Guy and I stood motionless, both transfixed by the folded bills he gripped in his fist. As the bus came to a halt, the brakes whirred and groaned and the wings of the doors flapped open with a breathy whoosh. Guy crammed the money into the pocket of his jeans. "You make me sick," he hissed, and he turned on his heel, leaving me on the curb.

I didn't know if I'd been repudiated or skillfully scammed. I stood there, watching the passengers file into the bus, until I was certain Guy was on it. Then, in case he got back off, I decided to wait until the doors were closed. After that it seemed the best course to be sure the bus actually pulled away from the curb and rolled off into the night. When I couldn't see it at all, I rubbed my eyes and looked again. Only then did a sensation of deep release and relief allow me to turn away and walk back to the boardinghouse where Eve, languidly rocking herself on the porch swing, waited for me.

The next day I wrote a check for one hundred dollars, leaving twelve dollars in my account, put the check in an envelope, and because I didn't know Guy's address, sent it to him care of his agent, Bev Arbuckle. I didn't want to do it, but I didn't not want to do it, either. Guy's melodramatic description of Madeleine as "a girl in trouble," which struck me as something from a '50s soap opera, stung me—you can't turn your back on a girl in trouble. But Madeleine wasn't some misguided teenager; she was an adult, perfectly capable of making her own decisions. Trusting Guy to give the money to Madeleine kept me from having to contact her directly. I honestly believed, I still do, that it was up to her to tell me what she wanted me to know, yet knowing what I now did, I wanted to help her. I liked the anonymity of my admittedly small contribution to her well-being. And I liked especially that she clearly had no intention of involving me in her predicament. I had another month in Connecticut and by the time I got back to the city, Madeleine would presumably be as she had been and we could go from there.

In the meantime, Marlene, by example and by design, was teaching me what I needed to be an actor. Interestingly it was a combination of egomania and complete selflessness. In the process of taking on a character, some essence of the self must remain intact. "Never lose yourself on the stage," Stanislavski famously advised. I saw in Marlene, day after day, something essentially unaltered that absorbed the character she played. She didn't become Alexandra del Lago, Alexandra del Lago became Marlene Webern. It's difficult to describe, it sounds abstract and absurd, but for me at that time, it was transformative, allowing for subtleties of interpretation and impression that had hitherto eluded me. Marlene watched me literally like a hawk; it was as if her eye was equipped with a zoom lens that saw straight into the heart of me. Especially when we were onstage together, I could feel that probing eye on me and it charged our time together with what reviewers call "electricity." Yet she was not, by any means, always focused upon me. Her eyes often wandered away, resting on some prop item or on her own hands. Sometimes she lifted her chin in my direction but let her eyes go maddeningly out of focus, with that inward smile of hers and an attitude of listening. When she wasn't watching me, she was intensely listening to me.

I became conscious of how rarely people actually look at or listen to each other in ordinary life, or if they do, how often it's with ill intent. Marlene's attention was nonjudgmental, curious, and serene, neither hot nor cold, and it was like that onstage and off.

One Sunday afternoon in the last week of the season, I found myself at loose ends after the children's production, in which I had a role as a wolf. Acting for children is relaxing; they're such an open, rambunctious audience, eager to go on the wildest flights of fancy, their little mouths open in helpless ohs and ahs, their eyes dancing with delight at each revelation of the simplistic plot. I'd taken off my wolf makeup and hung up my wolf suit for the last time, and I felt sad about that.

The others had all gone off in a rush after the show. It was a clear, hot day, one in a string of them, and they had planned an outing to the coast for a swim, an opportunity I had declined. I wasn't up for the beach just yet. As I stepped from the dark theater into the blazing sun the sensation of carrying a weight of gloom became so pronounced I owned it. "I'm sad," I said to no one, and sat down on the step. I fished in my pocket for a cigarette, lit up, and breathed in the pungent, lethal smoke. Soon I'd be back in the city looking for a job. I heard the creak of the screen door behind me, but I didn't bother to look up. The stairs were wide, I wasn't blocking the way. A pair of tanned feet in red sandals appeared on the wood next to my hip. "I thought everyone went to the shore," Marlene said. The sun was behind her and I squinted up at her. Her eyes were hidden behind her dark glasses, her hair was loose, her full lips were slightly parted; star power wafted from her like a breeze from another planet. How was it possible that I knew this extraterrestrial beauty? "I don't care for the beach," I said.

"I don't either," she said, smoothly dropping down on the step beside me. "All that sun is bad for the skin and sand is very unpleasant."

"You speak against sand?"

"It sticks to everything. It gets into everything."

I took another drag on my cigarette. "That's true," I said.

"You do look the picture of despondency," she observed. "Has something happened?"

"Not really."

"Romantic entanglement? Financial reverses?"

"I'm depressed because the summer is nearly over," I said, "and you're going back to L.A. and I may never see you again."

"It has been an excellent season. But you should be energized; you've grown as an actor."

"Have I?"

"Oh, immensely. Don't you feel it?"

"I feel it when I'm with you."

"We had a lot of fun with our play."

"I'll miss kissing you. I really love kissing you."

She laughed. "That's very sweet."

"No. It's not."

"You'll be kissing someone lovely on the stage in no time."

"It would help if you'd say you didn't actually mind kissing me."

She turned away from me, as if she heard someone approaching, but there was no one. "Actually those scenes were disturbing to me. You remind me so much of my son."

"Good God," I said.

"I didn't want to tell you because I thought it might inhibit you."

I hadn't given much thought to Marlene as a mother. When I'd heard about the son, I'd pictured a boy in grammar school, a little leaguer or soccer enthusiast. "How old is your son?" I asked.

"He's twenty."

"How is that possible?" I said.

"I was young when he was born."

"Do I look like him?"

"Not really. It's something about the way you move. Your gestures remind me of him. You're much more alive than he is. He's an unhappy young man, I'm afraid. Not very lively."

"Why is he unhappy?"

"Probably because his mother is an actress."

"Is he in school?"

"No. He didn't do well in school. There were drug problems and he's very independent, he doesn't take . . ." she paused, searching for the right word, "direction."

"Does he want to be an actor?"

"Oh no. He despises acting."

"That's not great," I said, pointlessly.

Marlene drew herself up and removed her sunglasses. Her

eyes were moist, and her voice, when she spoke, quavered slightly, as from emotion. "I'm worried. Tell me, what is the matter with my son? Why is he so sad and so austere?"

"Chekhov, right?"

She slid the glasses back into place. "Very good," she said. "It's Arkadina in *The Seagull*. I'll be doing it in the spring in Pasadena. So you see, everything is of use."

"You're always working."

"Yes," she said. "I've been fortunate. But you will be too."

"Not if I don't find an agent."

"I thought you had one."

"No. I don't."

"I'll send you to Barney. He'll be perfect for you and you for him." She opened an absurdly small purse and took out her wallet, not, I noted, the one I'd snatched from the bag in the immortal improv. She extracted a card and wrote a name and phone number on the back. "Call him when you get back," she said. "Tell him I sent you. And I'll call him to tell him about you. He'll be expecting you."

I took the card and studied the name, Barney Marker. "You're something with these cards that change my life."

"You're very talented, you should be encouraged. But I want to advise you about your training. Sandy is a wonderful teacher. Listen to everything he says, but don't take his criticism too much to heart. There's a coldness in you that he'll take offense to, he'll try to root it out of you, but I think ultimately it will be your strength."

"You think I'm cold?"

"Part of you is. Yes. The other part is very hot, very passionate. It's your temperament, and it's a gift. Not many actors can stand still the way you do."

"Are you like that?"

"Like what?"

"Hot and cold."

"I was. These days I'm mostly weary. But when I'm working, I'm all right."

"I think you're brilliant," I said.

She rested her hand on my knee sending a bolt of liquid heat straight to my groin. "I know you do, Edward," she said. "And that's very gratifying to me." My brain, joining in the excitement in my groin, was churning out torrid images.

"Could I ask you something?" I said.

"Of course."

"You know that photograph you had in your wallet that first time, at school? When we did the improv?"

Her eyebrows knit over the glasses. "No," she said. "What photo?"

"The one of you, on the couch."

She drew her hand away and pressed her fingertips against her lips in an expression of deep puzzlement. "A photograph of me?" she said.

"On a couch."

"My driver's license is in my wallet. But I'm not on a couch."

"You're acting," I said.

"In the photo?"

"No. Now. You're having me on."

She fumbled with the bag. "Would you like to see my wallet?"

"No," I said. "It's not the same one."

She opened the purse and closed it again, emanating mystification from every pore.

"Forget about it," I said, stubbing out my cigarette next to my shoe.

So I was never to know anything about the photograph and Marlene was such a good actress that I suddenly doubted whether I had actually seen it.

"I must be off," she said, glancing at her watch. "I'm lunching with the board."

I slipped the card into my shirt pocket. "Thanks for this," I said. "It means a lot."

"Let me know what happens. My address is on the front."

"I will," I promised, and I did. When I got back to the city the third call I made was to Barney Marker. "Mr. Day," his assistant said. "Yes, Ms. Webern spoke with Mr. Marker about you. Can you come in on Wednesday in the afternoon?"

The second call I made was to Teddy.

"You're back at last," Teddy said. "Come over at seven and we'll go get dinner somewhere. I've got a lot to tell you."

The first call was to Madeleine. I left a message with the service. "Tell her I'm back," I said. "She knows the number."

"Oh my God, you're a blond," Teddy cried when he opened the door. "It's a totally new you."

"Not for long," I said as we exchanged an awkward hug. "Getting it done is torture and it fries your hair." I followed him into his kitchen where he immediately began pouring out glasses of Scotch.

"Let's have a drink before we go out," he said.

Teddy looked different too, though just how I couldn't say. He seemed lighter, more buoyant. He was wearing a stylish beige linen jacket, expensive, definitely Italian, which was odd, because Teddy was generally indifferent to fashion. His ironic woebegoneness, partly attributable to his face and partly to his disposition, was in place, but there was a brightness about him I'd never seen before. His habitual lethargy had been replaced by something more sinuous and expansive. "You look great," I said.

"Did I look bad before?"

"I don't know. You look happy."

"I am. I really am."

"Do you have a job?"

This made him laugh. "Not exactly, but in a way yes, I do. Or maybe not." He handed me a glass and we went out to the sitting room. There was a large painting I hadn't seen before hanging over the fake fireplace, very dark with dots of bright color that made me think of lights on a bridge at night.

"That's new," I observed.

"It is," he said. We sat in the armchairs which had been turned to face the painting. "So how was it? Were you a success?"

"I was," I said. "It was great. It changed my life."

"I've had a transforming summer myself."

"So what do you mean about the job? Do you have one or don't you?"

"I do. It's a new part for me. I'm in love."

"That's not true. You're always in love," I said.

"But this time it's different."

"It's requited," I suggested.

"It is so requited." He sipped his drink, his eyes alight with amusement.

"Is it Jasmine?"

"No. But that's a good guess. It is someone in her family."

"She has a sister?"

"No. She has a brother, no sisters."

"It's not Mrs. Lee!"

He sputtered with delight. "No, no, not Mrs. Lee."

"You look like you're going to pop," I said. "Who is it?"

"It's Jasmine's brother," he said. "Wayne."

"You're joking," I said. And it was a good joke, but I failed to see the point of it.

"I've never been more serious in my life."

My jaw went slack with amazement. "I see you've been keeping something from me," I said.

"I've been keeping something from myself. And it's been killing me. Slowly, slowly, year after year."

"I'm dumbfounded," I said.

"I know you are. I was too."

"Give me a little more Scotch for the shock and tell me exactly how this happened," I said.

"I can't wait to tell you," he said, passing the bottle. I settled in my chair, ready for a story packed with my favorite subject, unexpected and powerfully conflicted emotions.

"You know Jasmine and I hit it off that night we met her at the restaurant, and after you left we went out a few times. Mindy was giving me such a hard time and Jasmine is a sprite and so undemanding it was a relief to be with her. One night she invited me to dinner with the family—to taste real Chinese food, she said—though I think she'd already figured out more about me than I knew about myself The inscrutable Chinese, you know. We don't get them but they see right through us.

"So I went down there and it was her parents, the aunt, Mrs. Lee, who you met, and her husband—he doesn't speak English—and Jasmine's brother, Wayne, who was in the kitchen when I arrived. He's an incredible cook. I was sitting at the table with the family when he came in carrying a tray of the most fabulous dumplings and when I saw him my heart just stopped. All I thought was, What a handsome man. Jasmine introduced him and I stood up to shake hands, and I tell you Ed, the look he gave me went through me like a skewer through a hot dog. Then we all sat down and pitched into the dumplings and everyone started talking half in Chinese and half in English. This went on for about six courses. At one point Wayne was bringing out a platter of noodles and he lowered it to the table from behind me. I said something idiotic like 'I love noodles,' and he laughed. Then he put his hand on my shoulder, just the lightest squeeze and he said, 'So you like Chinese noodles,' and everyone laughed hysterically. They're very giddy, that family; they laugh a lot. So different from dinner at the pater's; I can't tell you.

"The evening wore on and I learned that Wayne was a painter and he's even had a few pictures in shows. He works in a gallery in SoHo and has a studio in the East Village, and everyone in the family knows he'll be a great painter and they're proud of him. Again, the opposite of my experience."

"East meets West," I said.

"It was just mind-boggling. I kept drinking rice wine and trying not to look at Wayne, but it was hopeless. And I was having a good time. Jasmine was being enormously sweet, and the mother wanted to know all about Stella Adler—she thinks Jasmine should study with her. The mother is completely informed about theater, which is astounding. Anyway, somehow I got through it without fainting away, and as I was leaving Wayne said I really should come by his studio to see his work. I said I'd be very interested in that, and he said, 'Come tomorrow,' which was a Sunday. 'I'll be there all day.' So I said I would come around four and he told me the address and that was that."

"So you went to the studio," I said.

"I did. But first I came home, of course, and tried to make some sense of what had happened to me. I sat in this chair and drank a big glass of Scotch and halfway through I started crying."

"You felt sad?"

"I felt scared. I was scared to death. I decided not to go. I couldn't deal with it. Then I'd think of that little squeeze on my shoulder and I knew I had to go, and that made me cry harder. I cried all night. I hardly slept at all. On Sunday I just read the paper and drank coffee all day, trying not to know what was going to happen. I told myself he was just a friendly Chinese man and I'd go see the pictures and we'd have a nice chat about the art scene. The hours dragged by; I think I read every single line of the entire Sunday *Times.* Then, at last, it was time to go. I was wired to the limit from no sleep and the tears and then all the coffee; I'd eaten one piece of toast. I arrived at the door— it's more like a garage door, it slides open—and I rang the bell. There was this sound like the gate of a prison rolling back and there he was.

"We went inside and he offered me some herbal tea which was really welcome. We started talking about the dinner and the family and what Jasmine should do about her career. I felt completely comfortable. I took my tea and he showed me around the studio—it's pretty bare, very Zen, though Wayne's not a Buddhist—and I walked around looking at the paintings everywhere. He's done a lot of work. Some were stacked against the walls and some were hung up. I went along admiring each one and I stopped at this one." Teddy looked up at the painting over the fireplace. "This fantastic picture."

"It's his?" I said needlessly.

"Oh yes. Do you like it?"

"Yes," I said. "I do."

"I stopped in front of it and I said something, who knows what. What did I say? My heart was just racing. Wayne came up beside me and he did the dearest thing; he just put his arm around my shoulder and he said, 'You like this one particularly?'

" 'I do,' I said. He took the teacup away from me and put it on the floor and then he stood between me and the picture and put his arms around me and kissed me. And all I could think was, God help me, I'm in love with a Chinese man." Teddy paused, allowing me to savor the moment.

"Amazing story," I said.

"It is," he agreed. "I've been waiting for you to get back so I could tell you."

"Does anyone else know about it?"

"Oh yes. But not the details. And of course my family knows nothing about it yet. The pater will disinherit me when he finds out."

"That's big."

"It is. But there's nothing to be done about it." He said this frankly, without self-pity, as if he was describing an approaching weather system.

"So," I said. "You're out of the closet."

He frowned. "I've never liked that expression. But it's apt, I guess. That whole business about being in a closet, it irritates me. I always picture this absurd fag standing just behind the door, stripping down to his briefs and then—BAM—he kicks that door open and leaps out singing, 'I Gotta Be Me.' " He sang this line in a thin falsetto that made me laugh.

"But I wasn't just behind the door, Ed, I was way, way back in the darkest corner of the closet, behind the coats and the old badminton sets, and the snow boots, just crouched back there like a little mouse nibbling on crumbs I found in the coat pockets, and it was dark and I was scared, and also sad. I've been so sad for so long."

I considered this confession. "It made you kind," I said. "And it made you an actor."

"But not a *good* actor. That's one of the things I've been sad about. And here's a really funny part. A few weeks after that kiss, I had to do a scene for Ms. Adler and I just ripped right through it; I felt absolutely confident and powerful as I never have before, and when it was over she said, 'Well, Mr. Winterbottom, I see that I am a very talented teacher.' Poor old lady, she thought it was her teaching that finally got me to some kind of breakthrough, but it had nothing to do with her. It was my wonderful, beautiful Wayne who led me out of that suffocating darkness I'd been trying to thrive in and into the glorious light that is just pouring over me now, just blinding me with the joy and the freedom of it. When I think of how close I came to marrying Mindy Banks my blood runs cold. My God, Ed, I wake up in the morning feeling absolutely great. I can't wait to jump out of bed and spend another day basking in this wonderful, wonderful light."

He'd gotten out of his chair at some point and finished his aria standing beneath the painting, his arms opened wide to embrace his new self. It occurred to me that he'd probably bought the picture from Wayne. Teddy was, after all, rich, at least temporarily, and Wayne was surely poor. "That picture is actually rather dark," I observed.

Teddy smiled beatifically down upon me. "It is, isn't it?" he said and we both laughed.

"How did Mindy take the news?"

"Not well. She thinks Wayne will break my heart and I'll come crawling back to her."

I thought so too, but I wasn't going to tell Teddy; it would have been cruel. The whole idea of Teddy's Chinese man gave me the creeps. I imagined Jasmine had figured out Teddy was rich and ripe for exploitation by her brother. The whole family may have been in on it. But whatever happened, Teddy was visibly, seriously altered, and I believed what he said about his acting having been hampered by the denial of his sexual attraction to other men. That part made sense. "It's not going to make your life any easier," I said. "But it doesn't look as if you've got any choice."

"Are you shocked?"

"Of course, I'm shocked. But we're still friends, I hope."

"I want you to meet Wayne."

I didn't want to meet Wayne. I wanted Teddy to get over Wayne and go back to being reserved, ironic, and up for late-night drinking sessions at the Cedar or Phebe's. "Let's just wait a little on that," I said.

He threw himself down in the chair. "No one is happy for me. I don't understand it."

"If you're happy, I'm happy for you. I just need a little time to get used to the new you."

"Everything's changing," he said. "The old crowd is pulling apart. You know about Guy and Madeleine."

The conjunction of these two names irritated me so much that I squirmed in my chair. "What about them?"

"They're married."

"You're joking," I said, because surely this was a joke.

"No. They got married a few weeks ago. They went to City Hall. Mindy was a witness."

"Is she out of her mind?"

"Mindy?"

"No, Madeleine."

"I don't think so. But there was motive for haste. She's pregnant."

"I know that," I said.

"She told you?"

"No. Guy told me."

"I guess it was an accident, but they seem pleased about it. Guy especially."

"So they're living together."

"They are, at his old place. But they're looking for something better, for when the baby comes."

Physically speaking, anger is a complex emotion. It takes many forms, depending upon the degree to which it is allowed to be expressed. In our society no one wants either to see it or own to feeling it, so it breaks out in all sorts of inappropriate hostility, particularly in the workplace. It can be slow in developing, gathering force over a long period of time. This is what we mean by the expression "the last straw." Or it can be quite sudden, full-blown, and overpowering, as in "I saw red." What I felt at Teddy's news was largely of this latter variety and I was at pains to conceal it, but there was also something of the slow simmer coming to a boil, something that had known from the first time I saw her that Madeleine would bring me to seeing red. "I can't believe this," I said.

"I see that," Teddy said. "You've gone pale. It looks like a bigger shock than my affair with Wayne."

"Jesus," I said. "Maybe it's the combination." But it wasn't. I hadn't felt much beyond surprise and interest in Teddy's confession; it didn't touch me. This news penetrated deep into my thoracic cavity, where my liver was briskly pumping out enough bile to digest a brick. The truth was bitter. I didn't want to marry Madeleine—I didn't want to marry anyone, the idea was appalling—but I didn't want anyone else to marry her and I most particularly did not want Guy Margate to marry her.

"Mr. and Mrs. Margate," I said sourly.

"Well," Teddy said. "She's not changing her name."

At dinner Teddy talked about nothing but Wayne. He was in the first giddy stages of infatuation, his ragged heart flapping on his sleeve for the whole world to see. I hardly knew what to say to him but it didn't matter because he wouldn't have heard me if I had. I pleaded fatigue and the necessity for an early wake-up call—I'd been laid off at Bloomingdale's and would have to scare up a new day job—and we parted after dinner, he to Wayne's studio, I to my apartment, which the Georgia peach had evidently spent the summer scrubbing down with bleach; even the dresser drawers reeked of it.

My brain was in an uproar. I paced up and down, muttering imprecations against Madeleine; how could she have done it, how brought herself to so low a pass? I dropped to the floor and did push-ups until my arms trembled. I put Jim Morrison on my record player and sang along with "The Crystal Ship" and "Back Door Man." At midnight I could stand my thoughts no longer and went out.

The streets were empty but for panhandlers and unsavory types, so I walked at a brisk pace down to Washington Square, across to Broadway, and back up to Union Square, where there was an all-night bar patronized by models and Hispanic drug dealers. I had a quick drink there, exchanging pleasantries with a beanpole of a model who called herself Vakushka, "You know like in that movie."

"Verushka," I corrected her.

"No, I'm sure it's Vakushka," she replied. I set out again, across to Fifth Avenue and back down to Washington Square. The night was damp and progressively cooler. As I crossed into SoHo a light rain began to fall and by the time I got to Spring Street it was a downpour. I turned back toward the Village. There was still a smattering of nightlife going on, people rushing into and out of cabs and cars, lights flickering from the open doors of a few bars and restaurants. I cut across toward Bowery, thinking I might dry out at Phebe's if they were still open. The street widened, light posts were farther apart, the rain clattered, running off the gutters, puddling around the plastic garbage bags lining the curb. A torn bag rustled ominously as I passed and in the next moment a rat rushed out at me. "Get away!" I snarled, revving up to a trot. At the corner I turned north again, shielding my eyes with my hand to see through the sheeting water.

A man sporting an umbrella appeared on the opposite sidewalk, moving swiftly, as I was, and in the same direction. For a block he mirrored me. I could sense him there more than see him, and at the next corner he crossed to my side and came up behind me. The umbrella, a cumbersome and sensible accoutrement, made me think he was unlikely to be a thief or a thug. Phebe's lights glimmered in the near distance; he was clearly headed there as well. I glanced as surreptitiously as I could over my shoulder, but all I could see was the umbrella and a loose jacket flapping open as its owner hastened along.

"Why don't you slow down and share my umbrella?" he said. "We've still got a block to go."

It was Guy. My first impulse, which was to run away, gave way to my second, which was a burning curiosity to find out something about Madeleine. "How did you know it was me?" I asked, as he extended the umbrella over my head.

"I knew it as soon as I turned the corner. You walk like a dog with your head down."

"Ever observant," I said. "Can you do an impression of me?"

"As a matter of fact I have a very good impression of you. I'll show it to you someday."

The thought gave me pause. Did he do an impression of me for Madeleine? Did she laugh? Did she correct him on certain intimate details? An unpleasant scenario played out in my head as we covered the last block and stepped in under Phebe's awning. The chairs were stacked on the tables but there were a few stragglers at the bar, waiting out the storm. We went in; I shook myself off and passed a handkerchief over my hair. As he folded his umbrella and propped it primly against the door-frame I took a closer look at Madeleine's husband.

He'd changed again. His face was haggard, his hair was greased and slicked back, his skin was sallow, there were dark circles beneath his eyes. Married life. The jacket was bomber style, not new, shiny, probably water resistant. The sleeves were too short. There was something seedy about him, but his good posture and bones combined to give him an air of shabby gentility. He knew I was examining him and allowed a moment before he turned to me, his expression flat as a foot, and said, "I could use a drink."

"Me too," I agreed. We went to the bar.

"Miserable night," said the bartender. "What will you have?"

We had bourbon. "I understand you're to be congratulated," I said, lifting my glass in a mini-toast.

"News travels fast," he said. "Who told you?"

"Teddy. I just had dinner with him."

"Did you meet Wayne?"

"No. But I heard a lot about him."

"Teddy's not serious," he observed.

"He says he's never been more serious in his life."

"Not about Wayne. About being an actor. He's not serious and Wayne is a way out."

"He says his acting has improved."

Guy snorted. "Do you believe that?"

"Well," I said, "if he's been repressing a whole part of himself and now he's not, it stands to reason he'll be a better actor. He has access to more of himself. I mean, before he was acting even when he wasn't playing a part. Now he's not, so there should be more truth to his work."

"You sound like Madeleine."

"Do I?" I said. Madeleine often carped about "truth" until I was stultified with boredom. "Maybe she's right."

Guy rolled his eyes dramatically. "There's no way around playing a part," he said. "There's no truth to be known. You make it up as you go along. If anyone should know that, it's you."

"Does Madeleine know you think like this?"

"Of course not. I'm not stupid."

So he had contempt for Madeleine too. "How is she?" I asked.

He swirled his bourbon in the glass and knocked it back. "She's asleep."

Of course, I thought. He knew when Madeleine was asleep and when she was awake. And when she washed her hair, and what brand of toothbrush she preferred, and how carefully she placed those cotton balls between her toes when she painted her toenails. What Guy must know about Madeleine depressed me. "So you're on the prowl," I said.

"I have trouble sleeping," he said. "I walk around at night. But you know that."

We all stayed up late and burned the candle at both ends, so it had not, until that moment, occurred to me that Guy was an insomniac. It was sleeplessness, he implied, that had drawn him out on the pier that night. He was searching for sleep and he'd found a drowning man. And now he'd left Madeleine alone in a dingy apartment somewhere because he was too restless to lie by her side. The longer I spent with Guy the more I wanted to talk to Madeleine, but he was between us now, like an ogre guarding a princess, and he couldn't even be counted upon to fall asleep long enough to get past him. All my anger against her had been washed out of me by the rain and I could feel the cold, wet shirt against my back, the squishy toes of my socks. I was a miserable wet dog in the manger if ever there was one.

"Is she working?" I asked.

"She's not acting, if that's what you mean. She's got a job at the bookstore with me. She gets tired out pretty easily; the doctor says she's anemic. She's not going back to classes when they start up again."

"I'd like to talk to her," I said.

He pushed a few bills across the bar, studying me with his dark eyes. "I'm sure you would," he said.

She doesn't love him, I thought. How could she? He'd caught her at a weak moment. She had no one else to turn to and he was there. He twisted his mouth into something like a smile and gave a quick chuck to my shoulder with the back of his hand. "She liked that photo I took of you," he said.

"What photo?"

"In Connecticut."

My brain contracted around this information like an octopus engulfing a bivalve. "But you told me she didn't know you were coming to see me."

"She didn't know then. But when I got back I told her. And I gave her the money you sent. She appreciated that."

"I asked you not to tell her it came from me."

"I'm not going to lie to Madeleine for you. She's my wife."

I rested my elbows on the bar and lowered my head into my hands. "Oh, man," I said.

Guy buttoned his jacket. "I'm off," he said. "Nice running into you, Ed."

"Oh, man," I said again. I didn't lift my head until I heard the door swing closed behind him.

He'd laid a trap for me and I'd waltzed right into it. God knew what he'd told Madeleine about our meeting in Connecticut. How could I talk to her? She clearly wasn't going to return my calls, she wasn't going to classes, and she worked in the same place as her husband. And even if I did manage it, what could I possibly say? *It's your own fault,* I upbraided myself. *You wanted to get away from her, you wanted a break, you welcomed it.*

That's true, I protested in my defense. *But it wasn't supposed to turn out like this!*

The next morning I went down to SoHo to see if I could get my old job back. I was welcomed by my employer like the prodigal son. He was shorthanded; two waiters had quit by simply not showing up. He offered me a flexible schedule, including lunches and enough hours so that I wouldn't need a second job. On Wednesday I met with Barney Marker, an avuncular, fast-talking hipster from Brooklyn who asked me a number of questions, the last of which was did I think I was up to Pinter. He knew the director for a production of *The Birthday Party* coming up at the Roundabout, which had recently moved from a supermarket basement to a theater on Twenty-third Street. It was Equity, reputable, and regularly reviewed. With a pair of glasses, Barney said, I would be perfect for the part of Stanley.

I bought the glasses and a few days after that I read for the part, got a callback the next day, and by the end of the week signed up for my first substantial role in New York.

I felt great; things were definitely looking up. I wanted to tell everyone; most particularly I wanted to tell Madeleine. But I realized that I didn't even know where she lived.

I called Mindy Banks. "I don't think she wants to see you," she said, but not coldly.

"I need to talk to her," I pleaded. "I don't know what Guy told her but I'm pretty sure it was all lies. She won't return my calls. I'll have to go where she is, but I don't know where that is."

"She works at a bookstore," she said.

"I know that, but where is it?"

Mindy hesitated, consulting some code of female fealty. "It's at Columbus Circle. She works on Monday and Wednesday night. They stay open late."

"Is Guy there too?"

Again she paused.

"Mindy, I'm desperate."

"He's not there on Monday nights."

"Bless you," I said.

"Do you see Teddy?" she asked.

"Only once since I've been back."

"Have you met this Wayne character?"

"No, I don't want to. Have you?"

"I've seen him," she confided. "I went by the gallery he works in. He thought I was looking at the pictures."

"What did you think?"

"I think he's a Chinese devil."

I laughed.

"It's not funny," Mindy said. "Do me a favor and take a look for yourself. I'm so worried about Teddy it's making me sick."

A surprising number of customers were in the bookstore, scanning the tall shelves and thumbing through the volumes on the display tables. The place was vast, wall-to-wall books, various niches and corners formed by free-standing shelves and an information desk that looked like a bar at the center where two clerks, neither of them Madeleine, dispensed helpful hints to the shoppers. I had no idea how she would feel about being accosted in her workplace and I was nervous. I glanced about, pretending to read the placards over the shelves: Science, History, Chess. At a checkout counter near the door a businessman unfolded his wallet before a youthful clerk, not Madeleine, dressed in the equivalent of a dashiki. A murmur of female voices drew me into the Fiction aisle but the two women who halted their conversation at my approach were bespectacled and white-haired. I passed them with a nod and entered Poetry, an impressive collection, just in time to see the heel of a black shoe and the flare of a red skirt disappear into Religion/Philosophy. I followed; she turned again into Occult. She was carrying a book, and as I came around the corner, she stopped before a shelf and, stretching up on her toes, carefully slid the volume into place. Her hair was pulled back in an ill-contained knot. She was wearing a cerulean blue cardigan I'd never seen before that made her eyes, when she turned them upon me, glisten like captured bits of sky.

"Madeleine?" I said, tentative as a schoolboy.

Not a pause, not a moment of reserve or recrimination, no weighing of options or just deserts; she came down on her heels, her lips parting in a smile of such warmth that I moved quickly toward her, holding out my hands. "Edward," she said, stepping into my embrace, her arms circling my neck, nestling her head against my chest. My heart swelled with surprise and then pity. What on earth had we done to ourselves? I pressed my lips into her hair, that familiar spicy fragrance, and tightened my arms around her back. "I missed you so," she murmured.

A theatrical "ahem," issued from a professorial type happening upon us in his quest for an essential tome. We separated, holding hands. She didn't look pregnant, I thought, and she certainly didn't look anemic. "When do you get off?" I asked. "I'll wait for you. I've got to see you."

"It's impossible," she said. "Guy comes to meet me at eleven; that's when we close."

Guy, I thought, Guy Margate. Her husband. How was it possible? "Can you leave now for a while? Can you make some excuse?"

"I could go out for a few minutes."

"That's no good," I said. "Where can we go?"

She gazed at the professor, flagrantly fingering book spines near the end of the aisle. A sly smile played at the corners of her mouth. "Follow me," she said softly, and I did, awash with desire, past Theater, through Nonfiction, which went on and on, to a door marked DO NOT ENTER. We entered. It was a narrow dark office with a desk, a chair, and a battered leather couch. Oh, blessed couch. We made for it without a word, pulling our clothes aside, eager and abandoned, just as we were that first night under the staircase on the Jersey shore, that night when Guy Margate saved my life.

It didn't take long. Madeleine was stifling laughter near the end; she'd told me before that she found the "state" I got into amusing, which was another thing I liked about her. We gasped for a few moments, pulling ourselves apart. "God, Madeleine," I whispered.

She sat up, demurely rearranging her clothing, but I was too whacked to bother. "I'm going to go out first," she said. "You can stay here a few minutes. No one comes in here at night."

"Don't go yet," I said.

"I have to. I don't want to lose my job."

"When can I see you?"

"I don't know. It's difficult," she said. She was feeling around for her hairpins, thrusting them into her hair.

"Can't you call me? Will you just call me, so we can talk? I don't know what's going on."

"I know you don't," she said. She stood up, brushing down her skirt. "It's so dark in here."

"Will you call me?"

She guided herself to the door by clinging to the edge of the desk. "When you go out," she said, "don't look for me. You should leave the store." Carefully she opened the door a crack and peered through it. A thin shaft of light dashed across the floor and up the opposite wall. "I'll call you," she said. Without looking back she pulled the door just wide enough to pass and slipped away, leaving me on the couch with my pants around my ankles, satiated, stunned, and, as usual, completely in the dark.

For two days I stayed close to the phone and checked messages when I couldn't, but there were no calls from Madeleine. I called her service and left a message to call me at midnight. I figured Guy would be out walking. I got back from work at eleven forty-five and sat next to the phone, making notes on my Pinter script. Pinter is an actor's playwright, there's a lot of room in those loaded exchanges, a lot of choices to make, a lot to do or not do. I was finding it hard to concentrate; I kept staring at the phone, which was an old dial model, ponderous and obtrusive. Like Pinter it had a quality of menace. At twelve thirty it rang. "Talk to me," I said.

"Were you asleep?" she asked.

"No. I'm studying my play and I'm waiting for you to call me."

"You didn't tell me you had a job."

I laughed. "We didn't talk, sweetheart."

"What is it? Where is it?"

"The Birthday Party, Stanley, the Roundabout."

"That's incredible," she said. "That's fantastic."

"It is," I agreed. "I'm excited. When can I see you?"

"That's easier said than done."

This response irritated me. "Whose fault is that?" I snipped.

There was a long Pinteresque silence which I steadfastly refused to enter. I listened to Madeleine's breathing. Was it uneven? She was a weeper; was she weeping?

"Yours, actually," she said calmly.

The eruption of mutual recrimination that followed went on for some time. It was unpleasant, but some errors were cleared up on both sides. In the midst of my lame explanation of the compromising Connecticut pub photo, she exclaimed, "Stop, darling, I can't talk, he's here."

"When can I see you?" I pleaded. "Where?"

"Tuesday night," she said. "At nine. I'll come to you."

"I'll be here," I promised.

"I won't have much time." The line went dead.

What was I supposed to think of Madeleine? She was a complete puzzle to me, yet I felt, as I had during those weeks when we were pounding the streets for work, a bond of goodwill between us. She was married and pregnant and there was nothing either of us could do about that. I wasn't excited about the prospect of a baby, to say the least, and I wasn't looking forward to seeing her swelled up in that awful, ungainly, explosive way I find so disturbing. It would just get worse when the creature was out in the world, mewing, spitting, and shitting; demanding all the attention in the room. I've always known I wasn't cut out for fatherhood. What man is? It's a service role after all, unless one decides to take prisoners and call it family life. I wanted none of it.

But just to demonstrate how truly perverse human nature is, Teddy, having discovered that he was not biologically inclined to perpetuate the species, was in a nesting mood. "Come by," he said in his phone message. "I'm having a drinks party. Wayne is moving in and we're celebrating. Saturday. Anytime after eight."

Within the hour Mindy called. "Go with me, Ed," she pleaded. "I can't face this by myself."

To buck ourselves up for whatever was in store for us, Mindy and I agreed to have dinner before the party. We were determined not to be early, so we met at eight in a little place she'd chosen near NYU where the food was cheap. She was looking great. She'd lost weight and she was dressed to kill. I wanted to talk about Madeleine but Mindy wanted to talk about Teddy. She feared Wayne would be the ruin of him. So far he hadn't told his family about his mad affair, but this moving in together, which was so unnecessary, was bound to get back to them. His father came to the city regularly on business. Suppose he stopped by unexpectedly and the Chinese boyfriend answered the door in his kimono.

"He could just be a friend," I suggested.

"Wait until you see him," she said.

We split a bottle of not good wine and picked at our food, comrades in rejection. When I asked how soon after my departure for Connecticut Madeleine and Guy had become an item, she was evasive. "We were both so busy, I hardly saw her all summer," she said. "And then she called to say she was getting married and needed a witness."

"Did she say it was because she was pregnant?"

Mindy chewed a lettuce leaf, considering my question. "She didn't," she said. "I thought she was in love."

"So maybe she wasn't pregnant."

"I think she must have been."

"She doesn't look pregnant," I said.

"So you've seen her."

"Briefly," I admitted. "I went to the bookstore."

"That's good," Mindy said. "You two should be friends. I know she's very fond of you."

"Fond," I said.

"She cares about you."

I finished the wine. "Let's go meet the Chinese," I said.

A party, after all, is a kind of play. There are entrances, exits, sudden outbursts of emotion, affection, or hostility, lines drawn, tales told out of school, and there's a set. Many plays contain party scenes. Chekhov is fond of having them offstage, with characters drifting in and out and shouts going up from unseen guests. The eponymous birthday party that transpires in Pinter's play is a kind of anti-party, a grim affair that includes threats, seduction, and a nervous breakdown but there is a song, a sweet love long, in the midst of the general decline. I wondered how my director would see this moment.

Which brings me to the important difference between a party in a play and a party at a friend's apartment in Manhattan: at the latter there's no director.

Teddy's party was well under way by the time we arrived; we could hear the sound of laughter and the gaggle of conversation from the hall. A young man I didn't recognize opened the door and waved us in urgently, as if he was on a boat pulling away from a dock. "Drinks in the kitchen," he instructed as we came aboard, returning his attention to a short, pale girl dressed in a tie-dyed caftan. Mindy stuck to my side as we made our way through the crowd, which was composed of small groups that yielded like amoebas to let us pass. I saw Gary Santos near a window, and Jasmine, poised beneath her brother's artwork, in heels and a tight red dress, hollering into the ear of a seriously older man. I recognized a few others as actors, but most of the guests were strangers to me. "These must be Wayne's friends," I ventured to Mindy.

"He's over there," she said, rolling her eyes stagily to my left. I looked past her shoulder and spotted Wayne without difficulty—indeed he would have stood out in any crowd.

"Good God," I said.

"Don't stare," Mindy cautioned, prodding me on.

"He looks like Genghis Khan," I whispered.

Which was true. Wayne had an amazing face, bizarrely flat with black slits for eyes and a shock of stiff black hair that stood out in all directions. A Mongol face that made the word "steppes" leap to mind. One could picture him wearing a yak-fur hat and a yak-skin coat, astride a tough little pony. Instead he wore a gray V-necked sweater that looked like cashmere over blue-and-red-plaid bell-bottom pants and loafers without socks. He was tall, slender, elegant; his hands were as delicate as a girl's. I made these observations on closer inspection. In that first glance all I saw was that he looked completely foreign, not just from another world but from another time.

In the kitchen we found Teddy setting out bite-size dumplings on a plate. The counters were freighted with trays of brightly colored snacks. He looked polished up, bright, as a painting does after it's been cleaned; his colors were refreshed. "Here you are," he said. "Come try these before they get snapped up. They're fantastic." Mindy approached him tentatively, as if she expected a rebuff, but he passed his free arm around her waist, kissed her cheek, and popped a dumpling into her mouth. "How are you, dear?" he said. "I'm glad you could come."

"Good," she replied through the dumpling.

"It's delicious, isn't it?" Teddy said. "Wayne made them. He was up all night." He raised his arm in an introductory flourish. "Chinese party food!"

"One hour later you power hungry," I quipped.

"Now, Ed," Teddy chided, "let's not have any low ethnic humor."

I poured myself a Scotch. I felt uncomfortable and defensive, as if I was waiting for an audition. "Who are these people?" I asked.

"This is the art scene," Teddy said. "They're a fascinating bunch. Painters aren't like us at all. They have these funny things called identities."

"That sounds gloomy," I said.

"It isn't very playful," he agreed. "Wayne thinks it's hilarious so of course they're all in awe of him. Have you met Wayne?"

Though this was a simple yes or no question, Mindy and I exchanged perplexed looks. "You two look lost," Teddy said. "Grab a tray; go play waiters at a party."

I threw back my Scotch, took up a tray, and led the way into the scene. Clever Teddy had assigned me a role I knew I could play to perfection. A pod of guests opened before me and I lowered my tray skillfully before them. "Will you try one of these?" I offered. A lady with a prodigious nose snatched up a shrimp toast. "And here's a napkin," I offered. Our eyes met, I read her thought—what a handsome waiter! I raised my tray and moved on. Two hirsute young men, vacantly repeating the name "Cy Twombly" at each other, paused to load their flimsy napkins with treats. I looked past them into the kitchen where Mindy and Teddy still stood face-to-face over the dumplings. He was rubbing his hands together, his eyes cast down, his mouth slightly ajar. Mindy was talking earnestly, wagging her head with the force of her argument. Teddy took up a paper napkin and passed it to her. She dabbed her eyes with it, but she didn't stop talking. Poor Mindy. Teddy had tried to help her out, but she had refused the part.

My progress led me away from the painful confrontation going forward in the kitchen to the blithe and exotic author of that suffering. Wayne was leaning against a bookcase in conversation with a large blonde who pursed her lips skeptically when it was not her turn to talk. I eased my tray between them.

"You're Edward Day, aren't you?" Wayne said.

"No," I replied. "I'm just a waiter."

He narrowed his impossibly narrow eyes at me, lifting the corners of his mouth. "That's funny," he said.

"Why is it funny?" asked the pursing lady.

"Because we didn't hire any waiters."

"What makes you think I'm this Edward person?" I asked.

"Teddy has a photo of you, at the beach house."

"Ah," I said. "The beach house."

A surge in the conversational volume near the door caught Wayne's attention. I had my back to it but I recognized a too-hearty laugh, followed by a squeal that could only be Mindy Banks in the rapture of greeting an old friend. "Now I'm confused," Wayne said. "I think that could be Edward Day too."

"They do look alike," his large friend agreed.

I pulled my tray in close to my chest and turned to see Mr. and Mrs. Margate arriving at the festivities. Guy's head, visible above the company, swiveled from left to right, taking in the scene. He had cut his hair short and was clean shaven. All I could see of Madeleine was her hair; Mindy's fond embrace blocked the rest of her. "Take this, would you?" I said to Wayne, pressing the tray upon him.

"No, no," he protested. "I don't want to be a waiter."

"Just put it down," the large woman said testily.

I took her advice, ditching the snacks on a nearby coffee table where they were instantly decimated by ravenous artists. I made for the door where Madeleine, having been released by Mindy, stood facing me. She was dressed in an off-the-shoulder blue peasant dress with a black Mexican shawl, very flattering, but what I noticed next was that she looked ill. She was what my mother called "green around the gills." Her eyes, which had been so sparkling and mischievous only a few days before, were dull and sunk in dark circles. As I approached, she hunched over abruptly, pressing both hands against her abdomen. Her eyes closed, she took in a frantic gasp of air. I reached her side.

"Jesus," I said. "What's wrong? Are you OK?"

She clutched my arm and straightened, giving me a wan smile. "I'm not sure," she said. She glanced about at the cheerful partygoers, none of whom had observed her distress. "I guess I shouldn't have come. Guy tried to talk me out of it, but I wanted to see Teddy and his friend."

"Have you been sick?"

"I was throwing up this morning, but that's not unusual. I had a terrific headache last night. Now it's gone but I'm getting these sharp pains. I don't know what it is."

I laid my palm across her forehead; it was much too warm. "I think you have a fever. You need to lie down."

"It would be good if you get me to the bathroom," she said.

"This way," I said, passing my arm around her shoulder. It was at this point that Guy desisted from ogling his potential audience and turned his attention to his wife.

"Hello, Ed," he said, encroaching upon us as we edged along the wall. "I thought you might be here."

"Madeleine's sick," I said. "She should be in bed."

"What?" he said. He squeezed himself in on her other side, bending over her so that his mouth was close to her ear, "Sweetie, are you feeling punk?" he whispered. It was so close to baby talk my hackles went up. Madeleine leaned into him and I was forced to loosen my hold on her.

"I just need to get to the bathroom," she said. This destination was nearby and fortunately empty when we arrived, cosseting Madeleine between us.

"Should I come in with you?" Guy offered as she opened the door.

"No," she said, waving him away. "I'll be fine. Just wait for me."

Guy and I stood on either side of the door, like fresh recruits in the Royal Guard, while the sounds of Madeleine retching, running water, flushing the toilet, and retching again drifted through. Word got out that a guest was vomiting in the bathroom and Teddy appeared, emanating concern. "What can I do?" he asked.

"Nothing," Guy replied with an air of sufferance. "It can't last much longer. She hasn't eaten anything all day."

"Why did you bring her?" I snarled. "You can look at her and see she's sick. She has a fever."

"I'm sure you know all about it," he said.

Another round of heaving and flushing sounds issued from the inner chamber.

"Honey," Guy addressed the door. "Can I do anything?"

We heard the sound of water running, then silence. We men looked at one another, wide-eyed and helpless. Jasmine appeared, all competence in spite of the red dress. "What's going on?" she said.

"Madeleine's sick in there," Teddy said. "We don't know what to do."

Jasmine tapped the door. "Madeleine," she said. "Do you need help?"

No answer. No sound at all.

"Is it locked?" Jasmine asked, trying the knob, which turned easily. She opened the door a crack, peered in, then, casting us a look of frank dismay, slipped inside and closed it behind her.

Wayne's large blond friend bustled up, wanting to use the facility.

"You'll have to wait," Guy informed her. "My wife is very ill."

She backed away, screwing up her mouth in her habitual moue, scrutinizing Guy and then me. "So which one of you is Edward Day?" she asked.

The bathroom door opened narrowly and Jasmine's head appeared in the gap. "Teddy," she said. "Call 911. And then bring me some towels."

This was too much for me. "I'm coming in," I said, pushing past Jasmine, who offered no resistance. She closed the door and leaned her back against it. Madeleine was slumped on the floor, propped against the cabinet, holding a blood-soaked towel between her legs. Another one, wadded and cast aside, was so saturated it had formed a thick brownish pool at the edges.

"Oh, darling," I said, kneeling next to her.

"My shoulder is killing me," she said weakly, lifting her eyes to look at me. Her face was porcelain white, unearthly, her eyes unfocused, the pupils dilated. Jasmine opened the door again and Guy, bristling with importance, charged in.

"The ambulance is on the way," he announced.

At the sight of him, Madeleine burst into sobs. The room was too small for four people so I got to my feet, making way for Guy. We brushed shoulders as he dropped to his knees beside his wife. "Oh, oh," he wailed, "the baby, the baby." Madeleine moaned, leaning into the towel with both hands. I backed away. Jasmine was wringing out a washcloth at the sink.

"Is it a miscarriage?" I asked her.

"I think it's worse than that," she replied.

The turbulent intrusion of EMTs dangling stethoscopes and unfurling a nifty stretcher is reliably the death of a party. Barks of "Stand back" and "Out" were the extent of their contribution to the festive repartee, and they didn't stop to sample the dumplings. Guy, who was still on his knees on the bathroom floor, was the object of the second command. "What is it?" he whimpered as he backed out the door. "What's happening to her?" I was standing just outside and I could see Madeleine, collapsed sideways, eerily still, her eyes glazed, the greenish tinge around her mouth definitively shifted to blue. "She's going into shock," the female of the rescue team informed us, and before you could say "hypovolemic" they had her on the stretcher and were heading for the street. "I'm her husband," Guy repeated, escorting them, like Moses, through the parting sea of wide-eyed guests. "Come with us," Ms. Medic ordered and they were out the door. A dazed group, myself among them, spilled out into the hall, clutching our drinks and watching mutely as the rescued and the rescuers disappeared into the elevator. Teddy put his arm around me. "That was awful," he said.

"Where will they take her?" I asked.

"St. Vincent's, I guess. It's the closest."

"Where is it?"

"Twelfth and Seventh Avenue."

"That's good. I can walk over."

"Maybe you should wait a little while so they can get her admitted," he advised. "They don't encourage you to visit the emergency room unless you have to, if you see what I mean."

"I see what you mean," I said. The guests filed back inside, several making straight to the kitchen for refills. The talk was about who had seen what part of what had just happened. One claimed he knew nothing until the medics burst through the door and he thought, at first, it was some kind of raid. Another had noticed an odd gathering of concerned faces near the bathroom door and concluded the toilet was overflowing. Jasmine, looking like some fetishist's fantasy, passed through the hall in her red dress and high heels hoisting a mop and a bucket full of bloody towels. "I'll put this in the closet for now," she said to Teddy. "We can deal with it later."

As his sister passed with her grisly trophy, Wayne, who was driving a corkscrew into a bottle of wine, lifted his upper lip in a sneer of disgust. "Just get it out of sight," he snapped, thereby earning my eternal enmity. The cork came free with a cheery pop. "Let's get back to the fun part," he said, nimbly dispensing the golden liquid among the glasses pressed upon him.

I set my glass in the sink. When I looked up I saw that

Teddy was watching me and that he had deciphered my feelings about his paramour. His brow was furrowed, his eyes full and sad, his lips pressed in a thin line, as if to keep in words that might best be reconsidered. He was a social creature to his bones and it was important to him that his friends accepted his new love, his new life, his new self. He looked uncomfortable and on edge, whereas Wayne was having a fine time and appeared perfectly at ease. No good will come of it, I thought, ducking back into the living room. Wayne's paintings now covered most of the wall space and made the room feel dark and cramped. The partygoers were trying to get back in the swing of things, but it was heavy going. I picked up a dumpling from a tray near the door on my way out.

Difficult as it is to imagine now, nobody had a computer in those days, so finding someone in a hospital involved a lot of phoning and consultation with charts attached to clipboards. At length I was informed that Madeleine was on the fifth floor and directed to an elevator which would take me to a desk where I could make further inquiries. At this stop, a space station manned by aliens, I was told that Madeleine was in surgery. If I wished, I could proceed to the waiting room down the hall, first right, then straight ahead. I did so wish. After a longish stroll, past many doors opening upon scenes of human suffering unfolding in front of televised scenes of human suffering, I came to a glass-fronted room in which Guy Margate was pacing manically up and down.

"I don't know what's going on," he announced upon my entrance. "It's making me crazy. Do you have any cigarettes?"

I had, in fact, an unopened pack. "I'm trying to cut down," I said as I tore off the cellophane wrapper and pulled out the bit of foil.

"Now is not the time," said Guy. He produced a flip-top lighter and we lit up companionably.

"So what *do* you know?" I asked.

"She needs a blood transfusion. I picked that up from the medics. I haven't seen a doctor."

"That sounds bad."

"Have you ever ridden in an ambulance?" he asked. "It's totally weird."

"No," I said.

"It's completely weird."

"It must be," I agreed.

He puffed at his cigarette, paced to an ashtray on a couch-side table, and tapped off the ash. "What did Teddy say?"

"He said it was awful."

He charged back to the door, looking out at the empty hall. "I can't stand this," he said.

"Just keep walking," I said.

He headed for the water fountain. "You're calm. Why is that?"

"I'm not calm," I said. "I just don't find walking up and down like a caged animal helps much."

"You should try it."

I stalked to the door and back to the couches, crossing

Guy's path as he went from the fountain to the wall. "No," I said. "This doesn't work for me. I'm going to sit down and jigger my leg." Which is what I did.

"Be my guest," Guy said, moving on.

"Was she conscious?" I asked.

"No. I think they knocked her out in the ambulance."

"And they didn't say anything about what was wrong."

"They said she'd lost a lot of blood."

"I'll say," I said.

"I had to sign papers, releases, you know, about how they're not responsible if she dies. But she won't die. I'm sure she won't die."

"Don't even say that."

"You're right. That's bad luck. She's strong."

"She is."

"But she's anemic. That means not enough blood."

"It means not enough red blood cells. But there's the same amount of blood."

"So she has a normal amount of blood."

"I would think so."

He stubbed out his cigarette. "I feel helpless. That's what's making me crazy."

"Have another cigarette," I said, brandishing the pack.

"Thanks," he said. "Thanks for coming."

"Wouldn't have missed it," I said. Guy pulled out his lighter and we lit up again.

By the time the blood-stained doctor from Mars opened the door, we were down to three cigarettes. He stepped inside, rested his hands on his hips, and looked from Guy to me and back again. "Which one of you is the husband?" he inquired.

"That's me," Guy replied, whirling upon him. "For God's sake, tell me she's not going to die."

"She's not going to die," he said firmly.

Tears sprang from Guy's eyes. "Thank God," he said. "What happened to her? What did you do?"

What happened to Madeleine, the doctor explained, was an ectopic pregnancy which—Jasmine was right—is a lot worse than a miscarriage. I now know it means the fertilized embryo has lodged in the fallopian tube instead of in the uterus where it belongs, and if you are a pregnant woman and you have bleeding, abdominal pain on one side, and, for some strange reason having to do with nerves, severe pain in one shoulder, get yourself to a hospital pronto. Madeleine, our medical expert informed us, had nearly died. Sometime between her upright entrance at Teddy's party and her prostrate exit on the stretcher, the fallopian tube had burst. "Of course we had to terminate the pregnancy," the doctor explained. "It was a mess in there. The tube was destroyed, fibroids all over the place; I saved the ovaries, but I had to take the uterus. She won't be able to conceive again."

"Oh no," Guy whispered at this news. "Oh, that's terrible. Did you hear that?" he said, turning to me.

"I did," I replied.

The doctor agreed that it was too bad. But, he assured us, the surgery was successful, the patient was young and strong, and in a few weeks she would be fine. She was stable though still unconscious and Guy was welcome to sit in the room with her until she came to.

"Let's go," Guy said, breaking for the door. The doctor raised his eyebrows at me and followed the eager husband. "I'll phone you," Guy called back to me as he and the doctor disappeared down the hall.

I went back to the couch, sat down, and broke into a cold sweat.

What actors know about emotions is that they come in pairs, often in direct opposition to each other. That's what it is to be conflicted. We want what we should not want and we know it. We desire that which is dangerous or forbidden and might cause us to suffer. We fear success, embrace failure. We strive to be independent, longing at the same time to surrender to a burning passion. We hold ourselves aloof from the people we need and seek the approval of those who have no use for us.

Or at least I do. I was sweating with relief as well as anxiety, relief that Madeleine would recover and be herself again, anxiety that she would be different, that she would decide to leave me out of her life and cleave to her husband. There was an element of incredulity and anger that she might do that, for I couldn't persuade myself that she was in love with Guy. Now there would be no other reason for her to stay with him. I thought there was a possibility that she would continue to play us somehow, that we were sport to her, which made me anxious, but also relieved, because then I wouldn't be responsible for anything, for any of it. I confess that I had felt only relief at the news that she would not be able to have a child, which was enormously cruel and selfish of me, but there it is. I felt that. But I was also made anxious because I feared she would respond to her condition recklessly; it might make her bitter and angry and she might detect my indifference to the matter and hate me for it.

I took out a cigarette, examined it closely, and put it back in the pack. I recollected the shocking vision of Madeleine huddled on Teddy's bathroom floor, pressing into the mound of bloody towels between her legs, and another of her glazed eyes and blue lips as the medics descended upon her and the art scene outside yielded briefly to the life-threatening-emergency scene. It had all happened so quickly; I'd felt side-lined, a voyeur. Guy had been at the center of the action, forcefully taking his rightful place, which galled me, yet I had not wanted to be in the ambulance, was relieved to be left behind.

Marlene Webern's steady voice came to me: "There's a coldness in you."

She was right, I thought. Guy had accused me of being calm, and I had replied that I was not, which was true, I was beyond calm. He had his act down: he was nervous, erratic, abrupt, he couldn't keep still, he couldn't stop speculating about what might go wrong or right, he was frightened and hopeful by turns. When the news finally came, he was tearful. But all I had felt throughout the ordeal, and what I felt then, alone in that chilly room designed to accommodate desperate people in the throes of powerful emotions, was a generalized sadness and a humbling conviction that somehow I had been exposed and that everyone concerned now knew I was entirely unequal to my part.

———

It was a long time before I saw Madeleine again. Guy didn't call me from the hospital. Instead he called Madeleine's mother, with whom she had a difficult relationship. Madeleine, too weak to argue, agreed to go home to Cleveland.

I was absorbed in rehearsals for the Pinter and then in performances, so the only information I got about Madeleine and Guy was through conversations with Mindy. It was partly from her and partly from idle gossip, some of it in the pages of *Back Stage,* that I followed the ensuing roller-coaster ride that was Guy Margate's career.

While Madeleine was in Cleveland, Guy was offered a job as assistant stage manager and understudy to the lead in a Broadway-bound play that was going into tryouts in Philadelphia. He expressed mixed feelings about this prospect to everyone who would listen, but was eventually persuaded by Bev Arbuckle that it was a good option, as he had nothing else going and was desperate for cash. The lead, a talented actor named Marc Trilby, took a dislike to Guy from the start. Early in the rehearsals, the story went, he announced that Guy would never get a chance to play the role for an audience, not once, so he should just forget about it. In the meantime Madeleine, her health improved, frantic to get away from her mother, and determined that, as she could not have a family, she would have a career, joined her husband in Philadelphia, where she quickly landed a role in a revival of Shaw's *Heartbreak House* at a regional theater.

Guy's play opened to excellent notices. Marc Trilby was

particularly well received and the producers, buoyed by their success in the provinces, prepared to move the show to Broadway. At the end of the Philadelphia run the actors, all save Guy, were euphoric to have a hit on their hands. They arrived in town and immediately began their rehearsals on the new stage.

A few nights before the opening, Marc Trilby was having dinner with well-heeled friends in a new Italian restaurant on the Upper West Side. It was a tall, narrow building with dining rooms on two floors, the kitchen and bathrooms tucked away below street level. In its previous incarnation there was a dining room on the third floor, but in the renovation this space was consigned to storage. Late in the evening, Marc Trilby, well lubricated by alcohol and the praise of his fellows, excused himself from the table and wandered off in search of the men's room. Somehow he persuaded himself that it was up one flight instead of down two. He climbed the carpeted stairs, crossed a dimly lit landing, opened a likely-looking door, stepped into an open shaft that had once served as a dumbwaiter, fell through two floors, and landed, to the astonishment of the line chef, on a prep table in the kitchen. Both of his legs were broken in the fall.

Two nights later, Guy Margate made his Broadway debut.

The New York critics were unanimous in their contempt. The script, the direction, the acting, were variously disparaged, but one thing all agreed upon was the inadequacy of the lead, one Guy Margate, who, it was acknowledged, had leaped into the fray because of an unfortunate accident to the estimable Marc Trilby. Audiences, so warned, stayed away. In two weeks the producers were forced to admit the failure of their enterprise and the play quietly closed.

I didn't see it—it was during my Pinter run—but Mindy did and even her charitable heart could find nothing kind to say about Guy's performance. "He's just not right for the role," she concluded. "And, of course, the reviews have been so brutal he's terrified and it shows."

Did Madeleine witness her husband's humiliation upon the boards? I didn't know. I'd heard not one word from her since the night she nearly died. I didn't know how to reach her, but she knew where I was, so I concluded, not unreasonably I think, that her silence was purposeful, and that I'd lost her one more time.

Part III

I'd like to skip ahead six years to the winter of 1982, but having so carefully detailed the events of a short period I fear my readers will require a summary of this gap. For myself, I can do it in two words: I worked. The Pinter was a success, my Stanley hailed as "hilariously punchy," "as startled and startling as a deer in the headlights" (I loved that one), and "sheer madness fueled by paranoia and delusions of shabby grandeur." I was nominated for an award that William Hurt won. Barney had a good strategy which kept me busy, and I was lucky—or so my friends thought. Gradually I had to phase out my waiter's job because I was acting too much to keep it. Not that I was making any money. The explosion of Off and Off-Off theater in the '70s put a lot of actors out there, but the exciting new work was often at non-Equity theaters which paid less than union wage. A common practice was to use a pseudonym, wrapping, in effect, an actor who wasn't in the union around an actor who was. Mine was Dale Edwards, not terribly original, I admit, but I've never wanted to get too far from myself. It was a heady but discouraging time; I was in a production with an elaborate $20,000 set where the actors were paid literally nothing but the honor of working with that scenery. Another short run in a tiny midtown theater paid $50 a week. At the Roundabout, when the paychecks arrived, the techies put down their hammers and saws, left the lights on, and marched off to the bank in a herd, because they knew if they waited until the following morning, the checks would bounce. Many fine actors, reduced to doing commercials, driving cabs, or juggling temp jobs, gave up and went to California. Some tied themselves to regional companies where they had job security of a sort. My way was slow, but it was steady. I was single and parsimonious, and my apartment was rent-controlled. Others had it a lot harder. Al Pacino, famously, slept on the stage in a ratty theater on the Lower East Side.

' I saw Teddy rarely, usually backstage, because, stalwart friend that he was, he attended every play I was in, no matter how small the part or tattered the venue. Wayne was never along. As it turned out, Wayne had no interest in theater, but Teddy maintained this didn't affect the amatory bliss of their cohabitation. What did put a strain on it was, as everyone had predicted, Teddy's father, who had gotten wind of his son's attachment and recalled him to the family manse for a serious talk. "He told me he'd always known I would disgrace the family," Teddy confided, "but he said he was impressed by the originality of my failure, and how many parts it had to it: first the acting thing, which was pathetic, then the homosexual thing, which was disgusting, and then the Chinese thing, which was so appalling he didn't want to speak of it."

"Did he cut you off?" I asked.

"We're in a standoff," Teddy explained. "It's all very Oscar

Wildesville, except Wayne has no fortune to lose. The pater has agreed to continue my allowance for the meantime. It actually comes from my grandfather's estate so he would have to make an effort to hold it back and I could conceivably sue and win."

"You've consulted a lawyer?"

"Wayne did," Teddy said. "I can't be bothered, frankly."

I considered the implications of this last revelation to be of the worst sort possible.

Back to the deep freeze of December 1982. An actor was in the White House and all was right with the world. I had auditioned for the part of Jean, the valet in Strindberg's *Miss Julie*, which was being revived at a now extinct theater in the East Village. It's a delicious role, full of menace, subtle seduction, and all manner of imposture. Jean is a valet who takes total control of his vivacious and temperamental mistress; in the end she is so completely under his spell that he persuades her to kill herself. The theater was Equity and with good reviews might support an extended run. I read for the callback with a beautiful actress, Sylvia Brent, who went on to have a career in a long-running soap opera, a fate she didn't deserve. She wasn't brilliant, it can't be denied, and I could tell she was nervous, so I played into her insecurity and we came off strongly. I got the part, she didn't.

We opened in icy January to good notices and receptive audiences, all pleased to be warm for a few hours in a darkened theater while class warfare played out convincingly on the stage before them. Our six-week run was extended an extra two, though it was clear that we wouldn't be sustainable beyond that, the Strindberg ceiling being understandably low. One dark Sunday afternoon in February, when the streets were glazed with ice and the wind was rattling the windows so forcefully one expected to see Catherine Earnshaw peering in looking for Heathcliff, I was in the dressing room after the show, dreading the gauntlet to the subway. We'd played to a diminished audience of committed Strindberg enthusiasts and stalwarts from the sticks. *Miss Julie* is a three-person piece, just the valet, Jean; his mistress, the eponymous Julie; and the kitchen maid, Kirstin, who may or may not be Jean's fiancée. Our trio shared a comfortable, old-fashioned dressing room/ greenroom with a mirrored counter, a screen, a couch that sometimes served as a stage prop, a coffee table, a sink, and an impressive British-style electric kettle. The ladies had gone, having agreed to share a cab, as they both lived midtown. Feeling mildly depressed by the low turnout, I had prepared myself a mug of tea and settled on the couch. The play was in its last week and I was, as always, uncertain about what I would do next. I knew what I wanted to do, however, and I was on the very cusp of doing it. I had an audition for the part of Astrov in a new production of *Uncle Vanya* scheduled at the Public Theater, a part I wanted more than I cared to let myself know. The casting director had seen both my Stanley and my Jean. She had called Barney and invited me to audition, so my hopes were perilously high.

To appear at the Public Theater in a Chekhov play would qualify as an enormous coup, but it was also a dangerous gamble. One could still be flayed alive by the critics, but it would never be the fault of the play—one would have failed to come up to the standard of an acknowledged genius.

I was reading, for the hundredth time, Astrov's prophetic speech about the deforestation of the district, and his despair of saving the natural habitat that once flourished and provided food and shade and spiritual sustenance for the peasants who, deluded by the siren call of progress, relentlessly cut down trees and cleared land. In two of Chekhov's plays, *The Cherry Orchard* and *Uncle Vanya,* the fate of trees is of nearly as much interest as the fate of the characters. *The Cherry Orchard* ends with the clanging of the ax, and the audience experiences this sound as dread.

There came a light rapping at the dressing-room door; nothing like an ax, but startling nonetheless. At first I thought it was the wind, effecting some structural creaking—the theater was old and full of complaints—but then it came again, a light drumming as of fingernails against the wood. "Come in," I said.

At this point I hardly need tell you the name of the actor who entered the scene. But I will remind you that I hadn't seen Guy Margate in six years, so, though you may be feeling very smug, I was taken completely by surprise. Guy, as was his habit, came on in medias res.

"I've got to hand it to you," he said, "when it comes to playing the brute with women, you're totally credible."

I closed my script and laid it on the coffee table. "Guy," I said. "I can hardly believe it. I thought you were in Philadelphia."

He stepped into the light, taking in the furnishings with his ever critical eye. "Isn't this cozy," he said. "You could practically live in here."

"It is," I said. "Have a seat. I can offer you a cup of tea."

"That would be fine," he said. I got up to tend the kettle while he stood there awkwardly, trying to decide whether to sit on the couch or pull up a stool from the counter.

"What brings you to town?" I asked.

"We're transitioning back to the city. Philly's just not what Maddie needs at this point. She has an important audition that could make the difference. She was too nervous to come alone, so I came with her."

"Black or herbal?" I asked.

"Black," he said.

As I busied myself with the tea, I sneaked brief glimpses at my unexpected guest. He'd gone through a fairly marked physical transformation. There was less of everything, less hair, less weight, less color. He looked as though he'd been laundered once too often. His eyes were odd—they bulged in a way I didn't remember—and his lips were dry and chapped. He was clean shaven, his hair was short, the hollows in his cheeks were deep, and there were two grooves, like quotation marks, between his brows. He looked older than me, and I wondered if he actually was. He wore a heavy green wool coat, too wide in the shoulders, too long at the sleeves. "Take your coat off," I suggested.

He shrugged off the garment, glancing about for a place to put it.

"There's a hook on that screen," I said.

"It's bitter out there," he said, hanging up the coat. He'd developed a slight stoop, as well as a corrective habit of lifting his shoulders and rolling them back and down.

"How did you know I was here?" I asked.

"Teddy told us. We saw him last night."

"But Madeleine didn't come with you."

"She's off with Mindy somewhere."

"Did she know you were coming to my show?" The water was bubbling and I handed him a stained mug with a tea bag in it, which he looked into ruefully. "It's just tea stains," I said.

"No. She doesn't know I'm here," he said. He held out his cup. As I filled it with boiling water, the old familiar distrust and physical revulsion was aroused in me, sharp and pungent as a scent, and I drew away from him.

"How is she?" I asked.

Guy pulled out a stool and propped himself upon it, letting his long legs splay apart and cradling the warm mug between his hands. His pants legs hiked up over the top of his well-worn boots. Horrific argyle socks clung to his thin shanks. I looked away. "She's good," he said. "Well, you know Maddie, she's good and she's not good."

"You call her Maddie."

"She doesn't mind. She likes it, actually. You were wrong about that."

"So what's not good?"

"Her nerves. She's working a lot. Her career is really taking off. In fact, I've pretty much had to put my own on hold because even though she's working, she's not making much

money, of course, she's an actress, and we have to live somewhere and we have to eat and someone has to put food in front
of her or she won't eat."

"So you've got a day job."

"At a bookstore. I've been there a few years. I'm a manager
now."

I didn't entirely buy this tale of husbandly self-sacrifice.
Rumor had it that after the Broadway disaster Guy had tried
out for a lot of roles in New York and Philadelphia but no one
had any use for him. There was a particularly cruel bit of gossip, put out by an actor who should have known better, that a
playwright impressed by Guy's audition was warned by the director, "Forget it. What you just saw is all you're ever going
to get."

This vicious tidbit came to mind as I watched Guy sipping
his tea. "Well, that's good," I said.

He swallowed, craning his neck and doing the thing with
his shoulders. "Really," he said. "What's good about it?"

"Well, that you're a manager."

"I'm killing myself," he said. "Managers don't get overtime
and work twice as many hours. It's a trap."

"I didn't know that."

"I have to do everything, the shopping, the cooking, pay
all the bills, keep Maddie calmed down. I never sleep."

I recalled the arduous business of keeping Madeleine
calmed down. "But her career is taking off."

"Regional stuff, but solid roles. Shakespeare, she did Desdemona last year. Rave reviews. She went up to Yale this fall

and did a new play. There was a write-up in the *Times*; you probably saw it."

"No," I admitted. "I missed it."

"He said the play was a bomb but Maddie was a star."

Every time he called Madeleine "Maddie" I flinched and he noticed it. I had the sense that he was doing it on purpose to irritate me. I imagined how persistent he must have been to wear her down to the point where she accepted this diminutive, because I knew she hated it.

Guy sipped his tea, watching me over the rim. What was he up to? What did he want from me? Was it money?

"You've been doing OK, I hear," he said.

Money, I thought. "I've been working. I don't get paid much, but I scrape by."

He took this in without comment. I pulled out a stool and sat facing him. "So, what's the audition?"

He rubbed his chin between his thumb and forefinger, pulling the flesh in to a wedge. "Bev thinks it could be the turning point for her," he said. "I do too. She's got a good shot at it. The director saw her at the Yale thing and liked what he saw."

"What's the part?"

"It's Elena in *Uncle Vanya*. A new production at the Public."

"Wow," I said.

"She would be fantastic in that part."

"She would indeed," I agreed. My heart rate increased to keep up with my careening brain. Madeleine as Elena, me as

Astrov, it would be a triumph of casting. The electricity would dim the houselights. The play depends on the audience's apprehension of the intense physical attraction between these two characters. Elena is a difficult role. She's a prisoner of her own beauty, she has no ambition, no life force, but she drives everyone around her to the limit of endurance. Psychologically she's opaque and she's made a decision no one can understand; she's married an old man and not a rich old man, either. Madeleine had just the right quality of unexamined stubbornness. The role would be a natural fit for her. And she was so lovely and she was so hot. As I sat there, with Guy's eyes probing me, I was filled with such a physical craving to see her, to be with her, that I got up, pretending I needed to refresh my tea. Other anxieties crowded in, one of which was the copy of the script I'd left on the coffee table. I didn't want Guy to see it. I didn't want him to know. When my back was to him, I shot a glance at the table. Yes, there it was and I had laid it facedown.

"It's a great play. A difficult play," Guy observed.

"Chekhov is always a challenge," I said, pouring water into my mug. Why should I tell him? After all, I might not get the part. A piquant moment of silence passed between us.

"I know you have an audition for Astrov," Guy said.

So that was it.

"Who told you?"

"A little bird." He said this slowly, mocking me.

"Teddy?" But I knew I hadn't told Teddy. I hadn't told anyone.

"I don't have to say."

"Well, it's true," I said. "So what."

"So I don't think it's a good idea."

"I'll certainly take that into account," I said.

"I think you should," he said, giving me a meaningful look.

"OK, I'll bite," I said. "Why is it not a good idea?"

"Maddie's feelings about you are complicated," he said. "Now is not the time for her to be forced to . . . explore all that. There's too much at stake for her in this project and she's going to need all her concentration to get through it."

"Bulletin, Guy," I said. "Madeleine is an actress. She's a professional. And so am I. That's what we do."

"You like to talk to me as if I don't know anything about acting," he said. "You've always done that. I may not be working right now, but I'm an actor."

"Then act like one," I said. "Or better yet, act like a man."

"I'm acting like a husband," he replied. "And one who cherishes his wife. You haven't given Maddie a second thought for six years, but I've spent every minute of that time taking care of her. She's a talented, brilliant actress, there's nothing she can't do, but she's fragile, she's a fragile woman."

Everything about this eruption of drivel offended me, but particularly egregious was the assertion that I'd given no thought to Madeleine over the intervening years. I thought of her all the time. I was like the guy in the Dylan song, I'd seen a lot of women, but Madeleine never left my mind. I felt I knew her better than Guy, and I was sure she saw right through his absurd posturing which was designed to disguise the obvious fact that she could act circles around him. At that moment I felt Guy's presence in my dressing room was an outrage against her. What would she say if she could see him, suited up as Guy the

Protector, with his bulging eyes and his ultra-earnest manner? I rapped my mug down sharply against the counter. "My God," I said, "she must be sick of you."

This surprised him. "That's not true," he said. "Maddie loves me."

"You're so fucking insensitive you call her by a babified name she hates and you tell yourself she likes it."

"You know nothing about it," he countered. "You've never had a loving relationship with anyone. All you think about is yourself; you can't be relied upon for anything, and believe me, no one knows that better than Maddie."

"What are you talking about?"

"Don't pretend you care about her. You used her when it was convenient, and when it wasn't, you couldn't be bothered."

"Did she say that?"

"She doesn't have to say it. I was there."

"That's right," I said. "You were there and that's why I never got a chance to do anything. You took over, that's what you do. You butt in where no one wants you and you take over. That's what you're doing right now. If Madeleine knew you were here, she'd be totally humiliated."

He blinked at me as if he couldn't focus, rolling his shoulders up and back. "So you insist on doing the audition," he said.

"Relax," I said. "I might not get the part. Or she might not. You've got odds, if you can figure out what they are."

"I think I have a fair idea of what the odds are," he said.

A heavy odds-calculating silence fell between us. Guy got

up, slid his mug onto the counter, and sat down again. I ambled over to the couch where, just to irritate him, I picked up the bright-yellow script and stood solemnly leafing through it. I was a bit young to play Astrov, the only thing I had against me. Astrov is thirty-seven. He fears his life is over, he's lost his looks. I'd have to feel forty. Madeleine was actually a little old to play Elena, but I didn't think that would be a problem, not with her slim figure and flashing eyes. Of course I hadn't seen her in six years, in which time her husband had lost half his hair. Guy sat pressing his fingertips to his eyes, rubbing hard. "I'm just exhausted," he said.

"Why don't you take sleeping pills?"

"I do, but they don't work for me." He dropped his hands to his lap and took in a long, slow breath, such as one takes before the commencement of a disagreeable task, a breath in which I sensed the drawing out of a tide between us. He exhaled through his nose, pressing his lips together and meeting my eyes coldly. "I should have let you drown," he said.

Here it comes, I thought. "I didn't ask you to save me," I said, which was a stupid thing to say. Guy pounced on it. He flashed his predator smile and then he did something profoundly unnerving: he flung his arms into the air and cried out in my voice, "Help, help, don't leave me."

It wasn't just my voice, it was my inflection, my manner, my peculiar combination of actuated facial muscles, my eyes wide with terror, my mouth trembling with fatigue, it was me, drowning, but only for a moment, and then it was Guy again, chuckling at his own cleverness.

"Very funny," I said.

"Very funny," he echoed. It was eerily like looking in a mirror.

"So you think you should have let me drown, but you didn't. What should I do, kill myself?"

"I'm not asking you to kill yourself."

"Not yet."

"Though in some cultures I do have that right."

"You've been doing research."

"I have. In the Eastern view, I'm responsible for you. Because I saved your life, I'm required to look out for you. But here in the West, you owe me your life. Basically, you belong to me."

"Any place where it's just a happy accident not necessitating a further relationship?"

"You'd like that, wouldn't you?"

"I think a case can be made for it."

He looked thoughtful. "I'm afraid not. It's universally understood that our relationship is special. It's mythic, actually. You were supposed to die that night, you were a goner, and I had to rob death to save you. At some personal risk, I might add, though you seem to discount that for obvious reasons."

"I don't discount it," I said quietly. He'd brought it all back with his cruel impression of me and his talk of robbing death. I remembered how I had struggled with him in the water, how certain I was that death had a grip on me and there was no escape, yet how desperate I was to be saved. I had no lucid thoughts, only terror and a belligerent conviction that I was too young, too vital, that it was unfair. How could death be indifferent to the injustice of it? And not just indifferent, but avid, pulling me down again and again, gagging me with gallons of water, wearing my will down to a fine thread of naked resolve. It was just at the moment when that thread snapped, when the waters closed silently over my head and I gave in to my fate, that Guy thudded into me in the darkness, his arms tightening around me, lifting me, while I squirmed and sputtered, dragging me back into the world.

"This seems like such a silly demand," I said. "It doesn't have enough gravity. I mean, it's serious, I really want to do this audition, but why would you insist on something so . . . I don't know, so personal? It doesn't seem fair."

Guy emitted a series of breathy clicks through his nose which I took to be laughter.

"This doesn't have anything to do with Madeleine, does it?" I asked. "That was just a cover."

"It was a test," he said. "And you failed."

"So if I back out of the audition because I think it's best for Madeleine, I pass the test, but since I failed the test, I have to give up the audition because you saved my life."

"I couldn't have put it better myself."

"It's crazy," I said.

He stood up, shaking down his pants legs over the appalling socks. "I know you got good reviews for this Strindberg thing," he said. "But I just don't get it. You're way off, there's no subtlety, it's a totally wooden performance. Everybody says you're up and coming, but Astrov is a complex role. It's not like this nasty valet thing. You're not ready for it; that's what I'm worried about. And Ed, you don't want to flop at the Public in an important role, take my word for that. It could be the end of your career."

"Jesus, Guy," I exclaimed. "Where are you from? It's hell, isn't it? It really is hell."

He wrested his coat from the hook, wrapped himself inside it, and fussily fastening every button, turned on me a sympathetic smile. "You're hysterical because you know I'm right. Think about that." He ambled to the door. "I've got to meet Maddie," he said. "Thanks for the tea."

"Wow," Teddy said. "He really worked you over."

This was true. I felt bruised by the latest scene with Guy and I'd run to Teddy for moral support. "Did Madeleine seem like a crazy person to you?" I asked.

"It's hard to say. She's a good actress. Now that I think about it, she didn't talk much. Maybe she was a little tense. Guy went on and on about the audition. He was more excited than she was."

"Did you talk about me?"

"I did. I told them about the Strindberg. But I didn't know about this audition. Why didn't you call me?"

"I didn't call anyone. I'm superstitious about this one, it feels big. I'm almost afraid to talk to myself about it."

"How did Guy find out?"

"That's what I'd like to know," I said. "Jesus, what am I going to do? I'm wrecked now. I'm completely unsure of myself."

"You're seriously thinking of backing out?"

"Barney will murder me."

"Is it because of what Guy said about Madeleine, or what he said about your acting? Or the other thing?"

"The debt?"

"The debt," Teddy said.

"Do you think he has the right to ask me to do this?"

"He wasn't exactly asking."

"That's true. He never asks. He doesn't think he has to."

Teddy said nothing, gazing into his Scotch, letting me work it out for myself.

"Is there some kind of cosmic thing that will backfire on me and ruin my career if I defy Guy Margate?"

Teddy dug into the ice bucket on the table and added a few cubes to his glass. The spirit of Wayne hung over the room; every inch of wall space was covered with his paintings. We were munching Chinese rice crackers. All agreed, it was impressive that Teddy and Wayne had stayed together so long, though Mindy maintained their longevity was the result of Teddy's willingness to support Wayne in a style to which he had quickly become accustomed. I thought it had more to do with Wayne being exotic, the lure of the East and all that distantly smiling serenity. I recalled Guy's description of the Eastern view, that because he had saved me, he was obligated to look after me. Was it possible that in his mixed-up brain he thought that was what he was doing? "Do you think he's trying to save me from myself?" I said.

"When's the audition?" Teddy said.

"Thursday."

He rubbed his cheek with the palm of his hand, ruminating upon my case.

"There's no guarantee I'll get the part," I said. "Especially now, since I'm going to be completely conflicted about it."

"I can't tell you what to do," Teddy said.

"I know."

"But I can tell you that what Guy said about your acting isn't true. You're a gifted actor; everyone knows it."

"Thanks."

"I envy you. So does Guy. That's what this is about."

I nodded, stuck for something to say. Teddy had left Stella Adler years ago and gone to Meisner for a while, then he tried Uta Hagen and then Julie Bovasso; he was a connoisseur of acting teachers, evidently unwilling to give up being a student. His performances were in showcases and rare at that. I'd seen him a few times over the years, always in small parts that he made the best of, but there was something inhibited about his work. I recalled how certain he'd been at the dawn of Wayne that the acknowledgment of his sexual identity would have a liberating effect on his acting, but that hadn't happened. If anything he was less confident, more tentative. Wayne's complete indifference to what was, after all, Teddy's art didn't help. Before Wayne, his friends were all actors, comrades-in-arms; now he spent his time at gallery openings, where painters sniped at one another, or at gay bars where one's professional aspirations were not the subject. He stayed in acting classes because it was the only way he could still fancy himself an actor.

"I've been lucky," I said.

"You have in some ways," Teddy agreed. "Though not in love."

"I'd sure like to see Madeleine," I said.

"Best wait until this audition thing is behind you both."

"That's true," I agreed. "I don't want to muck up her chances. How does she look?"

"She's more beautiful than ever," Teddy said.

"How could she have married that guy?"

"Guy," Teddy said. We smirked.

"He looks terrible," I said. "What's with his eyes? Is he on drugs?"

"He's on desperation," Teddy said.

"It's so unfair," I said. "If I had to drown, I don't see why someone decent couldn't have saved me. Why couldn't *you* have saved me? I wouldn't mind owing you my life for a second."

Teddy's expression was wistful. "I can't swim," he said.

I left Teddy in a mood as black and bitter as the frigid streets I walked through. I had to make a decision but I didn't want to think about it: I knew thinking wasn't going to help. Guy had attacked on three emotional fronts: my feelings for Madeleine, my personal sense of obligation to him for saving my life, and my insecurity as an actor. I might rationally decide that I would or would not undertake the audition, but emotionally I was a shambles.

It wasn't late, but the streets were quiet. A taxi whooshed by, ferrying a lone, pale citizen swathed in fur. A few pedestrians hurried from building to building, paddling the air with their bulky arms, simultaneously urged to speed by the cold and to caution by the ice. The Village was just entering the long period of gentrification which would not end until all but the most litigious of its residents were driven to points east and south. My building, which had so far escaped even a cosmetic coat of paint, huddled before me, the shabbiest on the block. The windows were dark, save the third-floor front, where an impoverished novelist, who would later enjoy a small but respectable following, scribbled into the wee hours of morning. I grasped the stair rail with my gloved hand and mounted the sticky, salt-strewn steps to the front door. Like most New York apartments, mine was overheated, and I was looking forward to the blast of warm air that would greet me after the long haul to the fourth floor. Somewhere between the first and second landing a memory eluded the thought police and burst into the full sensory-surround screen of my consciousness. It was Madeleine leaning into me on this staircase, her arm wrapped around my back, her hand resting on my shoulder, her eyes and lips raised to mine, that night after we'd come back from the Jersey shore, when I'd outwaited and outwitted Guy at the bar. How long ago that was; it seemed another world, though the truth I didn't know then was that I hadn't changed at all. I would change later.

As I trudged ever upward with this ghost of Madeleine clinging to my side, regret and anger percolated in my gut, while fatigue closed down various circuits in my brain. I flipped the locks on the apartment door and headed straight for bed. Madeleine was everywhere I looked, but especially behind my eyelids. As I drifted into sleep I heard her voice guiding me. "This way, Edward. This way." I thought about the scene at the bookstore, that night before the last night I'd seen her. "You shocking girl," I said, feeling pleased with myself. I knew I would dream of her and I did.

This was my dream. It was so odd that in the morning I wrote it down, so the details are exact. Madeleine and I entered a bedroom that looked a bit like a stage set. The furniture was oversized and crowded together; there were two doors, stage right and left, and upstage a heavy maroon curtain covered the entire wall. The bed was unmade, the sheets rumpled, a wadded quilt, resembling a dead body, hung over the foot. Madeleine turned to me and we kissed. I was eager to get her into the bed, but enjoying the deep openmouthed kiss too much to break it off. At length she pulled away and said, "Are you hungry?"

I knew then that I was famished. "Yes," I said. She stepped behind the curtain, reappearing almost at once with a plate of roast turkey balanced on one open hand, a knife, fork, and white napkin in the other. All this she arranged on the dressing table, motioning me to take a seat on the poufy stool in front of it. "I have to get ready for bed," she said. "Eat this and I'll be right back."

I settled down to the repast. Dream efficiency supplied a glass of cold white wine. As Madeleine went off behind the curtain, I took up the knife and fork and began to eat. The turkey was superb; I was certain I'd never had better. It was tender and moist, warm and flavorful. It's not easy to cook turkey this well, I thought. It's usually dry and stringy, like chewing a wrung-out mop, but this meat fairly melted in my mouth. Sleeping or waking, I know I've never come across a better bird.

As these cheerful observations passed through my brain, and the turkey disappeared down my gullet, I heard a shuffling outside the stage-right door. I put down my cutlery and stared at the door's reflection in the mirror of the dresser, moved by a dim premonition of what was about to happen. Abruptly the door flew open and Guy Margate stepped in. "What?" he exclaimed, observing me on my pouf. "You here?" Our eyes barely crossed in the mirror. He went to the bed, pulled his sweater off and tossed it on the floor. Then he did the same with his T-shirt, belt, pants, socks, and underpants. I watched him in the mirror as I finished the remains of the turkey. It made me uncomfortable, especially the girlish grin he sent me as he stripped off his underwear and dropped them, with a flourish, onto the pile, but I wasn't going to give him the satisfaction of ruining my meal. Naked, he fell to rearranging the pillows, straightening the sheets, shaking out the quilt. Then he slipped under the covers and turned his back to me.

I drained my wineglass. I could hear Madeleine behind the curtain, running water, brushing her teeth. "I'll be right there, darling," she said. Guy didn't move. The curtain rustled and she appeared, dressed in a scrumptious negligee, her hair falling loosely over her bare shoulders. She passed me without speaking and climbed into the bed, scooting close to Guy and pressing her lips against the nape of his neck, his back. "Darling," she said.

She thinks he's me, I thought.

Guy flipped over like a fish tossed on a dock, kicking off the quilt. Madeleine screamed. She jumped up on her hands and knees and crawled to the side of the bed. At last she saw me, my back was to her, and I watched her in the mirror as she swung her legs over the edge, covered her face with her hands, and burst into sobs. Guy, very still now, eyed her coldly. It struck me as funny; I don't know why. I laughed and Guy laughed. We laughed together at poor Madeleine, who wept inconsolably. I woke up.

What a ridiculous dream. I didn't even get to have sex with Madeleine; all I'd managed was a kiss. And why the turkey? What was the significance of the turkey?

I don't put much credit in dreams, but Madeleine always did. When we lived together she liked to hear my dreams and to speculate about the meaning of their random components. I have such odd ones—sometimes they're more like stories and I'm not even in them. Madeleine had a book she'd picked up somewhere, a dictionary of dream symbols, which gave the ancient prophetic interpretations of an astonishing array of terms. Once I'd had a dream in which I struggled with an enormous piece of tree bark. "Tree bark," Madeleine read. "A danger-go-slow warning in regard to the opposite sex." We both shouted with laughter, for it was the night after she'd moved her records and books into my apartment. "Too late," she said. "Poor Edward, it's too late to go slow now."

Another night I'd spent my dream time trying to warm myself by a cold radiator. "Remorse over an alienated friend is signified in a dream of a cold radiator."

"What could the ancients possibly have known about radiators?" I scoffed.

"The Romans had hot water," she correctly observed. "They had steam heat."

Thus my memory of Madeleine on the stair provoked a foolish dream and now the dream led me to recollections of daily life with Madeleine. I sat up in the bed and regarded my impressive erection. The erotically charged atmosphere of the dream had not yet dissipated: the kiss, then the turkey, then Guy's surprise entrance. He'd taken my place in the bed, but it didn't do him any good because it was me Madeleine wanted. The sight of him made her scream.

To act or not to act; that was the question.

My eyes fell on the Chekhov script I'd left atop my clothes piled on the floor. *You're a sly one,* Astrov says to Elena, when she quizzes him about his feelings for poor, plain Sonya. *You beautiful, fluffy little weasel . . . you must have victims.* I picked up the script and turned to that confrontation. Was it *"you* beautiful weasel" or *"a* beautiful weasel"? It was *a.* At the end of the speech Astrov folds his arms, bows his head. *I submit,* he says. *Here I am, devour me!* It's a declaration rich with irony, he's teasing her, but it's not entirely a jest. Astrov is a sensible man, a doctor, and a botanist; he cares about what future generations will think of his generation. He has little hope that the destruction of the local environment can be stopped, but he has to try, so he plants trees. His attraction to Elena, a lazy, selfish, desperate, beautiful siren who enchants him from the first moment he sees her, is serious. He knows this passion could be the wreck of him, yet he can't resist it.

I put down the script and stood up, thinking of myself as Astrov and Madeleine as Elena. How would she play her response to my plea to be devoured? Her line is simple: *You are out of your mind!* Does she believe that? It would depend on what I gave her. I crossed my arms and announced to the dresser: "I submit, here I am." I dropped to my knees, opening my arms, offering my naked plea: "Devour me!"

Then I got up, felt around for my slippers, and padded off to the bathroom. "Elena, you vixen," I shouted. "Your Astrov is coming to save you."

That was how I reached my decision—lightly. Playfully, as an actor, not as a friend of one or a lover of the other, not in defiance or in anger, but as one who is offered a prize and reaches out to take it. The audition was the following afternoon. I had purchased a bottle of dye to add silver at my temples and a tin of shadow to darken the light creases under my eyes. As I applied it, I thought of how much older Guy appeared than me; his looks, like Astrov's, were ruined. I raised my eyebrows to bug my eyes out like his, but that wasn't right. Astrov was exhausted, not tense. I recalled the stoop of Guy's shoulders, his tic of correcting it. I'm tall; I carry my shoulders back and low. I practiced at the mirror, trying out various degrees of slouch. I discovered it wasn't only at the shoulders; it started at the diaphragm. The belly was slack. I stepped back from the mirror to get a longer view. Years, I thought with satisfaction. It added years.

I read with the stage manager, a compact middle-aged matron who fed me my lines crisply, like sugared wafers. The director asked me a few personal questions. I was lucid and friendly, like Astrov, ironic and curious about the world around me. I got the callback the next morning. This time I read with Rory Behenny, a fine actor who had just finished a successful run at the fledgling Brooklyn Academy of Music. Rory was the reason our director had decided to take on the play. We did the scene in which Astrov and Vanya argue about a missing bottle of morphine. Vanya is suicidal; Astrov scoffs at him. Rory was like a quick fox, daring me to catch him. We had a lively skirmish and at the end our little audience of professionals gave us a lusty round of applause.

Barney called me the next morning, sounding glum. "Well," he said, "they've cast the Chekhov."

"And?" I said.

There was a pause, but I didn't hang on it; I was that confident.

"Rehearsals start Monday," he said.

Yesterday, as I was cleaning out the attic of our house, I came across a box of Madeleine's books. It had been hastily packed for the move from Philadelphia to New York, unpacked in the East Village apartment where Guy and Madeleine briefly lived, then packed again, by me this time, and shipped to Connecticut. At first I imagined that Madeleine might ask for her books, but it soon became clear that she was unlikely to do that, so the box became a disheartening reminder of all that I had lost, and I stowed it away. It wasn't a large box. It occurred to me that there might be something in it of use in composing this memoir; at least it would refresh my memory of what Madeleine was like then, what she chose to take with her on what was to be a harrowing trip to oblivion. I brought the box to my crowded study under the eaves and cut the tape with a utility knife. One by one I unpacked the books. A dictionary, a Bartlett's quotations, a complete Shakespeare, a complete Chekhov, three plays by Ibsen, a stack of the bright-yellow scripts Madeleine had collected for auditions, or just because she was curious about something new and a script was cheaper than a ticket. Stanislavski's *An Actor Prepares,* several nineteenth-century novels, Hardy, Eliot, *Middlemarch*—she loved *Middlemarch*. Shurtleff's *Audition*—every actor had that one then and I've noticed it's still in print. The collected poems of Yeats and Blake, and, of course, the *Dreamer's Dictionary.* Serendipity! I'd just been writing about it. I took it up and flipped through it gingerly, with the creepy sensation that someone was watching me. A musty odor arose from the pages, long cooped up and eager to interpret those vagrant dreams. All right, all right, I thought. What have you got for turkey?

Honestly, I didn't expect to find anything; turkey is a New World bird, after all, but there it was, a longish entry between "tunnel" (an obstacle dream) and "turnip: see vegetable(s)." For all you dreamers of poultry, here's the entire scoop on the gobbler that was beat out by the eagle for the role of our national bird. If you see a strutting turkey in your dream it portends a period of confusion; a flock of turkeys predicts public honors; if you kill a turkey, expect a stroke of good luck; if you cook, dress, and serve the bird, you'll enjoy a period of prosperity. However, if you do what I all unknowing did, if you eat the turkey, "you are likely to make a serious error of judgment, so be very careful regarding any important matters which may be pending."

I snapped the book closed and dropped it back into the box.

I admit, as prophecy, the turkey dream isn't exactly Birnam wood, but as I piled the other books back on top of the malevolent dictionary, I had a sense of my fate having ambushed me with a spitefulness I could never have anticipated.

Not much happens at a first rehearsal, but the atmosphere is fraught with tension. The action largely consists of what unclever people call a meet and greet, followed by a reading of the play. Our *Vanya* cast assembled at a rehearsal stage at the Public Theater, a large room with low ceilings, bare white walls, and a polished wooden floor. A few straight-backed chairs were scattered around, an upright piano loomed in one corner. There was a side table set up with coffee urn and pastry tray, and, at the center, a long rectangular table on metal trestles with ten green plastic chairs drawn up to it, the setting for our first run at Anton Pavlovich Chekhov.

Repertory actors have an easy time; they're like a team of draft horses accustomed to pulling heavy loads in tandem. They just want someone to point out the road and off they go. They may even genuinely like one another. But a cast of actors chosen through auditions are more like chickens in a coop, each actor strutting the length and breadth of the limited territory, secretly terrified yet determined to appear nonchalant. We have our parts; that's not the problem. It's the pecking order that needs establishing and that's going to be up to that big, mysterious rooster, the director, who grins and grins as we come in one by one, his eyes like black beads in which we see ourselves reflected in ludicrous miniature. A consistent first-rehearsal behavior I've observed over the years is this: if there is a window in the room, within fifteen minutes of arrival every actor will meander to it and stand looking wistfully out.

I arrived in turmoil. I knew it was going to be impossible for me to concentrate on anything but Madeleine, and I was vexed that this public setting was to be the scene of our first meeting in so many years. I had hoped that she would call me, that we might even manage a brief meeting, but no such luck. Now I would be forced to make lighthearted, self-aggrandizing chatter with my fellow actors and pretend I was, like them, absorbed in the business of the first read, when all I really wanted was to get Madeleine alone and talk to her. Seriously. I just wanted to talk to her.

When I joined the company she hadn't yet arrived, so I had a few minutes to take part in the jovial introductions. Here was Gwen Post, a mad, wild-eyed bag lady who would play Marina, our dear old Nanny; here was a gloomy, intense collection of outraged nerve ends named Sally Divers, who was our Sonya, the girl who cherishes an unrequited passion for Astrov. Rory Behenny, the eponymous Uncle Vanya, who had read with me at the audition, ambled among us, dressed in a bizarre outfit, part tuxedo and part tracksuit. He pumped my hand and announced to all that he hoped I'd remember to bring the morphine. My enthusiastic response was without pretense; Rory was a truly gifted actor. He died a few years later of pancreatic cancer, which meant the stealth attack of lethally reproducing cells was probably under way as we stood in the rehearsal room joking about the pressing need for morphine.

Peter Smythe, our director, a combination of sprite and gremlin, with milky-blue eyes and bright-red hair cut in a bowl like the early Beatles, moved among us making introductions and encouraging us to help ourselves to the refreshments. Anton Schoitek, a hulk of a Russian with a head like a wild boar, perfect for the part of the faithful retainer Telyegin, came in with a roar and lifted Peter off the floor, hugging him to his massive chest and growling "Peter, Peter, Peter." As we were laughing at this spectacle, the door opened again and Madeleine slipped into the room.

One by one the company focused on her. Peter slid down the front of the Russian, announcing her name. I was leaning on the piano, not directly in her line of sight, and I watched as her eyes passed among the others and lit at last upon me. Lit is the correct word; I felt as if I was standing in a single spot, with the rest of the stage and all the people on it cast into darkness. Peter, running through the names, arrived at mine. "Ed Day," he said. "Our good doctor Astrov."

"We've met," Madeleine said, smiling modestly.

Rory, who was next to me, sent a sharp look from Madeleine to me and back again, making a show of being caught in an electric charge. "I'll say," he said, and everyone laughed.

I'm an actor; I don't get caught out by my emotions, but it took a conscious effort to hold myself in check. My impulse was to cross the room and fold Madeleine in my arms, and I could have done it, in actor-display mode. No one would have thought a thing about it. But I didn't move. Nor did she. Our eyes met and I drank in her presence, detecting the subtle changes in her that only I could see. She was a little thinner, which made her seem taller. Her abundant hair was tied back; the front cut short, curling over her brow cherub-style, which contrasted interestingly with her high un-cherubic cheekbones. She was wearing a lavender sweater that shifted her changeable eyes toward gray. Her eyes were different. That was what kept me from moving. The brows were drawn slightly down and together. She regarded me from farther away than the actual distance between us. Indeed so defensive was her expression that her head was drawn back on the pale column of her neck. Her upper lip lifted slightly, revealing the line of her teeth. In the next moment she blinked and turned her attention to our director who directed her to consider the delights on the refreshment table. But I knew what I'd seen in her eyes, and it unnerved me: it was fear. Why should Madeleine ever be afraid of me?

Another actor arrived, I don't remember who, and then another, and then our company was complete. We were invited to carry our coffee and rolls to the table where the business of the play would begin. Peter assigned our seats and asked us to take out our wallets, a request I thought very odd, but it turned out to be an introductory exercise in which each of us chose something we carried with us, a photo or card or memento, and told a little story about why we kept it with us. I remember little about this process except that I had nothing more personal than my Equity card, a fact I described as "sad" to the amusement of the group. Only the Russian came up with less. He had nothing in his wallet but a twenty-dollar bill. "This is America," he said. "Who cares who you are, only money counts."

What was it that Madeleine always carried with her? I don't remember. The afternoon passed in a blur of distraction. My brain came up with various clever ways to disguise the fact that I wasn't entirely there. Peter wanted a cold reading, which was a relief. I couldn't have interpreted a nursery rhyme. Madeleine was sitting two chairs down from me so that I couldn't see her. Her voice, so rich and so familiar, vibrated in my ear. It was music, and I closed my eyes to take it in.

At last it was over and we were free to pull on our boots, coats, hats, scarves, and gloves and go out into the cold. I sidled next to Madeleine and waited for her to finish an exchange with Rory, who had worked with the director of a play she'd done at Yale. He asked if she shared his opinion that the guy was impossible.

"My audition lasted three hours," Madeleine said. "He kept asking for more and more personal stuff. He wanted to break me down. I was so angry that I started to cry and I figured I'd lost the role. But that turned out to be just what he wanted."

"He's a sadist," Rory said.

"He is," Madeleine agreed.

While Rory occupied himself with wrapping a long multi-colored scarf around and around his throat, Madeleine turned to me and, with commendable calm, said, "How are you, Edward?"

"I'm fine," I said. "Where are you staying?"

"At a hotel," she said. "They put me up. It's just a few blocks."

"Can I walk you over?"

"Sure," she said.

We didn't speak again until we were on the street and out of earshot of our dispersing colleagues. "Is Guy with you?" I asked.

"Not yet," she said. "He's coming in on the train late tonight."

I took her hand and we walked another block in silence. At the light I put my arm around her shoulder. She was trembling so violently her teeth chattered. "Are you cold?" I asked.

"No," she said.

The hotel lobby was a dreary hall with a dim chandelier, a faded carpet, and a single bored attendant at the desk. We passed without greeting and stood in front of the elevator for an eternity.

"This elevator is really slow," Madeleine observed.

"I read an article," I said. "Some guy did a study. The average time it takes until a person waiting for an elevator shows visible signs of agitation is fourteen seconds."

"Fourteen seconds?" she said.

"Right."

"I'll remember that." The elevator dinged and the doors shuddered open upon a blood-red interior. We stepped inside. Madeleine pushed the button for the seventh floor. "At last," I said when the doors had closed. She turned to me, raising her arms around my neck, and the kiss of seven floors began. When the doors opened I kept my hand on her waist and we hurried down the empty hall to the room door. On the way Madeleine loosened her scarf and unbuttoned her coat. She had trouble with the key, turning it left and right and then left again, but nothing happened. I nuzzled her neck, peeling the collar of her coat away with my teeth. "Too slow," I whispered. She laughed. "I know," she said. The mechanism clicked and the door drifted open. I pulled her in for another kiss, which we held on to as I backed her inside and kicked the door closed behind me. It was a tiny, hot, dark room filled by a double bed, which was fine with us. Madeleine unbuttoned my coat; I pushed hers off her shoulders and worked on the sweater. In no time we were free of our clothes and tangled in each other on the lumpy mattress. Sex can be estranging; it can drive two otherwise compatible people apart. I'd had that experience a few times over the intervening years, but with Madeleine I had the sense that sex could actually hold us together. I couldn't go wrong, she was always with me. We kept at it quite a while, rolling off the bed to the floor at one point. At another the bed frame gave a shriek and a loud crack. "Oh no," Madeleine cried and we clutched each other, expecting the mattress to collapse beneath us, but it didn't. I made a lot of noise right at the end. She was nicely twisted with her hips turned one way and her shoulders the other, laughing and gasping for breath. My heart announced its ecstatic condition with a roar and I collapsed on top of her. After a few moments she eased her head out from beneath my shoulder and we had one more distressingly tender kiss. When that was over I rolled off of her and we lay side by side, washed up. The expression "flotsam and jetsam" came to mind, and then, like flotsam and jetsam, drifted away. "I thought that rehearsal would never end," I said.

"Me too."

"Every time you read a line I had to cross my legs."

"Does that help?"

"No," I said. "Only one thing really helps."

She snorted. I turned onto my side and smoothed her hair back with my palm. "I like your hair like this."

"I think Elena will pull it all up."

"But with the curls in the front."

"Um," she said. We were quiet then while the world fell back into place.

"So," I said. "How have you been?"

She gave me an incredulous smile. "Pretty good. Up until last Wednesday."

"What happened then?"

"I found out you were playing Astrov."

"And that was bad news?"

"That was shocking news."

"How did Guy take it?"

"Not well."

"That doesn't surprise me."

"No?" She was pressing little kisses down the inside of my forearm.

"Did he tell you he came to see me?"

She closed her eyes, taking in a slow breath. "When?" she said softly.

"When you were here for the audition. He came to my play and he came to the dressing room and he tried to talk me out of doing the audition."

"I think I don't need to know this," she said.

This annoyed me. "I wish I didn't know it," I said. She was silent. "Do you have any idea how he found out I was up for the part?"

"No," she said. We were very still then, while the specter of Guy Margate slid into the bed between us. "He's been having a hard time," she said, turning away from me.

"I know. He told me."

"What did he say?"

"He said he was killing himself."

"I feel sorry for him."

"You've a funny way of showing it."

She looked back over her shoulder. "What do you mean?"

I gestured to the room, the wreck of the bed, our clothes commingled on the floor.

"He must never know about this."

"He thinks you love him."

"Did he say that?"

"Yes. He said, 'Maddie loves me.' "

She turned over to face me, frowning.

"Maddie," I said. A blush started at her throat and swept up to her cheeks.

"I don't know what to tell you," she said.

"You could start by telling me why you married him."

"I was pregnant. You rejected me. He was so kind, he loves me so much."

"I rejected you?"

"You sent that chilly postcard."

"That wasn't rejection, Madeleine. That was a postcard. I never got the chance to reject you."

"But you would have. I knew that."

I rushed past this arguable point. "Another thing I'd like to know is when you started sleeping with him. Was it before I left for Connecticut?"

She pursed her lips and fluttered her eyelashes.

"It was before, right?"

"By sleeping with him, you mean when did I first have sex with him, right?"

"Exactly. When did you start fucking him? That's my question."

She allowed a dramatic pause, concentrating on the ceiling while tears welled up in her eyes. "I've never had sex with Guy," she said.

"Oh please," I said.

"It's unbelievable, isn't it?" she said.

"Completely."

"Nevertheless, it's true."

I suppose my mouth dropped open and some version of amazement sat upon my brow. It was as if she'd handed me one of those sudoku puzzles everyone is so mad for these days; I was conscious of a pattern I'd never noticed before and certain numbers were falling neatly into place. "So, he's gay," I said.

She gave a sad smile to the ceiling. "I wish it was that simple," she said.

"Madeleine," I said. "What are you telling me?"

She glanced fleetingly at my face then resolutely back at the ceiling. "Guy is impotent," she said. Immediately upon this revelation the tears overflowed and a strangled sob burst from her throat. I rolled upon my back, staring blankly at her crumpled profile and the tears streaming down her cheeks into her ears.

"You mean—" I said.

"Completely," she whimpered.

I rubbed my forehead with the heel of my hand. "So you've been married six years and there's no sex?"

She squeezed her eyes closed, nodding her head.

"He gets in bed with you and he can't get it up?"

A moan, sniffing, and gasping. "I swore to myself I'd never tell you," she said. "I've betrayed him."

"So you haven't had sex in six years?"

"Mumble, director, mumble, mumble Yale."

"What?"

Big sigh. "I had an affair with the director of the Yale play last fall. It was awful. That's the only time, until now."

"There was that time in the bookstore."

"You're right. I should never have done that."

"So you feel guilty for wanting to have sex every few years."

"You don't understand."

"It's crazy," I said. "You know that, don't you?"

She nodded again.

"It's just not normal. Has he been to a doctor?"

"It's psychological. He had a brutal childhood, his father left, his mother did sick things to him."

"You've got to leave him."

She put her hands over her face, wiping the tears away. "I can't. It would kill him."

"It won't kill him," I said. "You're just being dramatic. He has no right to ask you to live like this."

"He took care of me when I needed him."

"That was his choice," I said.

"And he saved your life."

"As he never fails to remind me."

"We owe him so much."

"That doesn't mean we have to like him."

She considered this. "We don't have to like him. But we can't try to destroy him. You must feel that, Edward."

I sat up and swung my legs over the bedside. "I don't feel it," I protested. "I know I should, I know I'm obligated to him. He saved my life and I'm obligated to him, but I don't feel it. I just don't feel it."

Madeleine said nothing. She'd stopped crying and when I looked back she was arranging a pillow under her head. "He told me he wished he'd let me drown," I concluded.

"Perhaps he does."

"So why do I have to care what happens to him when he wishes I was dead?"

"Because he would never do anything to hurt you."

"You think not?"

She pondered this. "He has his own demons."

"Great," I said. "The demon has demons." I got up and went to the bathroom, where I drank a glass of water and looked at myself in the mirror. I had an incipient mustache; I was growing it for Astrov, who talks about his mustache in the first act. It made me look older, sinister. I didn't like it. I raised my eyebrows and made my eyes bug out like Guy's. "What time is he coming?" I called back to Madeleine.

"Late," she said. "His train gets in at ten thirty."

I stood in the doorway looking down at her. She was stretched out with her head propped up, her hair waving out in all directions over the pillow. I felt enormously sad. The cruel irony of her fate wasn't lost on me. She'd been dealt a very poor hand and had tried to make the best of it, but she'd lost the game.

"Are you living with anyone?" she asked.

"No," I said. "There's a woman I see. She's a lighting tech."

"Are you in love with her?"

"No. It's not serious."

"Oh," she said, idly scratching the inside of her thigh. This caused the breast resting against her arm to jiggle lightly. She lifted one knee, the better to get at the thigh, her eyes all the while resting on me. I felt a pleasant tingling in the groin, which resulted in a visible indicator of my emotions. Cause and effect—where would we be without it?

"Oh, look," Madeleine said, pointing at me with girlish surprise.

"What can I say," I said, looking down at my steadily lifting member.

"As I understand it," she said, "only one thing works." She patted the sheet and I crossed the narrow space, clambering in beside her.

Madeleine was as flexible as a reed. She had a remarkably strong back and open hips; she could do a backbend from a standing position and sit in the demanding full lotus for hours on end. She liked being pulled about, folded and unfolded like an accordion. Her ankles were over my shoulders and her knees pressed into the mattress when we heard three sharp raps at the door. We froze, our eyes locked in alarm. "Who is it?" Madeleine called sweetly. There was no answer. "Wrong room!" I exclaimed. Madeleine was sweating; her upper lip gleamed in the dim light. We heard the key slide into the lock—one click. The door, scraping against the cheap carpet, said "Shhh" as Guy, lugging a suitcase, stepped into the room.

Let's play this as a comic scene. The only sound is the obscene pop of my cock coming free of Madeleine as I lurch backward and she dives for the floor. Guy stands speechless in the open doorway with what I take at first to be a grin on his face. Madeleine is scrambling, pulling in articles of her clothing. I arrange myself cross-legged on the edge of the mattress facing him, but he does not move. "For God's sake," I say to him. "Close the door."

His face is a mask, the grin not glee but terror. His eyes take in the room, his panicked wife on the floor, his own reflection in the mirror over the dresser, the disheveled bed, and the unabashedly naked me, facing him, waiting upon his next move. What's odd is how calm I feel, how guiltless. As our eyes meet he apprehends this; it does something to him. In that moment it's out in the open between us: we are enemies.

Quietly, still clutching the suitcase, he steps back into the hall, pulling the door closed behind him. Madeleine is sobbing on the floor. "Oh God," she repeats, though I know she is not a believer. No sound from the hall; he's just standing on the other side of the door. Will he change his mind and reappear, charged for confrontation? "Calm down," I advise Madeleine, who sits up dazedly, pulling her blouse over her head. "He's going."

Another moment. She's holding her breath. Then we hear the creak of the floorboards as Guy, yielding the stage, treads stolidly off into the wings.

After Guy left, Madeleine and I argued about what we should do. I wanted her to leave with me at once; she wanted to wait for Guy's return. She was certain he would come back. In the end I left and she waited. Near eleven, the time when he had been originally expected, Guy appeared at the hotel-room door, shaken but resolved. He described himself as disappointed in Madeleine, though not surprised that I would take advantage of her weakness.

"Your weakness," I said. "What century is he living in?"

"He cried all night," she said. "He's had such a hard time. You and I have been working; we can't understand what he's going through. It's as if he's been shut out of the theater and now we have these great parts and the minute we're together we betray him. He trusted us, and we betrayed him."

"He cried?"

"I didn't sleep ten minutes."

"So what is he going to do?" I asked. We were speaking softly in the hall outside the rehearsal stage.

"He's quitting his job," she said. "He's moving to the hotel until we can find an apartment. He's delivering me to rehearsals in the morning and picking me up at night."

"But that's absurd," I said. "You're not his prisoner."

She smiled, misty eyed. "I'm a prisoner of this play. So is Elena."

"What is this, method acting?"

She rested a trembling hand on my forearm. "I can only see you here and only kiss you as Elena."

"I can't stand this," I said. "I'm going to follow you when you leave and punch his nose in."

"Don't," she said. A trio of our fellow actors, exiting the elevator, filed past us to the door. "Don't try to hurt him."

"You've got to leave him, Madeleine."

"Not yet. Not now. I can't be that cruel."

Peter Smythe, peeking gnomically from the open door, announced, "Here they are in the hall. Aren't you coming in, lovebirds?"

In general the actor's memoir is divided into two parts: stirring tales of my youthful artistic suffering followed by charming profiles of all the famous people who admire me. I'm not sure why this genre is popular, as nothing could be more boring than an actor's life and actors are such a self-absorbed and narcissistic lot, they're unlikely to make good narrators. Katharine Hepburn got it right when she titled her tiresome paean to herself simply *Me*.

Fortunately for my readers, this memoir is different. In this memoir something memorable actually happened. If you are over forty you may have read about it in the papers, though it was far from front-page news. It was a curious item quickly buried in the back pages.

Now, as I approach the big event, it occurs to me that there may be those among you who, through some fault in your stars or your education, are unfamiliar with Anton Chekhov's *Uncle Vanya*. In this case you must fail to appreciate how bizarrely the events Madeleine and I acted out upon the stage echoed the anxious lives we put on hold to take our parts. For this reason I pause at what I hope is a suspenseful moment to tell you a little about the play.

There's no summarizing the plot of a Chekhov play. One might say they all have the same plot. A group of unhappy characters come together at a provincial estate and complain about the emptiness of their lives, the hopelessness of trying to do any good in the world or to find satisfaction in work or love. Invariably they imagine real life is elsewhere, most likely in Moscow. The "action" of the play takes place offstage, thereby circumventing melodrama. Dispossession, either of property, of virtue, or of hope for the future, is the process the characters unwittingly facilitate. The world outside the estate is changing. It is coarsening; it is being deforested, developed, and exploited. Through indolence, ignorance, or indifference, in the course of the play each of the privileged characters will lose what he or she most values.

Uncle Vanya concerns a family in possession of a country estate that brings in less and less money each year, despite the efforts of the eponymous Uncle Vanya and his niece, Sonya, who labor incessantly to keep it solvent. Of the older generation, only the mother, Maria, a tract-reading feminist in thrall to her son-in-law, survives. The son-in-law, Serebryakov, is a professor of literature at a distant university. His wife, Vanya's sister, Petrovna, has died. It is the visit of this revered professor, in reality an aging windbag in declining health, with his young and beautiful second wife Elena that springs the action of the play. Mikhail Astrov, the family doctor and friend to Vanya, is called in to care for the hypochondriac Serebryakov. In spite of himself Astrov is struck by Elena's beauty and drawn to her. Vanya too is madly, hopelessly, openly in love with her and makes a comic show of his feelings, following her about, teasing her about her laziness and uselessness, complaining to Astrov about what a crime it is that she is faithful to the professor. *To deceive an old husband you can't endure—that's immoral; but to try to stifle your pitiful youth and vital feelings—is not immoral,* he tells Astrov.

Of course, as this is Chekhov, there's a gun and eventually it goes off, though, in this case, ineffectually.

So, in summary, my character, Astrov, is bewitched by the beautiful, useless Elena, who out of sheer perversity has married an old and impotent husband, and now wanders about the run-down estate tantalizing all who see her.

From the first day of our rehearsals, our director expressed his astonishment at the naturalness and sensitivity of Madeleine's interpretation of Elena. He thought she was acting. I wasn't so sure.

Now, one last scene before we proceed to the drama.

It is my habit to arrive early at the theater for rehearsals. I get up, shower, dress quickly, and hit the streets, still in the daze of sleep. At the hall I drink two cups of coffee and eat whatever sugary roll or doughnut is on the table, putting my nerves on the alert for the work to come. I enjoy watching my fellow actors make their entrances, one by one, greeting one another and milling about the ample space. There are always a few who are habitually late, flustered and apologetic, with wild excuses that vary from day to day until their creative faculties are exhausted and they resort to blaming the subway.

It wasn't the subway—the theater was an easy walk from my apartment—but my alarm clock that failed me on the third day of our rehearsals for *Vanya*. I woke half an hour late, curtailed the shower, dressed frantically, and rushed into the street with my hair still wet, hoping my fellow actors would not have eaten all the cheese Danish by the time I arrived. It was a blustery, chilly, gray morning, threatening the dreaded wintry mix, and I bustled along with my cold damp head bowed against the wind. As I ducked under the theater awning, the glass door flew open and a man, his face drawn in under the hood of a heavy parka, burst out, nearly colliding with me. We drew apart and our eyes met. As he ducked past me, an expression of revulsion and outrage which struck me as completely disproportionate to the provocation narrowed his eyes, inflated his nostrils, and doubled his chin. In that moment I recognized him—it was Guy.

This was a confrontation I would have preferred to avoid, but I was still too close to the numbing embrace of sleep to feel anything beyond a mild vexation and surprise. I didn't greet him; how could I? Our coats brushed as he pushed past me, leaping awkwardly upon a wedge of packed and blackened snow at the curb. His boot soles were slick and could find no purchase. Briefly his feet performed a pas de deux on the ice, but he had lost his balance and in the next moment his legs buckled, his arms flew up, he emitted a low cry of alarm, and down he went, flat on his back in the street. His head was protected by the hood, but it was dangerously close to the passing traffic and as I watched in fascinated horror, a car whooshing past threw up a spray of half-frozen muck that caught him square across the face. I released the door handle, and, careful of the ice, hastened to assist him. By the time I got to him he had risen on one elbow, occupied in wiping the slush from his eyes. I bent over, offering my hand. "Are you OK?" I said.

"Get away from me!" he shouted. "Don't come near me!" I stepped back, meeting the apprehensive gaze of a passing pedestrian who veered toward the building to avoid the two crazies at the curb. Dripping gutter water, Guy got to his feet and staggered into the traffic.

"Be careful," I warned. A car swerving to avoid hitting him sent a wave of slush over my shoes. "Christ," I exclaimed.

"Stay away from me," Guy shouted. I watched as he dodged another car and gained the opposite sidewalk, where he stopped, turning to scowl back at me. His face was streaked with dirt, his eyes fierce, and his cheeks flushed with rage. This interested me. Guy had always seemed so studied to me, conniving and artificial, but this was raw emotion.

"Fine," I replied, "that's fine with me," and I stalked back to the theater. I opened the door upon the warm, inviting lobby, puzzling over the whole complicated history of my connection to Guy Margate, the man who saved my life. The cliché "no good deed ever goes unpunished" came to mind. What was that from? I looked back through the glass door and saw, to my surprise, that Guy was still on the opposite sidewalk. He was smoking a cigarette, his back pressed to the building, glaring across the traffic at the door. I doubted that he could see me, but without thinking, as I mounted the marble steps, I raised my hand and waved goodbye.

The rehearsal period for our *Vanya* was intense; we had four weeks to put up a long and complex show. We started in the morning at nine, broke for lunch, which was sandwiches sent in from the deli down the street, and then went on until eight. In the first week we got the blocking down and worked on various separate scenes, but after that we had the whole cast in all the time. It's an eight-character play and the scenes require from two to six at all times, the family passing in and out of the set, just as they would in an ordinary home. At one point Serebryakov remarks that the house contains "twenty-six enormous rooms, people wander off in all directions and you never can find anyone," so there's a sense of brooding and empty space outside the circle of warmth where the characters confront one another with their suffering.

Peter Smythe had clear ideas about what he wanted and the ability to express these ideas coherently, which is about as rare in the theater as the ivory-billed woodpecker is in the forest. He was interested in his actors and gave us leeway, even adjusted his own view in the light of an interpretation that he hadn't considered. Soon, with his guidance, we began to cohere into something very like a small orchestra, each instrument in tune with every other and clear about the score. I never worked more confidently and I think the other actors felt as I did. At night I was generally too exhausted to do much but have dinner with a few of the cast. Madeleine was never with us, having been disappeared by her husband for who knows what sort of dinner, a jolly evening of browbeating and guilt-tripping and kvetching. In the second week she told me Guy had found an apartment in the East Village and that Sunday they had driven to Philly with a truck, packed their meager possessions, and moved in. "Is he going to get a job?" I asked.

"Not yet," she said.

We had five days to rehearse on the theater stage itself. The first two were devoted to the ordeal known as tech rehearsal, in which the actors are required to sit or stand for hours on end while the lighting director and the sound director make minute adjustments to their equipment, and the stagehands figure out how they're going to get the furniture moved between scenes, and the set designer instructs the actors about the dangers of the set, which parts move and which are permanent, which doors open in, which out. The union allows two eleven-hour days and we filled every minute of that time, breaking for dinner and then back in the theater until midnight. During the waiting around we familiarized ourselves with the stage, the backstage, and the dressing rooms.

At last we did a full dress rehearsal and I finally got to kiss Madeleine as passionately as I wanted with no interference from our director. She struggled, as Elena must, but I held her tightly until Vanya appeared with his roses and ruined everything.

Peter's notes were brief: an adjustment to the blocking here ("How did everyone get balled up in the corner?"), a suggestion about timing there ("Sonya, start leaving before she says 'Go on' "). In conclusion, he said, "Astrov and Elena, about that kiss."

Madeleine stepped forward, eager for the critique, but I hung back and said coldly, "What about it?"

"Well," Peter said, "actually." He left a nice pause for effect. "Actually, it's perfect."

Uncle Vanya opened at the Public in March to notices so overheated you could warm your hands by them. Rory Behenny in the title role was "brilliant, as always," and brought to the outraged Vanya "a wry intensity." Edward Day's performance was "astonishing," also "complex, nuanced, ironic," possessing—I liked this one—"a range Chekhov would have applauded." In Astrov, Day "showed us reason and desire in mortal combat." Madeleine Delavergne was "born to play Elena," her beauty "delicate, ravishing, haunted," her Elena "longing to live but unwilling to sully herself in ordinary life, mesmerizing." "When Astrov and Elena steal their brief kiss, the audience holds its collective breath."

Our director, Peter Smythe, was praised for his "apprehension of the tragic strain in the comic situation of these trivial characters who can't bear the tedium of their existence."

Et cetera. Tickets were hot; cast and crew settled in for a nice long run.

I've never much liked the whole setup of Christianity, with its emphasis on being saved, thereby acknowledging a debt that can only be paid by a lifetime of sacrifice and devotion. Must God's love have strings attached? People who crave salvation should think about how they're going to feel if it turns out that this God who saved them is, upon closer acquaintance, completely alien. He, possibly she (or, more likely, it), is not now and never has been one of us. Jesus clearly was not one of us, with his crypto-stories about the prodigal who is more beloved by the father than the dutiful son and the sliding pay scale for field hands, with his magic powers that run the gamut from improving the wedding beverage to blasting trees to raising the dead. These days we have born-agains everywhere, even in the White House, carping about how clear and meaningful everything is now that they've seen the light and accepted Christ as their Savior. There they were, just sinning along aimlessly, drinking and fornicating down that slippery slope lined with good intentions and ending you know where, when suddenly Jesus reached out or down or across and saved them. And now they feel grateful all the time, every day. If things go wrong, that's God's way of testing their faith, and if they are successful and make lots of money, that proves they have been chosen by God.

It's supposed to be all about free will, but there's not much freedom in it. And if God is really so eager to save the desperate from themselves, where was he when my mother was knocking back the Seconal with her lunatic girlfriend from hell.

These musings are by way of preparation for the climactic scene of our drama, which takes place, appropriately (though perhaps you'll disagree), in a dressing room at the Public Theater between acts 2 and 3 of Chekhov's *Uncle Vanya*.

Mikhail Astrov isn't onstage for the last part of act 2 and he doesn't appear again until several minutes into act 3, so it was my habit to retreat to my dressing room and stay there through the intermission until I appeared in act 3 toting my geographical surveys. Rory Behenny and our Russian, Anton Schoitek, shared the room with me but they had a serious long-running card game going in the greenroom, so I generally had the space to myself.

In the third week of our run I was backstage, exchanging witticisms with the Russian, when Madeleine arrived looking harried and made a beeline for her dressing room. "You're late, my angel," I said, following her. At the door she turned to me. "We've been fighting all day," she said. "Even in the subway. He wouldn't let up."

"Where is he now?" I asked.

"He's here somewhere." She laid her hand on my forearm, her eyes searching mine. "If I leave him, can I stay with you?"

Did I hesitate? Not more than a breath, I swear. "Yes," I said. She squeezed my arm and her eyes softened. Then she disappeared into the room.

The audience that night was a live one; we could feel their attention. Sweet ripples of soft laughter ran up and down the aisles at various points and we fed on them, pumping up the irony, which in this play is sometimes too subtle for lazy auditors. I delivered my last line to Sonya in act 2 and exited stage right. My dressing room was around a corner and down a few steps. I paused on the landing, noticing that the door, which I knew I'd closed, was open.

So no entrance: this time he was waiting for me. The room was long and narrow, the usual bare bulbs and faux-leather chairs lined up before a dressing shelf, a full-length mirror at the far end and two sinks tucked behind the door. He was slumped in one of the chairs, rummaging through an open backpack in his lap. He had on a light jacket, similar to the one I wore as Astrov, and he had a mustache trimmed in the same absurd nineteenth-century style I'd chosen for my part. "Look at this enormous mustache I've grown," Astrov tells the old servant Marina. "A ridiculous mustache. I've become an eccentric." I pushed the door open a few more inches with my foot. Guy looked up from the backpack, raising his hand unconsciously to stroke the bristles over his mouth. "Is it real?" I said, entering the scene.

He frowned. "Is what real?"

"The mustache."

He dropped his hand. "Of course it is," he said.

"How did you get in here?"

"It wasn't difficult."

I crossed to the mirror where Astrov's reflection greeted me. "I'll have to ask you to come back after the play," I said. "I don't like to break character in the middle of a performance."

"Don't then," he said. "That Astrov character is as big a heel as you are. And I've got the same problem with him."

I plant trees, I told myself, because I want future generations to be happy because of me. "And what problem is that?" I asked.

"He's trying to steal my wife."

"Why not come back later and we can talk this over like gentlemen."

He shook his head wearily. "I asked you not to take this part. I knew it would be too much for her. I know you have no sense of obligation to me, you've made that perfectly clear, but you owe it to her to let her get on with her life."

I breathed deep into my diaphragm, lifted my shoulders and rolled them back, shrugging off Mikhail Astrov. "You're always so preoccupied with who owes who what," I said. "It's a real failing of yours."

"How do you sleep at night," he said. It wasn't a question.

"Well," I said. "I sleep well. You're the one who doesn't sleep."

"I don't sleep because I care about other people. If I see someone struggling, someone in trouble, I try to help. I don't just let them drown."

Oh, here we go, I thought. "Look," I said, "I know I've been a big disappointment to you but I just can't keep my mind focused every second of the day on how grateful I am to you."

The sound of applause, like a thousand ping-pong balls simultaneously dropped into play, pattered in over the intercom. The intermission had begun. Guy lurched to his feet, clutching the backpack to his stomach, and with a crabbed sideways step brought his shoulder to the door and eased it closed. Panic turned a screw in my chest and tightened the cords in my throat. The murmuring of my fellow actors as they drifted to their dressing rooms, a cough, a laugh I recognized as Rory's, a ribald exchange as he and Anton sat down to their card game, the creak of shoe soles against linoleum, the glug of water running in the pipes, all these familiar sounds of our daily routine were improbably dear to me. Why was I trapped with this crazed loser and his backpack? I could have pushed past him, pulled the door open, and ordered him out, but I didn't. If I made him leave he would run straight to Madeleine's dressing room and start in on her. She'd gotten through the first act well enough, tearing up prettily during her brief and marvelous response to Vanya's teasing. *Everyone looks at me with pity, poor thing, she has an old husband! This sympathy for me, how I understand it.* Her voice quavered on the last line in a way I hadn't heard before. Our big scene was coming up and I didn't want her distracted, so I decided to have it out, whatever "it" was, with her husband. He had resumed his seat, hunching over the bag like some beggar going through the day's collection of rags and bottles. "What is it you want from me, Guy?" I asked.

He glanced up sharply over the bag. "Don't ask me that," he snapped. "If you had any interest in what I want, we wouldn't be here."

I could think of no response to this assertion, which was, I recognized, indisputable. I twisted the waxed tip of my mustache, gazing upon my unwelcome guest. I knew too much about him, I thought, and though some of what I knew should have made me pity him, what I felt was a steadily mounting irritation, such as a buzzing fly produces of a Sunday morning when one is trying to read the papers. Just as, while rolling up the book review for use as a weapon, one may succumb to a grudging admiration for the doomed insect, I admitted that there was in Guy's persistence, as well as his supremely confident appropriation of the moral higher ground, something impressive. He seemed incapable of seeing himself as anything but wronged. So be it, I thought. "You're right," I said. "I don't care what you want."

He returned his attention to the bag. "That's better. At least you're being honest."

"Has it ever occurred to you to ask yourself what *I* want?"

"I know what you want."

"Do you?" I said. "And what is that?"

I assumed he would say *my wife,* and I was prepared with my response, which was that his wife could make her own decisions. But instead he lifted his head and considered me thoughtfully, his eyes fixed vacantly on my forehead as if he were reading a scroll on a video screen. "You want to be rid of me."

A hoot of laughter followed by a shout of "In your

dreams!" echoed from the card game outside. Then came the rapping knuckles and the repeated warning, "Five minutes, five minutes," from the stage manager making his rounds. I turned to the dressing shelf and opened a stick of liner. "I don't have time for this," I said.

Guy made a sound somewhere between a gargle and a laugh. I could see him in the mirror, pressing his palm into his forehead, smoothing back the hair from his temples. "I think you do," he replied.

"Has she told you that she's leaving you?" I said. "Is that what this is all about?"

"She's not leaving me. What makes you say that?"

"Jesus, Guy," I said. "Why should she stay with you? You keep her like a jailer. She's young, beautiful, talented, she's a successful actress. Once she's free of you, the world's at her feet. Do you think she doesn't know that?"

"Did she tell you that?"

"She doesn't have to tell me. Take a look in the mirror." I stepped aside and his eyes shifted to the mirror in which we were both reflected, but he didn't look at himself. He glared at my reflection. For an eerie moment our eyes met on the surface of the glass.

"Three minutes," the call came from the hall. "Three minutes."

Doors snapped and creaked and the atmosphere between us thickened as the bustle of actors heated up in the hall. Madeleine was out there. When the lights came up in three minutes, she would be onstage, complaining to Vanya about how bored she was. I tried to distinguish her voice, her tread, but it was impossible. Guy wasn't listening. He was back at the bag, which had evidently an endless potential for engaging his interest. He reminded me of Beckett's character Winnie, in *Happy Days,* buried to her waist in sand, reaching for her purse whenever her ruminations veer too close to the abyss. "There is, of course, the bag," she says.

"Look," I said to Guy, "you can wait in here until I get back."

"But you're not going anywhere," he said. He had extracted something new from the bag, something I couldn't make out at first because his head was down and he was turning it over in his hands, fiddling with it. Then he parted his legs, the bag slipped to the floor with a thud, and I saw that he was holding an extremely nasty-looking revolver and pointing it directly at me.

The apprehension of a tight spot always commences with a flush of incredulity. There's a mistake here. This isn't really happening. So it was, without any sense of the ironic potential which strikes me now as charmingly piquant, that I asked, "Is it real?"

"Oh yes," Guy said, narrowing his eyes at me in a way that struck me as absurd. Was he taking aim? Why bother, the pistol was huge and we weren't five feet apart. "It's real, it's loaded, and I've just removed the safety."

I wasn't afraid, though I should have been. The gun affected me as a provocation rather than a threat. I felt elated, light on my feet, and ready to match wits. "I hope you've considered the consequences of your actions," I cautioned.

He rearranged his mouth into a sneer and tilted his head as

if listening to an inner dictate. A sour, metallic smell wafted off of him and I noted a line of perspiration gathering over his brow. "I have, actually," he said.

"Because even though I know you're unhappy and disgruntled, and rightly so, I don't deny that you have a legitimate complaint, I don't see how what you're doing can help matters. Not for Madeleine, and not for you, and certainly not for me."

"You will be the biggest loser," he agreed.

The intercom crackled overhead. Act 3 had begun. *The Herr Professor has graciously expressed the desire that we should all assemble in this room at one o'clock today*, Vanya said.

"That may be," I said, "but you'll lose Madeleine either way."

He blinked, pushing the pistol out over his knees. Madeleine's voice, falsely amplified, said, *It's probably business.*

"This isn't about Madeleine," Guy said. "It never was."

I pressed on. "You tell yourself you care for her, but think about the impossibility of her situation. She can't have children; she's stuck in a sexless marriage. It's unbearable."

Wrong card. We both watched his index finger stretch over the trigger. "What are you talking about?" he said.

"What do you think I'm talking about?"

I'm dying of boredom, Elena lamented above our heads. *I don't know what to do.* With a flourish of my hand I indicated the intercom speaker.

Guy followed my gesture, his eyebrows knit, his upper lip lifted over his teeth, completely mystified. "That's good," I said. "You're good in this part."

He returned his puzzled attention to me. "She's not stuck in a sexless marriage," he said. "That's ridiculous. We have sex all the time."

You must be a witch, Sonya chided Elena.

I nodded sympathetically. "It's nothing to be ashamed of," I said. "It can happen to any man."

He laughed. "This is rich," he said. "There's nothing she won't say when she wants to get laid. And she's insatiable, but you know that. We had great makeup sex that night after I found you in the hotel room, she was really hot. We called you the warm-up act."

"Guy," I said, "give it up."

Now Sonya confessed her love for Astrov to Elena. *I love him more than my own mother. Every minute I seem to hear him, feel the pressure of his hand.*

It was my cue to head for the stage. I moved closer to the door, oblivious to the armed threat in the chair. The theater chestnut called "Chekhov's rule" popped into my brain: a pistol on the wall in the first act must go off in the third. Guy was still chuckling over the joke he and Madeleine had enjoyed at my expense. "No, really," he said. "She told you we didn't have sex and you believed her?" So great was his amusement that his hand relaxed and the barrel of the gun tilted toward the floor.

I took the chance to push past him, throwing open the door. His head came up and he jerked around in the chair, leveling the gun at me. Who knows what came over me, a near fatal curiosity, an irresistible impulse to risk my life, but I paused at the door and looked back at him. He was hunched forward awkwardly over the gun, as if it was alive and he had to struggle to keep it from pulling him out of the chair. His chin was down, and his eyes, rolled up and fixed on me, brimmed with hatred such as I have never seen before or since. It shocked me, that look, it frightened me, and I dodged away. He's going to hurt someone, I thought as I rounded the corner and darted up the steps to the wings where a stagehand waited to hand me the roll of maps I would display to the indifferent Elena. "Listen closely," I said to him. "There's a man with a gun in my dressing room. Don't go down there. Tell Peter to call the police." His eyes grew wide and solemn and he nodded his head, glancing anxiously past me at the stairs. "Just don't go down there," I said. He nodded, wandering away into the wings.

Sonya came offstage and stood quietly to one side. We both watched Elena, who was alone before the audience, debating with herself the pros and cons of yielding to Astrov's charms. *But I'm a coward. My conscience would torment me. He comes here every day, I can guess why, and even now I feel guilty.*

Gripping my charts, I moved to the dark at the edge of the stage. Elena paced during her monologue, not in agitation, but aimlessly, tormented by her thoughts, too lazy to act, to put herself out of her own misery. *I am ready to fall on my knees before Sonya, and ask her to forgive me, to weep.*

I stepped into the lights, advancing strongly upon this beautiful intruder who was destroying my orderly life. *Good Day!* I said, and we shook hands.

In this scene Astrov has come to show Elena his passion, the geographical charts he has made which detail the gradual degradation of the flora and fauna in the neighborhood. Elena has expressed an interest in seeing them, but this is a ruse; what she wants is to tell him that Sonya is in love with him and, thereby, to draw him out on the subject of his heart, which she believes herself to have captured. I spread out my charts across the table before Elena, fixing them with clips, and began my lecture on ecology. *Now look at this. This is a map of our district as it was fifty years ago. The dark and light green represent forests.*

I loved this speech. Even the most indifferent members of the audience were stirred by the prophetic vision of our nineteenth-century playwright. It's a mighty plea for environmental stewardship but it's also an argument for the vital necessity of art. *On this lake there were swans, geese, ducks, and, as the old people say, a powerful lot of birds of all sorts, no end of them; they flew in clouds.* I raised my hand, indicating an imaginary flock darkening the sky and inviting Elena with an eager, schoolboy earnestness to humor me, to stretch her limited imagination to a sense of natural wonder. Of course, she couldn't do it. She gave me a look of frustrated sadness. She was bound by law and by social stricture to a sick, tyrannical old man who kept her awake all night moaning about his gout. Why should she care if there had once been geese honking across the horizon, wild goats and elk startling the weary traveler in the woods at night?

I returned to my chart. I was dead center at the heart of Doctor Mikhail Astrov, a moody, lonely, cynical man, yet passionate about life and driven to do something worth doing in this world, longing at this moment to share his despair of the present and dim hope for the future with a beautiful, desirable, sexually frustrated woman who is bored by what interests him.

Edward Day was gone; Guy Margate a nonentity, a disturbing dream from which Astrov has awakened. *Besides villages and hamlets,* I continued, *you can see scattered here and there, various settlements, small farms, hermitages of the Old Believers.* I lowered my chin and raised my eyes, letting her in on my skepticism about the "Old Believers."

She isn't listening, I thought. Her mind is wandering. But I won't stop yet. I want her to understand how much is at stake in this world, because men are indifferent to beauty. *This is how it was twenty-five years ago.* I rolled up the top sheet exposing a second chart. *Already one-third of the area is woodland. There are no longer any goats.* I went on, but she resisted me. I made the case that it wasn't a matter of progress, the old giving way to the new, but rather of *a degeneration due to stagnation, ignorance, complete lack of understanding.* When I lifted my finger from my meticulously drawn map, I saw that her eyes were glazed with boredom. I drew away, closing my heart to her. *But I can see by your face that this doesn't interest you.*

I understand so little of all this, she said.

In frustration I rolled up my charts. *There's nothing to understand; it's simply uninteresting.*

She gave me her coy smile; really, she was enough to try a saint. *To be quite frank, my thoughts were elsewhere.*

Then we had the whole fraudulent business of her sounding me out about my feelings for Sonya.

Emotionally this is an intensely complicated scene; it's a showstopper. Elena and Astrov are attracted to each other and have been repressing this attraction for reasons that are both personal and social. The attraction is purely sexual; it has been growing on a daily basis for a month in which they have been constantly together but never alone. Now, at last, they are alone. They are as concentrated as two people can be. A tiger could leap through the window and they won't notice. He declares himself: *I submit. Here I am, devour me!* And she puts up a flimsy show of resistance: *Oh, I am not so low—I am not so bad as you think!* But it's a sham. He takes her in his arms, she struggles, but weakly. *Where shall we meet?* he begs her. *Someone may come in, tell me quickly . . . what a wonderful, glorious . . . one kiss.*

And at last, they kiss. We kissed.

Because of the arrangement of the entrances near the stage, the gunshot sounded as if it came from the audience in the right orchestra seats. It startled a few cries out of those closest to the door, but no one bolted. Madeleine jerked in my arms. Had he shot her? I held her fast, running my hands along her spine, releasing her lips and lifting her face so that I could look into her eyes. Her gaze was clouded by desire and she brought her hand to the back of my neck, stretching up to meet my lips with hers. As there was no reaction from anyone resembling an authority, and no further disturbance of the airwaves, the moment passed. Some innocents may have thought the shot was part of the play. I held Madeleine fast, stroking her hair and pulling her in close at the waist, so overcome by desire that I wanted to force her down onto the floor and have at it right there in front of the audience. Who cares? I thought, my brain sparking like a power line cut loose by a lightning bolt. I've got her now. She eased her mouth from mine and I pressed her cheek against my chest, allowing my other hand to stray over her hips. Behind me, Vanya entered stage right, carrying the bouquet of roses he'd gathered for her. Neither of us could see him yet.

Somewhere in my consciousness the gunshot was being judiciously minimized and filed away. There would be some harmless explanation for it; it could have been the blank gun Vanya would fire in the next act, or perhaps it wasn't a gun at all, but some amp blowing out—there was a lot of voltage out there. Elena was strangely limp in my arms. I felt a hiccup against my collarbone—was she weeping? I lifted her chin and looked into her wet eyes. As the tears overflowed she said something that startled me almost as much as the gunshot. *I am not so bad as you think.*

It wasn't her line. The prompter whispered the correction. I held her by the wrist and shoulder, turning her to face Vanya, but she didn't see him. She was sobbing now, but she caught her breath and said, *I am not so bad as you think.* She was supposed to break away from me and run to the window. Again the prompter gave her the line: *This is awful.*

Never mind, never mind, Vanya said. He and I exchanged a look freighted with worry. I launched into my little speech about the weather, after which I was to make a hasty, embarrassed exit stage right, while Elena must remain onstage through the long scene in which Serebryakov threatens to sell the house, and Vanya, in a fury, tries to shoot him with the pistol.

I'm not so bad as you think, Elena said again.

Vanya dropped the flowers. *I saw everything, Helene.*

I'm not so bad as you think, she repeated.

I paused at the entrance to the wings, opening my hands to

Vanya who understood my gesture. We had to get Madeleine offstage. Serebryakov, Sonya, Telyegin, and Marina were beginning their entrance stage left. Madeleine didn't move. She stood there like Lucia di Lammermoor, a pale and fading rose, her eyes clouded, her lips parted, gazing hopelessly beyond the audience, as lost as a soul in hell. I glanced at the prompter, his eyes aghast over his bifocals, giving her, for the third time, her line—*I must leave here*—but she was indifferent to him. Vanya approached her. *You must leave here,* he said. He took her arm and to the relief of the entire cast and crew, now frozen in apprehension, she didn't struggle. *You must leave here this very day*, Vanya said. Cautiously he guided her to me as the others entered the stage in the midst of an idle conversation about the vicissitudes of age. Serebryakov, whose line was *Where are the others?,* cleverly adjusted it to *Where is Maria Vasilyevna?* I didn't get to hear how they improvised for the now absent Elena because Peter Smythe appeared, sweating but competent, motioning me into the wings. Together we led Madeleine through the dark backstage to the lighted landing above the dressing rooms. "I'll send in the understudy for the last act," he said. "It'll be a mess, but we don't have a choice. They'll have to fake it through the rest of this scene."

"She doesn't have many lines," I said. Madeleine stiffened between us, staring in wide-eyed panic at my open dressing-room door. Three policemen were gathered there, two engaged in conversation, the third speaking loudly into a bulky cell-phone precursor. "No," she said, pulling away from us. Peter stepped in front of her, blocking her view. We steered her toward the dimly lit kitchen off the greenroom. "It's all right,"

Peter said calmly. "Let's go in here and I'll fix you a nice cup of tea." Madeleine craned her neck, looking past me. "Is someone in there?" she asked.

"It's OK, sweetheart," I said. "It's nothing for you to worry about."

She gave me an uncomprehending look. Her face was tear-streaked, her nose red and damp. She sniffed, bringing the back of her hand to her nostrils. I pulled my handkerchief from my pocket. "Here," I said, "use this."

"Thank you," she said. She blew her nose discreetly, folded the cloth, and handed it back to me, a faint, diffident smile on her lips. "I don't believe we've met," she said.

To this day I don't know how we managed to get through the fourth act. Of course the audience noticed that Madeleine had been replaced by her understudy, and as they trundled out into the street, they doubtless speculated about what might have happened. Was she taken ill or had some emergency required her to leave the stage? If they read the Metro section the next day in the *Times* they might have noticed a brief article about the suicide of an unemployed actor in a dressing room at the Public Theater. Otherwise, Guy's exit went unnoticed by the wide, searching eye of the press.

Because I was the last to see Guy alive, I was subjected to an interview with Detective DiBanco, a short, hirsute investigator with a Napoleonic gleam in his eye. He was waiting for me in the wings at the end of the show, and he escorted me to the door of my dressing room. The other actors were encouraged by the attending officers to gather their belongings and leave the theater. Guy's body had been removed and Madeleine spirited away by Peter Smythe. Orange tape was stretched across the open door to the dressing room. I tried to avoid looking at the pool of brownish blood congealing on the floor.

It was unusual, Detective DiBanco informed me, for a suicide to shoot himself in the chest. "It's hard to be accurate," he said. "Most choose the temple, or they just put the barrel in their mouths."

"Well," I said, "he was an actor."

"Why does that make a difference?"

I gaped at his innocence. "An actor doesn't want to mess up his face."

"Was he a friend of yours?"

I wasn't sure how to answer this. The scene had a dreamy artificiality about it, and my emotions had simply shut down. I couldn't feel a thing. DiBanco was a professional; he hung on my answer with actor-worthy concentration. What should I tell him? Should I begin on the Jersey shore? At last I punted. "I hadn't seen him in a long time," I said.

"So he just dropped by your dressing room to kill himself?"

I searched for a shorthand version. "His wife is in the play," I said. "We were lovers, he was jealous. I think he planned to shoot me, but he didn't have the courage."

Detective DiBanco pulled down the corners of his mouth, nodding his head ponderously, for all the world like a cop in a TV drama. "Did he threaten you?" he asked.

"In a way. Yes. I'd say he did."

He gazed up at me; he had to lift his chin to do this, and I noticed a red notch on the jawbone where he'd nicked himself shaving the thick stubble that surged over his chin. "He left a kind of note," he said. "But it doesn't make any sense. Maybe it will make sense to you."

"A kind of note?"

"I'll show you," he said, pulling the tape aside. Reluctantly I followed him, keeping as much distance between my feet and the blood as I could. Guy's blood, I thought, and a reflex of nausea fired an acrid shot of vomit into my throat which I swallowed back manfully.

"It's on the mirror," DiBanco said, unnecessarily, for as he spoke my eyes discovered Guy's final condemnation. He'd used a brown liner crayon to draw a picture frame with a small rectangle at the base, like a title plate, in which he'd carefully inscribed my name. Above the frame, scrawled in startling red lipstick, was a single word: INGRATE.

I took my place as he'd known I would, so that I filled the frame. It made me smile, this last joke of Guy's; it was so sophomoric, so ridiculous, so totally Guy.

"I see it makes sense to you," Detective DiBanco observed.

"A long time ago," I confessed, "Guy Margate saved my life."

At my apartment, to my relief, there was a phone message from Peter Smythe, which I returned at once. "How is she?" I asked.

"She's asleep," he said.

"Does she know what happened?"

"It's very strange," he said. "She's calm, but she doesn't

know anything, who I am, where she is. I don't think she recognizes her own name, but she's decided to believe I know it."

"This is terrible," I said.

"I called a shrink I know. He said she may snap out of it. She said she was tired, so Mary gave her a gown and a toothbrush, showed her the guest room, and she went to bed. The door is open; we'll hear her if she gets up in the night. Are you OK?"

"I have no idea," I said.

"Can you do the matinee tomorrow?"

"Yes," I said. "I can do it."

"Call me in the morning," he said. "We'll figure out what to do. Do you know Madeleine's family?"

"No," I said. "Guy knew her mother. I never did."

"Jesus, what a thing to do. What was wrong with that guy?"

"Guy?" I said. "I guess he snapped. He couldn't get a job."

"Yeah, yeah, it's a hell of a profession," Peter said. "We're all crazy from it."

"That's true," I agreed.

After I hung up the phone I switched off the lamp and sat in the dark for a few minutes. I could hear Guy laughing at me. "We called you the warm-up act." Was that the last thing he said to me? Was there any possibility that it was true, that he and Madeleine were in some sort of complicity against me, that there was another cruel story I didn't know anything about? Or was it just another of Guy's ploys, right there at the end, to shake my confidence, to get even with me because I had succeeded and he had failed?

Naturally I preferred the latter proposition, but I also admitted that I would probably never be sure, as Guy was gone and Madeleine, if she could even remember her story, would have a strong personal interest in sticking to it.

Guy is gone, I said to the empty darkness pressing against me. But I hadn't seen his body. They'd taken him and the backpack and the pistol away sometime during the last act. A sinister doubt crept in from the dime-store-mystery plotting lobe of the brain: What if Guy wasn't really dead? Then the police would have to be in on it, also Peter, who had identified Guy. Impossible, right? But no sooner had the thought crossed my mind than a creak and crunch issued from the bedroom, as of someone rising from the bed. My trembling fingers shot out for the lamp switch, but it wasn't where it had always been. "Christ," I muttered, feeling around until I found it exactly where it had always been.

The light blasted my eyes. The bedroom door was ajar. I could see the empty bed and the dresser, just as I had left them, but I had to get up, cross the room, and look behind the door. That was when I decided to go out. It was midnight and it was chilly; people with sense were all in bed. I didn't want to talk to strangers; I didn't want to be alone. I called Teddy.

He was awake; he had, he said, just come in, and how was I.

"Not great," I said. "Guy Margate shot himself in my dressing room during the show tonight."

"My God," Teddy said. "Are you serious?"

"Yes. He's dead, and Madeleine doesn't know who she is."

"Ed," Teddy said. "Where are you?"

"I'm in my apartment, but I can't stay here. I'm too creeped out. I need a drink. Can you come out and meet me somewhere?"

"Hold on," he said. He talked to someone, Wayne no doubt, but I couldn't make out what he was saying. "I'll meet you at Phebe's," he said. "I'll leave right now."

"Thanks," I said. "I'll be there."

Teddy was waiting on the porch but as soon as he saw me he came out and steered me into the small room behind the bar. He had evidently spoken to the bartender, for a bottle of whiskey and two glasses with ice cubes melting in them were set up on a table. This dark room wasn't ordinarily open unless the crowd overflowed, so we had it to ourselves. "I would have told you to come to the apartment," Teddy said, "but Wayne invited some people from the opening in for drinks. Do you want something to eat?"

"Wayne had an opening?" I said.

"No. It wasn't his. A friend. Awful pictures." He poured the whiskey over the ice, his eyes moving from his hand to me and back again, animated by solicitude. He slid the glass to me. After I swilled a good draught, I thumped the glass down on the table with a sigh. "Thanks," I said. "That helps."

Teddy sipped his drink thoughtfully. "So Guy is dead," he said.

"Yes."

"I can hardly believe it."

"Me neither."

"And what did you mean; Madeleine doesn't know who she is?"

"She just lost it all," I said. "Right in the middle of the third act. We heard the shot and she was sobbing in my arms and she kept repeating her line over and over. We had to get her offstage and then I gave her my handkerchief and she asked me if we'd ever met."

"What was the line?"

"What?"

"What was the line she was repeating?"

"What?" I took another drink, washing back the impatience I felt at this question. "I'm not as bad as you think."

"That was the line?"

"Yes," I said. "That was the line. I'm not as bad as you think. Why is that important?"

"Where is she now?"

"Peter took her home."

"Peter?"

"Smythe. The director. He said she doesn't know who she is. He called a psychiatrist who said she might snap out of it. She went to sleep."

"This is awful," Teddy said.

"I don't know what I'm going to do," I agreed.

"No," Teddy said. "I'm sure you don't."

"For one thing, the understudy has a completely different interpretation of Elena. It's all vanity and irritation. I'm not saying it's wrong, but it's just completely different. I'll have to start from scratch."

Teddy was quiet, rotating his glass on the coaster, drying the moisture from the bottom before he lifted it for another cautious sip. His eyes rested upon me with a distant, friendly

curiosity, such as one might show for a child who has charmingly botched a recitation.

"I know that sounds incredibly callous," I admitted.

"Well," Teddy said, "it is *one* of the things you'll have to
worry about."

I slept poorly and arrived at Peter's apartment fifteen minutes
early. He came to the door in his robe and slippers, his eyes
bleary, his mop of hair sticking out in all directions. "Come in,
come in," he said. "What a night. I didn't get back from the
hospital until four."

"What hospital?" I said, looking about the gloomy living
room. Why was it so dark?

"Bellevue," Peter said. He shuffled to the window and
pulled the curtain cord, vaporizing the gloom. "God it's bright
out there."

Bellevue. My legs went rubbery and I sank onto a handy
hassock. "Oh no," I said.

"We didn't have any choice. She woke up screaming
and we couldn't calm her down. She wanted to get out of
the apartment, didn't know who we were, said someone had
stolen a baby, at least I think that's what she said. Mary called
Dr. Hershey and he said to call 911 and meet him at Bellevue.
So that's what we did."

"Did she calm down?"

"They gave her a shot. Then she was just moaning."

I stood up, making for the door. "I've got to see her."

"They won't let you see her," Peter said. "Sit down, have a cup of coffee."

"What will they do to her?"

"It's a hospital. They'll take care of her. You can call Hershey later. She's his patient now. She needs help, psychiatric help. Hershey said she was in a fugue state."

I sat back down again. So Guy was right, I thought. Madeleine was fragile. I hadn't believed it because she was so ambitious and talented and beautiful and sexy, but he knew it, probably from the start, which is why his suicide is so completely inexcusable. He knew what it would do to her; he even made sure she would bear a crippling weight of guilt. He'd kept her up all night, berating her, threatening to kill himself if she left him, and then he sat in the dressing room listening to the play on the intercom, waiting for that moment when her lips met mine, and then he pulled the trigger. When she heard the shot she knew exactly what it was. In the annals of suicide has there ever been a more ignoble performance? If there was any justice and if there was a hell, I thought, Guy was surely in it. I would not waste a moment's pity on him.

Peter brought me a mug of coffee. "Do you want milk?" he asked.

"No," I said. "Black is good."

"Are you sure you can do the matinee? We can get the understudy if we call him now."

"No," I said. "I can do it."

———

The matinee was a shambles. We were running on nerves, parroting our lines like politicians, all save the understudy, who was in the unenviable position of benefiting from another actor's misfortune. She'd decided to throw herself at the role with a passion that was at odds with the character she was playing. She shivered and fidgeted, had starts and fits. The audience, composed of blockheads with hearing aids, thought she was terrific.

After the show I headed uptown to the offices of Dr. Seymour Hershey, a dour, bespectacled individual with heavy dark lips like two prunes folded under his big nose. He greeted me indifferently, even disappearing behind the desk to pick up a pencil while I inquired about Madeleine's prognosis.

Amnesia, he explained, is a rare condition, usually brought on by an injury, such as a blow to the head. In such cases the effects were sometimes reversible, though not, as so often happens in fiction and film, as the result of a second blow. In Madeleine's case the loss of memory was the result of a psychic trauma. "Typically," he said, "these patients were sexually abused as children. Do you know anything about her childhood?"

"Not much," I admitted. "She didn't like her mother."

"Well," he said, psychiatrically, "she would have buried that too."

"She's an actress," I said. "There's nothing buried in there. She has complete access to her emotions. That's what actors do."

"Pretending to have emotions you don't feel doesn't open the portals of the unconscious," he said.

"We're not pretending. That's the point," I countered.

He probed his chin with his thumb, scanning his desk for something of interest. "Actually in my experience, actors are extremely unstable personalities," he said.

"Will she get her memory back?" I asked.

"If she wants to," he said. "But her memory loss is the least of her problems."

"Will she get well?"

"If she wants to," he repeated maddeningly.

"So your deep professional wisdom is that Madeleine wants to be extremely unstable."

He ran his eyes over me critically, like an antique dealer inspecting a table, checking for cracks in the veneer. "Not consciously, of course," he said.

"Can she come home?"

"Oh no. Not now. She needs to be clinically evaluated. There are medications that may help. I can recommend a mental health facility that should be able to take her."

"An asylum?"

"We don't actually call them that anymore."

"Where is it?"

"In Westchester. It has an excellent reputation. It's called Benthaven."

I sputtered. "Benthaven?"

He removed his glasses and rubbed the lenses with a square of red cloth he kept on the desk for just that purpose. Absolutely humorless, I thought. My poor Madeleine. "Once we get her stabilized I can have her transferred there," he said.

"Can I see her before she goes?"

"Oh, yes. You can see her. It might be helpful; I don't think it can hurt. You should bring her some food. She's refusing to eat anything they offer her at the hospital."

"Why does she do that?"

He gave me another long, magnified look, opening and closing his prune lips a few times like a fish trying to catch a wafer of food in an aquarium. "Why do you think she would do that?"

"I have no idea."

"Then what makes you think I would know?"

"You're her doctor."

"And you're her what? Her friend? More than that?"

I had to think this over. Whatever I was, I knew I was committed to getting Madeleine out from under the thumb of Dr. Seymour Hershey.

"I'm the one who knows what she likes to eat," I said.

In the days that followed, Teddy and I began the process of freeing Madeleine from the mental health authorities. Hershey was having a picnic because Madeleine wasn't capable of making decisions and we couldn't find anyone related to her who was. I knew her father had died when she was in high school and Teddy's investigations revealed that her mother too had died of cancer the previous year. Madeleine was a widow and an orphan.

By the time I got to see her, she was "stabilized," but she hadn't, as hoped, snapped out of it. She wasn't hysterical or frightened, she was unfailingly polite, but she didn't recognize either Teddy or me, nor did she understand why she was in a hospital. Mostly she was hungry, but, as Hershey had told me, she wouldn't touch anything that didn't come from outside. Teddy and I took turns bringing meals from nearby restaurants. One night, as I was opening another white carton of her favorite Chinese takeout, she confided, "If you eat the food they make here, you can never leave."

"So it's not that you don't like it," I said, handing her the box.

She stabbed a water chestnut with the plastic fork. "I'm sure it's perfectly nice," she said in her new affectless voice.

"They make it nice," I suggested, "to tempt you to eat it."

She sent me a conspiratorial glance over the carton. There was just the flicker of a smile at the corners of her mouth as she lifted a long noodle above the edge. "Exactly," she said.

She's still in there, I thought. I just have to find a way to get her back.

Teddy helped me with the other problem that (I can't resist the pun) gravely needed clearing up, which was the earthly remains of Guy Margate. He too was without traceable relations. "We can't just leave him to the city to dispose of," Teddy said. "Should we buy a plot somewhere?"

"I want him cremated," I said.

"Should we scatter his ashes?"

"No," I said. "I want him cremated and in an urn and buried. I want him put to rest."

Teddy, puzzled by my vehemence, acquiesced. "I can arrange that," he said.

Getting Guy out of the morgue and into a grave proved a complicated and expensive process. Teddy took on the funerary arrangements and, with the help of Detective DiBanco, I navigated the murky legal channels. In the process I had to sign a document that made me responsible for Guy's interment, an obligation that gave me a full moment's pause.

"Do you want to see him?" the detective inquired.

"No," I said, scribbling my name on the dotted line.

"We'll release his stuff to you. The backpack has keys in it; must be to his apartment. We'll keep the gun."

"Yes, do. Please," I said.

"We checked him out from his license. He didn't have a record."

"That's comforting."

"You know where he lives, right?"

"Lower East Side," I said. "But I don't know where exactly."

He took up a pen and jotted down the address on a yellow pad. "You actors are an odd bunch," he said. He ripped off the sheet and held it out to me.

"In what way?" I asked. I had the sense that he was about to make some deep and revelatory observation, so I gave him my full attention.

"You know, like a bunch of children. Always in the fantasyland, always waiting for a break, playing make-believe. Your friend was wearing a fake mustache. You'd think if you was going to kill yourself you'd take off the costume."

So the mustache wasn't real.

"It's a calling," I said to DiBanco.

"Yeah, right. Like I was called to be a detective."

"Weren't you?"

"No, I wanted to play baseball. But I had to be realistic. That's the difference."

I took Guy's bag back to my apartment, dropped it on my kitchen table, and made myself a cup of coffee, postponing this final encounter with all things Guy. It had seemed bulky when he had it on his lap, but in fact there wasn't much in it. A shabby wallet with his license, a bookstore ID, one credit card, and thirty dollars in cash, one of those collapsible leather coin purses containing sixty-seven cents in change, a leather key ring with five keys. A travel toothbrush and a travel-size tube of Colgate toothpaste. A comb. A wool muffler. A pair of wool socks and an unopened box of white Jockey briefs. A blank notebook and a pen. A copy of the *Playbill* for *Uncle Vanya*. A paperback sci-fi novel, *God Emperor of Dune*. I flipped through the *Playbill*. My name on the cast list had been scratched out with a red marker; my listing in the Who's Who box was entirely blotted out in red.

The sun streamed through my kitchen window as I drank my coffee, considering the last hours of Guy's unhappy, un-lucky life. According to Madeleine they had been fighting all night, even on the subway. At some point, either before or during that argument, he'd packed this backpack. What was he planning? The underwear and toothbrush suggested he in-tended to be away, at least overnight. The gun must have been in the bag already. Did Madeleine know he had it? Was that why, when she heard the shot, she knew what it was? The mustache, I thought, why the mustache? Did he plan to murder me and then take my place onstage after the intermission? What a bizarre idea, but not impracticable.

I put everything but the keys back in the bag and stowed it in my closet. Someone had to clear out the apartment and let the landlord know his tenants wouldn't be returning. I dug the address Detective DiBanco had written for me from my coat pocket, took up the keys, and went out into the street. Maybe there would be some clue—a diary, perhaps—that would clear up the mystery of Guy's intentions toward me.

The East Village is still a gritty territory where the opportunities to enjoy a tattoo session are limitless, but it was worse then. An evening stroll required making a choice between dodging the rats on the street or the dope peddlers on the sidewalk. These denizens weren't much in evidence in daylight, but the occasional syringe or strung-out, babbling addict lolling curbside provided helpful reminders for those who might be duped by the run-down gentility of the buildings. One had to circumvent the black steel doors flung open like bat's wings over steps descending vertiginously into the gloom of various basements, a vast underworld of violence and criminality.

The Margates' apartment was in a brick-fronted building with a fire escape laced across the front. Steel steps rose over the used-clothing store at street level to a bright-red, triple-locked steel door that had been installed during a recent, hopeful makeover. I mounted the steps and plied the keys until I found the ones that fit, hauled the heavy door open, and stepped into the foyer. It wasn't bad. Black-and-white tile floor, red walls, a line of steel mailboxes, and a dusty but solid concrete staircase leading to the upper regions. Apartment E was on the third floor, behind a wooden door with only two locks. I tried the keys again; the door glided open before me.

I'd been expecting penury and grubbiness, but this was bourgeois respectability. Guy and Madeleine had been playing house. Very small house, there were only two rooms and a bath, but house all the same. Dishes stacked in the kitchen cupboard, geraniums on the windowsill off the fire escape, a flowered cloth on the two-seater table tucked into the corner between the fridge and the sink. They'd only been in the place for a month, but it was seriously furnished. Well, I told myself, they'd been together for six years and they'd acquired stuff. A painted bookcase containing the books I would later pack up and move to Connecticut, a wicker couch with paisley cushions, a lady's desk with a few envelopes on top, a swiveling desk chair on wheels. A curtain of the same paisley cloth as the cushions hung from brass rings, pulled partially aside to separate the space. Behind it was the bed, an iron bed frame painted shiny black. The patterned sheets and quilt were thrown halfway back over the mattress, as if the sleepers had leapt up and rushed away. Perhaps they had, I thought. Homely items, fuzzy slippers, hers, and leather slippers, his, a half-full glass of water on the night table, a dresser with one of her blouses folded neatly on top. Oddest of all was the double frame with two photos propped on a ledge that must once have been a fireplace mantel. The frame was hinged and had an antique look to it, black glass mat and pewter filigree edging. The photos were professional head shots, his and hers. They appeared to be looking at each other, his expression cool, masculine, serious; hers demure, but with a frank sexuality about the mouth. I laid the frame flat and stood looking down at them. His wasn't recent; he had more hair. "This is too sad," I said to the empty room. They slept in this bed every night as innocently as children, with these artificial selves framed and elevated like devotional images of saints gazing at each other in the upper atmosphere.

Or perhaps they didn't sleep like children. Perhaps they had screaming fights all night, as Madeleine claimed, or perhaps they had, as Guy insisted, sex all the time.

I left the bedroom feeling oddly chastened, and approached the desk. The papers were just bills and lists. I opened the drawer: a box of paper clips, an open package of loose-leaf paper, a checkbook. It was a joint account, Guy Margate and Madeleine Delavergne. I found the name of the realty company to which they were paying the enormous sum of four hundred dollars a month. Guy had written a check for twelve hundred the month before, first month, last month, and damage deposit. The second payment was overdue by a few days; the balance in the account was three hundred and seventy-five dollars.

This was sad, too, so sad that I sat down on the desk chair, completely enervated by the turmoil of my emotions. Noise from the street assaulted the building, shouts, cars, sirens, trucks with the reverberating backup beeps, a revving roar that sounded like a leaf blower, though there were no dead leaves in the world just yet, a dog barking and barking, and beneath all this the persistent thrumming hum that was the city itself, the living, breathing, pulsing, all-consuming heart of it, the never-ending beat that elated some and pursued others to oblivion.

That was when I decided that once I got Madeleine out of the hospital I would take her out of the city.

I put the checkbook in my pocket—I would contact the Realtor and arrange to pack up the apartment—and let myself out the door. I had only an hour before I had to be at the theater. The understudy wasn't bad, but I couldn't warm up to her. When Madeleine's Elena complained that she was bored it was a shameful confession. In the understudy's interpretation it was an accusation. My Astrov was becoming something of a clown, frantically trying to amuse her.

The next morning Teddy called to consult with me about the urn for Guy's ashes.

"I don't care," I said. "Just make sure the lid is tight."

"Should it be metal or ceramic? Wayne thinks it should be bronze."

"Do they have lead?"

There was a moment of silence. "Here's one that's copper lined in lead. Not bad-looking."

"Get that one."

We had a simple ceremony at a funeral home in Queens that Wayne recommended because two of his uncles were interred in the adjoining mausoleum. Teddy put an announcement in the papers, and to our surprise a few people showed up—two clerks from the store in Philadelphia, the manager of the Columbus Circle store, and a few actors Guy had worked with in the Italian play and the Broadway disaster. His agent, Bev Arbuckle, didn't show, though I'd left her a message on her answering machine.

I got Guy's birth date from his driver's license and Teddy

had his name and dates carved on a marble panel, behind which the urn was safely sealed away. Teddy had paid for something called "perpetual care," which meant, once Guy was stowed in his slot, we didn't have to come back.

Guy was thirty-nine years old. He shot himself in the heart a week before his fortieth birthday.

Now for a final leap across a canyon of twenty years to the present. Madeleine and I are married and live in a small Connecticut town near the regional playhouse where I spent that mystical summer with Marlene Webern and where I now serve on the board. As it turns out, I have a knack for fund-raising and am much valued both by the playhouse and by the local prep school where I chair the theater program. We do a lot of dining out with the well-heeled.

In that first year Madeleine was in and out of Benthaven having her mood swings adjusted and calibrated and gradually recovering most of her memory. There are still gaps, the night Guy died being most notable. She knows it happened because she's been told, but she has no memory of it. She generally dislikes talking about the past and I sometimes suspect that considerable swatches are still largely blank. Every morning she takes an antidepressant pill; she never forgets that. It alters something fundamental in her; it narrows her range. For obvious reasons, but also, I think, because of this medication, she has no interest in acting. She doesn't like going to plays; she says the theater makes her anxious. She prefers movies.

Yet she often quotes lines from plays. She still has a lot of

Shakespeare, which crops up in her ordinary conversation. If I read her a bit from the newspaper about political skulduggery, she nods quietly and observes "Some rise by sin, and some by virtue fall" or "Knavery's plain face is never seen till used," that sort of thing. These lines drop from her lips without intonation, like a bag of chips falling into the tray of a vending machine when the correct code has been punched.

She's Madeleine but not Madeleine, though she doesn't know it. She laughs more easily, seldom weeps, has no ambition, is affectionate and loving and warm, but she's not passionate about anything, including me. She's a serious gardener, but she's still a miserable cook.

I don't act much anymore myself, though occasionally I take a small role in a school production or fill in for a bit at the playhouse. I keep track of what's on in the city and go in whenever Teddy has a role, which, these days, is more and more often.

In the '80s, as everyone knows, AIDS wiped out a sizable percentage of the arts community in New York; Wayne Lee was a casualty. Teddy spent two desperate years trying to find some way to save his partner, but there was almost nothing available in the way of treatment, and Wayne's last months were gruesome. To make matters worse, some secrets about Wayne's financial dealings and, of course, sexual meanderings surfaced, and Teddy was forced to see his beloved in an unflattering light even as he was giving every ounce of his energy and patience and affection to the dying man. Was Wayne grateful? I went so far as to ask this once, and Teddy replied without hesitation, "I couldn't care less. I'm losing him."

By the time Wayne died, Teddy was mentally and physically worn out. He couldn't bear being in the city, where everything reminded him of his lost happiness. Around that time I bought the small house I still live in, with a big yard which Madeleine straightway turned into an Eden complete with apple tree. There was a guest cottage at the back which I fitted out. Teddy became a regular visitor; especially welcome for his cooking skills. Often we stayed up late, after Madeleine had retired for the night, drinking and talking. At first all we talked about was Wayne, but gradually the subject turned to old times and to acting. I encouraged him to go upon the boards again and he admitted that he missed the theater, though he never wanted to attend an acting class again in his life. I pulled a string or two and he got a slot in the company at the playhouse. He spent the summer living in the boardinghouse, working hard and sleeping well, absorbed in an energetic group of actors, mostly younger than he was. He played Malvolio in a production of *Twelfth Night* to great acclaim—he was riotously funny, with such perfect comic timing that the audience began tittering the moment he stepped onto the stage. His fellow actors admired him, he made a few connections, and in the fall, when he returned to the city, he acquired an agent and threw himself, with a good will, into the grinding business of auditions. He began to get parts, mostly comic, and to live the life of a working actor. Young men were drawn to him because he was kindhearted and he fell in and out of love, but he has never lived with anyone again. He's working too hard.

So happy ending all round, more or less. I know you're relieved. But much as we might imagine we can leave the past behind, it has a nasty way of pressing its hoary old face against the window just as we are sitting down to the feast.

About a month ago I was taking the train down to the city to meet with a select group of theatrical high rollers who might throw some money Connecticut-ward, and to see a new play in which Teddy had a role. It was a chilly January day. Madeleine dislikes going to the city in the winter, so she opted to stay at home. I was staying over in a hotel because the rollers did business at breakfast, so I packed an overnight bag. I was closing the lid of my faithful but battered sidekick of many years when the zipper jammed. Pulling it back didn't work; it locked up like a safe and wouldn't budge in either direction. Bracing against the bed with knee, gripping of the tiny metal tab, furious yanking accompanied by imprecations followed by the sudden disheartening thweeeet as the placket parted company with the suitcase, ensued. Renewed curses brought my lovely wife to the bedroom door. "Is something wrong, darling?" she said mildly.

"My suitcase is completely fucked!" I exclaimed.

She joined me in examining the damage and agreed with my diagnosis. "Take mine," she offered.

"I don't like yours. It's too big."

"I used to have a smaller one," she said. "Where is it? Is it in the attic? I think it's in the attic."

Together we ambled down the hall to the attic door. As I climbed the narrow steps ahead of her, it occurred to me that a trip to the attic is an excursion into history, and that all over the world the present unravels beneath the stored detritus of the past; that's what attics are for. At the top I pulled the light cord and turned to watch Madeleine trudging up behind me. The harsh light from the bare bulb illuminated the fine creases around her eyes, the deeper lines around her mouth. She is still a beautiful woman; age only serves to accentuate her aura of refinement and sexuality. Her face was lifted to mine and she was smiling in a distant, distracted way. "Don't look back," she said.

"Why not?" I asked.

"You might lose me," she said, arriving at my side. "I think it's inside a bigger case. It's part of a set."

We proceeded to examine the area I call Mount Luggage, a museum of the improvements in the design of the wheeled suitcase over the years, including the steel-trap-on-wheels that pinched so many fingers around the world and the equally hazardous four-wheeled hard-side. "It's here," Madeleine said, pulling out a gray two-wheeler.

"Why did you say I might lose you?" I asked.

She bent over the case and unzipped the top, revealing the promised smaller bag within. "I was following you in the dark and then you turned on the light and I thought I might be coming up from the underworld."

"Like Eurydice," I said.

"And then you looked back." She pulled the smaller case out and set it between us. "Will this do?"

I put my arms around her, resting my cheek against her hair. "It's fine," I said, but I was thinking, as I often do, *What is in my wife's head?* My hand strayed to her breast.

"You'll make yourself late," she cautioned.

She was right. I snatched the bag, carried it back to the bedroom, transferred my travel togs, kissed my helpmeet, and headed for the door.

"You have time," Madeleine cautioned as I picked my way around the ice on the walk. "Don't rush. Drive carefully."

A few hours later in the hotel room I unpacked Madeleine's bag, carefully hanging my cashmere turtleneck and Armani jacket in the closet, so as to appear fresh, stylish, and wrinkle-free for the millionaires on the morn. I removed my underwear and socks and slid my fingers inside the back pocket where, in my rush to change bags, I had stuffed my oral hygiene products. In this process a card, stuck against the side of the case, was dislodged. As I extracted my toothpaste, the card edge peeped mischievously out at me. I pulled it loose. It was a note card with a faded Japanese block print on the front: a waterfall, pedestrians with umbrellas crossing a bridge. The edges had been pressed together so long they were joined and I had to pry the top loose with a fingernail.

Inside I recognized Madeleine's handwriting.

> *My Darling,*
>
> *Your beautiful flowers were in the dressing room when I arrived. How heartening to read your sweet note with the fragrance of roses filling the air. I got right over my jitters and the performance went amazingly well. I died beautifully, everyone agreed.*
>
> *I can hardly wait to see you and you to see the play and tell me all your thoughts. Dearest, I miss you awfully. "The*

heavens forbid but that our loves and comforts should increase, even as our days do grow!"

And grow. Come as soon as you can and rescue me from
this villainous Moor. He's killing me.

Love, kisses, M.

I sat on the bed and read this billet-doux a few times over.
The quote I dimly recognized, Desdemona to Othello. It took
about three minutes to commit the whole message to memory.
Then I put it in my jacket pocket, changed my shoes, and went
out to the street. Teddy's play was a longish walk from the hotel, but I had only one thought, which my brain repeated every
step of the way: So she loved him.

The play was at the Laura Pels, a fairly new theater, small
and well-appointed. It was a comedy about a dysfunctional
family, not great but not bad, not very funny, though Teddy
was ripping in the role of the father who can't say consonants, a
little quote from an old Feydeau farce brought nicely up-to-
date. All the acting was top-notch and the audience liked it
well enough. One feels relieved these days when a play is not
like television.

I concentrated on the stage doings with difficulty, distracted
by a voice from the past, one I'd never heard before. "Dearest, I
miss you awfully." Guy too was piping up from the memory vault.
"She did Desdemona last year. Rave reviews." And of course the
immortal line "We called you the warm-up act" smacked around
the walls of my brain like a racquetball. It was sickening.

After the show I met Teddy at the dressing-room door and

we walked a few blocks to the West Side Café, a place I like because there are usually a few actors hanging around and the food is good. I praised Teddy's performance and we discussed the merits of the play and the reviewers' comments, which had been largely positive. "It's a great group," Teddy said. "We all get along. No one is crazy. It's good fun."

"It's always better when no one is crazy," I agreed. When we were seated, with drinks in hand and had ordered our dinners, I pulled the card from my pocket and passed it to Teddy. "I want you to look at this," I said. "I'll tell you what it is after I ask you a question about it."

"It looks old," he said. "Is it something mysterious?"

"Just read it," I said. I sipped my wine while he gave the writing close attention.

"All right," he said. "Who is it?"

"I'll tell you in a minute. I want your opinion."

"It's very sweet. She's playing Desdemona. That's the quote, right?"

"Yes," I said. "It is."

"So what's the question?"

"In your opinion, is the person who wrote that note having sex with the person she's writing to?"

"Well, it's very affectionate. She misses him. Or her. I suppose it could be between two women. But yes, I'd say they were lovers."

"I thought so too."

"So, who's it from?"

"It's from Madeleine. To Guy."

"And?"

"I found it in her old suitcase, tonight, just before the play, at the hotel."

"In *her* suitcase?"

"I borrowed it. I broke mine."

"So maybe she never mailed it."

"Possibly. I figured he used the suitcase later and left it in there."

"That could be. They were married a long time."

"That's what I thought."

Our meals arrived and we had a moment's banter with the waiter. Teddy broke a piece of bread, frowning in puzzlement. "I don't get it," he said.

"What?"

"Your question. About the sex."

I laid down the fork I had picked up. "Madeleine told me she and Guy never had sex."

Teddy sawed at the small roasted bird on his plate. "Wow," he said. "She told you that?"

"A long time ago."

"Why would she tell you that?"

"Exactly. Why would she make something like that up?"

"So he was gay. Wayne thought he was."

"Really?"

"He thought Guy was in love with you."

"He did?"

"He just said it to be catty; he hardly knew either of you. Wayne thought everyone was gay, actually, just half the world represses it, hence the human race."

"So he thought I was gay."

"He thought you and Guy were in love but you were both in denial and used Madeleine to get at each other." He slathered butter onto his bread. "You're not eating."

I picked up my fork again and speared a green bean. "I'm dumbfounded," I said, chewing the bean. "That's so ugly."

"It is. I never believed it."

"Anyway, Madeleine said Guy wasn't gay. She said he was just completely impotent."

"Wayne would love that."

"Can we just leave Wayne out of this?"

Teddy pulled his chin in and made his eyes round. "Touchy," he said.

"I'm just trying to figure out what the truth is."

"Guy's been gone a long time. He was a terribly unhappy man."

"He denied it."

"That he was unhappy?"

"That he was impotent."

Teddy took a swallow of his wine. "You asked him?"

"I didn't ask him. I told him I knew and that it was too bad and could happen to any man."

"When was this?"

"That night. In the dressing room."

"Oh, my lord," Teddy said slowly, addressing his quail.

"He said Madeleine made fun of me. He said they had sex all the time and they made fun of me."

Teddy pulled a tiny bone clean between his front teeth. "This is sick," he said.

"I assumed he was lying. I always have. Then I found this note."

Teddy picked up the card and read it over again. "There's nothing in here that proves anything either way," he said. "She doesn't say, 'I miss your erect penis,' or anything; it's just affectionate. So maybe she was telling you the truth."

"But it's very affectionate. You can't deny that."

"Why don't you just ask her, Ed?" he said softly.

This irritated me. "You can't ask her anything about Guy. She just says she doesn't remember. Her memory is full of holes. She doesn't want to talk about anything that happened before we were married."

"Well, then, why don't you forget about it too?"

"It's just that I've always believed she didn't love him. I thought he trapped her, and then he made her feel sorry for him, but that really she disliked him as much as I did."

"No one disliked Guy as much as you did."

This surprised me. "Did you like him?" I asked.

"Guy was OK. He was funny sometimes, and he was so awkward and he had such bad luck, I felt sorry for him. I didn't agree with Wayne. I think he was madly in love with Madeleine. And she was fond of him. Sex or no sex, they had a close relationship. Whatever it was that held them together, it lasted several years."

As Teddy advanced this reasonable view, I tried to eat another bean, but it stuck in my throat. I started to cough. I was thinking of the photo in their apartment, Guy and Madeleine on the mantel over a scene of domestic harmony. The cough turned into a frightening wheeze. I couldn't catch my breath. I clutched my throat and tears filled my eyes. The attention of our fellow diners began to coalesce upon our table. Teddy got up and, with remarkable ease and speed, whacked me twice high on my back. This helped. A brief series of coughs, through which I was able to suck in a few swallows of water, opened my windpipe. Teddy sat down again as I pressed my napkin against my lips, holding it there while I breathed in slowly through my nose.

"Are you OK?" Teddy asked.

I nodded behind the napkin.

"I think you should throw this note away and forget you ever saw it. Send Madeleine some roses and tell her you love her."

I nodded again. He was right, of course. But not roses; she didn't approve of out-of-season flowers. Chocolates. I knew her favorite shop, Upper West Side. I pictured her, brightening up at the sight of the cunning brown box. I lowered the napkin and drank a swallow of wine.

But that our loves and comforts should increase, even as our days do grow!

Guy, opening the card, moving his lips over that line.

Maybe I was just tired. I hadn't slept well the night before. Or the night before that. In fact, I hadn't slept well in years. I didn't like thinking about the past, it was pointless, it was over, but as I sat there it all came stamping up around the table legs, hauling me down like a pack of demons into a dark and fiery furnace, where Guy Margate rolled over on a spit and fixed me with the burning coals that were his eyes.

"Are you OK?" Teddy asked again.

A shudder ran up my back, gripped my neck, and rustled my jowls. My throat felt tight. My eyes were stinging and I squeezed them shut.

"Ed?" Teddy said.

My head was filling up with fluid. I sniffed as it slid down my nose and I opened my eyes, releasing a mini-flood of tears. "I don't know what it is," I blubbered. "All of a sudden I feel . . ." A sob strangled whatever it was I felt, so moist and respiratorially calamitous a sob that, once again, our fellow diners turned our way. What was I thinking about? I hardly knew.

Death? My mother's and Guy's, a frame of suicides, one pushing me into the theater, the other driving me out, and my own mortality, and the thought that Madeleine might die, and Teddy, my dear friend, he might die. I opened the napkin and swabbed my eyes and nose, but it just kept coming, this viscous flood, and I wondered how a head, which looks relatively dry from the outside, could dump, without warning, so much liquid. "I'm sorry," I gasped, covering my face with the cool linen and boohooing like a diva. I heard Teddy fending off the tentative approach of a concerned waiter. "We're breaking up," he said in a voice so arch and fey that I laughed through my tears. I lowered the napkin; all eyes were on us. Teddy was holding his hands out, his mouth set in an insipid pout, turning from one group of alarmed diners to another, repeating vapidly, "We're breaking up. What can I sa-ay, we're breaking up."

"You're killing me," I moaned, hiding behind the napkin

again. The fit was easing off, but, in spite of how Teddy amused me, at bottom I was still sad. I dried my eyes and dabbed my nose, while he returned to crunching up his quail. "I hope you don't mind," he said, between bites. "I'm really hungry."

"Go right ahead," I said.

"So what was that all about?"

"I'm not sure," I said, tearing up again. "It's that stupid note. It brought the whole thing with Guy back. I never could figure out what was going on there. I couldn't get to the bottom of it. And now I guess I never will."

"So you were moved by your own touching saga."

I drank some water, dried the last tears, took out my handkerchief, and gave the nose a serious blow. "Yes," I agreed. "I was."

"Well, it is a good story. You ought to write it down."

"No one would believe it." I straightened my spine and slid my eyes along the tables nearest us. The chatter level had returned to normal, clinking cutlery provided a reassuring white noise. At the bar a woman with a loud laugh laughed loudly and, as I glanced toward her, a tall, dark-haired man, dressed in an impeccable three-piece suit, came into view. Our eyes crossed, his intent on contact, mine on escape. He approached us, gliding stealthily among the tables.

"Do you know this guy?" I asked Teddy, tilting my head to indicate the potential interloper.

"Never seen him before," Teddy said. "Great suit."

Then he was upon us, his handsome face emanating goodwill. "Excuse me," he said. He nodded first to me, then to Teddy, and back again to me, feigning hesitancy. "I'm sorry to disturb you, but, I hope you won't mind, I just had to ask, are you, by any chance, Edward Day?"

I set down my fork and gave him my attention. He had the manner of a supplicant. He was blushing, his eyelids flickered nervously, but his voice gave him away. It was an actor's voice, perfectly controlled and pitched for this complex public space. "I am," I said.

"You are," he agreed. "I thought you must be." A self-conscious, oh-silly-me laugh escaped him and he shifted his weight from one foot to the other.

"Do I know you?" I asked.

"No. That is, we've never met. I saw you on the stage, years ago, it was at a theater downtown, very small. You played the valet in a Strindberg play."

"*Miss Julie,*" I said.

"Yes. It was an incredible performance."

Teddy leaned over the table, grinning from ear to ear. "This is great," he said.

"It's kind of you to say so," I said, frowning at Teddy.

"That play changed my life."

Teddy was chortling. "But you must have been, what, twelve years old?" he said.

"I was eighteen," my fan replied. "It was in my first year at NYU. I wasn't certain what I wanted to do. I'd always loved the theater, but I'd never seen anything like that play. Your performance, well, this may sound odd, but I'd never understood what the expression 'truth' in acting meant until I saw . . ." He paused, opening his palm to acknowledge the master, "Edward Day in *Miss Julie*. When I left that theater I knew I wanted to be an actor."

"Really," I said.

"You changed my life," he said.

Acknowledgments

I want to thank, in roughly chronological order, the following actors, playwrights, and theater enthusiasts who helped me along the way to this novel: Christine Farrell, Robin Day, Laura Shaine Cunningham, Anthony Giardina, Patrick Pacheco, Peter Schneider, Sarah Harden, Nicole Quinn, Jack Kroll, Janet Nurre, Mikhail Horowitz, Christine Crawfis, Ean Kessler, Walter Bobbie, Mary Willis, and Geri Loughery. Thanks also to playwright Nina Shengold, who responded to my query about the possibility of talking to actors with the message, "You want actors, I'll give you actors." The next thing I knew I was at a rehearsal of a Broadway play. I am grateful to Adam LeFevre, Robyn Henry, and Christopher Durang, for graciously agreeing to let me watch.

Thanks are also due to Erin Quinn, who unknowingly suggested the plot; Nicole Drespel, who gave me a backstage tour of the Public Theater; Peter Skolnik, who answered my questions promptly and told great stories in the process; Ronit Feldman, who gave the manuscript an early and actor-oriented reading, and my energetic and hardworking agent, Molly Friedrich.

I owe a special debt to John Pleshette, who was there then. His memory for detail is truly astonishing, and his descriptions of the daily grind of the actor were harrowing. There may be actors who remember what they got paid in 1973, but I suspect not many recall what the set cost as well. John also read the manuscript and offered invaluable suggestions.

I am and will continue to be indebted to Nikki Smith, my most trenchant reader and valued friend.

For the unwavering support and enthusiasm of my nearest and dearest, John Cullen, Adrienne Martin, and Christopher Hayes, I am continually grateful.

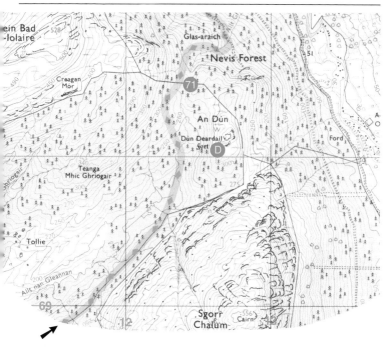

The Way reaches a fence **71** where a new path has been created to allow walkers to visit the Iron Age hill-fort of Dùn Deardail **D**. It is only a short detour and does provide an opportunity to see an archaeological curiosity. Hill-forts were common in Britain during the period which lasted from roughly 500 BC to the first century AD. Some were large enough to contain regular settlements, others simply places where people could retreat if attacked. Dùn Deardail is what is known as a vitrified fort, one in which the stone defences have been subjected to such intense heat that silicate materials in the rock, such as quartz, have melted to form a glassy mass. There are numerous theories as to how this happened, but the likeliest explanation is that the drystone walls that surrounded the summit were braced with timber cross-pieces. If these caught fire, intense heat would have been generated, causing vitrification. No one can now discover whether such fires were caused by accident or as part of an attack on the fort. From here there is a splendid view of Ben Nevis while down in the glen there is a glimpse of the houses on the outskirts of Fort William, indicating the end of the Way.

The nature of the walk now changes again, as it follows a broad track through the Nevis Forest. Much of the woodland has been felled, leaving scarred hillsides. Now the long descent to the bottom of Glen Nevis begins with great sweeping bends. The hillside above the walk is laced by streams, while down below a narrow strip of green fields separates the woodland from the lower slopes of Ben Nevis. Where the track reaches a gentler slope **72** a second track appears on the right, doubling back to the Youth Hostel and the road up Glen Nevis. The main route continues straight ahead to a point where a narrow path crosses the track **73**. Turn right to go steeply downhill; and where the path immediately divides, take the fork to the left. The conifers are now left behind for an area of deciduous woodland bordering a stream, which makes a pleasant change. It zig-zags down past a small cemetery. Go through the wooden gate at the edge of the wood and carry straight on down the track to the road **74**. Turn left and stay on the road to the end of the walk. It is a somewhat disappointing finale to an invigorating trek through wild country to end on a pavement beside a road, but there are things of interest along the way. A vast roadside boulder is described as a Counsel or Wishing Stone. There are various legends attached to the stone, including one that claims that at certain times the whole rock magically rotates and settles down again. It will, of course, only perform when no one is there to see it. Falls on the river form an attractive feature, but the outskirts of Fort William, when they appear, are not very prepossessing. On arriving at a roundabout **75**, proceed to Nevis Bridge, which crosses the river and marks the official end of the West Highland Way. The centre of Fort William is reached by carrying straight on down the road.

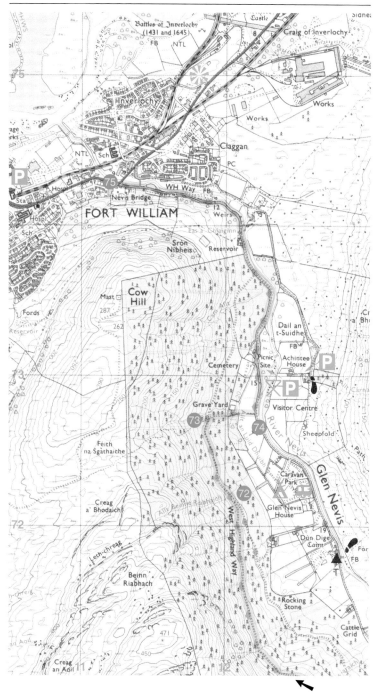

THE ASCENT OF BEN NEVIS

12½ miles (18km) return trip   *(see map on pages 134–5*

There are some who feel that though the West Highland Way is a magnificent walk, the end comes as an anti-climax. This need not be so, for anyone with a day to spare can, in the right conditions, add their own climax, with an ascent of Britain's highest mountain, Ben Nevis. But this is one of those climbs that needs to be taken seriously. In good weather, all that is needed is the stamina for the long haul to the summit. In winter – and winter on Ben Nevis can begin in October and last right through to May – only properly equipped and experienced mountaineers should attempt it. Even in high summer there are potential dangers. Weather changes very rapidly in this part of the world, and a walk that begins in sunshine can end with cloud covering the mountain and driving rain. The ascent up the obvious track may be simple enough, but once the top has been reached it is essential to locate the same route down again. It is easy in bad weather to roam the summit plateau and lose all sense of direction, and there are crags and steep falls for the unwary. Map and compass are, as always, the essential tools of the hill walker; and provided one knows how to use them and is suitably equipped for the walk, there should be few problems. The first essential is to check local weather forecasts and then prepare accordingly.

There are two starting places for walkers on the West Highland Way. The most popular route takes the road that crosses Nevis Bridge at the end of the Way and turns down the valley on the opposite bank of the river to end at Achintee Farm, which offers bunkhouse accommodation. From here there is a clear track all the way to the summit. This bridleway was first constructed in 1883 to provide access to a weather observatory, so it takes the easiest line, offering a steady but never excessively steep climb. It passes beneath the face of Meall an t-Suidhe, then swings left to climb up Red Burn Gully, near the top of which it again swings round to the left to provide a more comfortable ascent. It emerges by a lochan, sitting in a hollow halfway up the mountain.

The path now crosses the Red Burn and then proceeds to zigzag its way to the summit plateau. It does not feel like a summit, more a bewildering, rocky wilderness, marked by the ruins of the observatory, abandoned in 1904, and the Peace Cairn, built to commemorate those who died in the Second World War. Again it is important to stress that there are dangers here, sharp drops and snow cornices that can last well into late spring, but common sense is the main defence against accidents. Do not stray too close to the edges, especially in bad weather, and be very sure that a patch of snow covers solid rock and not empty air. The descent follows exactly the same route back down again.

The alternative starting point is the Glen Nevis Youth Hostel. Cross the footbridge over the river opposite the hostel and follow the very obvious path that zig-zags up the steep hillside. It joins the bridleway on the rocky slope of Meall an t-Suidhe and then follows the route already described.

Is this a more appropriate end to the West Highland Way than a suburban traffic island? That is up to the individual to decide. Some will say that the ascent of Ben Nevis is little more than a hard, unremitting slog with little in the way of scenic delights when the top is finally reached; others would argue that to climb Britain's highest mountain is its own reward. But whichever ending is selected, busy Fort William or wild Ben Nevis, nothing can take away from the satisfaction and delights of one of Britain's greatest long-distance walks.

The West Highland Way stays on the valley floor, but Ben Nevis offers a more challenging grand finale to the walk.

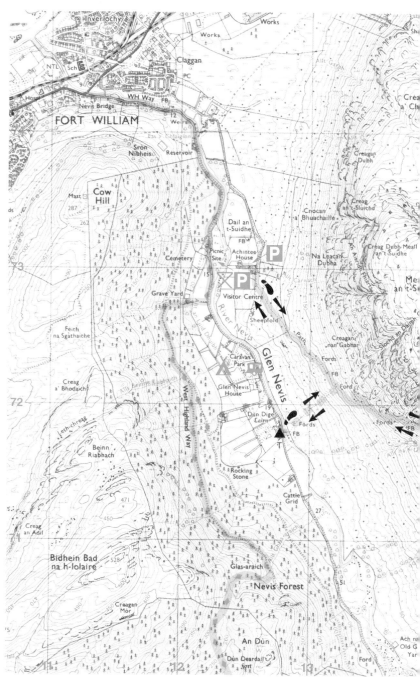

Scale is approx 2¼ inches to 1 mile

134

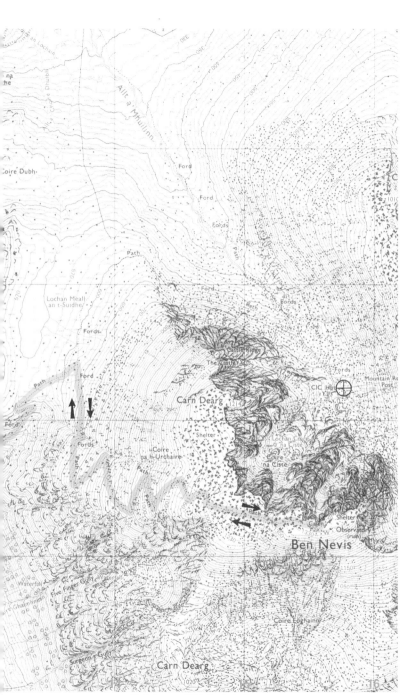

Scale is approx 2¼ inches to 1 mile

135

Useful
Information

TRANSPORT

Information on transport can be obtained from Tourist Information Centres in Scotland. There are also rail and coach centres which will be able to give specific information on timetables.

Rail Enquiries
National Rail Travel Passenger Enquiries (tel. 0345 484 950)

Coach Enquiries
Scottish Citylink Coaches and National Express (tel. 0141 332 9644/ 0990 505050)

Getting to the start of the West Highland Way at Milngavie
If you are walking from the south to the north you will have a choice of transport to Milngavie. A regular rail service operates from the main line termini at Glasgow Queen Street Station or Central Station. Journey time is approximately 20 minutes. There is a frequent bus service from Buchanan Street Bus Station in Glasgow.

Returning to the start from Fort William after your walk
It is possible to return to Glasgow by rail or by coach from Fort William.

Passenger Ferry Services on Loch Lomond

Rowardennan to Inverbeg
Loch Lomond Ferry Service, Rowardennan Hotel
Weekends only until mid-May
April to September (tel. 01360 870273)
10 am, 2 pm, 6 pm, returning 10.30 am, 2.30 pm, 6.30 pm
Inversnaid to Inveruglas
Inversnaid Hotel, Inversnaid
March to 2 January (tel. 01877 386223)
Daily passenger service. Times vary from week to week – at least twice a day.

Ardlui (West Highland Way and Islands)
Service on request, returning by arrangement. Please phone ahead to arrange transportation from West Highland Way to Ardlui campsite. Easter till October, daylight hours on request.
Cuillins Yacht Charters, The Flat-a-Float, Ardlui
(tel. 013014 244/01301 704244)

Ardlui West Side (Loch Lomond to Ardleish East Side)
12-passenger ferry operating between Ardlui Marina Pier and Ardleish Jetty on the West Highland Way.
1 April to 31 October. 9 am, 10 am, 1 pm, 4 pm, 5.30 pm, 7 pm.
Also on demand by raising ball on flagpole when on east side.
Ardlui Hotel Marina, Ardlui (tel. 01301 704243)

Boat Trips
Balmaha Boatyard, McFarlane & Son (tel. 01360 870214)
Sailings to Inchcalloch Nature Reserve Island and daily cruises.

ACCOMMODATION

A leaflet, *West Highland Way Long Distance Footpath*, giving information on accommodation is published annually by Loch Lomond Park Authority and is available from Tourist Information Centres. Information is given on hotels, bed-and-breakfast houses, guest houses, camping facilities, bunkhouses and bothies. *West Highland Wayfarer* is a holiday freesheet produced by Famedram Publishers Ltd, send SAE to PO Box 3, Ellon, AB41 9EA. *Stilwell's National Trail Companion* is available from bookshops and contains information on accommodation

Youth Hostels
There are three on or close by the Way at:

Rowardennan	GR 359992	(tel. 01360 870259)
Crianlarich	GR 386250	(tel. 01838 300260)
Glen Nevis	GR 127718	(tel. 01397 702336)

Further information can be obtained from the Scottish Youth Hostels Association at 7 Glebe Crescent, Stirling FK8 2JA (tel. 01786 451181).

There are **bothies** at:

Rowchoish	GR 336044
Doune	GR 333145

Tourist Information Centres

Scottish Tourist Board, 23 Ravelston Terrace, Edinburgh
EH4 3EU (tel. 0131 332 2433)
Fort William and Lochaber Tourist Board, Cameron Centre,
Cameron Square, Fort William, Inverness-shire PH33 6AJ
(tel. 01397 703781)
Greater Glasgow Tourist Board and Convention Bureau,
35 St Vincent Place, Glasgow G1 2ER (tel. 0141 204 4400)
Loch Lomond, Stirling and Trossachs Tourist Board,
41 Dumbarton Road, Stirling FK8 2QQ (tel. 01786 475019)

Summer only
Balloch: Balloch Road (April to October tel. 01389 753533)
Drymen: Drymen Library, The Square, Drymen (May to
September tel. 01360 660068)
Tarbet: Main Street, Tarbet (April to October tel. 01301 702260)
Tyndrum: Main Street, Tyndrum (April to October
tel. 01838 400246)

Useful addresses

British Trust for Ornithology, Beech Grove, Tring, Hertfordshire
HP12 5NR
Forestry Commission, 231 Corstophine Road, Edinburgh
EH12 7AT (tel. 0131 334 0303)
Glasgow Weather Centre, 118 Waterloo Street, Glasgow
(tel. 0141 248 3451)
Historic Scotland, Longmore House, Salisbury Place, Edinburgh
EH9 1SH (tel. 0131 244 3101)
National Trust for Scotland, 5 Charlotte Square, Edinburgh
EH2 4DU (tel. 0131 226 5922)
Ordnance Survey, Romsey Road, Maybush, Southampton
SO16 4GU
Ramblers Association (Scotland), 23 Crusader House, Haig
Business Park, Markinch, Fife KY7 6AQ (tel. 01592 611177)
Royal Society for the Protection of Birds and
The Scottish Wildlife Trust, Cramond House, Kirk Cramond,
Cramond Glebe Road, Edinburgh EH4 6NS (tel. 0131 557 3136)
Scottish Natural Heritage, Battleby, Redgorton, Perth PH1 3EW
(tel. 01738 627921)
Scottish Youth Hostels Association, 7 Glebe Crescent, Stirling
FK8 2JA (tel. 01786 451181)

close in and the path plunges downhill with wooden stairs to help on the steepest section at the bottom. It ends with a bridge over a rocky gorge, where a stream, its banks dotted with silver birch, splashes delicate green and white against the darker conifers. Now, inevitably, there is a climb up the other side, though the effort is eased by the enticing glimpses of mountain scenery through the trees. The gradient eases and the walk becomes a long, steady ascent, past a craggy ridge which pushes up above the trees that clamber up the slopes but stop just short of the summit. Throughout this section the path dips, rises and turns so that there is never any lack of interest along the way.

The forest track opens out to provide one of the more dramatic views of Ben Nevis.

as if it were determined to keep going all the way to the summit. Another stile **70** is crossed to a patch of open ground, followed immediately by a return to the woods and what will turn out to be a very rugged section of walking. At first the going is easy, and the walker can enjoy birdsong and the company of remarkably tame chaffinches and thrushes. There is a pleasant, open feel to the walk and constant views of hills and mountains. Then the trees

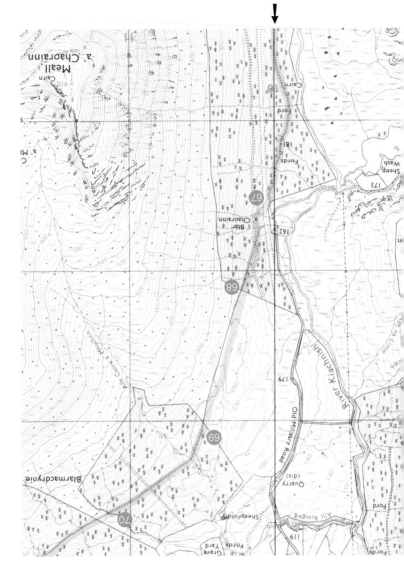

PREFACE

june 26th

My best friend, Mandy, is getting married, and no one is suffering more than my secretary, Kate.

KATE
I'm an administrative assistant. Not a
security guard.

ME
And I appreciate everything you do for me. Didn't I
get you that gift certificate from Saks last Christmas?

KATE
Macy's.[1]

ME
Whatever you say. But I can't talk to Mandy right
now. Just take a message.

KATE
I already did that. Six times.

ME
What'd she say?

KATE
"Urgent—Call me."

ME
It's a bluff. Tell her I'm in a meeting.

---

[1] Don't be fooled. The Macy's in Manhattan is really nice. It's their FLAGSHIP store.
She was just angling for sympathy.

KATE

That's what I said the first time she called.

ME

I'm in the ladies' room.

KATE

Used it twice. Once more and we'll be saying
urinary tract infection.

ME

Hey, that's a —

KATE

Forget it. I have my pride.

ME

All right. Put her through. But if I'm not
off the phone in three minutes call my
other line.

KATE

You know, this wasn't in my job
description.[2]

Kate struts out of my office. I wish I could go with her.
Instead I pick up the phone.

ME

Hi, Mandy. What's going on?

MANDY

Just the usual bridal nightmares.

---

[2] Technically an argument could be made against this comment. One of the nice
things about working for a big corporation like Hind Publications is the way the
employment contracts use broad, undefined terms such as "general support,"
thus leading the way for grand abuses of power like the one you're seeing here.

ME

What nightmares? You found the guy. He found
you. In just three months it'll be eternal bliss —

MANDY

Three months and two days.

ME

Like I said . . . Now relax and enjoy yourself.

MANDY

Oh, you couldn't possibly understand, Amy. You've
never been married.

ME

Then why'd you call me?

MANDY

What?

ME

Never mind. Just tell your spinster friend what's
ailing you.

MANDY

You're mocking me. Don't mock me.

ME

I'm not mocking you.[3]

Suddenly there's loud sniffling on the other end of the phone.

ME

Don't cry, Mandy. Everything's going to be okay.[4]

---

[3] I was totally mocking her.
[4] That's right. Throw me a huge party, buy me an expensive dress, make me the
center of attention, and to top it all off, shower me with gifts of my choosing,
and I'll cry too.

MANDY

I'm just so tired. Today the florist called to say that
her original quote on Holland tulips was under by
fifteen-point-seven-eight percent.

ME

Wow! Fifteen-point-seven-eight percent? How'd
you even figure out how much that was?

The sniffles become sobs. Did I say the wrong thing? My
other phone begins to ring. Kate's just earned a pay raise.

ME

Oops, there's my other line. I've gotta go. Just
remember this is about you and Jon getting married.
That's all that matters.

MANDY

But the tulips are an integral part of our floral concept.

ME

We'll talk soon!

I hang up. I know I should feel guilty, but all I feel is relief.
Moments later Kate returns to my office with a scowl.

KATE

We both know she's calling back in an hour.

Kate — So young. So wise.

ME

You're probably right. Now tell me why getting
married turns normal people into total freaks?

KATE

Don't ask me, Ms. Thomas. I'm not married.

ME
That's why I like you, Kate.[5]

It's true and you know it. People who are about to be married magically transform into raging narcissists. They're like those robot dolls we had as kids. The ones that transformed from a human to a car to a prehistoric animal. Well, put a veil and a string of pearls on one of those T-Rexes and you've got yourself a bride-to-be whose personal evolution is powerful enough to sweep every living man, woman, and child into its turmoil. And that's not malicious. Just fact.

Trust me. I know.

Mandy's asked me to be a bridesmaid at her wedding this September. On a certain level it's flattering. She's been one of my closest friends since sophomore year in college. Stunning, determined—and extremely high maintenance—she's the only person I've ever known who arranged her clothes by season. It's an odd mix of awe and incredulity that seals our friendship.

But now the terms of that friendship dictate that I appear at her nuptial soiree in a yellow satin dress with an empire waistline. Mandy has convinced herself that the "buttercup" color and the empire waistline are a subtle yet elegant interpretation of Camelot-era gowns.[6]

Yeah, right.

First off, the fabric may be called "buttercup," but it's really "pucker-mouth lemon"—like cheap mustard at picnics and ballparks. Or New York City taxicabs. And only young girls with eating disorders look elegant in empire

---

[5] That, and the fact that I love being called "Ms. Thomas," even if it is by a twenty-one-year-old who has a Backstreet Boys screen saver on her computer.

[6] That's Camelot as in Sir Arthur, *not* Jackie O.

waistlines. The rest of us look pregnant and dumpy. So you can forget Camelot.

But I'll wear it and smile. Because Mandy loves it and I love her.

Besides, I'm secure enough to appear in public as a livery vehicle. I'm an attractive twenty-nine-year-old brunette. I've even been told that I look like Julia Roberts. The Size 10 version. But shorter. With smaller boobs. So for one day I can endure the shame and humiliation of joining seven other women in pucker-mouth lemon dresses as we cruise down Mandy's wedding aisle to the tune of three hundred bucks a pop.

Oh, did I forget to mention *that* part?

And the spewing wallet doesn't stop there. There's still the engagement gift, the shower gift, the wedding gift—it all adds up.[7] Then there are the eight groomsmen who have to buy suits or top hats or full-body armor (I've been too afraid to ask). Not to mention the 250 guests she's invited to share in this intimate event, which she's been painstakingly planning for twelve long and laborious months . . .

I sound callous. I hate that, because I'm not. In fact, I try to be as patient and understanding as possible. I try to remember, as Mandy constantly reminds me, that I've never been through this. I really *don't* know what it feels like to endure the tumultuous storms that mysteriously accompany weddings. I try to remember that all those insane brides used to be my thoughtful, intelligent, truly enjoyable

---

[7] People always say you don't have to bring a gift to the engagement party. They're lying. They never forget who brought what and who showed up empty-handed. The first person who told me engagement gifts weren't expected is still waiting by the mailbox for my present to arrive. That was four years ago. She stopped speaking to me after two. But I don't care. I'm not sending it on principle: liars really tick me off.

LAURA WOLF

friends. Women I loved being with. The whole "do unto others as you would have them do unto you" doo-doo.

But it's difficult. It's like they've been stricken with some Mad Bride Disease. And it's not their fault—it's the diet powder they've turned to in a desperate attempt to shed those extra ten pounds that they've failed to lose for the last thirty years.

Yet not for a second do I begrudge them their happiness— or their hysteria. I'm thrilled they've found soul mates, partners, whipping boys, playthings . . . Heck, life's hard. A spouse is an invaluable bonus. No one prepares us for the lonely weekends watching mediocre TV, wishing we had something better to do. Sure, I've got a great boyfriend and terrific friends. But boyfriends come and go and friends make other plans. A spouse is always on-call. You can stay at home and do nothing, because you're doing it *together*.

But enough is enough. These days every time the phone rings it's another person calling to say she's getting married. They're bursting with excitement, spewing from the mouth, as their joy overfloweth for hours and hours and hours . . . Wedding dates, seating charts, flowers, registries, hors d'oeuvres, and gifts. Next they'll be calling about babies and twins and in-vitro fertilization. Hours of birthing details. Placentas, epidurals, and tearing. Do they *have* to talk about the tearing? Then it'll be Little League and Cub Scouts and car pools and extramarital affairs and couples therapy and divorce court . . . Soon I'll have to get a second phone just to order Chinese food!

Breathe. I must remember to breathe.

The thing that I really don't understand is the whole *desperation* to marry. I wasn't one of those little girls who sat around and fantasized about my wedding dress. I didn't know how I'd wear my hair or what type of flowers I'd hold. And I certainly didn't have visions of myself floating

down the aisle as hundreds of guests quietly weep into handkerchiefs while whispering in hushed tones about my exquisite beauty. My remarkable poise. My stellar choice of veil.

In fact, I pretty much assumed I'd never get married. I mean, why bother? I'm not religious. My family doesn't really care. And I have a sister who made it clear from infancy that she intended to lead the most June Cleaver existence possible, thereby assuring my family of at least one joyful nuptial.

I still remember the first week of college, when a girl in my literature class told me in all seriousness that college was our last chance to find a husband. According to her it was the last time we'd be in an environment with an abundance of men of the appropriate age, educational background, and financial strata. I was horrified. Here was an intelligent, good-looking, very young woman declaring that her main goal in college was to meet a mate.[8] College was simply an episode of *The Dating Game* honed to its sharpest point.

By junior year she was engaged to a guy with chronic dandruff and a history of kleptomania. She liked his sense of humor and thought his love of tennis would make him a good dad. She stopped talking to her friends and socialized exclusively with his. They were married two years later. I'm no devil-worshiping Satanist, but I just don't get it. Wasn't the whole point about birth control to liberate us from these shackles of dependency? Isn't that why we had the 1970s? Wasn't that why halter tops were invented?

And it's not like I'm "out of touch." As the Associate Features Editor of *Round-Up* magazine, it's my job to know what people in New York are thinking and doing. And not just the Donald Trumps and models of the moment but

---

[8] The degree she was getting in macrobiology? Merely a footnote.

real people, who worry about public school violence and look forward to eating hot zeppoli at the next street fair. In fact, I'm so "in touch" that I've been appointed editor of next year's "Faces in the City" issue. So I know weddings are important and meaningful events. I just don't understand why they diminish my girlfriends' capacity for rational thought, increase their ability to cry tenfold, and entirely vanquish their fashion IQ. I mean, for God's sake, *I look like a taxicab with dyed-to-match shoes*.

I think my sister, Nicole, innately understands my genetic inability to deal with marriage. Nicole, my vaguely younger sister, got married five years ago to her college sweetheart, Chet. A sincerely great guy. So storybook-touching it almost made me puke. But she was smart enough to plan the whole thing while I was backpacking through Europe. I returned just in time to slip into a pale pink spaghetti-strap dress and march down the aisle along with four of Nicole's nearest and dearest girlfriends.

The photos from that day are beautiful. People are joyful and excited, and then there's me. My eyeliner smeared into raccoon eyes and my pale pink dress so close to my skin tone that it looks like flesh.

Yeah, that's me. I'm the haggard naked chick on the left.

Nicole knew what I've suspected for a very long time. Weddings just aren't my bag.

july 10th

We're in Frutto di Sole, a little Italian restaurant in the West Village that we've been coming to since the day we graduated college. Small and cozy, it's filled with checked tablecloths, cheap wine, and woven baskets of flour-dusted bread. Its owner, Rocco Marconi, a stocky old man with a Neapolitan accent,[9] calls our favorite table—the one in the back near the fireplace—the "Sirens" table. He claims it's because my girlfriends and I are so pretty. But I know it's because we're louder than most emergency vehicles. Which makes sense, because Frutto di Sole is where we toast promotions and curse unfaithful boyfriends. Where we celebrate birthdays and mourn birthdays. Depending on the year.

But tonight, Mandy, Jon, Stephen, and I have come just to relax and spend time together. Something that's been difficult to do since Mandy and Jon got engaged. Except it's already 8:30 P.M. and Stephen's late.

MANDY
So we've decided that you and Stephen should
get married.

Here it comes. The international conspiracy of married people just itching to have you join their cult.

ME
Like I've told you before, Stephen and I are happy
with the way things are. Besides, I'm in no rush to
get married. Maybe I'll *never* get married.

You should see them shudder when I use that one.

---

9 Despite the fact that he's from Bayside, Queens.

JON
Single women always say that.

Did I mention that Jon's a real ass? And that Mandy could
have done a lot better if she hadn't freaked out when she
saw thirty approaching?

ME
Well, some of us mean it.

MANDY
Of course you do. It's just that you and Stephen
have been going out for almost a year now. You guys
are great together. He adores you and he's gainfully
employed. Why wouldn't you get married?

ME
I've known the cashier at my dry cleaner for over a
year now and he's gainfully employed. Why don't
I marry him?

MANDY
Because Stephen's in *software development*. It's the
plastics of the 21st century.

ME
You sound like your mother.

MANDY
Yes. And my mother's a very smart woman. You'd be
wise to follow her example.

Mandy's mother—like her mother before her—is a stickler
for detail, a tyrant for tradition, and a devotee of Emily
Post. Oh yeah, and she married the senior legal counsel for
a huge conglomerate. Thankfully Mandy has broadened
the example to include a career—in real estate.

ME

Well, you're right about one thing. Stephen and I are
happy. Things are perfect. So why screw it up
by getting married?

JON

It sounds like you're in denial. No offense.

ME

Don't be ridiculous. Why would your telling me I'm
in denial offend me, Jon? On the contrary, it
strengthens my belief that married people push
single people to wed because they're uncomfortable
with their *own* decision to devote themselves
exclusively to one person for the rest of their lives.

That's right, Jon. Smell the coffee. No more Winona Ryder
fantasies for you, you little perv.

MANDY

Well, it wouldn't hurt you to at least consider
marriage. Let's face it, you're not
twenty-five anymore.

ME

So?

MANDY

So if you don't want kids that come through a mail-
order catalog, you'll need to settle down soon.[10]

JON

Plus, looks don't last forever.

---

[10] Why do people keep telling me to "settle down"? I *am* settled. I'm Associate
Features Editor of *Round-Up* magazine. I have cable television. I get junk mail in
my own name!

Jeez, I hate this guy.

Sure, I think about getting married. How could I not with all this badgering? But it doesn't feel right yet. It's not my time. It may never be my time. And that's okay. I'm a well-educated, intelligent woman who loves her career and has plenty of friends. And yes, I have a terrific boyfriend. I'm really happy. So why do I need to get married?

The answer is, I don't. And I certainly don't need to be married in order to have kids. Anyone who's ever played Doctor knows that. Besides, I can always offer sanctuary to Jon and Mandy's devil offspring, who will undoubtedly grow to loathe and despise their father the minute they gain the ability to understand the English language.

ME

Oh, Jon. You always know exactly what to say.

july 12th

Stephen and I first met at a birthday party for our mutual friend James. In his birthday cheer it occurred to James that Stephen, recently split from his onerous ex-girlfriend Diane, and I, single for so long that I'd blocked it from my memory, might hit it off. We did.

I knew nothing about computer programming and he'd never read *Round-Up*. But we both liked Dick Francis novels, Chinese food, and having sex. I don't exactly remember how that came up, but it did. So we did. Three nights later in his apartment. And for the record, it was *really* good.

But that night at James's party I had no idea that the sex would be so good. All I knew was that this handsome, thirty-one-year-old guy with light brown hair, hazel eyes, and a smile that tilted to the left was single and didn't seem

like a stalker. Furthermore, he was intelligent (his knowledge of politics extended beyond sound bites), he was charming (he told me I had the prettiest blue eyes he'd ever seen), and he was endearingly awkward (after mistakenly calling me "Ann" he apologized profusely, then blushed for the next twenty minutes).

But what I remember most from our first meeting was his willingness to laugh.

Soulful and embracing, that laugh enveloped me. And I was gone. Lost in the euphoric haze that precedes first kisses and tells your heart to beat faster.

Four months later, after dating steadily, I happened to be searching Stephen's wallet for change of a twenty. Instead I found a picture of myself. Lovingly protected in a clear plastic slip and tucked neatly behind his driver's license — there I was, asleep in a hammock during a trip we'd taken to Fire Island. The words "Amy takes a nap" had been lightly inscribed on the reverse side with a pencil.

Right then, I fell in love.

july 15th

Stephen and I played hooky today. Instead of going to work we went to the beach.

It's one of Stephen's most attractive qualities — spontaneity.

Unlike the rest of us, when he gets an idea in his head he actually pursues it with gusto. So while my inner voice is telling me that I have to go to work and be a dutiful employee, Stephen's inner voice is saying, "Mmmm . . . beach weather." And it's not like he's irresponsible. In fact, it's his hyper sense of responsibility that keeps him at the office for twelve-hour days. But today he saw an opportunity and

seized it. So who was I to be a party pooper? Besides, I may be a control freak, but even I recognize the value of occasionally cutting loose.

Or at least I did the minute my toes were wiggling through the sand and the ocean breeze was fluttering across my bare skin. And when my mind wandered back to work and deadlines and calls I had to make, Stephen gently calmed me with a kiss.

Mandy's mother is wrong. A ring couldn't possibly make this any better.

july 17th

On a superficial level, summer is pure fun. Concerts in the park, tons of daylight and iced tea. But the truth is that Memorial Day to Labor Day is like one big walk down the aisle.

It's difficult not to feel a little disenfranchised.

Invitations fill your mailbox. Wedding dates thwart vacation plans. And television commercials use tearful fathers[11] walking their "little girls" toward the altar in an effort to massage our heartstrings and awaken our fears so that multinational companies can sell us everything from expensive champagne to wedding insurance.

The business of marriage is being rammed down our throats and my gag reflex is working overtime.

For a person who's not engaged, I find myself thinking about marriage a lot. Which can't be healthy. It's like thinking about an insulin shot when you're not a diabetic. It'd be a fabulous boost but would ultimately kill you.

---

[11] Why do we still assume fathers are paying for these events?

Not that marriage itself is bad. But the Cult of the Married is lethal. It annoys me, angers me, and, more often than I care to admit, it makes me feel like utter crap. As if being single says more about me than the fact that I don't have a husband.

> Humiliating: When people want you to marry so they can stop "worrying" about you. So they won't feel obligated to call you on the weekend or live in fear that when you're old and alone you'll expect them to entertain you.

The minute I expect Jon to entertain me is the minute I welcome anyone with a side arm to blow a bullet through my brain.

> Frustrating: When the love bug bites married people so hard that it causes amnesia. Suddenly all their memories prior to marriage are erased and they're unable to fathom another lifestyle.

This IS Mandy. Trust me, back when we were nineteen Mandy was *not* looking to get married. Sure, there were girls who were. But not Mandy. She wanted to lay anything that moved and wore a football jersey. Choosy she wasn't. And marriage was certainly not on the agenda. But here she is years later, reincarnated as her mother, preaching to the Single on the evils of going it alone.[12]

> And the Ultimate Nail in the Coffin of Decency: The fact that men are rarely badgered on the topic of marriage.

---

[12] "Alone" being defined as any state other than legally married. As if Stephen is simply a sexy mirage.

Sure, the times they are a-changin' and the occasional homophobic parent will prod their son toward marriage. But parity on this subject? No way. When I'm with Stephen no one utters a word about our getting married. And if they do, they let it rest with our initial response that we're not interested. None of the needling and shaming. And among men, forget about it. It's rare that any man will turn to another man and say, "Hey, Joe, shit or get off the pot." NO man wants the responsibility of pushing his friend to the altar.

It's like aggressively advocating vasectomy to your best buds—there are certain regions of life you just don't mess with.

july 18th

After a particularly taxing day at work Stephen came over to my apartment, where we went to bed early and played Connect the Dots.

With a can of whipped cream.

Anything that is vaguely round on your partner's body qualifies as a dot. You'd be surprised how many portions of the male anatomy are round.

july 30th

Stephen's been distracted and edgy these past two weeks and it's starting to get on my nerves. Last night he became apoplectic because I made plans to see Anita on Saturday night when he and I had already agreed to see a movie. So I'll reschedule with Anita, right? Wrong. It was like I'd told him I was planning on canceling his cable just

before the playoffs. "How could you do that? What were you thinking?!"

"I was thinking it'd be nice to see Anita. But it's fine. I'll just see her some other time."

"I certainly hope so, because we have *plans*. We've *planned* to go to the movies."

"Relax. You're totally overreacting."

This is where he became defensive. "I'm not overreacting. I'm reacting in a manner that is perfectly acceptable, considering the fact that we made plans, days in advance, which you completely forgot about. Now tell me you honestly can't understand what the problem is here."

"Okay. I honestly can't understand what the problem is here."

It wasn't the response Stephen was hoping for. But he was pissing me off. And I really didn't appreciate him acting like I was the one with a problem. One thing I'm sure of—*I* don't have a problem.

As much as I hate to admit it, I think the end is near. Either he's trying to precipitate a breakup or he's getting really possessive. Either way, it's a clear signal to bail. Which is depressing as hell. It's not like I was planning on marrying the guy, but I was positive we'd last well into my thirties. He just seemed so right for me. He's intelligent, he's handsome, and he likes four of my five favorite things: laughing, eating, reading, and sex. So what if he's not big on shopping?

And I was actually beginning to tolerate his fanatic love of sports![13]

How could this not work out? Why are some people destined for good fortune in relationships while the rest

---

[13] Okay, fine. Maybe I wasn't learning to tolerate his love of sports. But I was definitely learning to ignore it.

🍸 LAURA WOLF

of us play giddyap on the merry-go-round of losers and creeps?

Maybe I should just break up with him tomorrow night and see Anita on Saturday. After all, I haven't seen her since she started her new job at *Teen Flair* magazine. Maybe she knows someone I could go out with. Maybe there's a cute sixteen-year-old in her "Acne Before the Prom" focus group. Or maybe I should find a really old guy who's been divorced a couple of times. Someone who wants to subsidize our purely meaningless fun . . .

Ick.

What am I talking about? I can't dump Stephen. I mean, I could, but I don't want to. I love him. I was about to suggest we move in together. This is just my defense mechanism kicking in. But it's always better to be the dumper than the dumpee. Right? And what if he's about to give me the boot? Shouldn't I spare myself the humiliation?

Absolutely!

Except I can't imagine living without him.

august 1st

I'm getting married!!!!!!!!

august 1st—11 P.M.

Stephen's been a pain in the ass because he was so nervous about ASKING ME TO MARRY HIM! Some jerk at his office told him this horrible story about proposing to a woman. Instead of saying yes the woman turned him down, told him off, then married his brother. No wonder

Stephen was a mess. He *hates* his brother. But so do I! And now we're getting married!

There I was at the movie theater concessions counter with Stephen, about to see the new Jackie Chan film, wishing that I were going to see the new Sandra Bullock movie instead, still deliberating whether or not I should break up with Stephen before he dumps me when—Boom! Before I can ask for a medium Diet Coke and a bag of Gummi Bears, Stephen drops to one knee and asks me to marry him. In front of everyone. I couldn't believe it. The next thing I know, the women on line are screaming for me to say yes and some guy at the back is yelling at us to hurry it up so he can get his nachos and Sprite before the previews start and all I can think is—

How much I love Stephen.

How this feels more right than anything else in the world.

How I wish I could stop crying long enough to say "YES!"

And who the hell orders *nachos* at the movie theater?

august 2nd—3 A.M.

I can't sleep. Every time I close my eyes the words "I'm getting married!" roar through my head. It's definitely surreal. But does it count if I haven't told anyone yet? Is it like when a tree falls in the woods and no one hears it? Or is that "No one can hear you scream in space"? I don't know. I can't think straight. My mind just keeps spinning and spinning like a ballerina pumped full of amphetamines.

Holy shit! "YES."

Just one word and my whole future has changed. I can't handle this. *I am going to explode.*

I had to wake Stephen up.

ME
Do you realize that this is the only moment in our entire lives when only you and I know that we're engaged? We should cherish this moment.

Stephen's eyes vaguely crack open.

STEPHEN
You're right, honey. I do cherish it.

His hand reaches out limply to stroke my arm.

STEPHEN
But could we talk about it tomorrow? I've got an 8 A.M. conference call and I really need to sleep.

Puckering his lips, he manages a kissy sound before passing out.

Do I get annoyed that he won't cherish this moment with me, or do I rejoice that even at 4 A.M. he's considerate enough to call me "honey" before blowing me off to go back to sleep? I go with loving and responsible. After all, he does have an 8 A.M. meeting and he could have gone back to his apartment to sleep, but he wanted to spend our engagement night together.

I'm marrying a man who's romantic AND gainfully employed. What a rush! Good-bye, losers!

- Jonas the painter: An "abstract-impressionist"?
- Anthony the inventor: Who's going to wear Velcro swimwear?

- Rick the conga drum player: Constantly sweet-talked me into doing his laundry. What was I thinking?

It all seems like ages ago. As if my decision to marry has suddenly put decades of distance between my life before Stephen and now. Our commitment to each other has solidified our union and built this impregnable wall around us. This is forever.

august 2nd

Work was a complete waste today. I couldn't stop smiling and I had the attention span of an A.D.D. poster child. I was certain that someone would figure it out. I mean, for Christ's sake, I was glowing! All during the department meeting—glow, smile, glow, smile, glow, smile . . .

But no one noticed. Which is strange, because I work at New York's least read magazine. No one ever smiles. Or glows.

Further complicating matters was the fact that I couldn't tell anyone about my engagement. I decided on my way to work that my mother should be the first person to know. After all, she gave me life, right? It's a matter of respect. So here I was with the greatest news since control-top pantyhose and I'd sworn myself to silence.

Silence isn't my style. Just ask my secretary, Kate, who pops Advil throughout the day and routinely complains of carpal tunnel syndrome when I dictate letters.

I decided to take the commuter train upstate this weekend and tell my mother in person. Face-to-face so we can embrace in this most intimate of mother-daughter moments.

The minute I got to my office I called to tell her I'd be arriving on Friday night.

Unfortunately the woman who gave me life is too busy to see me for the next two weeks.

School starts in less than a month and she's got to prepare a new curriculum for her fourth-grade class. So I'll wait. I may have to staple my mouth shut, but I'll wait so those lice-infested, snot-encrusted nine-year-olds can have a shot at a decent education. But it's worth it. After all, how many times does a girl get to tell her mother she's getting married?

august 3rd

This silence thing is killing me. Stephen thinks I'm crazy. I think I'm driving him crazy. He's the only one I can talk to about the engagement so I've called him forty-six times since yesterday morning. That's approximately once every half hour. I've gotten no work done and he's forwarded his calls to voice mail.

So in an effort to contain myself I channeled my exuberance toward a worthy cause: shoe shopping.

I pass the Kenneth Cole shoe store every day, and this was the first time I noticed the display of bridal shoes in the window. After work I tried on a pair of simple, classic, reasonably priced white satin sling-backs. I actually considered buying them before it occurred to me—

I'VE ONLY BEEN ENGAGED FOR SEVENTY-TWO HOURS AND ALREADY I'M BUYING FOOT-WEAR?!

Talk about overzealous. It's like preparing the spit before you've shot the pig. How Mandy of me! So I hurried

out of the store and bought a low-fat blueberry muffin instead.[14]

august 5th

I don't understand why people have such trouble organizing weddings. All you need is a good list.

Luckily, I'm the list queen.

I've always made lists. That's why I'm so good at my job. I'm organized and in control. I'm on top of the situation, always. As a fast-rising magazine editor I've overseen articles on housing scandals, crack babies, and boat shows. Not to mention a six-part series on yo-yo dieting. I think I can handle a wedding.

It drives me nuts to think that people like Mandy actually spend thousands of dollars to hire a wedding planner. Sure she wants everything done "just right," but how about putting that money into something practical? Like an IRA. Or a new vacuum cleaner. Those are investments. But thousands of dollars on a wedding planner? Another couple thousand on flowers? Not to mention the million-dollar dress you only wear once. Forget it. I refuse to wake up in debt the day after my wedding.

---

[14] But not by choice. Trust me, delusion doesn't live here. . . . She's over at Jenny Craig's house. They were sold out of my favorite full-fat chocolate chip muffins with the powder sugar top.

LIST OF THINGS TO DO
FOR WEDDING:

1. Choose wedding date
2. Tell boss wedding date
3. Vacation time for honeymoon
4. Decide on honeymoon
5. Get minister
6. Choose reception venue
7. Make guest list
8. Choose maid of honor
9. Choose best man
10. Register for gifts
11. Arrange for engagement party
12. Buy engagement ring
13. Buy wedding rings
14. Buy wedding dress
15. Choose maid of honor dress
16. Order wedding cake
17. Hire caterer
18. Hire band for reception
19. Order flowers for ceremony
20. Buy shoes

august 6th

It started as a lark. Since I can't actually talk about my wedding I figured I should at least use my time wisely and get all the planning out of the way. You know, zip through that "Things To Do" list, then get back to the important things in life, like my story ideas for the October

issue of *Round-Up*. So, looking for guidance, I stopped at the newsstand to buy a bridal magazine.

Except it wasn't that simple.

I work in the magazine industry and even I never realized how many bridal magazines there are. And they cost a fortune. Ten dollars a pop? That's what some guys get for sperm donations. And sperm's got a longer shelf life. These magazines are useless after I'm married. Even if I give them to a girlfriend, she's got to get married within the next year or the dresses will be out of fashion, the prices will have changed, and the vendors will have moved.

And they're 90 percent ads.

But which one to buy? I probably should've waited to ask Mandy, but I still have eight LONG and TORTUR-OUS days of silence left, and I see no reason to be idle. So I purchased ten. I'm too busy *living* to waste a second agonizing over how to choose a bridal magazine.

august 7th

After studying the bridal magazines and weeding through all the advertisements, it seems I left a few things off my list.

Although only freaks and Mandys would seriously consider numbers 30, 31, 36, 38, and 39.

LIST OF THINGS TO DO FOR WEDDING (AMENDED):

1. Choose wedding date
2. Tell boss wedding date
3. Vacation time for honeymoon
4. Decide on honeymoon
5. Get minister
6. Choose reception venue
7. Make guest list
8. Choose maid of honor
9. Choose best man
10. Register for gifts
11. Arrange for engagement party
12. Buy engagement ring
13. Buy wedding rings
14. Buy wedding dress
15. Choose maid of honor dress
16. Order wedding cake
17. Hire caterer
18. Hire band for reception
19. Order flowers for ceremony
20. Buy shoes
21. Plan rehearsal dinner
22. Invites to rehearsal dinner
23. Hire musicians for ceremony
24. Decide on dress code
25. Get marriage license
26. Hire videographer
27. Hire photographer
28. Order table flowers

29. Order bouquets
30. Order boutonnieres for men
31. Order nosegays for women
32. Order invitations
33. Decide on wine selection
34. Postage for invitations
35. Choose hairstyle and makeup
36. Buy gifts for attendants
37. Buy thank-you notes
38. Announce wedding in newspaper
39. Buy headpiece

august 9th

I showed my list to Stephen. After looking it over he felt confident that I'd remembered everything. And just as I suspected, he agrees that we should not, under any circumstances, allow our parents to get involved with the planning. Stephen's folks live only a few towns away from my parents upstate, so it's not like it'd be impossible for them to commute to the city and help. But where my parents can be overbearing, especially my mother, the Stewarts are just plain insane. That's Stephen's word, not mine.

Mr. Stewart owns an electrical repair company and Mrs. Stewart's an interior decorator with a passion for dogs—in particular, her little chow named Chuffy, whom she carries everywhere in her handbag. The Stewarts separated ten months ago after thirty-five years of marriage. Mr. Stewart now lives in a bachelor pad across town and is dating a woman with whom Stephen and his brother, Tom, went to high school. Perhaps "insane" doesn't really begin to capture

the family gestalt. In any event, we'll take their money with sincere gratitude, then handle all the details ourselves.

Actually, it looks like *I'll* be handling most of the details. Although I've been given the enviable responsibility of overseeing next fall's "Faces in the City" issue of *Round-Up*, Stephen's entire company is relying on him to complete production of a new software program by June so they can release it in September. He hasn't got a moment of free time. So he's agreed to let me handle all the wedding details—except the band, which he wants to choose. The only thing he asks is that the meal be "real." He hates finger food.

Not a problem. I've got plenty of time, my trusty list, and an easygoing fiancé who I adore.

How hard can this be?

august 10th

ittle Women was on TV tonight. Overwhelmed with love, Professor Bhaer proposes to Jo in the pouring rain.

No movie theater, no concession stand, no artificial butter-flavored popcorn. Just romance.

august 11th

t's my first mini-crisis. The Maid of Honor Dilemma. Mandy, Anita, or my sister, Nicole? It seems so small and insignificant a decision, but the more I think about this the bigger the problem gets. A misstep so early in the wedding process could seriously cripple my chances for smooth and

harmonious sailing, not to mention lay the foundation for years of bitterness and latent hostility.

I guess Nicole's the easiest to edge out since she didn't ask me to be her maid of honor, and honestly, we may be sisters but we're not that close. I mean, let's be real. She's Mr. Coffee and I'm a double espresso. Blood may be thicker than water, but unlike me, she'd know exactly what cleansing product to use to get it out of your carpet.

But Mandy or Anita? My yin or my yang? I'm not Mandy's maid of honor, and Anita will never have a maid of honor, since hell will freeze over before she ties the knot, so I can't use the "payback" principle. On a practical level, Mandy is better able to handle the responsibilities. After all, she is the repository of all wedding knowledge. And I doubt Anita even knows about bridal showers, let alone that it's the maid of honor's responsibility to throw one. But certainly a party spearheaded by Anita would be significantly more fun than the Stepford Wives luncheon Mandy's likely to pull together.

It's the difference between Sabrina the teenage witch and Buffy the vampire slayer. Neither is truly "right" for the job, but somebody's got to do it.

august 13th

I went over to Stephen's apartment last night to work on the wedding.

We decided on an evening ceremony with "festive attire," which means sharp and elegant. Although Stephen and his best man will definitely wear tuxedos. After all, Stephen *is* the groom.

But it wasn't the planning that alarmed me that evening. It was his apartment. I've been there a hundred times since

we started dating. We've had meals there, entertained friends there, had sex in his bedroom, his bathroom, and on his kitchen floor. But this visit was different. This was the first time I ever really *looked* at his apartment. The apartment of the man with whom I am going to share my life and my living space. Sure, it's well-lit and fairly clean, but when did it get so TACKY?!

Is he going to keep that horrible plaid couch after we're married? Not to mention the light-blue toilet seat, the collection of plastic cups from his favorite sporting events, the neon bar sign that reads "HOT ICE," and don't get me started on the entertainment center with the remote-controlled doors.

Sure, these things were cute and fun when we were dating, but now that we're going to be sharing an apartment they're positively TERRIFYING. I can't live with a neon bar sign.

Never before have I thought about the concept of joint property. His stuff is my stuff and my stuff is his. By virtue of our marriage I practically own that entertainment center. What an awesome sense of culpability that brings. And whoever thought I'd be the proud owner of a vintage 1990 *Playboy* magazine featuring Pamela Anderson as Playmate of the Year? On a brighter note, I also own the foot massager, the big-screen TV, and the framed Ansel Adams prints.

But the couch!

august 14th

I went two weeks, two TORTUROUS weeks, without telling anyone about my engagement because I felt it was important to tell my mother first, in person, at our monthly

family meal. After all, she *is* the one who gave me life. Did she not birth me? Did she not scream in agonizing labor for thirty-six hours so that I could come into existence?

I actually kept quiet about the most outrageous thing that's happened to me since my orgasmic one-night stand with the guy who played Tom Cruise's younger brother in that pirate movie. That's right. I slept with what's-his-name. But this was bigger. Better. The best news I've ever had, and I saved it for my dear sweet mother.

Who couldn't have been less enthusiastic if she'd been doped up on cough syrup.

Sure, she smiled. She hugged me. She told me how happy she was and how great she thinks Stephen is. But then she turned around and finished scrubbing the grout on the kitchen counter.

No champagne. No euphoria-induced prancing throughout the house. Just grout. Grout so clean you could perform invasive surgery on it.

Dad gave me a hug. A big generous hug followed by a litany of questions ranging from how it felt to be engaged to whether Stephen's family was planning on splitting the expenses.

And while Chet and Nicole congratulated me, there was none of the weeping hysteria I was expecting from classics like *Beaches* and *Steel Magnolias*.

NICOLE
That's terrific. I'm really happy for the two of you.

ME
That's it?

That's our *femme à femme* bonding? Thirteen years I share a bedroom with you and that's all you've got to give?

NICOLE
What do you mean, "That's it?"

ME
I mean, here I am sharing some pretty incredible
news. No, correct that. The *most* incredible news
I've ever told you –

NICOLE
I don't know. Sleeping with the guy from the pirate
movie was pretty cool.

ME
Cool, yes. Incredible? No!

CHET
What guy?

NICOLE
The one who played Tom Cruise's younger bro—

ME
Can we focus here? I'm getting married and all you
can say is "I'm happy for you"?

NICOLE
Well, I am happy for you, Amy. Stephen's a really
nice guy and I know you love each other. I guess I'm
just a little surprised.

ME
By what?

NICOLE
By the fact that you're actually getting
married. I've never thought of you as the
marrying kind.

There it is. Here we go. The gloves are off.

ME

What's that supposed to mean? What's the marrying
kind? And why am I not it?!

NICOLE

I just can't imagine you settling down with one
person.

CHET

Did you and Stephen consider living together first?

ME

Yeah, but we decided to get *married* instead.

Thank God Stephen was sick with the flu and didn't witness this delightful family tableau.

NICOLE

I didn't mean it as an insult. I just meant that some
people seem better suited to marriage than others.
Maybe that's just a part of your personality that I'm
not aware of.

ME

How could you not be aware of that? Even Mandy's
mealymouthed fiancé, Jon, knows that I'm the
marrying kind. He thinks it's a great idea!

CHET

Jon, the guy you said had the IQ of dog shit
on a stick?

ME

Yeah, Chet. That's the one. And by the way, thanks
for listening.

I can't believe this! Chet is a Social Studies teacher at the neighborhood junior high. Nicole is a paralegal for a local law firm. They *are* Ward and June Cleaver. So why are they advising me to live with Stephen instead of marrying him? My head began to spin and for the first time in my life I literally could not speak.

Why wasn't my family happy for me? Was I expecting too much? Or did they know something I didn't? Had I jumped too quickly? Was I making a mistake?

My palms were suddenly cold and clammy, and as I walked to the living room, I realized that my feet had gone numb. Thank God Gram was sitting on the sofa.

GRAM
I heard the exciting news. How wonderful!

Gram moved in with my parents after my grandfather died two years ago. It seemed the natural thing for her to do. Once a large, regal woman who had won a slew of tennis trophies, she had gracefully shrunk to become a silver-haired septuagenarian who insists that she's 5'5" although we all know she's 5'2". My only surviving grandparent, she has always been my favorite.

GRAM
Your Stephen's an absolute doll.

ME
Thanks, Gram. That means a lot to me.

GRAM
He's so dark and handsome. Just like Clark Gable.

ME
No, Gram. That was Jeremy. Stephen's shorter.
Lighter hair. You know, more of a runner's build.

GRAM
The Dan Quayle look-alike?

ME
Dan Quayle?

GRAM
A little around the face, but it doesn't matter. Come
here. Let me give you a big Grandma hug.

And just then, as she stood up from her armchair to give me
a hug, she tripped over the television cord and fell to the
ground. It was pretty horrifying. She didn't scream too
much, but it was clear from her expression that she was in
excruciating pain. The whole family had to carry her back
to the sofa. And while nothing was broken, she must have
smacked her head on the ground, because she kept complaining of a ringing in her ears. We spent the rest of the
evening bringing her tea and adjusting her pillows.

All because she wanted to give me a congratulatory hug.
Now, *that's* the spirit.

august 15th—12:30 A.M.

I just couldn't contain myself. The moment I got back from
upstate I had to call everyone. Sure, it was 11:45 P.M.,
but good news is good news no matter when you get it. And
wouldn't my dearest friends want to hear my good news regardless of what time it was?

—Hey, Mandy.
—It's a quarter to twelve.
—Yeah, at night. Listen, I'm sorry to wake you, but I've
got great news to tell you.

—No, actually it can't wait. If it could wait, I wouldn't be calling you at midnight, now would I?

—I'm *not* getting testy. Just listen to me. Stephen and I are getting married. Isn't that wonderful?

—No, we haven't set a date yet.

—Of course I remember that your wedding is on September 20th. You call me every friggin' day about it.

—Do you really think that I would schedule my wedding on the same day as yours?

—What's that? What's Jon saying? Oh, just put him on the phone.

—Yeah, that's right, Jon. You found me out. All the single girls just say they like being single. Boy are you clever. So listen, tell Mandy to call me tomorrow. And Jon, it's been a real pleasure sharing this intimate moment with you.

august 15th

Mandy called me back at 7 A.M. this morning. She apologized for being so sleepy last night, then got all crazy with excitement—but not before verifying that my getting married would not in any way conflict with my duties as her bridesmaid or interfere with her wedding. Clearly she's experiencing difficulty focusing beyond her own existence.

Freak.

We spent the next hour giggling like idiots . . . until Mandy asked if I was going to keep my name.

Of course I'm going to keep my name. I've been Amy Sarah Thomas my whole life. To suddenly change my name to Amy Sarah Stewart seems as logical as changing it to Amy Groucho Marx. Besides, I'm not Mrs. Stewart. Mrs.

Stewart is some recently divorced eccentric from upstate New York who carries a dog named Chuffy in her purse. I'm Ms. Thomas, a fast-rising magazine editor.

august 16th

I've spent the entire weekend calling people about the engagement. It's been educational. Just when you thought it was safe to divide the population into those who shave and those who wax, there appears a whole new criterion — those who can successfully feign enthusiasm and those who can't.

I just assumed that everyone would be delighted. After all, doesn't it signify my happiness and shouldn't that please my friends? Apparently not. People I figured would be mildly pleased were overwhelmed with joy and emotion, and those who I was certain would be elated weren't.

And I will never in my entire life forget who those people were. Yes, that *is* a threat. And a promise.

ANITA
Married? But why? You've always been so
anti-marriage.

ME
I'm not anti-marriage.

ANITA
Sure you are. You're the poster child for
non-legally-binding unions. You abhor
blood tests. Shirk at the thought of wearing
white. And you Krazy Glued your
toilet seat down.

ME

Is this some deeply coded way of congratulating me?

ANITA

Oh, screw congratulations. Of course I'm happy for
you. Stephen's a major piece of ass *and* he's got a
sense of humor. Just as long as you're certain this is
what you want.

Why would she ask such a thing?

august 17th

Last night was Stephen's turn to make the pilgrimage
upstate and tell his family about our engagement.
Considering his parents' acrimonious divorce he thought it
would be best if he went alone. Reading between the
lines—which in this case an illiterate could do—this means
that his parents are still duking it out over their financial
settlement, so the topic of marriage might not be met with
the usual enthusiasm.

Judging by the migraine that Stephen's had since his return, I think he was right. Apparently Mrs. Stewart was so
thrilled by the news that she fed Chuffy a fresh can of Beef
Feast before dissolving into a deep depression. Her comment, "My son's getting married. I'm getting old," set the
tone for the evening. After putting his mother and Chuffy
to bed, Stephen went across town to see his dad.

Mr. Stewart celebrated the news with a group hug:
Stephen, himself, and Misty—Mr. Stewart's new girlfriend
and Stephen's tenth-grade lab partner. Being wedged between his father's armpit and Misty's left breast was just

about all the happiness Stephen could take. But Misty insisted on a champagne toast. And though it's a gesture most clear-thinking adults would recognize as thoughtful and kind, Stephen was disgusted. He viewed it as Misty's self-serving attempt to ingratiate herself to the family, and specifically blames the champagne for his migraine.

And as the threesome drank champagne, Mr. Stewart made a toast. "To a happy marriage, and if necessary, a painless divorce!"

The minute he saw my jaw drop, Stephen knew he shouldn't have repeated it. I was livid. What kind of creep puts a divorce provision in the middle of a marriage toast?! But Stephen quickly reminded me that if I wanted to be pissed at his dad I'd have to take a number and get in line . . . behind him, his mom, his brother, and his sister. Apparently I have yet to earn my right to bitterness.

I met the Stewarts for the first time ten months ago. Mrs. Stewart had invited us to dinner so she and the rest of the family could meet me. Everyone was there, including Stephen's older brother, Tom, and his little sister, Kimberly.

It was a disaster. The entire family was completely nuts. Straight out of the Menendez family Christmas album. Mr. Stewart complained bitterly about the food, which Mrs. Stewart had made. Mrs. Stewart did her best to ignore him by spoon-feeding Chuffy at the table. Tom repeatedly told us how much smarter, better looking, and sexually active he is than his coworkers at the Xerox Corporation.[15] And Kimberly, who had recently graduated college and was about to start work at a local public-relations firm, was presented with a brand-new Honda Ac-

---

[15] Note to self: Consult doctor about the genetic probability of Stephen and I reproducing anything remotely resembling Tom.

Old farm machinery scattered over the valley floor near the abandoned farm of Tigh-na-Sleubhalch.

becomes a broad forest track, with the trees well set back so that it does not seem too claustrophobic, and firebreaks provide brief opportunities to enjoy the wider view. At the edge of the wood **67** turn off the forest track onto the narrower path to the right. Here a seat has been provided for those who would like to pause and enjoy the scenery. The end of Lochan Lùnn Dà-Bhrà can be seen, and for the first time since leaving Kinlochleven, a road. This is, in fact, following the line of the military road and provides an easy shorter walk into Fort William for anyone who needs it. The Way, however, now turns away from the old route for the very last time, and briefly plunges back into the woods.

Leave the woods by a very high stile **68** and climb straight up the small hill. This offers an even better view down over the whole of the lochan, in its setting of wild moorland and distant hills. The path now runs as a small terrace on the hillside with yet more dark woodland up ahead. But before the woods are reached the view opens out quite dramatically as Ben Nevis looms over the trees. The path now wriggles its way into the conifers, entering the woods via a wooden stile **69**. It crosses a mountain stream on a wooden bridge, and then heads straight on towards the mountain

ACKNOWLEDGMENTS

In praise of women . . .
All of whom helped to guide, shape,
and support this book.
My editor Kara Cesare, my literary agent Tracy
Fisher, Beth de Guzman, Cori J. Wellins,
and Lauren Sheftell.

In praise of friends . . .
Who took the time to read my early drafts
and to offer invaluable advice.
Garret Freymann-Weyr, Mikie Heilbrun, Albert
Knapp, Elizabeth Marx, Giuliana Santini,
and Matthew Snyder.

In praise of family . . .
Who have always given unwavering support
to my creative efforts, and who bear absolutely
no resemblance to the fictional families
that I've created.

And lastly to my father, who in a moment of
stunning clarity suggested I write a book.

For Karl
Who helped the writer to wake up
(And without whom I *never* would have been a bride)

A Delta Book
Published by
Dell Publishing
a division of
Random House, Inc.
1540 Broadway
New York, New York 10036

Book design by Lynn Newmark

Cataloging-in-Publication Data is on file with the Publisher.

ISBN: 0-385-33583-0

Manufactured in the United States of America

Published simultaneously in Canada

January 2002

10 9 8 7 6 5 4 3 2 1
BVG

Diary
of a
Mad Bride

Laura Wolf

Delta Trade Paperbacks

Diary of a Mad Bride

MY WEDDING WAS STARTING IN LESS THAN TWENTY MINUTES,

and I was stuck in a 7-Eleven parking lot with popcorn kernels wedged in my gums and vanilla ice cream melting on my dress. It was a disaster too large to comprehend. After an agonizing year spent planning my wedding, could it really end like this? The voices chronicling a year of wedding hysteria swirled in my head....

—My grandmother upon viewing my engagement ring

"What do you mean he gave you an emerald! Diamonds are eternal, emeralds say, maybe five years."

—My future father-in-law on the night of my engagement party

"To a happy marriage and, if necessary, a painless divorce!"

—My best friend, Anita

"Oh, screw congratulations. Of course I'm happy for you. Stephen's a major piece of ass and he's got a sense of humor. Just as long as you're certain this is what you want."

Would I survive this day after all....

There's no way I'm telling Barry about my concession-line proposal.

ME

Did you remember to wish Mr. Spaulding
happy birthday?

BARRY

His birthday isn't until June 15th. He's a Gemini.

ME

That's odd. He loved the birthday card I gave
him this morning.

And before you could say "brown-noser" he was out the door.

august 26th

I've decided to forgive Anita's less than enthusiastic endorsement of my wedding plans and ask her to be my maid of honor. She'll keep me laughing, honest, well dressed, and entertained—even if she maligns the concept of marriage in between shots of Jagermeister. Short of asking her to bear my child, it's the greatest compliment I can give her. And honestly, she's been my best friend since she hustled me into the ladies' room during a press conference, to inform me that I'd tucked my skirt into my pantyhose. So she deserves it. I just hope Mandy isn't too upset when she finds out.

Who am I kidding? Mandy's so self-absorbed these days she barely notices Jon.

ANITA

I know this is supposed to be an honor and
I'm flattered that you thought of me. But I just can't
get into it.

ME

What do you mean you can't get into it? Does that
mean you're saying no?

ANITA

Exactly.

ME

You can't say no. No one ever says no to that
question. Besides, you're my best friend. It's the
greatest compliment I can give you.

ANITA

Come on, Amy. You know how I feel about
marriage. From where I stand the only thing worse
than being someone's maid of honor would be
bearing their child.

august 28th

I knew Mandy would appreciate the maid of honor position. With her high regard for marriage and the "show of
shows" that are weddings, she would acquit herself ad-
mirably in the role. She will provide me with the perfect
balance of support, guidance, assistance—and, when necessary, fealty.

Crass as that sounds, I've begun to sense that fealty will

have its moments in this ritual. As will loose tea, pink balloons, and prissy little finger sandwiches at my Stepford Wives bridal shower.

ME

Listen, Mandy. You've been one of my best friends
since college and I can't think of a better way to
express my appreciation than to ask you to be my
maid of honor.

I practiced this speech several times before delivering it. I've cherished Mandy ever since she held back my hair while I vomited profusely from my first encounter with grain alcohol. So it was important to me that she knew my offer was sincere and heartfelt. Because it was.

But most of all I wanted to ensure that she'd say yes, because the thought of two people refusing to be my maid of honor was just too damn depressing.

MANDY

So you finally got around to asking me. I guess this
means Anita said no.

ME

Who told you?

MANDY

You did. Just now.

ME

Shit!

MANDY

What were you thinking, asking Anita to be your
maid of honor? That's like inviting Kate Moss to the
Betty Crocker Bake-Off.

ME
Well . . .

MANDY
Anyway, I'd be delighted to be your maid of honor.

ME
Oh thank goodness! It really means a lot.

MANDY
It should. You clearly need all the help you can get.
Although I can't possibly do anything until after
my own wedding.

ME
Of course. But what do you mean I need help? I've
got everything under control.

MANDY
Do you have a wedding date?

ME
No.

MANDY
A wedding dress?

ME
No.

MANDY
A wedding song?[16]

ME
No. But I've read all the bridal magazines and I've
compiled a detailed list of things to do.

---

[16] SONG?!

MANDY

No offense, but those magazines are worthless. With the possible exception of the one by Martha Stewart. Hey, she's not related to Stephen, is she?

ME

Not that I know of.

MANDY

Too bad. Anyway, the fact remains that any bride worth her floral budget knows that the single most essential tool when planning a wedding is the *Beautiful Bride* book.

So Mandy had been holding out on me. Sure, she *could* have mentioned the *Beautiful Bride* book weeks ago when I first announced my engagement. But no. She had to see me squirm until I finally got around to asking her to be my maid of honor. Talk about passive-aggressive.

Luckily I really do have things under control. The date and the dress can be chosen in under fifteen minutes. As for the song—has anyone ever heard a little ditty entitled "Here Comes the Bride"? Please. As much as I want to benefit from Mandy's experience, I refuse to succumb to her neuroses.

august 29th

Not surprisingly, *Beautiful Bride*'s glossy cover boasts a picture of an attractive blonde dressed like a bride. I've decided to name her Prudence.

Prudence has creamy white skin free of wrinkles, pores, and pimples. Her hair is molded into a massive bun that should protect her from falling debris in the event that she passes a construction site. But if she *is* wounded at a construction site, the tiaralike ornament mounted on top of her massive bun will undoubtedly transmit an emergency distress signal along any of the AM frequencies.

And don't for a minute think Prudence broke the bank on the tiara and skimped on the gown. Her elaborate taffeta dress could easily make bed skirts for all of Kensington Palace.

But what alarms me about Prudence is her smile.

It's big and long as if the corners of her mouth have been stretched back and taped to her earlobes, and her teeth, polished to a high-intensity white, bulge in an effort to break free.

It's the smile of someone struggling to convince herself she's happy.

august 30th

I introduced Stephen as my fiancé for the first time today. Very strange. It was like telling someone he's my brother. Or my gynecologist. It had to be a lie. How could he be my fiancé? That would mean I'm getting married. And how ridiculous is that?

So I dissolved into laughter.

august 31st

I have seen the future. It's not pretty.

Mandy's bridal shower was today. Her sister, Kendall, threw it in the Cranbrook Hotel. The Cranbrook is famous for its Women Only policy. When it realized that the policy had failed to ensure chastity within its hallowed halls it adopted a tacit, constitutionally illegal, albeit impossible to prove policy of no homosexuals. What a warm and embracing environment in which to celebrate love.

I only knew a handful of the shower guests from college. The rest were women whom Mandy had met over the years who share her love of shelter magazines, summers in the Hamptons, and QVC. Bubbly young women whose nail polish matched their lipstick and whose legs were always crossed.

For what seemed like an eternity we "oohed" and "aahed" over gifts, giggled innocently at lingerie barely racy enough to get a clock-radio started, and used the discarded ribbons to decorate a paper plate for Mandy to wear as a hat. As an expression of my affection and to assuage my guilt over not asking her to be my maid of honor first (especially since I was busted on it), I maxed out my credit card and bought Mandy an extraordinarily expensive tea set. I knew she'd love it. Martha Stewart did.

During this time I kept discussion of my own engagement to a minimum and actively avoided the topic of wedding proposals. The last thing I wanted was the outpouring of pity that my concession-stand wedding proposal was certain to elicit from this crowd.

The highlight of the event was seeing Mandy eat. She's been starving herself since May. If it's not steamed, poached, or in a Jenny Craig wrapper, she's not going for it. But today she celebrated by eating a slice of cake so thin you could shine a light through it. Afterward, to alleviate her potential consternation, one of the guests offered her an Ex-Lax. Clearly love has no bounds.

As I drank my peach-flavored iced tea I began to worry.

I don't want a bridal shower like this. A cookie-cutter affair that follows all the "rules" and bores me to tears. I'm not like those Bubbly Young Women. I'm creative. I'm rational. I don't cross my legs when I sit on the toilet! My bridal shower should be exciting. A gambling junket to Atlantic City. All-night club-hopping. Naked karaoke. Anything but a lobotomized gathering featuring laxatives and cake. Where's the fun in that?

Ugh.

september 1st

Beautiful Bride is closer to a computer circuitry book than a primer for weddings. It's filled with pointers, tips, rules, charts, diagrams, and a ton of very fine print.

I've only been engaged for a month and already I'm three months behind "schedule." Who knew I had a schedule? I don't even have a wedding date yet.

Additionally, it appears that I've left a number of very important items off my list.

Official THINGS TO DO List

1. *Choose wedding date*
2. *Tell boss wedding date*
3. *Vacation time for honeymoon*
4. *Decide on honeymoon*

5. Get minister
6. Choose reception venue
7. Make guest list
8. Choose maid of honor
9. Choose best man
10. Register for gifts
11. Arrange for engagement party
12. Buy engagement ring
13. Buy wedding rings
14. Buy wedding dress
15. Choose maid of honor dress
16. Order wedding cake
17. Hire caterer
18. Hire band for reception
19. Order flowers for ceremony
20. Buy shoes
21. Plan rehearsal dinner
22. Invites to rehearsal dinner
23. Hire musicians for ceremony
24. Decide on dress code
25. Get marriage license
26. Hire videographer
27. Hire photographer
28. Order table flowers
29. Order bouquets
30. Order boutonnieres for men
31. Order nosegays for women
32. Order invitations
33. Decide on wine selection
34. Postage for invitations
35. Choose hairstyle and makeup
36. Buy gifts for attendants

37. Buy thank-you notes
38. Announce wedding in newspaper
39. Buy headpiece
40. Buy traveler's checks for honeymoon
41. Apply for visas
42. Get shots and vaccinations
43. Order tent if necessary
44. Order chairs/tables if necessary
45. Make budget
46. Divide expenses
47. Make table-seating charts
48. Choose bridesmaid dress
49. Decide on menu
50. Decide on hors d'oeuvres
51. Decide on dinner-service style
52. Decide on staff-guest ratio
53. Decide seated or buffet
54. Reserve vegetarian meals
55. Reserve band/photographer/videographer meals
56. Make photo list
57. Choose hotel for wedding night
58. Hire limo for church-reception transport
59. Buy guest book for reception
60. Find hotel for out-of-towners
61. Decide on liquor selection
62. Hire bartenders
63. Verify wheelchair accessibility
64. Choose processional music
65. Choose recessional music
66. Choose cocktail music
67. Choose reception music

> 68. Choose ceremony readings
> 69. Prepare birdseed instead of rice
> 70. Schedule manicure/pedicure/wax

september 2nd

My parents keep their wedding album neatly filed between a biography of Eleanor Roosevelt and a Sidney Sheldon paperback that my baby-sitter left behind in 1976.

As kids, Nicole and I would flip through the album and laugh at how funny everyone was dressed. Our dad in a *beige* tuxedo. And Gram, impossible to miss, in her floor-length gown covered with giant gold sequins.

But now when I think about that wedding album it's my parents' youth that strikes me most. They were barely in their twenties. My father had just been hired as a manager at the local supermarket and my mother was studying for her teaching certificate. They had no idea what life had in store for them. Yet their joy is impossible to deny.

This is what I see in my relationship with Stephen—a love that's strong enough to brave an unknown future, joyfully.

september 4th

I met Mandy for lunch today. It's less than three weeks until her wedding, so I expected the usual hysteria about place cards and hors d'oeuvres and wine selections. But there was none. Far from hysterical, she was truly depressed. Apparently her mother and her aunt had a fight about her aunt not giving Mandy and Jon an engagement gift and now her aunt won't come to the wedding. It seems her aunt withholds gifts as a way of expressing her dissatisfaction. When pressed, she told Mandy's mother that she was dissatisfied with the graduation gift Mandy's family had given her own daughter three years earlier. It was too cheap and thoughtless. When Mandy's grandmother heard this she got so mad at the aunt that she decided to disinherit her. This made Mandy's cousins so angry that now they won't come to the wedding either. It all sounded ridiculously petty.

But it did make me appreciate my family. Bud and Terry Thomas may be stingy with their enthusiasm, but at least they're not dysfunctional. Which is good, because Stephen and I have chosen June 2nd as our wedding date, and nothing is more unpleasant than dysfunction under a hot summer sun.

september 5th

Wedding planners. What a joke. I've already made an impressive dent in my "Things To Do" list.

LAURA WOLF

Official THINGS TO DO List

1. Choose wedding date
2. Tell boss wedding date
3. Vacation time for honeymoon
4. Decide on honeymoon
5. Get minister
6. Choose reception venue
7. Make guest list
8. Choose maid of honor
9. Choose best man
10. Register for gifts
11. Arrange for engagement party
12. Buy engagement ring
13. Buy wedding rings
14. Buy wedding dress
15. Choose maid of honor dress
16. Order wedding cake
17. Hire caterer
18. Hire band for reception
19. Order flowers for ceremony
20. Buy shoes
21. Plan rehearsal dinner
22. Invites to rehearsal dinner
23. Hire musicians for ceremony
24. Decide on dress code
25. Get marriage license
26. Hire videographer

27. Hire photographer
28. Order table flowers
29. Order bouquets
30. Order boutonnieres for men
31. Order nosegays for women
32. Order invitations
33. Decide on wine selection
34. Postage for invitations
35. Choose hairstyle and makeup
36. Buy gifts for attendants
37. Buy thank-you notes
38. Announce wedding in newspaper
39. Buy headpiece
40. Buy traveler's checks for honeymoon
41. Apply for visas
42. Get shots and vaccinations
43. Order tent if necessary
44. Order chairs/tables if necessary
45. Make budget
46. Divide expenses
47. Make table-seating charts
48. Choose bridesmaid dress
49. Decide on menu
50. Decide on hors d'oeuvres
51. Decide on dinner-service style
52. Decide on staff-guest ratio
53. Decide seated or buffet
54. Reserve vegetarian meals
55. Reserve band/photographer/videographer meals
56. Make photo list
57. Choose hotel for wedding night

58. Hire limo for church-reception transport
59. Buy guest book for reception
60. Find hotel for out-of-towners
61. Decide on liquor selection
62. Hire bartenders
63. Verify wheelchair accessibility
64. Choose processional music
65. Choose recessional music
66. Choose cocktail music
67. Choose reception music
68. Choose ceremony readings
69. Prepare birdseed instead of rice
70. Schedule manicure/pedicure/wax

september 6th

According to *BB* I'm alarmingly late in reserving a venue for my wedding reception. Flirting with disaster. Treading that thin line between a life of happiness and a dream unfulfilled.

And it's starting to worry Prudence. I can tell by her refusal to blink.

It seems people typically reserve their venues a year in advance. I only have nine months. But I refuse to worry. If a human being can sprout in nine months from some spare biological matter, then I can plan a wedding. Besides, this is New York City. Not some little suburb with one church and a town hall. There are literally thousands of hotels, "event" spaces, and gardens for us to choose from. We could do a turn-of-the-century mansion, a hotel ballroom, a loft, a theater, a botanical garden, a private club, or a waterfront restaurant. And Lord knows, this city of sin isn't lacking in places of worship. Even Gomorrah had churches.

Besides, how bad can it be? After all, I'm going to be a June bride.

Holy shit.

september 8th

While compiling my guest list for the wedding[17] I realized that it's been a while since I've seen several of my friends.

This is strange, because I'm very social. I'm the one you call if you want to go out. I'm always up for a movie, a gallery show, or a meal. I love debating local politics and discussing career goals. Then it occurred to me that all these "lost" friends are married. I've only seen them a couple of times since their weddings. One by one my married friends have disappeared. How did this happen?

Where did they go?

I'm vowing here and now that THIS WILL NOT HAPPEN TO ME. I will not fall off the face of the Earth after June 2nd. I will not cease to exist.

I wonder if my married friends made the same vow?

september 9th—2 A.M.

I can't sleep. It's just occurred to me that marriage is emblematic for lodging.

The Jewish wedding canopy is symbolic of the roof on

---

[17] According to *BB*, you can't start looking for a reception venue until you know how many people you're inviting.

the couple's new home. The Catholic church is the *house* of the Lord. And then there's the "institution" of marriage, like the Institution of American Dentistry, which you "enter into," like a home, a supermarket, or a car wash. But do you ever come out? Will I fade into my friends' memories as that brunette with the great smile?

And what if the lodging is substandard, like a hut? Or a log cabin? Or a studio apartment with roaches and no hot water? Who do I complain to?

september 10th

I went to Frutto di Sole with the girls tonight. Anita, Jenny, Kathy, and Paula. We just laughed and bitched and ate really great bad food. I felt like I was back in college. Except Mandy wasn't there to complain about my use of profanity. She was too busy putting the fear of God into her wedding caterer.

Several times during the evening I thought to ask my girlfriends about wedding venues, dress suggestions, and creative party details . . . but I decided against it. I'm not going to be one of those brides who won't shut up about her wedding. As much as I love her, I'm no Mandy.

Furthermore, I'm going to make a point of doing this at least twice a month when I'm married. Going out with the girls. Kicking back and talking, maybe Rollerblading in the park . . . I just hope Stephen won't feel threatened. Forgotten. Left out. Neglected. Abandoned. Hurt. Ignored.

For Christ's sake! This is why I don't own a pet!

september 13th

Barry held the door open for me on the way into the conference room.

Something is very wrong.

september 14th

I went over to Stephen's apartment for dinner. We needed to buckle down and come up with a rough estimate on our guest list. And though I purposely sat on and tried to bond with his plaid couch, visions of Goodwill just danced in my head.

Since I always want sushi and he always wants Mexican, we generally compromise and order out for Chinese. But tonight Stephen surprised me with a homemade dinner. Seafood paella served by candlelight. And on our table was an ice sculpture the size of a milk carton, which Stephen himself had made.

The man can cook but he can't sculpt. He claimed it was a rose, and though I praised his artistry, I couldn't help but think how much it looked like a human brain. Shrinking and dripping before our very eyes onto a saucer. All through dinner—drip, drip, drip. And when I suggested that we move it away from the candles, Stephen insisted on keeping it where it was. Drip, drip, drip went the human brain.

Then, just as we were finishing dessert, and the human brain had shrunk to the size of a small tumor, I noticed something sparkling within it. Minutes later Stephen's hand-carved rose revealed a dazzling jewel. He plucked it out and slipping it onto my finger asked how I liked my engagement ring.

It was the most romantic, creative, thoughtful gesture. And the ring was sparkling and stunning and NOT A DIA-MOND.

It's a glorious emerald set in a gold band. Lovely and elegant but NOT A DIAMOND.

ME

Oh. Wow. It's an emerald. I don't know what to say.

STEPHEN

I'm so relieved you like it. I thought you might
prefer a diamond, but my grandmother convinced
me to give this to you. It belonged to her mother and
she's been keeping it all these years, waiting for one
of us to get married. I even had it sized to
fit your finger.

ME

Oh yeah, it fits great.

What could I say? It was his great-grandmother's ring. To refuse would be insulting four generations of his family. So what if his wedding proposal was cut-rate? The ring is stunning and he cooked me dinner and he hand-carved a human brain from a block of ice, but it's NOT A DIA-MOND.

I know this shouldn't bother me. After all, I'm the one who keeps insisting that we avoid the shackles of tradition, blah, blah, blah, but when else in my entire life am I going to get a diamond ring? Never. This was my one chance and I blew it.

EVERYONE IN THE ENTIRE WORLD
Your engagement ring is lovely.

ME
Thank you. It's a family heirloom.

EVERYONE IN THE ENTIRE WORLD
Ah, I was wondering why you didn't get a diamond.

Yeah, me too, asshole.

september 19th

Mandy's a walking time bomb. Say the wrong thing, touch her the wrong way, suggest she eat something more substantial than low-sodium consommé, and she'll snap your neck like a diseased twig.

But she smiled continuously from the wedding rehearsal to her rehearsal dinner at the oh-so-elegant Chez Jacques. And when Marcel, our snotty waiter, mistakenly referred to her as Madame instead of Mademoiselle, I swear I thought she'd take her butter knife to his heart. But her smile never once faltered. Like Prudence—only armed with cutlery.

And thank God for that cutlery, because the food was terrific. All sorts of delicacies you rarely get to eat because you're too old to order the children's portion but old enough to owe rent. Escargot, foie gras, baked brie, and pâté. Stephen and I ate everything that would fit in our mouths.

But not Mandy. No sluggishness, hangover, or water retention for this bride-to-be.

The highlight of the evening came when Mandy's dad made a toast. He praised her for growing up to be such a poised young woman. And while this made me suspect that he'd been out of town during her anguished search for place-card holders to coordinate with her burgundy organza overlays, it did make me teary. I mean, here was this sixty-something corporate lawyer who's spent the last forty years downsizing companies, facilitating hostile take-overs, and pink-slipping entire towns, choking up while publicly professing his love for his child. Sure, he'd deny his own mother medical treatment if her HMO didn't cover the procedure, but his love for his daughter was just so touching. In fact, the whole evening was loving and heartwarming and would have been perfect had Jon not been there. I mean, come on. Even *his* family doesn't seem to like him.

I can only imagine what tomorrow will bring.

As for our rehearsal dinner, I have to admit that I think it's old-fashioned to expect the groom's family to pay for it.[18] It's like a throwback to the days when women viewed their engagement rings as an insurance policy against their virtue. If they got dumped before the wedding, then their diamond's trade-in value would compensate for their sullied purity.

Well, these days purity is more about soap than sex, so I see no need to be prehistoric about our wedding costs. On the other hand, the Stewarts are a bit on the traditional side—except for Mr. Stewart's generationally challenged girlfriend. I wouldn't be surprised if they offered to pay for the whole thing. I just hope it's not too outlandish. As a decorator Mrs. Stewart spends every day preoccupied

---

[18] Although I'm certain the prospect of pawning their son off on another family was enough motivation for Jon's folks to shell out the cash.

 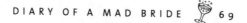

with appearance and taste and style. She may insist on turning it into a real "affair" at Le Cirque or Tavern on the Green.

I'd be happy with a celebratory gathering down in Chinatown. After all, nothing says I love you like a plate of sesame noodles.

september 20th

Talk about overkill. Mandy's wedding was more like a coronation than a blessed event. From the 250 guests to the doves and the horse-drawn carriage, EXCESS had its day. *Dynasty* meets Liberace, Marie Antoinette, and Cher.

And no, that's not the wind whistling. It's the jubilant cheers of a wedding planner putting an addition onto her house. Who knew Mandy's parents had so much disposable income?

Our pucker-mouth lemon dresses were UNDER-STATED in this setting. And Jon, what an idiot! He wore a morning coat at *night*. Do top hat and tails mean anything to anyone? If you're going to overdo it, at least do it right. Like Mandy. If you're going to act like a princess, then dress like one. Which she did. Right down to her ten-foot train that everyone stepped on. But she looked radiant.

The more weddings I see the more I thank God that I've got common sense. More is not necessarily better. Sometimes more is just annoying. The floral centerpieces, those damn out-of-season Holland tulips at 15.78 percent over their original quote, were so big that we couldn't see across our table.

And the entrees. Would you like fish or meat? The grilled

salmon or the beef medallions? How obvious. Where's the thought? The creativity?

And I know Stephen feels the same way. We simultaneously reached for each other's hand when the horse-drawn carriage appeared.

ME
Be afraid. Be very afraid.

STEPHEN
Trust me. I am.

And as one of the horses began to neigh uncontrollably, Stephen looked into my eyes, desperate.

STEPHEN
Please tell me you don't want livestock at our
wedding. Because honestly, I don't think I could
take the pressure.

Stephen can relax. The only animal at our wedding will be that jackass brother of his. In fact, Mandy's wedding really drove home how much I value Stephen and his down-to-earth sensibilities. It even helped me make peace with my engagement ring. So it's no marquis-cut diamond. Big whoop. It's stunning and it's unique.

september 22nd

A recent poll of my friends, presented as a potential story idea for the magazine, revealed what I suspected: My wedding proposal stank.

Margo: Husband delivered a personalized fortune cookie

to her at a Chinese restaurant. Done before? Sure. But it demonstrates good planning skills.

Mandy: Jon presented her with a two-carat diamond ring while they were watching the Boston regatta from his parents' waterfront penthouse. Proves the old adage: Birds of a feather . . .

Lisa: Hand in marriage asked for at Café des Artistes. No particular creativity, but illustrates ability to choose romantic locale.

Meghan: Got engaged while ice-skating at Rockefeller Center. Displays romance, youthful charm, and a solid knowledge of cheesy eighties movies such as *Ice Castles*.

Jessica: Husband proposed during a picnic lunch in an apple orchard. It doesn't get more Hallmark.

And then there's my SECRET SHAME . . .

Amy: The Multiplex Concession Stand Proposal.

Sure Stephen got down on his knee, and yes, we skipped the movie and celebrated with a nice dinner, but is this really the tale you want to tell for generations to come? Me, Stephen, and the unmistakable stench of stale popcorn? And it wasn't spur-of-the-moment. By his own account, this man who thrives on spontaneity had been planning it for months. He *chose* to ask me on the candy line. What does that say about him? What does it say about me?

september 23rd

Stephen and I have come up with a tentative guest list of seventy people, which I think is a nice intimate group for a meaningful experience. The last thing I want is one of those impersonal functions like Mandy's extravaganza where you're not sure whose wedding you're at.

"Did we take a wrong turn? Was it Ballroom Number One or Number Two?"

"Is this the Henson wedding or the Lieberman bar mitzvah?"

Size is especially important, since *BB* says the bride and groom are expected to personally thank each guest for attending the wedding. Smile and shake hands. Smile and shake hands. This would explain why Mandy was wearing a wrist guard by the end of her wedding. But there's no way I'm spending my big day shaking 250 hands. Not a chance. I won't have time to eat my pumpkin bisque.

Lobster risotto. Asparagus ravioli?

Our guest list includes friends and family, and allows everyone to bring their spouse or significant other. We decided that if someone's not seriously involved and they know other guests, then single folks will be invited alone. There's no reason to subsidize someone's dating life. And Lord knows Stephen's got plenty of cheapo friends who would just love to bring their gal du jour to a fancy wedding with a fabulous meal and an open bar—all free of charge. Well, forget it. That's what Club Med is for. Go buy some beads.

Besides, being realistic, I know that our parents will want to include some of their friends in the list, so we're bound to get up to eighty-five by the time all this is over.

Surprisingly, making the list, or rather agreeing on the list, was not as easy as I thought it would be. Stephen didn't want me to invite my friend Jane because he can't stand her, so I volunteered to bump her from the list on the condition that he not invite his ex-girlfriend Diane "I'm a Big Pain in the Ass" Martin. But he didn't want to bump Diane since she invited him (without me!) to her wedding last year and he didn't want to seem petty. I also wasn't so crazy about him inviting the guys he plays softball with on the weekends. I've only met them once. After hours of arguing we finally compromised with him inviting Diane and her husband but not the softball gang, and my not inviting Jane but getting to seat Diane off in some corner with my cousin Eddie, who suffers from chronic halitosis.

The one thing we immediately agreed on is that neither of us wants to invite Stephen's brother, Tom.

september 24th

I still slip occasionally and call Stephen my boyfriend. It's going to take a while to get used to calling him my fiancé. Especially without laughing. And by then it'll be time to call him my HUSBAND!

september 25th

Today was crazy. We had an early-morning staff meeting to discuss the December issue. I came armed with story ideas but somehow forgot that December means holiday issue. I've been spending so much time thinking about next June that the holidays just seem like a minor inconvenience on the way to the rest of my life. Needless to say, my pitches on sanitation negligence, cabbie cover-ups, and a profile on a woman who recycles hypodermic needles were met with hesitance. And when I quickly suggested a profile on city caterers (slyly figuring that the research could be useful to my wedding), Barry gallantly praised my "clever" idea, then sideswiped me by insisting that by the time the December issue hits the stands most of the city's caterers will be booked for the holidays. Meanwhile his lengthy list of story ideas ranged from the ever-trite "Who Are the Men Who Play Santa Claus" to a search for the perfect eggnog.

Like anyone really drinks eggnog.

In front of all the other editors, associates, and assistants, my boss, Mr. Spaulding, made a point of asking me to submit a new list of holiday-oriented pitches by tomorrow. A serious blow to my image of authority. Besides, it's going to be near impossible to make that list by tomorrow, since I looked at two potential reception venues after work today and have another one scheduled before work tomorrow morning.

The venues I saw tonight, a famous hotel and a swanky nightclub, were all wrong. The hotel ballroom was too big and the nightclub was fine until you turned up the lights. Both were incredibly expensive.

And our time is quickly dwindling. Soon we'll be eight months away from our wedding. According to *BB* we may as well elope. So to expedite the process, I've given Kate a list of thirty-five potential venues to call and make viewing appointments. After all, we really are open to anything.

Except boats and riverfront restaurants. Stephen has an aunt who's afraid of water.

september 26th

This morning we saw a photographer's loft down in Chinatown. Very hip, open, and all white. The right size for a group of eighty-five and could easily be transformed into a romantic setting with some clever decorations. The photographer even offered to throw in a couple of backdrops for free. But the neighborhood was too seedy. It's one thing to step over restaurant trash on your way to a celebrity photo shoot, but for a wedding reception?

I composed my list of holiday-oriented story ideas on the bus ride to work.

Kate's gotten in touch with twenty-two of the reception sites I asked her to call. Half were already booked for our date. She scheduled appointments for the remaining eleven. Unfortunately, Stephen's so busy with his project at work that it looks like I'll be seeing most of them myself. Hopefully Kate will be able to contact the remaining thirteen places.

As for the ceremony, Stephen and I have chosen a church on the Upper East Side—First American Presbyterian. Since Stephen's family is Presbyterian and my family is only vaguely Protestant, it makes the most sense. It's beautiful and classy and available for our date. We have an appointment to meet the minister next Saturday.

While Stephen thinks his mother will be disappointed that we're not being married by his family minister, Reverend MacKenzie, in the church that he attended as a child, he's fairly certain that she'll accept our decision to marry in the city. After all, First American is on the Upper East Side.

Besides, Stephen says Reverend MacKenzie gives him the creeps.

As for my parents, I'm certain they won't care. They didn't bat an eye when Nicole and Chet were married by Chet's renegade Baptist minister cousin who arrived five minutes before the ceremony after driving sixteen hours from Louisiana without stopping to shower. Trust me. The guy didn't shower.

I just hope my parents understand why I want to get married in the city instead of their backyard. Unlike Nicole, who's permanently ensconced herself in our hometown, I am no fan. Just going back to see my parents gives me the shakes. It's quiet, it's manicured, it's boring. It's like the whole place is on life support. Getting married there would be tantamount to running a lawn mower over my head.

Not to mention the fact that if we get married in the city, our folks will be too far away to attempt a coup. I've seen *Betsy's Wedding* a thousand times on cable and I'm determined that this wedding be our personal expression, not some parental fantasy come true.

september 29th

My mother and Gram came down to the city to do some shopping today. Before heading home they stopped by my office. While my mother was in the ladies' room I proudly held out my hand to show Gram my engagement ring. Gram took one look at my ring and clapped her hands in delight. "Would you look at that! It's lovely!"

"Stephen gave it to me. It's my engagement ring."

Gram's delight turned to concern. She looked me straight in the eye as if she were about to tell me I had male-pattern baldness, and said, "But that's an emerald. Engagement rings are supposed to be diamond."

"Typically yes, but there's no reason to be trapped by the shackles of tradition."

Gram shook her head. "Sure there is. Diamonds are tough as nails. They symbolize strength and fidelity. Emeralds are weak and unreliable. Liz Taylor wears them all the time."

Weak and unreliable? Elizabeth Taylor? Was she kidding?

"Come on, Gram. You don't really believe that. Besides, this ring belonged to Stephen's great-grandmother."

Gram clutched her heart. "You mean he didn't even buy it?"

"No. It's a family heirloom."

"Heirloom? That means *free*. He should've spent some money on my beautiful granddaughter."

Forget that this ring and I have bonded. And that it makes me smile every day. All of that meant nothing. Because in under thirty seconds Gram had somehow managed to turn my stunning emerald ring into a stinging source of shame. Like the magician pulling a rabbit from a hat—you don't know how it happens, but it does.

Just then my mother returned from the bathroom. I stuffed my hand into my pocket and quickly asked about their train schedule. I'd show her my ring some other time. Maybe in a year or ten. But right now I'd had all the family support I could bear.

Minutes later I was putting them on the elevator as Barry was stepping out. "What do we have here? Don't tell me. Three generations of Thomas women. No doubt in town to make wedding preparations. How exciting! You know, Amy, you never did tell me how your Dream Boy proposed."

But before I could dodge the question Gram responded, "On the candy line at the multiplex on Broadway. The one next to the adult bookstore." I'm not sure whether I screamed or just felt like it.

Barry smiled. "A 'concession' proposal. That's original . . . *and* telling." Then he and his shit-eating grin sashayed away, his howls of laughter ringing throughout the halls.

I turned to Gram in disbelief. But she was clueless.

"What's so funny? I'm certain that's what Stephen told me." Looking at her sweet, innocent face I remember thinking, If she weren't such a kind old lady I would definitely kick her teeth in.

october 1st

I saw five reception venues today as my lunch hour turned into a lunch afternoon. Two hotels—too expensive. One garden restaurant—affordable if I want to get married on a Tuesday night. A corporate event space in the East-Asian Cultural Building. Too impersonal. Too cold. Too scary. Do I really want a bust of Chairman Mao spotlit during my wedding reception? And a SoHo art gallery. Great except I'd have to buy a hefty insurance policy for the artwork, which would remain on the walls during my event. Scheduled for June 2nd—"High Heels and Hymens: Fetishistic Nude Photography."

october 3rd

Stephen's just informed me that his friends Mitch and Larry are going to be his best man and groomsman.

Mitch and Larry, who might as well be called Beavis and Butthead, are like Mandy—only emotionally stunted. Unable to maintain their appearance let alone jobs or relationships, they have little to do with who Stephen is now. They're more a part of his past than his future (God willing). They're his old fraternity brothers who have yet to realize that college is over, the frat house is gone, and those gray hairs in their goatee mean that forty-ounce beers are no longer for personal consumption.

I was really hoping that Stephen would choose one of his more interesting, *literate* friends. But no. He got all sentimental and clung to the gruesome twosome.

Marriage really is a package deal.

october 4th

We met with Father Anderson today. He's the only minister I've ever seen who wears a Rolex and carries a cell phone. His broker called three times during our meeting. Apparently there was a rally on Seagram's. Anyway, First American Presbyterian is ours on June 2nd. I just hope Father Anderson puts his phone on vibrate.

Official THINGS TO DO List

1. ~~Choose wedding date~~
2. ~~Tell boss wedding date~~
3. ~~Vacation time for honeymoon~~
4. Decide on honeymoon
5. ~~Get minister~~
6. Choose reception venue
7. Make guest list
8. ~~Choose maid of honor~~
9. ~~Choose best man~~
10. Register for gifts

11. Arrange for engagement party

12. Buy engagement ring

13. Buy wedding rings

14. Buy wedding dress

15. Choose maid of honor dress

16. Order wedding cake

17. Hire caterer

18. Hire band for reception

19. Order flowers for ceremony

20. Buy shoes

21. Plan rehearsal dinner

22. Invites to rehearsal dinner

23. Hire musicians for ceremony

24. Decide on dress code

25. Get marriage license

26. Hire videographer

27. Hire photographer

28. Order table flowers

29. Order bouquets

30. Order boutonnieres for men

31. Order nosegays for women

32. Order invitations

33. Decide on wine selection

34. Postage for invitations

35. Choose hairstyle and makeup

36. Buy gifts for attendants

37. Buy thank-you notes

38. Announce wedding in newspaper

39. Buy headpiece

40. Buy traveler's checks for honeymoon

41. Apply for visas

42. Get shots and vaccinations
43. Order tent if necessary
44. Order chairs/tables if necessary
45. Make budget
46. Divide expenses
47. Make table-seating charts
48. Choose bridesmaid dress
49. Decide on menu
50. Decide on hors d'oeuvres
51. Decide on dinner-service style
52. Decide on staff-guest ratio
53. Decide seated or buffet
54. Reserve vegetarian meals
55. Reserve band/photographer/videographer meals
56. Make photo list
57. Choose hotel for wedding night
58. Hire limo for church-reception transport
59. Buy guest book for reception
60. Find hotel for out-of-towners
61. Decide on liquor selection
62. Hire bartenders
63. Verify wheelchair accessibility
64. Choose processional music
65. Choose recessional music
66. Choose cocktail music
67. Choose reception music
68. Choose ceremony readings
69. Prepare birdseed instead of rice
70. Schedule manicure/pedicure/wax

october 5th

O ver a billion men on this planet and I found the one who puts the toilet seat down. It's like winning the lottery!

I am so in love.

october 6th

I 've seen seven more reception venues. None of them works. Of the remaining twenty-one that Kate has called, fifteen are booked for our date, and I'm scheduled to see the last six next week. What a disaster.

I'm going upstate this weekend to spend some time with my parents and to determine how much money they're giving us for the wedding. Even before the food, liquor, and entertainment costs, these venues are more expensive than I ever imagined. We'll definitely have to cut corners here and there. But I can't worry too much. After all, does it really matter if we serve California wine instead of French?

october 7th

T oday is my thirtieth birthday. Everyone said I'd be disappointed, devastated, depressed . . . but I'm thrilled. I have friends, family, and Stephen. Not to mention (somewhat) meaningful employment. What more could I ask for?

Well, I've had a RUDE awakening.
My parents are only giving us $5,000 for the wedding. That will barely pay for the food!

DAD

We're heading into retirement soon. If you'd done this a few years back, like your sister did, it would have been easier for us.

ME

Well, forgive me for not jumping on the first man I met just to ensure you'd pay for my wedding.

DAD

Oh, sweetheart, we're glad you didn't jump into marriage. Frankly, we didn't think you were the marrying kind.[19] It's just that it's a little late.

ME

Late? I'm only thirty!

MOM

I had two children by the time I was thirty.

ME

And look how we turned out!

MOM

You're getting hysterical.

ME

You bet I'm hysterical. I thought you'd be more supportive of my marriage.

---

[19] Again with the Marrying Kind?! Why do people keep saying that?

DAD

We're very supportive of your marriage. Stephen's
a nice, solid man. But our accountant's advising
us to be fiscally conservative. You know, Nicole
was quite pleased when she got $5,000 for
her wedding.

ME

First off, that was five years ago. If you calculate the
rate of inflation, $5,000 back then is like
$20,000 today.

DAD

I guess that's New Math.

ME

Second, Chet's family laid out twice as much as that.

DAD

Then Stephen should ask his family for the rest.

They were right. The only option is to ask the Stewarts to
shoulder the brunt of the cost. I hope they don't mind. It
could get as high as $15,000. But I suppose that's just a
drop in the bucket for them. After all, they've got a four-car
garage.

october 10th

Stephen has just informed me that his family's willing to
match my parents' $5,000, but that's it. Not a penny
more. After I regained consciousness I reminded him that
this isn't the Stone Age. The days of dowries, trousseaus,
and prized goats being offered by the bride's family are long
gone. The groom's family is more than welcome to shoulder

the financial burden of a wedding. Even *BB* says so. And Prudence agrees. I can see it in her eyes. Besides, the Stewarts are significantly more affluent than my family, so it just makes sense.

STEPHEN
I understand that it makes sense to you. But my family is pretty traditional.

ME
Your mother keeps a miniature chow in her handbag and your father's dating your lab partner from tenth grade.

STEPHEN
True. But we still go caroling at Christmas.

Yeah? Well, this year we may have to do it for profit, because there's no way $10,000 is paying for an elegant New York City wedding.

Stephen insists that we shouldn't worry. "We'll work it out." Sure, that's a terrific answer for a spontaneous person. But control freaks like me who can't sleep at night without triple-checking their Things To Do list need a real PLAN. Besides, he's so distracted by his damn computer program that "We'll work it out" is pass-the-buck language for "You deal with it, Amy."

october 10th—4 A.M.

I can't sleep. I keep reviewing the numbers in my head, and there's no way to have an elegant wedding for $10,000. After all, this is America. Not Taiwan.

And for the record, if I could, I'd be more than willing to

pay for this wedding myself. Except I work in magazines. It's a notoriously cheap industry. I do it for love, not money. Especially at *Round-Up*. So I can't pay for it out of my own pocket. I can barely afford clothes that have pockets. And despite Mandy's raving about how lucrative the software industry is, Stephen's at a start-up company, which is having trouble starting. He makes less than I do.

I'll just have to beg my parents for more money.

But what if they're being honest about their retirement fund? What if their accountant is right and they need to save now so they won't be in the street when it's time for premasticated foods and saltwater enemas? How selfish of me to bug them for more money. The very people who clothed and housed me and sent me to Girl Scout camp when I was twelve. Where do I get off deciding how they should spend their money?

On the other hand, it's not like they're impoverished. They both work, they both have pensions, and they own their house. They're debt-free: Nicole and I are repaying our college loans. And it's not like they'll starve—my dad's middle-management at a supermarket chain. They're even planning a trip to Europe next year for my mom's fifty-fifth birthday. So come on, people, ease up those purse strings!

And why is Stephen's family suddenly so tightfisted? I thought they were delighted about this marriage. Why else would they give me the coveted emerald ring?

october 13th

Barry interrupted our review of the December proofs to ask how many kids Stephen and I are going to have. Why's a guy I'd love to see sail the *Titanic* thinking about me procreating? He shouldn't even look at my briefcase, let alone envision me splayed out on a hospital bed with another life spewing from my loins.

ME

It's not something we're thinking about yet. How
long is your eggnog piece going to be?

BARRY

A double-page spread. I've always felt that six
children made a good-sized family. Very
Brady Bunch.

ME

My writer covering the city's various religious
celebrations says the piece is running over. He's
going to need another quarter page. And having
six children has been out of fashion since
medical science perfected that smallpox vaccine.
Besides, if Carol Brady actually birthed all
six of those kids she wouldn't have had
time to do the show.

BARRY

Why not? Shirley Partridge had five kids *and* a
band. And with those hips you could have an entire
litter if you wanted.

What the hell's wrong with my hips?!

But before I could respond he was out the door and complimenting Mr. Spaulding on his choice of tie.

october 14th

I saw two more reception venues today.

The first was a Veterans Administration party room. And they say war is hell. You should've seen this room. Throw a few certified morons in there and it could pass for the D.M.V. No wonder vets are so depressed.

The second was the ballroom at the Marrion hotel. It's where Stephen's ex-girlfriend Diane "I'm a Big Pain in the Ass" Martin got married. Sure that makes it a hand-me-down venue, but I figured with $10,000 I should just be happy it's not the Motel 6.

But even the Marrion wanted $4,000 just to rent the room. What are they, crazy? They're barely above the Days Inn on the hotel food chain, and they want more than a third of my entire wedding budget? Forget it. That would leave a buck-fifty for decorating, and even I can't be creative on a buck-fifty.

How the hell do people afford these things?

october 15th

My parents are holding their position—no more money. Stephen's parents are taking their cue—no more money.

Apparently the Stewarts are so busy arguing over the terms of their divorce that the mere mention of money sends shivers down their spines.

Well, they'll be sure to shiver when Stephen and I are married at the homeless shelter at Port Authority.

october 17th

Kate expressed concern about my wedding today. She claims that it's consuming too much of her time. She's fallen behind on her filing, her typing, her interoffice memos . . . and Barry's starting to complain that she isn't paying enough attention to *his* needs.

I don't get it. I'm an easygoing boss. She should be happy I'm not asking her to retype my file labels in a more "stylish" font like Barry did last month. Besides, if she's got time to give herself a manicure in the middle of the day, then she's got time to call the Chambers of Commerce for all the metropolitan areas in the greater tristate region, in search of a potential reception venue.

I know how this sounds. I know it sounds bad.

The greater tristate region? Who the hell wants to get married there? But I'm afraid it's come to this. No matter how creative I get there's just no way $10,000 will pay for a unique and creative eighty-five-person wedding in New York City.

Stamford, Connecticut, still beats my hometown. Trust me.

october 20th

Our parents have given us the names of people they want to invite to our wedding. All 135 of them!!! My parents had twenty-six, Mr. Stewart had eighteen, and Mrs. Stewart rang in with *ninety-one*. We don't even know most of these people. For instance, who the hell is Hans Lindstrom? And how are we supposed to pay for his lobster risotto with a budget of $10,000?!

october 23rd

Mandy, who is still perfectly tan from her honeymoon in Hawaii, just told me that she and Jon exchanged engagement gifts. Who knew people even did this? Apparently *BB* discusses this custom in Chapter Sixteen. I'm still on Chapter Eight.

Well, there's no way Stephen and I can afford engagement gifts right now. He has to save money for his tuxedo, I have to save money for my stress management seminar, and we both have to save money for Hans Lindstrom's lobster risotto!

I wonder if he'd like a subscription to *Round-Up*.

october 24th

I had lunch with our staff writer Julie Browning. She's spent the last two months doing an article on karaoke's impact on New York nightlife, and we needed to hammer out a new angle since the latest issue of *Glamour* featured the exact same story. Did I mention that *Round-Up* is New York's least read magazine?

While we were eating, Julie noticed my engagement ring. Turns out emerald is her favorite stone. Classy lady. We started to talk about marriage and life and work. Julie used to be a senior editor at a magazine in D.C. I always assumed that she'd left because she preferred the freedom of a writer's lifestyle. WRONG. Seems that once her boss got wind of her plans to marry she was surreptitiously edged out of her job. She was no longer invited to big corporate meetings, she was left out of the loop on major issues, and her story ideas were routinely passed over.

I told her that I wasn't worried about that since, unlike her socially conservative magazine in D.C., *Round-Up* is a very liberal glossy. But Julie wouldn't waver. She kept warning me to watch my back. "People assume that marriage, specifically being a WIFE, will affect your dedication to the job. They assume you'll devote your energies to your husband's career and turn your own into dilettantism. And of course, they assume you'll be quitting any day to have six kids."

I suddenly flashed to Barry, Carol Brady, and the arrangement of lilies. The flowers of death and funerals! What a fool I'd been! And when I returned to the office, there he was — Mr. Bridal Booster himself — eyeing my corner office.

Rank with the stench of coup d'état.

october 25th

Kate's had no luck with her search. She's called all the major metropolitan areas in the tristate region in search of a reception venue in our price range that can accommodate anywhere from 85 to 220 people (we've yet to settle this issue with our parents). Apparently she's come up empty-handed. Or at least she says she has. I doubt she truly applied herself to the task. I can't help but think that if I'd asked her to find the address of Ricky Martin's summer home or Brad Pitt's shoe size she would have had better luck.

But I can't complain too much. I've got to keep a low profile on my wedding. Julie's cautionary tale really spooked me and I don't want to provide anyone, especially Barry, with ammunition to take my job.

So I spent the rest of the day reworking an article on the efforts of hot-dog vendors to unionize.

october 27th

Bianca Sheppard called me last night. I've known Bianca since the third day of college, when she hip-checked me across the room while charging toward our handsome dorm adviser. To this day she swears she tripped. Since then she's been Bianca Sheppard, Douglas, Izzard, Santos, and Rabinowitz. Marriage seems to agree with her. Repeatedly. Hence her nickname "Repeat Offender," or "RP" for short. She marries, it lasts about two years, then she decides it's not what she wants and splits. A month later she's getting married again.

At a certain point, going to her weddings stopped feeling like romantic unions and started feeling like biannual wine tastings. Needless to say, she was the last person I'd think of for wedding advice.

But a natural resource for wedding dresses. She knew exactly where to go. After all, she's already had four.

october 28th—12:30 A.M.

I've become an insomniac.

Which is crazy, because I've never had trouble sleeping. Back in college I had to chew espresso beans in order to stay awake. But now the minute my eyes shut my mind races—venues, menus, bridesmaid, bands. Bands! I've got to ask Stephen if he's started to look for a band.

Breathe. I must remember to breathe.

But not Stephen. Somehow he's managing to breathe *and* sleep. Ever since the engagement we've been trying to spend each night together. Usually at my house since I need more stuff in the morning. It's a strange sensation to see him lying next to me—his adorable little snores, the cute way he drapes his arm over my chest—and to realize that I'm going to spend the rest of my life with this man. Every night for the rest of my life I'll roll over and see him.

How the hell did I get so lucky?

november 1st

Last night we went to Larry and Mitch's Halloween party. Larry went as a groom and Mitch went as a bride. They did it to needle Stephen, who thought it was hysterical. I thought it was totally obnoxious.

STEPHEN
Come on. He's even wearing a garter belt. You've
got to admit it's pretty funny.

There was nothing funny about the fact that Mitch had a wedding dress before I did. Besides, most brides wax their backs before the big day.

ME
It'd be a whole lot funnier if Larry didn't have
the word "sucker" written across his forehead
in lipstick.

STEPHEN
I admit that borders offensive, but you have to
understand it's their way of showing support. They
dressed up *for* us.

I could tell Stephen was trying to endear his Neanderthal pals to me. But it wasn't working. They weren't carnie freaks passing through town in a traveling show.

The show's permanent. They're here to stay.

Stephen wrapped his arm around my waist and gave me a hug.

STEPHEN
You have to remember, they've never been wildly
in love. Larry hasn't had a date in over a year
because he's too nervous to call a woman. And
Mitch is so insecure that he'll sleep with anyone
with a futon.

That's half of New York. Suddenly the article we did last May on the rise of venereal disease was starting to make sense.

STEPHEN
Trust me. Once they're more comfortable around
you they'll start to relax and show you their more
interesting side. I swear it's there.

ME
That'd be a lot easier to believe if Mitch was wearing
underwear.

As I pointed across the room, Stephen saw what I did—the bride sitting on the sofa, straddling a giant bong, giving everyone a glimpse at his full-frontal.

november 3rd

Today at the staff meeting Barry made a not-so-subtle remark about the "Faces in the City" issue being behind schedule.

Which it's not. I've got it all in my head. I just need to commit it to paper, have Kate type it up, and get Mr. Spaulding's approval before distributing it throughout the office.

The issue focuses on ten of the city's most influential and intriguing residents. So far I've come up with nine. I'm certain the last one will come to me any day now. I've done an enormous amount of research, but I've been stuck on number ten ever since the Concessions Stand Proposal. And since it's my first issue as editor, I want it to shine. I want it to have my distinctive mark. Especially now that Barry's on the prowl.

I assured everyone that they'd have my complete list of ten "Faces" within the week.

november 5th

I couldn't stand it anymore. I've spent the last three months trying to pretend it didn't matter. But it does. So I finally broke down and asked Stephen why he chose the candy line of a stinky movie theater on Broadway to ask me the most important question of our entire lives.

The minute I asked I knew I'd done something horribly wrong. He looked like I'd told him the NBA Championships had been canceled.

STEPHEN

I was trying to be romantic. Don't you remember?
We had our first kiss on the candy line of that stinky
movie theater.

Oh, God. He's right.

STEPHEN

We were waiting to buy popcorn and all of a sudden
I couldn't stop myself. I just had to kiss you. You
were just so beautiful.

I remember that kiss. Pure spontaneity. It made me tingle from my head to my toes. It was the nicest kiss I ever got. And I had entirely forgotten about it.

But not Stephen. He made the world's most romantic gesture by proposing to me at the very same spot as that fabulous kiss and I screwed it all up by complaining. My fiancé may defy his gender's genetic coding with his sensitivity, his tenderness, and his affection, but I've disgraced mine by acting like such a GUY!

How can he ever forgive me? How can I ever forgive myself?

november 6th

I'm assuming Stephen still wants to marry me despite the fact that I'm a heartless bitch, because he's been arguing with his parents about their outrageous guest lists for our wedding. He's managed to get his dad's list down to ten, but his mom is still hovering at sixty-five—including the ever-popular Hans Lindstrom, who, it turns out, is her optometrist *and* favorite client. She redid his cabin in the Adirondacks last spring.

If I were the one doing the arguing I'd point out that $5,000 buys a limited number of seats to our nuptial celebration. And that the only venue we'll be able to afford with that budget is the school auditorium in Love Canal.

But then, that's me. Stephen's got a whole other way of handling things. Being a software developer/computer programmer, he focuses on the "logic" of the situation. Logically speaking, would Hans really be insulted if he weren't invited?

For the record—the answer was yes.

november 10th

I presented my list of "Faces" to Mr. Spaulding today. He was thrilled with my choices. Particularly number ten— Reverend Dai-Jung Choi, a minister from the Unified Church who's married over four thousand New York–area couples in the last twenty years.[20]

november 11th

The guest list debacle rages on. My parents are down to ten, Mrs. Stewart's holding at twenty, and Mr. Stewart has stopped at five. Unfortunately those five include Misty and two of her relatives. Stephen is furious. He's argued all week with his father, but Mr. Stewart won't budge. To him, accepting Misty's relatives at our wedding is synonymous with accepting Misty as his lover.

---

[20] And who's cited in the index of *BB* as an authority on wedding legalities.

Well, Stephen doesn't accept Misty, and the mere act of Mr. Stewart referring to her as his "lover" made Stephen physically ill—and has set Mrs. Stewart on a rampage. First she told Mr. Stewart's college alumni magazine that he left her for a man. Now she's threatening to set fire to the wooden elf he spent years carving and which, being in the backyard, qualifies as her property. This was the first I'd heard about an elf statue. Stephen says it's beyond ugly but that his mother kept it all these years for sentimental reasons. Now she wants to torch it.

It reminded me of the ice rose/human brain that Stephen carved for me. Apparently a lack of artistic talent runs in the family. Thankfully Stephen's got the sense to work in a temporary medium.

And while I have to assume that our guest list won't come down much below the current 120, Chapter Nineteen of *BB* claims that an average of 25 percent of invitees will be unable to attend the wedding. This leaves us at 90, which is 20 more than we originally wanted but 130 less than when we started this debate, so I won't complain.

Official THINGS TO DO List

~~1. Choose wedding date~~
~~2. Tell boss wedding date~~
~~3. Vacation time for honeymoon~~
4. Decide on honeymoon
~~5. Get minister~~

6. Choose reception venue
7. ~~Make guest list~~
8. ~~Choose maid of honor~~
9. ~~Choose best man~~
10. Register for gifts
11. Arrange for engagement party
12. ~~Buy engagement ring~~
13. Buy wedding rings
14. Buy wedding dress
15. Choose maid of honor dress
16. Order wedding cake
17. Hire caterer
18. Hire band for reception
19. Order flowers for ceremony
20. Buy shoes
21. Plan rehearsal dinner
22. Invites to rehearsal dinner
23. Hire musicians for ceremony
24. ~~Decide on dress code~~
25. Get marriage license
26. Hire videographer
27. Hire photographer
28. Order table flowers
29. Order bouquets
30. Order boutonnieres for men
31. Order nosegays for women
32. Order invitations
33. Decide on wine selection
34. Postage for invitations
35. Choose hairstyle and makeup
36. Buy gifts for attendants

37. Buy thank-you notes
38. Announce wedding in newspaper
39. Buy headpiece
40. Buy traveler's checks for honeymoon
41. Apply for visas
42. Get shots and vaccinations
43. Order tent if necessary
44. Order chairs/tables if necessary
45. Make budget
46. Divide expenses
47. Make table-seating charts
48. Choose bridesmaid dress
49. Decide on menu
50. Decide on hors d'oeuvres
51. Decide on dinner-service style
52. Decide on staff-guest ratio
53. Decide seated or buffet
54. Reserve vegetarian meals
55. Reserve band/photographer/videographer meals
56. Make photo list
57. Choose hotel for wedding night
58. Hire limo for church-reception transport
59. Buy guest book for reception
60. Find hotel for out-of-towners
61. Decide on liquor selection
62. Hire bartenders
63. Verify wheelchair accessibility
64. Choose processional music
65. Choose recessional music
66. Choose cocktail music

67. Choose reception music
68. Choose ceremony readings
69. Prepare birdseed instead of rice
70. Schedule manicure/pedicure/wax

november 14th

We're less than seven months away from our wedding and we still don't have a venue. I'm afraid it's time to face the music. Even Prudence has that "all right, already" look.

We'll have to get married at one of our parents' houses.

Since Mr. Stewart now lives in a singles complex, I'm ruling him out immediately. In theory, we could get married at my parents' house, but I don't see why we should since Mrs. Stewart's house is bigger, more beautiful, and infinitely more comfortable for a wedding. After all, she's got a tennis court, and two bathrooms on the first floor.

november 15th

Stephen refuses to ask his mother if we can get married at her house. He said the last thing he wants to deal with is his mother's insanity. He's worried that she'll smother us with questions, concerns, and demands and that she'd make everyone, especially him, miserable.

Not to mention the fact that she'd sooner eat Chuffy with a knife and fork than allow Misty and two of her relatives into the house.

I reminded Stephen that we are now six months and eighteen days away from our wedding, without a place to hold the reception. But he wouldn't budge.

Now I know how Joseph and Mary felt.

november 18th

After combing through bridal magazines I decided to begin shopping for the most important, most photographed, most expensive item of clothing I will ever wear once in my life — my wedding dress.

Luckily *BB* has several tips on the subject:

1) Make sure it's not too small. You may not lose those ten pounds.
2) Make sure it's flattering from behind. The ceremony gives everyone a nice long look at your rear.
3) Make sure you can raise your arms to dance. It'd be horrible to rip it during the reception.
4) Make sure it photographs nicely.

I already knew that I didn't want any of that Cinderella ball gown nonsense that you see in the movies. My wedding dress will be elegant and fashionable. Like an evening gown you'd see at the Oscars. I want an ankle-length dress with a narrow silhouette in silk jersey and off-the-shoulder cap sleeves. Sure it'll be white, but it'll be sophisticated.

november 19th

The only thing I look worse in than a bikini is a narrow silhouette dress in silk jersey with off-the-shoulder cap sleeves.

First off, silk jersey has no shape of its own. It just falls where you do. Every bump, bulge, and roll you've got is nicely highlighted. And underwear? Forget it. It's not going to happen.

Second, the narrow silhouette is seen so often on catwalks and at the Oscars because only supermodels and famous actors can afford the liposuction necessary to fit into it.

Third, cap sleeves were not designed for anyone with an upper arm thicker than a baguette. They draw your eye to the widest part of the arm and leave plenty of room beneath it for that extra roll of skin to flap freely in the wind.

Oh, and the last thing—either Bianca Sheppard's cleaning up in alimony or she's selling her internal organs to science, because these dresses cost thousands of dollars.

Vera Wang must have a house for every season.

november 20th

I'll be celebrating my wedding in the inner circle of hell. Commonly known as my parents' backyard.

november 22nd

Stephen didn't seem to mind the idea of having our wedding reception in my parents' backyard until I mentioned that it meant swapping our cell phone-toting Father Anderson for his family minister, Reverend MacKenzie.

But what can we do? Nothing. Stephen will just have to get over his dislike of Reverend MacKenzie.

Trust me. In the "Who's More Upset About the Way This Wedding's Turning Out" contest, I'm ahead by a mile.

november 23rd

After finally deciding to embrace my roots, to return to the homestead, to have my wedding reception in my parents' backyard . . .

They flat-out refused.

When I reminded them that they'd been more than happy to host Nicole's wedding, they reminded *me* that since then the house has been repainted and the backyard landscaped. My mom doesn't want dirty handprints all over the walls and my dad doesn't want people trampling the flower beds. Not to mention the reseeded lawn.

Just as I was about to start yelling I thought to myself— "What would Stephen do in this situation?" Logic. I calmly explained to my parents that their lovely backyard was the only choice Stephen and I had since we couldn't afford any place we liked in the city and because the Stewarts' acrimonious divorce currently precluded using their house. My mother mentioned that the local Lions Club had a very "pleasant" room, which was available for a reasonable fee. The image of a windowless basement crossed my mind. It took all my willpower not to cry.

Instead, I screamed. "Nicole got everyone's enthusiasm! Nicole got plenty of money! Nicole got to use the backyard!"

I was now *begging* to celebrate my wedding in my parents' backyard.

Oh, how the mighty fall.

november 23rd—9:30 P.M.

My mother called to suggest we scale back to a post-wedding celebration of cake and champagne on the church lawn.

Forget it. There are Teamster meetings that are more substantial.

november 25th

Thanksgiving was one long series of epiphanies.

Maybe those Pilgrims should've just stayed home.

It started with an early dinner at my parents' house. As we sat down to eat I noticed that my mother seated Nicole between my father and herself. I was seated at the other end of the table, next to Stephen and Gram. It suddenly occurred to me that Nicole's been seated between our parents for every meal since 1973. They used to say it was because she needed help cutting her food. She's now twenty-seven years old. Trust me, she's mastered cutlery. But have the seating assignments been revised? NO. And who was it that got all that money for her wedding? And who got to use the backyard? And whom does my mother invite every summer to join her at the Tanglewood Crafts Fair? It was all beginning to make sense.

They liked Nicole better!

Sure they toasted my wedding and maybe they would have waxed sentimental a bit longer if Gram hadn't started to choke on a piece of turkey fat—but it doesn't matter. It's just a drop in the bucket. Bud and Terry had chosen a favorite. No wonder I'd gotten the bottom bunk![21]

At least I know I'm Gram's favorite. She always pays special attention to me. And after we discussed the latest issue of *Round-Up*[22] I began to tell her about my wedding. I was telling her all the difficulties we'd been having because Mrs. Stewart didn't want Mr. Stewart to invite his girlfriend when Gram suddenly interrupted me. "You mean Stephen's parents are divorced?" I could have sworn she knew that. "Yeah. I told you that months ago." Clearly disturbed, Gram leaned forward and spoke in hushed tones. "Call off the marriage."

What?!

"Stephen seems like a nice man, even if he does look like Dan Quayle. But everyone knows that children of divorced families are not as committed to their own marriages."

Sweet Gram, always thinking of my best interests, no matter how antiquated her ideas are.

"Don't worry, Gram. Stephen will take our marriage very seriously. Besides, they say almost half of all marriages end in divorce, so the chances of meeting someone whose parents are still married are pretty slim."

"My point exactly. It's one of those cycles. Once you're in it, you're sucked up for good." So charmingly old-fashioned.

"I appreciate your concern, Gram. But divorce isn't a contagious disease." "Sure it is. *20/20* said most people whose parents are divorced will have marriages that fail." *20/20* said that? "Hugh Downs or Barbara Walters?" "Barbara Walters, so you know it's true. And remember, we've never had any divorces in our family." I was about to

---

[21] Despite the fact that Nicole was a bed wetter.
[22] She's an avid fan. Perhaps the only one.

remind her that she and Grandpa would have gotten a divorce if they each hadn't been so determined to collect the other one's life insurance—but I didn't. I just smiled.

Note to self: Have Kate verify Gram's sources.

After dinner Stephen and I drove an hour to his mom's house for dessert. I'd forgotten how beautiful it is. It makes me crazy to think that I'm begging to have my wedding reception in the dismal Americana of my parents' backyard when we could be celebrating in style at Mrs. Stewart's Shangri-la.

My parents' house is functional and clean. My mom's always decorated like she taught: quick and to the point. If you need a chair somewhere—boom, you've got a chair. So what if it doesn't match anything else in the room. It's got four legs and a seat. Now sit. But Mrs. Stewart treats her house like a showroom. Everything matches and shines and inspires a cozy sense of financial security and an endless supply of nourishing homemade meals. And the place is enormous. The three kids each had their own bed AND bathroom. Then there's the front lawn, the back lawn, and the clay tennis court. If only!

But no.

Mrs. Stewart served us homemade pecan pie and ice cream. Stephen's sister, Kimberly, was there, so we were four. But instead of sitting in the bright and happy breakfast nook, we sat in the dining room at the huge formal table for twelve. The only light in the entire room was a single candle. It was like dining at the haunted mansion at Walt Disney World.

I am beginning to understand Stephen's position about NOT having our reception at his mom's house. Mrs. Stewart is clearly experiencing post-divorce depression. Some days she's up, up, up—but most of the time she's down and irritated. It's impossible to watch without feeling terribly sorry for her. Not to mention the fact that it's hardly a desirable temperament in the person whose personal space you're about to invade with caterers and ninety wedding guests—including the architect of her devastation and his perky young girlfriend. Yes, I was beginning to see Stephen's point.

As Mrs. Stewart listlessly continued to feed her pie to Chuffy, Kimberly talked a blue streak about the new sofa she bought for her living room. Despite her self-absorbed monologue Kimberly did manage to get a few digs in at me: A disparaging reference to *Round-Up* and a pointed comment about women who hit thirty and marry out of desperation. I've always politely suffered her vacuousness, but her aggressive behavior really pissed me off.

So I called her on it as we were getting ready to leave. "Is something wrong?"

Kimberly looked at me, surveyed the room for witnesses, then turned back with an expression I can only describe as what Amy Fisher must have looked like before shooting Mary Jo Buttafuoco in the head. "Yeah." She pointed an accusatory finger at my engagement ring. "That's what's wrong. My grandmother must have been high on Citrucel to give it to you. That emerald belongs to me. It's been in our family for four generations. It's worth a *shitload* of money. And it should've been *mine*."

I wanted to tell the Honda-driving brat to kiss my ass and then some, but just then Stephen appeared, forcing me to smile and end our conversation with a terse "Tough luck, Kim."

After all, how dare she?

Then, waving good-bye to Stephen's depressed mother,

his bitter sister, and the sugar-high family pet, we drove across town to see his dad.

Mr. Stewart and Misty had eaten Thanksgiving dinner at a local restaurant with Tom. By the time we arrived at the condo, Mr. Stewart and Tom were splayed on the couch in food comas while Misty was in the tiny galley kitchen brewing coffee. Not surprisingly, Stephen opted to join his father on the couch and steer clear of Misty.

I'd only met Misty once, a few months ago when Stephen and I dropped something off at Mr. Stewart's apartment. But it was brief and we certainly didn't have a conversation. So all I knew about Misty was what Stephen had told me—she was a sick and manipulative woman in search of a father figure—and what I could tell by looking at her—she was pretty in a Jewel sort of way. Not much to go on.

After congratulating me on the engagement, Misty and I stood in the kitchen talking for the next half hour. Clearly she was in no hurry to join the Stewart men on the couch. And who could blame her? Tom's a pervert and Stephen's cold to her. She may not be a chess master but Misty isn't stupid. In fact, she's positively normal. Not exactly what you'd expect from a thirty-three-year-old woman who's romantically involved with a sixty-year-old man whose interests are limited to electrical wiring and golf.

Mr. Stewart himself does not play. He enjoys the sport from the comfort of his Ultrasuede recliner in a temperature-controlled environment.

Misty, on the other hand, can talk about everything from recent medical breakthroughs to Edith Wharton novels. *House of Mirth* is her favorite. Currently employed as a lab technician at a local hospital, she spent four years after college working on a cruise ship. They traveled ten months of the year and almost always in Europe. She spent the next two years in Madrid as a secretary for the European branch of an American clothing company. She moved back to her hometown when her sister had a baby, her nephew's birth rekindling her desire to be close to family.

Currently considering becoming a veterinarian, she wasn't my type, but she would have made a nice friend for Nicole.

If it weren't for her bizarre relationship with my future father-in-law. A relationship that she FINALLY mentioned at the end of our conversation. And *thank God*, because I was *dying* to know. After all, how does something like that happen? Don't you ever stop and think, "Hey, this guy is old enough to be my father." "He's got kids my age." "He's got gray pubic hair!" But Misty's story was short and sweet and void of salacious details—

They have the same auto mechanic and eight months ago they met at his garage.

That was it. No apologies and no explanations. Remorse is not what Misty is about.

When the coffee was ready I followed her out to the living room, where she lovingly patted Mr. Stewart's bulging belly as she handed him a cup. Stephen cringed at her affectionate gesture. And Tom misunderstood it. Slapping his father's gut, he shouted, "Yeah, Dad, you really packed it in tonight!" Mr. Stewart just shook his head. Then, thanking Misty for the coffee, he made space for her alongside him on the sofa.

As I watched Mr. Stewart and Misty together, snuggling on the sofa, I was surprised by how natural it all seemed. Sure, at first it looked like Misty was abnormally affectionate with her dad. And that her head should have been on Tom or Stephen's shoulder. But aside from the age disparity, they seemed to be well suited and extremely content. And even though I felt guilty about not hating Misty on Mrs. Stewart's behalf, the fact remains that I had seen the Stewarts' relationship, and it wasn't half as loving as this one.

Besides, isn't love what matters most? And who's to say what's appropriate? Jon and Mandy are the same age, but I'd never say their relationship was appropriate. It's not even comprehensible.

november 26th

My insomnia's getting worse. They say sleep deprivation can destroy your health with headaches, high blood pressure, and dementia—not to mention what it can do to your appearance.

And when I do manage to sleep it's generally accompanied by some horrible anxiety dream where I get married in an army bunker, or I walk down the aisle naked, or worse, halfway through the wedding reception I realize I've forgotten to invite someone I love, like my great-aunt Lucy or my mother. In my dream I run to a pay phone and call her. I try desperately to come up with some plausible, forgivable explanation as to why my wedding reception's in full swing and this is the first she's heard about it. I generally don't wake up before experiencing a torturous period of guilt and devastation. How will I ever make it up to her? How will I ever explain why I forgot to invite her to my wedding?

Clearly this wedding is getting the best of me. I'm *allowing* it to get the best of me. But no more! I'm bigger than this. I'm stronger than this. I can control this!

Breathe. I must remember to breathe.

november 27th—1 A.M.

My plan of action is set. I must lure Nicole over to my side, ally her with my cause, then send her into the enemy camp to negotiate on my behalf. After all, if my parents have decided to make Nicole their favorite, I should, at the very least, be allowed to manipulate this fact to my advantage.

november 27th

After reminding Nicole that I taught her how to feign illness in order to skip school, that I convinced our mother to allow her to wear a miniskirt to her junior prom, and that I helped her avoid punishment in 1987 when she got caught sneaking out to a Debbie Gibson concert (like that wasn't punishment enough), Nicole agreed to speak with our parents about letting me use their backyard.

november 28th

My parents have agreed to let us use their backyard for our wedding reception.

I beg for a month—zip. Nicole asks once—voilà! Apparently whatever Nicole wants . . .

Official THINGS TO DO List

1. ~~Choose wedding date~~
2. ~~Tell boss wedding date~~
3. ~~Vacation time for honeymoon~~
4. Decide on honeymoon
5. ~~Get minister~~
6. ~~Choose reception venue~~
7. ~~Make guest list~~
8. ~~Choose maid of honor~~
9. ~~Choose best man~~
10. Register for gifts
11. Arrange for engagement party
12. ~~Buy engagement ring~~
13. Buy wedding rings
14. Buy wedding dress
15. Buy maid of honor dress
16. Order wedding cake
17. Hire caterer
18. Hire band for reception
19. Order flowers for ceremony
20. Buy shoes
21. Plan rehearsal dinner
22. Invites to rehearsal dinner
23. Hire musicians for ceremony
24. ~~Decide on dress code~~
25. Get marriage license
26. Hire videographer

27. Hire photographer

28. Order table flowers

29. Order bouquets

30. Order boutonnieres for men

31. Order nosegays for women

32. Order invitations

33. Decide on wine selection

34. Postage for invitations

35. Choose hairstyle and makeup

36. Buy gifts for attendants

37. Buy thank-you notes

38. Announce wedding in newspaper

39. Buy headpiece

40. Buy traveler's checks for honeymoon

41. Apply for visas

42. Get shots and vaccinations

43. Order tent if necessary

44. Order chairs/tables if necessary

45. ~~Make budget~~

46. ~~Divide expenses~~

47. Make table-seating charts

48. Choose bridesmaid dress

49. Decide on menu

50. Decide on hors d'oeuvres

51. Decide on dinner-service style

52. Decide on staff-guest ratio

53. Decide seated or buffet

54. Reserve vegetarian meals

55. Reserve band/photographer/videographer meals

56. Make photo list

57. Choose hotel for wedding night

58. Hire limo for church-reception transport
59. Buy guest book for reception
60. Find hotel for out-of-towners
61. Decide on liquor selection
62. Hire bartenders
63. Verify wheelchair accessibility
64. Choose processional music
65. Choose recessional music
66. Choose cocktail music
67. Choose reception music
68. Choose ceremony readings
69. Prepare birdseed instead of rice
70. Schedule manicure/pedicure/wax

november 30th

Anita and I went to a symposium for women in journalism. As employees of *Teen Flair* and *Round-Up* we were seated in the back with a partially obstructed view.

Although the lectures were interesting I was hoping that the topic of married women in the workplace would be discussed. It wasn't. According to Anita it's old news: "What's to discuss? It's the same as if you were single—keep office romances quiet or you'll be considered a slut, and don't let your personal life interfere with your work."

What about discrimination? Hyphenated surnames? Spousal medical benefits?

During the cocktail reception, as Anita enjoyed the open bar, I spotted Janet Brearley. Janet profiles unique and noteworthy weddings for one of the city's biggest newspapers. I met her last year at the symposium, but now I had something to talk about. "Hi, Janet. I'm Amy Thomas from *Round-Up* magazine. We met last year." Janet smiled and shook my hand. She had bits of duck confit wedged between her front teeth. "So how's everything at the newspaper?" Blah, blah, blah. "Did I mention that I'm getting married in June?" I tried to be subtle. To go for the soft touch. I guess Janet gets that a lot, because her spine immediately stiffened.

"Is that so?" She rubbed her temples. "Why don't you tell me all about it." So I did. And she smiled the smile of pity. Like I was a dyslexic struggling to spell the word IMPORTANT. "How lovely. It doesn't sound like the type of wedding *my* paper would cover, but I wish you the best of luck."

And there it was. Janet Brearley had confirmed what I'd long suspected. My fiancé's in computers. I'm in second-rate publications. We're having our reception in my parents' backyard in upstate New York surrounded by Common Man. Neither poverty-stricken nor fabulously wealthy, we've never been arrested, broken a world record, nor been leaders of an extremist religious group. Our wedding was going to be a boring, connect-the-dots affair.

All in all, we're just another brick in the wall.

I joined Anita at the bar.

december 1st

My great-aunt Lucy is back in the hospital. A new drug designed to increase her circulation gave her an incredibly high fever instead. And while it's not life-threatening, the doctors felt it was best to admit her to the hospital. I called her room, but a nurse said she was sleeping.

Why do good people have to deal with such horrible things?

Here I am running around, moaning about my $10,000 wedding, and Lucy's in Milwaukee General fighting a hundred-plus fever. Priorities, anyone?

december 2nd

I'm going to be a wife. I can't be a wife. That's RIDICU-LOUS!

A wife is a chain-smoking, fifty-year-old woman who looks like Edith Bunker. I'm no wife. I'm too cute to be a wife!

Not to mention the fact that I still crack up when I refer to Stephen as my fiancé.

(Which I think he's beginning to take personally.)

december 3rd

Today was Stephen's thirty-second birthday. At six P.M. Mr. Spontaneity decided he wanted to celebrate at a Russian restaurant in Brighton Beach, Brooklyn. Two hours later, ten of us were knee-deep in frozen vodka.

I swear he's got some magic power to make things happen. Maybe it's his awkward charm. His tilted smile. His willingness to laugh . . .

It was a great evening. And I had a terrific time. But as I chewed my sturgeon, I couldn't help but wonder when Mr. Spontaneity was going to apply his magic power toward procuring us a wedding band.

december 4th

Mandy's agreed to go dress shopping with me later this week. After hearing Bianca's list she assured me we could do better. "Oh, please. Saks? Barney's? Bergdorf's? Those are flash-and-cash stores. They provide the flash, you hand over all your cash. Only bozos and tourists pay retail. The real bargains are in the outer boroughs and on Long Island. You'd be amazed at the deals you can find in Queens."

I have to admit I was impressed. This was not the whiny, pampered bride of months gone by. This was Superhero Mandy—frugal, irreverent, and sensible. "Is that where you bought your dress?" I hesitantly asked.

"Of course. At Helman's in Forest Hills, Queens. They have fabulous sales on discontinued styles. *And* they negotiate."

So even the rich economize? Even the rich haggle over dollars and cents? I find this incredibly comforting.

Now I just have to find a dress that brings out my inner beauty—and hides my saddlebags like Houdini. If nothing else, at least I know it will be white.

december 5th

The *Round-Up* holiday issue has only been out for a week and already we've gotten six complaints from readers who have actually made Barry's choice for the "best" eggnog in New York. The recipe came from a small pub on Staten Island named Scotty's. It appears Scotty's eggnog recipe tastes great but has a significant expulsive—read LAXATIVE—side effect. Sure it's got nutmeg and egg yolks, but that's not holiday cheer you're feeling. Two people have already gone to the hospital for dehydration.

A good editor would have tested the recipe before sending it to the printers. But this is Barry we're talking about. So instead he spent the whole day with the legal department, hammering out a defense strategy.

I bet my rejected story idea on caterers seems like a real winner just about now.

december 6th

Anita and I are going to the revival house to see Steve McQueen flex his wild thing in *The Getaway*. It seems like forever since Anita and I made a public spectacle of ourselves. I can't wait. I view the evening as an unofficial celebration of Barry's weeklong suspension without pay. Yippeee!!!

december 7th

Finally some frivolity!

My mom's decided to invite Stephen's family for a big Christmas Eve buffet in celebration of our engagement. Obviously this is the result of her conversation with Nicole. And while I'm thrilled at the prospect of an engagement party, it's further proof that Nicole's her favorite. I can't believe it took me this long to notice.

december 8th

Mandy and I dress shopped for ten hours today—and zip. Over sixty dresses later I'm still naked at the ball. Who knew there were so many shades of white?

I even followed all of *BB*'s helpful hints on the topic of "Shopping for Your Bridal Gown" (Chapter Twenty-two): I wore pantyhose, slip-on shoes, and an easily removable outfit. I brought a pair of pumps whose heel is similar to the heel I want on my bridal shoes, assuming I ever find any. And I sucked on hard candy all throughout the day, just to keep my energy up.

But no matter how much candy I sucked, I just couldn't get my blood sugar high enough to buy anything I saw. There were ugly dresses, atrocious dresses, flammable dresses, and dresses that were okay and passable, and even some that were very beautiful. But the very beautiful dresses weren't flattering on me, and if I'm bothering to get married, it better be "very beautiful."

Mandy found a skirt.

december 10th

It just dawned on me that Christmas is in two weeks and I still haven't shopped for presents. What rock have I been under? Oh, yeah. That wedding boulder.

december 11th

Stephen discussed our wedding date with those brain surgeon friends of his, Larry and Mitch. Together the Three Stooges decided that June 2nd is "not a great idea" because it might conflict with the NBA playoffs. Stephen doesn't want to make anyone choose between our wedding and a game.

I really thought he was kidding. I kept expecting him to say "Gotcha!"

But he was dead serious. After four months of being engaged he suddenly wants to change the date? This is no time for spontaneity. I couldn't believe it. A basketball game or someone's wedding—is it really *that* difficult a choice? I know my friends wouldn't have a problem with it. And somehow I don't see Mrs. Stewart running out to the sports arena. So what he's really saying is that Larry and Mitch might have a "conflict." Boo-hoo. I'll weep later.

As an alternate date Stephen proposed March 2nd—the middle of the basketball season but way before the playoffs. I needed no time to consider it. "Have you ever heard of anyone getting married in March?" "No." "Well that's because March is a horrible month. It's cold and it's gloomy." "But that's the great part. It's off-season. We'll get great bargains." Thank you, Homer Simpson. But I'm not getting married outside in three feet of snow unless someone pays *me*.

december 13th

We are now getting married on June 22nd, at which point, I've been assured, there is little chance of any professional sport being in the playoff, finals, or trophy stage of their season.

I must really love this guy.

december 15th

M r. Spaulding and I met today to discuss assigning the ten "Faces" profiles. Since the profiles are in-depth looks into the way these people live, work, and think, it's imperative that the writers have plenty of time to study their subjects. We spent an hour going through a list of possible writers. I lobbied hard for Julie Browning. In addition to Julie being a talented journalist, the karaoke story got killed because *Glamour* did it first, and I think anyone who gets edged out of a job for getting married deserves all the opportunities she can get. And while I didn't say anything, I secretly longed to profile the Unified wedding minister myself. But who am I kidding? I barely had time to buy Christmas gifts.

But not so for Barry. He made a big scene of presenting Kate with a cashmere sweater. He made certain that the whole office heard about his generosity, knew it was *two-ply* cashmere, and was aware of his close ties to the "support staff." Kate was so thrilled by her new sweater that she wore it for the rest of the day.

It really was nice.

Note to self: Exchange Kate's designer peanut brittle for nicer gift.

december 16th

T he company Stephen works for had their Christmas party last night. Not bad for a bunch of computer nerds pinning all their financial hopes on Stephen's ability to perfect a program that enables one type of computer to talk to another type of computer when something else is also going on. He's explained it to me thirty times and that's as much as I understand. But he can barely write a letter let alone a magazine article, so in the end we're well matched.

The company rented a Mexican restaurant in midtown and hired a live band whose upbeat salsa music I was really enjoying until I heard Stephen talk about hiring them for our wedding reception.

"That was a joke. Right, honey?" His fleeting nod did little to inspire my confidence. But it was more than enough to get Louise, one of Stephen's coworkers, to start talking about her own wedding plans.

Louise is like Central Casting's idea of a successful computer programmer. Barely in her twenties, she's 5'9", 130 pounds, blond, and beautiful. Nicole Kidman would play her in the movie. And despite what the packaging may lead you to suspect, she's also extremely intelligent and hard-working. I breathed a long sigh of relief when I learned of her engagement. Irrational as it may be, ever since she joined the company I've harbored a deeply rooted fear that Louise and Stephen would fall madly in love and run off to beget some dippy, albeit outrageously attractive colony of computer geeks named Byte, Ram, and Mouse. But no. Louise is marrying some guy she met in an on-line chat room.

Which is good, because she's recently been assigned to help Stephen develop his computer program. This means that every night Stephen's working late, he's working late with Louise.

Thank God for cyber-love.

Over one too many margaritas Louise told me about her mother, who was so distraught at the thought of "losing her baby" that she had channeled her grief into collecting an enormous *trousseau* of all the nightgowns, robes, and lingerie Louise will need for the REST OF HER LIFE. Louise was getting a friggin' trousseau!

My envy was only vaguely tempered by the fact that the thought of my mother buying me lingerie makes me queasy.

december 17th

It's official. I've seen every wedding dress on Long Island. And Mandy now has bunions.

december 18th

I forced myself to brave the holiday crowds and shop for wedding shoes after work. Result: nothing. I know I should wait until after New Year's. I might even catch some sales that way. But I can't. I'm desperate to feel some sense of accomplishment. Of progress. It's barely six months from our wedding day and all I've got is a backyard with a newly reseeded lawn.

Thank God I've got a groom. But he doesn't count. I had him before all this started.

According to the schedule in Chapter Three of *BB* I should be spending this time planning the menu with my caterer and engraving gifts for our attendants. But I don't have a caterer, a menu, or gifts.

At this rate I'll be walking down the aisle in a plastic trash bag and a pair of rubber flip-flops.

december 23rd

I must have been crazy to let my mother invite both our families for Christmas Eve. It's the first time I'll be meeting Stephen's grandparents. I want them to think I'm charming and beautiful and worthy of their grandson. Not to mention their heirloom emerald ring. I should have bought a new outfit.

Then there's the issue of Stephen's parents getting along with my parents. Not to mention with each other, since Mr. Stewart insists on bringing Misty. I'll have to put Nicole on the lookout to ensure that Mrs. Stewart doesn't quietly slash Misty's throat with a cake knife. That would just fuel Gram's argument about Stephen's genetic predisposition toward disastrous marriages. And I should probably watch my own back lest Kimberly decides to reclaim her precious emerald ring while my finger's still in it.

And then there's Tom. Maybe Chet can regale him with tales of suburban life. Or dish the dirt about seventh-grade Social Studies—the secret life of Pilgrims, why Columbus really sailed the ocean blue . . . anything to keep Tom away from my relatives.

Trust me, they don't need to know how highly sexed he is.

december 24th

Where do I begin?

I had intended to arrive at my parents house early this afternoon to help my mother prepare for the party. But I got there two hours later than planned because I missed my train at Grand Central Station. I missed the train because I was busy laboring over an extremely tricky and elaborate recipe for Sacher torte. At three in the morning I woke up and realized that despite the fact that this engagement party is in honor of Stephen and me, it is also the perfect opportunity for me to make a good impression on my future in-laws. I decided to accomplish that by making a Sacher torte—the traditional celebratory dessert of Austria.

By 7 A.M. I was at the grocery store getting the necessary ingredients. I'd never made a Sacher torte; in fact I hate cooking, but that didn't discourage me. I'd found a detailed recipe in my *New York Times* cookbook. Everything was fine except that my oven must cook at a particularly slow pace, because it took a full hour longer for the torte to bake than was indicated in the cookbook. But it looked great. Stephen went ahead to meet his own parents as I waited patiently for my torte to come into its own.

By the time I arrived at my parents' house everything was ready. Thankfully Nicole and Chet had come early that morning to help. After praising my culinary efforts we exchanged gifts, since we had all agreed that my engagement party would also serve as our Christmas celebration. We swapped the usual—sweaters, books, and CDs—but Gram didn't give me my annual Christmas check. Gram's given me a Christmas check for the last thirty years. And even though the amount—generally between twenty-five and fifty dollars—isn't going to change my life, I find the gesture comforting.

Gram must have sensed my distress, because she winked at me and said with a smile, "Christmas checks are for little girls. Not grown-up women who have decided to get married." What?! I failed to see how my marital status impacted my ability to receive my beloved Christmas check. Am I any less worthy this year than last? Does getting married mean that I'm no longer Gram's little girl? After all, aren't I her favorite?

Separation. Confusion. Abandonment. Suddenly I felt every one of them. That Christmas check represented a bond that would never be broken. And yet now it was. But what could I say? Gram's from a different generation. She probably feels like I belong to Stephen's family now. Swapped like a goat or some prized chickens.

The Stewarts arrived in two waves. First Stephen came with his mother and Chuffy, along with his sister, his grandparents, the Brocktons, who drove in from New Jersey. After all the introductions were made and people held drinks in their hands, everyone relaxed and got to know one another. It was fabulous—despite the fact that my mother momentarily lapsed into teacher mode when she had us go around the room and say our names.

Mrs. Stewart and my parents immediately hit it off (with my dad scoring big with his comment about loving dogs), while Nicole worked overtime to make Kimberly feel welcome. But it was the Brocktons who won the award for the most incredible couple ever. They showered me with kisses and raved about how happy they are about our engagement. Keeping an eye out for Kim, I proudly displayed the emerald ring and thanked them for their generosity.

Mr. Stewart arrived half an hour late, with Tom, Misty, and April—a cousin of Stephen's who's enrolled at NYU and had chosen not to go home to California for the holidays. A palpable chill went through the room, although we all tried to act normal. As Stephen informed me AFTER the party, it was the first time the Brocktons had seen Mr. Stewart since he left Mrs. Stewart. And it was the first time Mrs. Stewart had seen Misty since she and Tom graduated high school together. *This* he neglects to mention?

Accustomed to manipulating the attention of large groups, my mother the schoolteacher made quick introductions, then immediately announced dinner. Overwhelmed by the sudden need for comfort and security, people ran to the buffet table like deer during hunting season. Soon we were all face-deep in plates piled high with food. Except for Mrs. Stewart, who ate just enough to be polite to my parents without giving Misty the satisfaction of knowing that she had ruined her appetite. Although I doubt Misty noticed. She was far too busy chatting with Chet. Apparently she had been a C.I.T. at his sleep-away camp.

Since Gram was already seated with Nicole, I chose a seat next to Stephen and the Brocktons. After fifty-six years of marriage, the Brocktons, who still hold hands, can finish each other's sentences and practically read each other's minds. Simultaneously they both began to tell me about their wedding. Mr. Brockton deferred to Mrs. Brockton, who went on to recount their wedding ceremony in the back of her mother's house in Philadelphia. She sewed her own dress, and each of her twenty guests made food for the reception. Mr. Brockton had surprised her that morning with a bouquet of roses to carry down the aisle. For her part, Mrs. Brockton was eternally grateful that her husband had remembered to remove the thorns. It was an incredibly romantic story, and as she finished telling it Mrs. Brockton gave Mr. Brockton a kiss. "He still buys me roses."

The Brocktons are truly wonderful. "So, when are you two going to have kids?" And *pushy*. I thought for sure the ink on our marriage license would dry before the push toward procreation came. Hell, as far as the Brocktons are concerned we still haven't had sex. Keeping his grandparents blissfully ignorant of our rabid premarital sex life is one of the reasons Stephen and I never lived together. But Mrs. Brockton wouldn't let it rest. "You know, back in our day people got married to have babies."

Regretfully Misty chose that moment to join in our conversation. "That's just a euphemism. Back then people got married to have sex. These days people don't wait for a license. They're much more liberated. Aren't they?" And she turned to look at *ME*.

A tortured, gurgling noise erupted at the base of my throat. It was the sound of my innocent façade—drowning.

The Brocktons fell silent, Stephen changed the topic to his mother's new hairdo, and I swiftly escorted Misty across the room to Mr. Stewart's side. She knew she'd screwed up. "Oh my God, Amy. I'm so sorry! It never occurred to me that they didn't know you and Stephen were sleeping together. After all, you're *adults*."

Yes, yes, I'm a wimpy hypocrite who cowers in the face of octogenarian expectations. Sue me.

I ran to the bar for a glass of wine.

My grandmother no longer considers me her little girl, my future grandparents-in-law think I'm a tramp, and from where I stood, it looked like Tom was putting the moves on Nicole. I was suddenly overwhelmed with the urge to run and hide in my childhood bedroom.

Desperate, I turned my attention to Stephen's cousin April. When Mr. Stewart asked if he could bring April he neglected to mention that she'd be dressed like a refugee from a Kiss concert. Wearing black from head to toe, including her eyeliner, her lipstick, and her nail polish, April was the type of person who made you want to bathe. It was something about her nose ring. But since she was Stephen's cousin and just barely a freshman at college I struggled to find some compassion for her naïveté. Someday she'd look back at pictures of herself and feel appropriately ashamed. We all did.

Besides, April is a student at NYU Film School and has agreed to videotape our wedding for free with the school's equipment. I was duty bound to be patient with her. "How's school, April?"

April adjusted her nose ring. "Pretty cool. I'm minoring in Women's Studies." Oh, please. How can you minor in Women's Studies? It's a lifelong field of inquiry to any woman. "So why'd you and Stevie decide to get married?" *Stevie?* "Because we're in love." "So what? That doesn't mean you need a piece of paper from the government." Great. The last thing I need is some brash college freshman doing her Gloria Steinem impression at my engagement party. "Stephen and I want to celebrate our joy." April shrugged. "Well, you don't need the State for that."

This is where I SNAPPED.

"True, but you do need them for the medical benefits and the bequeathment rights. Now, don't think I'm not happy that you just completed your first semester of Women's Studies. But reading a few Erica Jong books and mastering that Martina Navratilova hairdo of yours hardly qualify you as an authority on female liberation, let alone a spokeswoman for everyone with a vagina. So why don't you relax and soak up some holiday cheer before I kick your P.C. ass into the street. Okeydokey?"

April was stunned. "Jesus Christ, I'm gonna be your cousin. You can't get all aggressive with me." And as she scurried across the room in search of a friendly face, I realized she was right. This Goth-attired, pain-in-the-ass, amateur feminist would soon be part of my family.

I looked around the room at all these people talking, eating, sharing, laughing, avoiding one another, and realized that in only five months and twenty-nine days we would all be related. We would all be next of kin, able to verify one another's identity in the morgue, ride in each other's ambulance, turn off life support.

All these people had come to celebrate our engagement. To celebrate *us*. How outrageously gracious and kind!

Just then my mother brought out my Sacher torte. "And here's a little something Amy made for the occasion." Everyone "oohed" and "aahed." Turns out Sacher torte is the Brocktons' favorite cake. I began to relax. I was being ridiculous. I was overreacting. I was becoming a "Mandy."

As my mother walked around serving the torte my father raised his beer and offered a toast. "I'd like to welcome you all to our house and to our family. Terry and I are very happy that Amy and Stephen found each other. Stephen's a wonderful man. Any father would be thrilled to have him marry their daughter. And Amy has grown from a little girl who used to teach her sister cusswords to a wonderful, intelligent . . ." It was a heartwarming speech. And as Stephen and I basked in the limelight of family love, it happened.

"Good Lord, how long did this torte bake? It's like a rock! I think I broke my bridge!" And there was Gram, hunched over and clutching her jaw in pain.

Suddenly everyone was converging upon her, running for ice, offering amateur dental assistance, *setting aside their Sacher torte.* My father's speech forever left unfinished as Gram soaked up all the attention.

That's when it hit me. Every time we start to celebrate my wedding Gram mysteriously injures herself. Tripping over the electrical cable when I first announced my engagement, choking on the turkey fat at Thanksgiving, and now this. The old woman was sticking it to me!

christmas day

After the excitement and chaos of yesterday Stephen and I decided to spend today cuddled in bed. We rented some movies (*Stage Door* for me, *North Dallas Forty* for him) and ordered in Chinese food.

We also exchanged Christmas gifts. I gave him a twelve-pack of toilet paper. Each roll had the entire history of basketball printed on it—statistics and all. He LOVED it so much, he practically unfurled a whole roll just reading it. Then he gave me a silver bracelet with a single charm. He said that every Christmas for the rest of our lives he's going to add a charm to the bracelet. The first one, a heart with a key.

It was the most romantic gesture. I cried straight through my wonton soup and well into my egg roll.

december 27th

I've got to do something about Gram. The more I think about her outrageous behavior the more I realize that my once-beloved grandmother is plotting a hostile takeover of my wedding glory.

- She tripped over the television cable when I announced my engagement.
- She insists my engagement ring symbolizes wantonness.
- She squealed to *Barry* about my cut-rate marriage proposal.
- She choked on turkey fat the minute my parents got sentimental about the wedding.
- She force-fed me divorce statistics.
- She maintains that my fiancé looks like Dan Quayle.
- And she humiliated me in front of my entire family, old and new, by claiming to have chipped her tooth on my Sacher torte!

Stephen thinks I'm overreacting. Anita thinks Gram's brilliant. Mandy suggested we institutionalize Gram until after the ceremony: "I told you families get nuts around weddings." And my mother says I'm paranoid: "Don't be ridiculous. She's an old woman."

Well, I've got this old woman's number! *666!*

december 29th

Lucy's back home from the hospital. I called to thank her for the blue enamel barrette she sent me as an engagement gift. It's belonged to Lucy since she was a child. She figured by June 22nd I'd have plenty of things that were old, new, and borrowed but that I might have difficulty finding something blue. I was amazed that despite her illness she'd found time to send me a gift, let alone something so thoughtful.

And for the record, it was the ONLY engagement gift we got. All those freeloaders at the engagement party came empty-handed. Don't they know "no gifts" is just a euphemism for "We know it's tacky to ask but bring something anyway"?

I'd been fantasizing about Lucy flying out for the party, but I knew it was unrealistic. Between the cost and her health it just wasn't going to happen. But since Lucy loves gossip (she subscribes to *The National Enquirer, Star,* and *People* magazine), I did my best to give her the gory details—Misty, the Brocktons, the Sacher torte, and most of all, Gram.

Lucy loved hearing every high and low point of the event. And she backed me up completely on the "Gram Is an Attention Stealing Octogenarian" theory. She said Gram's been a junkie for public adoration ever since 1956 when she appeared on the *Queen for a Day* show. Well, Gram will just have to face facts—

There's a new queen in town.

december 30th

At 1 P.M. this afternoon Stephen suddenly suggested we go sledding. Except there was no snow in the city and we didn't have a sled.

Stephen didn't bat an eye.

We ran to Grand Central Station, hopped a train, went to his mother's house, searched the attic, found his childhood sled, and spent the next four hours jockeying for the best runs with the local preteen set at the neighborhood park. It was a blast.

If only he'd apply that same sense of mission to planning our wedding.

new year's eve—9 P.M.

This is the last New Year's Eve that I will ever be single. Exciting, yet somehow extremely unnerving.

january 1st

New Year's Resolutions:

1. Be a better person.
2. Lose ten pounds.
3. Remember how lucky I am to have met Stephen.
4. Enjoy the wedding plans (don't become a "Mandy").
5. Stop making fun of Mandy.
6. Call Lucy twice a month.
7. Work harder at the magazine.
8. Be a more tolerant boss to Kate.

9. Resolve difficulties with Gram.
10. Keep my New Year's resolutions.

january 4th

Kate came back from the holidays in a major snit. Apparently she "evaluated the situation" and doesn't like the way my wedding "has imposed upon her work environment." Where does a twenty-one-year-old with a secretarial degree come up with this crap?

Too much Oprah. Or *Barry*.

And to think I gave her a real Kate Spade handbag for Christmas. Maybe I should have given her that designer peanut brittle and kept the handbag for myself. Lord knows I could use a new handbag—

WAIT! It's only four days into the new year and I'll be damned if I abandon my resolutions so soon. Number eight—Be a more tolerant boss to Kate. Tolerance.

Maybe Kate's having trouble at home. Maybe Barry scolded her for not placing his story ideas at the top of the distribution packet. Or maybe she's just cranky because that mangy Backstreet Boy still hasn't answered her fan letters. Who knows. But whatever it is I must try to understand her position and respect her feelings. Besides, what if my wedding really has become a burden to her?

january 5th

I couldn't sleep last night. At 4:39 A.M. I broke down and called the Psychic Phone Line. A woman with an oddly calm voice advised me to abandon all romantic plans.

Apparently Venus has descended into the House of Aquarius, where she's been shackled and held captive. Does anyone else find this alarming, or is it just me?

On a lighter note, my lucky numbers are 2 and 36.

january 6th

Face #2, Murray Coleman, New York's "Bagel King," has refused to be profiled in our annual issue.

Stephen tripped in a pothole on his way to work. After falling face-first onto the sidewalk he was taken to St. Luke's hospital, where he received thirty-six stitches above his left eye.

I will never call the Psychic Phone Line again.

january 7th

Mandy reached into her bag of tricks (a.k.a. her bottomless pit of well-informed wannabe-chic women) and located a dress shop known for its reasonably priced copies of famous designer wedding gowns. After a cab ride down to the Bowery then a harrowing walk into a neighborhood generally reserved for drug dealers and Mafias of various ethnicities, we finally reached an old tenement building. In the basement window a hand-written sign read:

DRESES

Okay. I'm not a snob. And I certainly don't consider myself easily flustered. But the minute I caught sight of that misspelled sign through a dirty glass window in the bowels of a dilapidated tenement building in the middle of a neighborhood that clearly God and the agents of gentrification had chosen to forget, I had only one thing to say—"TAXI!"

I was certain Mandy was already on her cell phone calling a cab.

But no. This was Superhero Mandy—able to go where no bride has gone before. She was marching down the basement stairs. Unwilling to be outbraved by *Mandy*, I anxiously followed behind.

The basement store was filled with racks of wedding gowns covered in plastic. Five young women sat hunched over sewing machines, and before you could say "sweatshop," a burly middle-aged woman with a thick neck and hairy forearms brusquely introduced herself as Gayle. She wore a Yankees T-shirt and culottes. I hadn't seen a pair of culottes since fifth grade. With anxiety constricting my esophagus Mandy took it upon herself to inform Gayle that I was looking for a wedding dress, preferably a Carolina Herrera or Vera Wang knockoff.

Gayle blanched. Then bellowed, "Knockoff?! I don't have any knockoffs. Only high-quality merchandise. All original!" A quick glance around the shop revealed bins filled with clothing labels marked "Escada," "Armani," "Vera Wang."

As the seamstresses frantically debated whether or not we were Immigration, Gayle continued to protest and wave her arms in the air. I gasped, certain I'd seen a pistol stuffed into the waistband of her culottes. Gayle was packing heat! Mandy rebuttoned her Anne Klein jacket and stood her ground. "Originals, designer imposters, whatever you like to call them, Gayle, is fine with us. But I think we both know what we're talking about. So how about showing us something nice in a cream silk satin with a princess neckline."

But Gayle was having none of it. "What are you two, anyway? Cops? Well, forget it, Charlie's Angels. We're closed."

Charlie's Angels? God, I hope I'm not Sabrina.

Mandy impatiently tapped her heel. "Look, Gayle, I didn't come down here after a long day's work just to be sent home."

Did I mention that Mandy sells residential real estate? In *Manhattan*. She does not take negotiations lightly. "Now, my friend would like to see some dresses, wouldn't you, Amy?"

Quick! Which is more important—finding the dress of my dreams or living to see my wedding day? Luckily Gayle made the choice for me. "Like I said, we're closed." She threw open the front door. And when Mandy strutted toward the exit, hissing, "I canceled an aromatherapy session to come here," Gayle just stared blankly.

During the cab ride home Mandy carped about the lack of professionalism in the garment industry while I thought wistfully about the chiffon dress with the Basque waistline hanging in the back of Gayle's shop.

Wasn't this supposed to be fun?

january 8th

If you can get past the whole "staples in your face" thing, Stephen actually looks pretty handsome with his stitches.

Sort of a young Charles Bronson.

Official THINGS TO DO List

~~1. Choose wedding date~~
~~2. Tell boss wedding date~~
~~3. Vacation time for honeymoon~~
4. Decide on honeymoon
~~5. Get minister~~
~~6. Choose reception venue~~
~~7. Make guest list~~
~~8. Choose maid of honor~~
~~9. Choose best man~~
10. Register for gifts
~~11. Arrange for engagement party~~
~~12. Buy engagement ring~~
13. Buy wedding rings
14. Buy wedding dress
15. Choose maid of honor dress
16. Order wedding cake
17. Hire caterer
18. Hire band for reception
19. Order flowers for ceremony
20. Buy shoes
21. Plan rehearsal dinner
22. Invites to rehearsal dinner
23. Hire musicians for ceremony
~~24. Decide on dress code~~
25. Get marriage license
~~26. Hire videographer~~

27. Hire photographer
28. Order table flowers
29. Order bouquets
30. Order boutonnieres for men
31. Order nosegays for women
32. Order invitations
33. Decide on wine selection
34. Postage for invitations
35. Choose hairstyle and makeup
36. Buy gifts for attendants
37. Buy thank-you notes
38. Announce wedding in newspaper
39. Buy headpiece
40. Buy traveler's checks for honeymoon
41. Apply for visas
42. Get shots and vaccinations
43. Order tent if necessary
44. Order chairs/tables if necessary
45. Make budget
46. Divide expenses
47. Make table-seating charts
48. Choose bridesmaid dress
49. Decide on menu
50. Decide on hors d'oeuvres
51. Decide on dinner-service style
52. Decide on staff-guest ratio
53. Decide seated or buffet
54. Reserve vegetarian meals
55. Reserve band/photographer/videographer meals
56. Make photo list
57. Choose hotel for wedding night

58. Hire limo for church-reception transport
59. Buy guest book for reception
60. Find hotel for out-of-towners
61. Decide on liquor selection
62. Hire bartenders
63. Verify wheelchair accessibility
64. Choose processional music
65. Choose recessional music
66. Choose cocktail music
67. Choose reception music
68. Choose ceremony readings
69. Prepare birdseed instead of rice
70. Schedule manicure/pedicure/wax

january 9th

Invigorated from the holidays, Barry swept into my office and inquired about the status of my wedding plans. Was there anything he could do?

Not in the mood for his crap, I decided to taunt him by saying that Stephen and I were reconsidering the whole marriage thing. Maybe we'd just keep dating. Barry looked sick. He begged me not to make a rash decision that I'd undoubtedly live to regret. "Good men are so hard to find!"

So are good jobs, and I'm keeping mine. Now step away from my desk, Barry.

Agitated and anxious, he exited my office. I couldn't help but smile. Then I began to wonder, of all the possible ways to taunt Barry why had I chosen that one?

I tracked down some of my long-lost married friends to ply them for information on photographers. No one had any recommendations. But they all had plenty of complaints. The photographers were late to show up, failed to show up, got drunk at the reception, were intrusive and distracting during the ceremony . . .

And they were all outrageously expensive. We're talking thousands of dollars.[23] It seems in addition to the film, the processing, and the photographer's hourly rate, you pay for the prints and the photo albums. Sure, you don't want to develop your wedding photos at the Quickie Foto stand in the mall, but do you really need to pay $15 per photo? Who cares if it's printed on archival paper that's guaranteed to last for a hundred years. *I'm* not guaranteed to last for a hundred years. And most of these photographers insist on owning or at least maintaining possession of your negatives, so you couldn't bring them to the Quickie Foto even if you wanted.

Then there's the issue of the photo albums. The book for your parents, your maid of honor, your sister . . .

Sure, I could forgo a real photographer and just buy a bunch of those disposable cameras and set them on the tables for guests to take pictures, but even that will cost a couple hundred dollars. And I still won't have a formal portrait suitable for framing of Stephen and me and our families. The kind of photo that you see on the walls of old-style Italian restaurants, with the bride and groom flanked by fifty of their closest relatives and the family pet.

You bet Chuffy will join in the fun, but will she help pay for it?

---

[23] The official monetary denomination of the wedding industry.

january 11th

The more time I spend with Prudence the more I wish she was the chatty type. She seems so levelheaded.

january 12th

Since Nicole is the family *darling*, I decided to talk to her about Gram. I told her Gram was going out of her way to draw attention to herself at the expense of my wedding. That she was purposely manipulating people, and that, in short, she was plotting outright sabotage.

Nicole looked at me like I was crazy. "You're kidding, right?"

I wish. "Look, I know she does the sweet old lady routine, but behind that façade lurks a woman with some bizarre chip on her shoulder and a selfish plan in her heart."

Nicole remained unconvinced. "The woman who sewed our Halloween costumes, who gave us fudge when we were sick, and who still shows a vital interest in our lives is secretly plotting to sabotage your wedding?"

"I told you that sweet old lady bit is just a front." "A front? For God's sake, Amy, she can barely walk." "She may be slow, but she's sly. Why else would she act so strange?"

"I don't know. Maybe she's lonely. Maybe she's come to depend on the family's attention. Or maybe you're just completely *paranoid*."

"Have you been talking to Mom?"

"See! You are paranoid. And no, I haven't talked to Mom. I may not be some big magazine editor, but I'm smart enough to realize how ridiculous this whole thing is."

Maybe Nicole was right. Maybe I am overreacting. Maybe this is like me thinking more about myself than

Lucy. Selfish. New Year's resolution #1—Be a better person. And worse yet, resolution #9—Resolve difficulties with Gram. What if Gram's behavior is just a desperate attempt to cling to her family's love? After all, she actually reads *Round-Up*. Could I be such a chump?

"All right. Maybe I am overreacting. But it's only because I haven't felt a lot of familial support for my wedding."

"What about the engagement party last month?" "That was great, but I have to be honest. I really expected more sustained enthusiasm from everyone. Including you." "Me?" "Yeah, you. I would have been happy with a lousy thumbs-up, but you've barely shown any interest at all."

"You mean like the interest you showed in my wedding?"

"What are you talking about? I was in Europe until the day before."

"Exactly. You didn't help or support or enthuse anything at my wedding. You just popped in a few hours before the ceremony."

And the problem would be . . . ? "You had all your girlfriends here. You didn't need me. Besides, I assumed you wouldn't want me there. I'm not the marrying kind, remember? Weddings just aren't my thing."

"Sure. Until now. How convenient."

So there it was. Nicole's pent-up resentment released five years after the fact. No screaming or crying. No thrown objects or spewed invectives. That's not Nicole's style. She's reserved. Repressed. Suburban.

We'd never make the talk-show circuit.

january 15th

Citing bunions, swollen ankles, and migraine headaches, Mandy refuses to shop for any more wedding dresses with me. The indefatigable wedding fanatic has declared me impossible to please. "I'll throw you a bridal shower, help you choose flowers, and give you a Valium before the ceremony—but no more dresses."

How can she abandon me like this?

She's my maid of honor. My right-hand gal. My YIN! What about fealty?!

january 17th

Paula and Kathy went dress shopping with me today. Big mistake. Paula kept pushing me toward the tarty dresses generally reserved for child brides from Tennessee. Skintight, sleeveless, backless, frontless, adhered to your body with a piece of double-stick tape. And Kathy, no fan of the Super Tramp collection, went right for the Elizabethan fantasy. High-collared, corseted, billowing poet-sleeves, with a twenty-foot train. Give me a chastity belt and a leg of mutton, and to the throne I go.

january 18th

My mother called to remind me not to forget my sister's birthday. Nicole's birthday has been on the same day for the last twenty-seven years. Trust me, I've memorized it by now. She was really calling to badger me into buying Nicole a gift. "I know she'd like some new gloves."

Well, la-de-dah. "Mom, do you harass Nicole about buying me birthday gifts?"

"No. But your birthday isn't three weeks after Christmas. Everyone always forgets Nicole's birthday."

"No one forgets Nicole's birthday, Mom. You do it because she's your favorite."

Well, the cat's out of the bag now.

"Don't be ridiculous, Amy. I love you both the same."

How many times have I heard *that* line? "Oh yeah? Who sits between you and Dad at every family meal?"

"We're all lefties. We sit together so we don't bump elbows."

Isn't that convenient. "And who got to use the backyard for their wedding?"

"Have you forgotten where you'll be on June 22nd?"

Sure, but I had to beg. "And who goes with you to the Tanglewood Crafts Fair every summer?"

"Nicole does, because she *enjoys* crafts. The time I took you, you told one vendor to keep her day job and another to shave her armpits."

She's right. I hate crafts. And underarm hair. I'm being a complete idiot.

Breathe.

january 19th

After careful scrutiny of *BB*'s index I've concluded that there are no formal guidelines for elopement.

Just checking.

january 21st

I met Mandy and Jon at Frutto di Sole last night. Stephen had to work late with Louise, so it was just the three of us. Between their wedding and now the planning for my wedding, it'd been a long time since we'd gotten together. Thankfully Jon couldn't pressure me about marriage anymore.

So he chose a new topic. "You lucked out. 'Amy Stewart' sounds pretty good. Very British royalty."[24]

"Actually, I'm not sure I'll be changing my name."

Jon rolled his eyes. "Don't tell me you're going to hyphenate."

"No, I may just keep my maiden name. It's who I am. It's part of my identity."

Jon shook his head. "It'd be one thing if you came from a famous family, or had something named after you.[25] But you don't. So what's the difference if you're a Stewart instead of a Thomas?"[26]

Mandy smiled and held Jon's hand. "Trust me, Amy. A shared name brings a greater sense of union."

Great. In order to join that union, Mandy Alexander had to become Mandy Skepperman. *And* she has to sleep with Jon.

january 22nd

T he word must be out, because no one will go dress shopping with me. Work commitments, family obligations, flulike symptoms, poor circulation, and flatulence. The list of excuses goes on and on. . . .

---

[24] That would be "Stuart," you moron.

[25] You mean like a toilet? Oh, sorry. That would be "john."

[26] Forgive me. I forgot that only the rich and famous are entitled to a sense of personal identity. What a pinhead this guy is. I don't know how Mandy refrains from smacking him. If he were my husband, I'd smack him every ten seconds. On second thought, if he were my husband, I'd just hang myself.

LAURA WOLF

And the timing couldn't be worse. The wedding "high season" is just around the corner, and new dresses are arriving in the stores every day. I just know my dress is out there. Somewhere.

But I can't go by myself. Shopping alone for a wedding dress is like confiding your first sexual experience to a pet rock. *BB* suggests going with a friend. Did that. Or a female relative. You couldn't pay me to do that.

I wonder who Prudence went shopping with.

january 23rd

Stephen and I ordered our wedding rings at Lancaster Jewelers near Rockefeller Center. Two simple, matching 14-karat gold bands.

It was really exciting, not just because it's the first big wedding task we've done together, but because these rings symbolize the depth of our commitment. We'll be wearing these rings until the day we *die*. I could tell Stephen was nervous. He kept commenting on how strange it would be to wear a ring all the time. He isn't accustomed to wearing jewelry. Not a class ring, and sometimes not even a watch. Although some married men choose not to wear wedding bands, Stephen feels pretty strongly about it. In fact it was his idea to have them engraved,

Bytes Infinitum

It's computerese for "Forever."

january 25th

Stephen, Mr. Spontaneity, wants us to start looking for a new apartment. Now.

According to Chapter Twenty-five of *BB*, weddings, moving, and death are the three most stressful events in a person's life. I'm already neck-deep in the first. If I do the second, then how far behind can the third be?

And while I can understand Stephen's desire to get this task out of the way, he's so busy at work that he can't even plan his own wedding. Lord knows I haven't heard a peep about that wedding band he was so eager to find for us.

And how easy will it be to find an affordable one-bedroom apartment on a safe block with at least two windows and no rodents? After all, this is Manhattan we're talking about. It took me eight months just to find my crummy studio, AND I had to pay a broker's fee. Not to mention all the delicate negotiations that will have to take place regarding the disposal of Stephen's "less than attractive" possessions.

Under no circumstances am I starting my marriage with a plaid couch in a fifth-floor walk-up.

As far as I'm concerned we can wait until after the wedding to find our new apartment. A love nest for Stephen, me, and Miss Pamela Anderson — 1990 Playmate of the Year.

january 27th

Not sleeping has certainly been educational. Who knew infomercials fill the airwaves from 1 to 5 A.M.? Whatever happened to the shot of the American flag waving in the wind? So proud, so brave, so stoic.

Screw it. I'm getting one of those Fatbuster 2000 grills. It's endorsed by four celebrity housewives, and that's good enough for me.

january 29th

It started very innocently. I was flipping through the newspaper on the bus ride to work when I noticed an advertisement for Elán Bridal Salon on Madison Avenue. They were having a one-day preview of Dalia Dolan's new bridal collection. *Preview.* The collection isn't due out for another month, but this preview would enable you to find your dress and place an order now. As in A.S.A.P. As in I'm getting married in four months and twenty-four days and need to act quick.

I love Dalia Dolan dresses. And she always has a "special" dress that is priced under a thousand dollars. Last year's was cut on the bias, so I couldn't get it past my hips. But somehow I knew this collection would be different. This year's "special" dress would have an A-line skirt. It would look ravishing on me.

One problem: The preview was scheduled for 11 A.M. I had an editorial meeting at 10:30 A.M. There was no way I could see the dress. Or was there?

Kate arrived to work fifteen minutes late. I told her not to worry about it. She spilled Diet Coke on my presentation packet. I told her just to print a new one. She accidentally erased part of yesterday's dictation. I told her we'd do it again. Then I sweetly asked her to do me a *favor*. If I gave her an extra long lunch break and spending money, would she buy a disposable camera, take a cab to Elán's, and photograph Dalia Dolan's "special" dress?

After squeezing me for an additional twenty bucks she

finally agreed. It cost me another ten to ensure that Barry wouldn't find out.

Who knew Elán's strictly prohibits photography in their store?

Something to do with design infringement and people making knockoffs: Gayle with her pistol and culottes. And no doubt Kate was anything but subtle with her task. So is it *my* fault that they confiscated the camera? Am *I* to blame that she was strip-searched by security then physically escorted out of the store?

Kate thinks so. She's filed for a stress-related leave of absence. Barry is livid. I am going to need a ton of Kate Spade handbags to fix this one.

january 30th

People keep asking if I'm going to change my name. As if my decision will help them to define who I am. If I change my name I'm a family-oriented wife. If I keep my name I'm an aggressive professional with a frosty interior. And if I hyphenate? I'm just plain stupid. It sounds old-fashioned, but you'd be amazed by how we cling, consciously or not, to these stereotypes.

So what's a girl to do? On the one hand everyone in this industry knows me as Amy Thomas.[27] But on the other hand Stephen thinks it'd be nice for our kids to share the same name as their parents.

I'm assuming he doesn't mean Thomas.

---

[27] Okay, maybe not everyone. I doubt anyone at *Condé Nast* has ever heard of me regardless of what my name is. But the fifty or so people I do know *definitely* know me as Amy Thomas.

january 31st

It was parent-teacher conference day, so my mom was free by 1 P.M. After she did some shopping in the city we met for dinner at T.G.I. Friday's. We always eat at T.G.I. Friday's, because it's well priced and the portions are large. My mother's criteria for a good meal. Value and size.

This explains so much about my wedding dilemmas.

Unwilling to appear paranoid or selfish, I went out of my way not to mention Gram. Instead we talked about the parents who refused to believe that their kids are nose-pickers, chronic potty mouths, or attention deficit. Inevitably the parents themselves are nose-pickers, potty mouths, or attention deficit. This always fascinates my mother, so she was in a particularly good mood. In fact, she was downright effusive. She even brought up my wedding.

Over Cobb salad and minestrone soup she asked if I'd found a caterer (I haven't), if I'd chosen a florist (I haven't), and if I had a dress yet (I don't). "You know, Amy, this may sound old-fashioned to you, but I still have the dress I wore when I married your father." News to me.

"The day you were born I did two things. I decided to name you Amy after my favorite of all the Little Women — well, actually Beth was my favorite, but she dies in the end and that didn't seem right — then I packed my wedding dress into a box in case the day came when you'd want to wear it. I saved it especially for you."

Finally, some mother-daughter bonding! It was my *Terms of Endearment* moment.[28] I was shocked. "I'd *love* to wear your wedding dress!"

---

[28] But without the whole death thing.

february 1st

I actually slept well last night. Since my mother offered me her wedding dress I feel like an enormous weight has been lifted from my shoulders. Her very own wedding dress. It's a token of her affection, it's family history. And it's a lucky charm—my parents have been happily married for over thirty years.

May we all be so fortunate.

And there's even more good news. One of Stephen's coworkers has a brother who's a freelance newspaper photographer but wants to expand into wedding photography. Since he needs to build his portfolio he's agreed to shoot our wedding for free! All we pay for is the film and the processing and the printing! No overly precious, able-to-withstand-nuclear-fallout $15 prints, and he'll give us the negatives!

A wedding dress. A photographer. Next thing you know I'll find shoes!

february 3rd

I went shoe shopping at Bendel's after work. I found nothing.

LAURA WOLF

Official THINGS TO DO List

1. Choose wedding date
2. Tell boss wedding date
3. Vacation time for honeymoon
4. Decide on honeymoon
5. Get minister
6. Choose reception venue
7. Make guest list
8. Choose maid of honor
9. Choose best man
10. Register for gifts
11. Arrange for engagement party
12. Buy engagement ring
13. Buy wedding rings
14. Buy wedding dress
15. Buy maid of honor dress
16. Order wedding cake
17. Hire caterer
18. Hire band for reception
19. Order flowers for ceremony
20. Buy shoes
21. Plan rehearsal dinner
22. Invites to rehearsal dinner
23. Hire musicians for ceremony
24. Decide on dress code
25. Get marriage license
26. Hire videographer

27. Hire photographer
28. Order table flowers
29. Order bouquets
30. Order boutonnieres for men
31. Order nosegays for women
32. Order invitations
33. Decide on wine selection
34. Postage for invitations
35. Choose hairstyle and makeup
36. Buy gifts for attendants
37. Buy thank-you notes
38. Announce wedding in newspaper
39. Buy headpiece
40. Buy traveler's checks for honeymoon
41. Apply for visas
42. Get shots and vaccinations
43. Order tent if necessary
44. Order chairs/tables if necessary
45. Make budget
46. Divide expenses
47. Make table-seating charts
48. Choose bridesmaid dress
49. Decide on menu
50. Decide on hors d'oeuvres
51. Decide on dinner-service style
52. Decide on staff-guest ratio
53. Decide seated or buffet
54. Reserve vegetarian meals
55. Reserve band/photographer/videographer meals
56. Make photo list
57. Choose hotel for wedding night

58. Hire limo for church-reception transport
59. Buy guest book for reception
60. Find hotel for out-of-towners
61. Decide on liquor selection
62. Hire bartenders
63. Verify wheelchair accessibility
64. Choose processional music
65. Choose recessional music
66. Choose cocktail music
67. Choose reception music
68. Choose ceremony readings
69. Prepare birdseed instead of rice
70. Schedule manicure/pedicure/wax

february 4th

I took the train upstate right after work to go see my mom's — my — wedding dress. I'd originally planned to go tomorrow morning, but I couldn't wait. I was on the 7 P.M. train.

I found my parents sitting down to watch a rerun of *Diagnosis Murder*. My father had already slipped into his pajamas. But that didn't matter. This moment was about us girls. It was a female thing.

Bursting with excitement, I followed my mother to her bedroom and into her closet — a place forever off-limits to my sister and me. Consequently a place forever filled with mystery and intrigue. As kids, Nicole and I spent hours speculating about what lay behind that closet door: boxes brimming with dazzling jewels, a safe filled with the family fortune, love letters from my mother's *previous* husband — a tall, dark figure whom my sister and I had inexplicably conjured up. A man who looked like Humphrey Bogart and took my mother to smoky bars where they swore. Even as adults we weren't allowed into that closet. And yet here I was, being shepherded in by my mother herself.

Shepherded into what had to be the world's most claustrophobic space. Crammed with shoes, clothing, old luggage, and forgotten sporting gear, it was poorly lit and smelled like mothballs. It was, indeed, our family's fortune. And from the back, under a pile of ancient *Good Housekeeping* magazines and some knit jumpers from the early eighties, my mom unearthed an enormous cardboard box. It was the box in which she'd kept her wedding dress, for decades, in hopes that one day *I* might wear it.

Together we carried the box to her bed. My heart was pounding. My mother lifted the lid and began gently to pull back layer upon layer of yellowed tissue paper.

Then, when the final layer of tissue paper was finally removed, I saw my wedding dress—and wept. Really wept. Not delicate girlie tears, but the kind of tears reserved for occasions of monumental joy. And horror. It was the ugliest thing I'd ever seen in my entire life. And it was all mine.

Not wishing to insult my mother, I quickly repacked the dress in its enormous cardboard box and took the next train home. Maybe, if I was lucky, I'd be robbed at gunpoint.

february 5th—2 A.M.

I can't sleep. When I close my eyes all I can see is that horrible dress—the high collar, the flowing sleeves, the pinafore front, and the hooplike skirt. I look like a cross between a *Little House on the Prairie* extra and a cast member from the road company of *Godspell*.

LAURA WOLF

It suddenly occurs to me that the photos of my mother at her wedding are shot exclusively in close-up.

Is there any way to get out of this without forever destroying the mother-daughter bond?

february 5th

I left a desperate message for Mandy this morning. She still hasn't called me back.

Meanwhile I returned home to a message on my answering machine from Gram. We haven't spoken since my engagement party and I'm not sure whether anyone's told her about my suspicions. In either event, her message was very sweet. Or was it?

"Amy, your mother's just told me that you're going to wear her wedding dress. I'm so pleased. I thought of that dress the minute I heard about your engagement. That's why I urged her to offer it to you."

So that's how all this started. My mom assumed I wouldn't want her dress, but GRAM convinced her to offer it to me.

A well-intentioned bad idea or a setup? Should I worry, or seek psychiatric attention for advanced stages of paranoia? It's so hard to tell these days.

february 7th

I'm falling behind at work. Two of my writers are late with their assignments for the April issue and I haven't even begun to think about May.

The good news is that after begging and pleading I think I've convinced Kate not to take a leave of absence. This is a difficult time for me. I need her more than ever. She knows where everything is filed, is familiar with the job, and she can read my handwriting. Sure, groveling at her feet was pathetic, but I think it tipped the scales in my favor. Few secretaries have the pleasure of bringing their bosses to their knees.

february 9th

Kate presented me with a typed list of demands ranging from her refusal to make phone calls or written inquiries relating to my wedding, to her request that wedding vendors be transferred directly to my voice mail, thereby relieving her of the apparently odious task of taking their messages. And then there's that little matter of my not discussing the wedding between the hours of 9 A.M. and 6 P.M. And though I sensed Barry's evil influence behind these demands, I readily agreed. What else could I do?

Meanwhile Stephen has become smitten with a woodwind band from Ecuador. He "discovered" them playing in the subway station by his apartment. He's just dying for them to play our wedding.

I fully support breaking with tradition. Soprano? Harpsichordist? String quartet? Forget 'em. Bring on the bamboo flute and bells. But shouldn't our band at least be familiar with American standards? If someone makes a musical request, shouldn't the bandleader be able to respond in English?

You bet. But this band issue is Stephen's domain. I'm not getting involved. No way. I'm keeping my mouth shut. Whatever he decides is fine. And he's decided on these Ecuadorian woodwind people. He says their music soothes him.

How nice.

But isn't that what *wives* are for? And how the hell do you play "Brick House" on a recorder? You don't.

Yet why quibble about that when my mother's just laid the "ground rules" for my wedding reception—in both the figurative and literal sense. Leave it to an elementary school teacher to be so clever.

Apparently the wedding reception must be wholly contained to the backyard and the first floor of the house. No one will be allowed upstairs. This means all ninety-five guests will have to share one bathroom, since Bud and Terry don't want a Porta Potti stationed in the backyard. Something about septic fluid and germs.

february 10th

Mandy finally came to my apartment to see the dress. She was furious. "You drag me all over the city and this is the dress you choose?"

Who chose? This isn't free will. This is a horrible mistake.

Her suggestion—start a fire in my apartment, then use the dress to snuff the flames. What could possibly please my mother more than to know her cherished wedding dress had saved my life?

february 10th—11 P.M.

No matter how long I hold the dress over the lit stovetop it still won't ignite. I've singed my hair and melted my nail polish, but the damn dress WILL NOT DIE.

Lucky me. An asbestos wedding dress. What next? A poison-ivy bouquet?

february 11th

On a lark I proposed James Royce as Face #2 for our annual issue. Royce is a best-selling crime novelist who's lived in and written about New York for the last twenty-seven years. He's also notorious for refusing interviews. Until now. Apparently he's ready to talk and is willing to do it in *my* "Faces in the City" issue of *Round-Up*!

Mr. Spaulding was thrilled. Barry was apoplectic. Stephen and I splurged on a fabulous steak dinner to celebrate. Who knew losing Murray Coleman as Face #2 was a stroke of enormous luck?

february 12th

It's hopeless. There is no acceptable reason why I can't wear my mother's wedding dress. It's in pristine condition and fits perfectly. Like a glove. Like a huge dishwashing glove soaking in a big vat of ugly. And how can I tell her *that* when she saved it especially for me?

february 13th

Stephen and I went upstate for the requisite "premarital counseling" with Reverend MacKenzie. Stephen complained the entire way there. "I can't believe we're letting MacKenzie counsel us, let alone join us in holy matrimony. If he asks about our sex life, just ignore him. If he pressures you, talk exclusively in generalizations. Under no circumstances should you divulge details."

"Would you relax? The guy can't be that bad. Your mother adores him."

Stephen held his ground. "Just wait until you meet him. You'll know exactly what I'm talking about."

"Is he forgetful? Rude? Verbally abusive?"

"No. It's more subtle. Like a bad vibe."

A bad vibe? He's a minister, not a pawnbroker. How ridiculous. I was certain Stephen's feelings for Reverend MacKenzie were colored by recollections of interminable church sermons about sacrifice and shame. As far as I was concerned, so long as Reverend MacKenzie didn't carry a cell phone we had no problems. We could talk loyalty, respect, and fidelity until the sun set. Then confirm my wedding date, speak highly of me to my mother-in-law, and I'll be on my way.

Stephen just continued to pout.

The United Presbyterian Church, where Stephen's family has belonged for the last twenty years, is like the country club of churches. It makes First American on the Upper East Side of Manhattan look like a Pentecostal storefront. Built in the early 1920s, it gleams from its spotless whitewash exterior to its overpolished red oak interior. The hymnbooks are covered in full-grain leather and every carved pew boasts a fluffy seat pad to cushion the strain of religious devotion. It's elegant, classy, and luxe.

As was Reverend MacKenzie, an affable albeit reserved man in his mid-sixties with a firm handshake and natty wing tips under his ministerial robe. Direct and expedient, he asked about our thoughts on marriage—what we expected from it, what it meant to us—then scheduled another meeting for the month of May. No inappropriate sexual questions and no shady solicitation of funds. Just the facts.

The minute we exited the church Stephen was on a roll. "See what I mean? He's creepy." But how creepy could the guy be? His nails were clean and his breath smelled like Listerine. The minty kind.

february 14th

L ove is about compromise.

The day started with Stephen sending a dozen long-stem roses to my office. Then ended with the two of us at his favorite video arcade.[29] We converted $30 into a bucket of quarters and went wild. He's sharp with the Kung Fu Kick Fighter II, but I can still whup his butt at Mission Control Stun Gun III.

Next Valentine's Day I'll be a WIFE.

february 18th

I cannot wear this hateful dress.

I must wear this hateful dress.

Thank goodness for friends.

Having heard about my disastrous wedding dress, Paula called to tell me about her friend Katrina—a clothing designer who's got her own studio in Greenwich Village. Apparently Katrina's agreed to take a look at Mom's dress and see if there's any way to redesign it. Who knows, I may end up with a custom wedding dress.

---

[29] Yes, my thirty-two-year-old fiancé has a *favorite* video arcade. It's his secret shame. Okay, so it's *my* secret shame about *him*. He's a rabid arcade junkie. He prances when he wins free games and yells when the preteens hog the machines. Thankfully, like a fondness for airline food or a sincere appreciation for Elvis impersonators, the opportunity to indulge in this obsession is limited. It's not so easy to find a good video arcade in Manhattan. Which is the *only* reason I'm in the game room of the Summit (read: Slum It) Hotel on Valentine's Day.

february 19th

It seems I hold only two points of interest.

Either you're wondering why my engagement ring's not a diamond, or you want to know if I'll be keeping my last name. So what's my answer?

I DON'T KNOW!

I've been Amy Sarah Thomas for the last thirty years. It's not like it's some TV character I've been playing. It's my real-life identity. And getting married doesn't change that. But part of me likes the idea of sharing a name with Stephen. Sure I know that love is the tie that binds, but the same name can't hurt. And on a practical level, it will make things a lot easier—restaurant reservations, legal documents, airline tickets . . .

Then there's the whole hyphenate thing. Mrs. Amy Jacob-Jingleheimer-Schmidt. Stupid? Damn straight. Yet suddenly it makes a little more sense. You get to keep your identity while publicly declaring your relationship to your spouse. But Amy Sarah Thomas-Stewart? It sounds like roll call at a white Anglo-Saxon Protestant support group.

And it will never fit on a credit card.

february 20th

Katrina howled with laughter when she saw my dress. None of the giggles or titters generally reserved for velour cowl necks or outdated swimwear. No sir. My goddamn wedding dress brought down the house.

Coincidentally, my insomnia has returned.

february 21st

Anita loves the idea of having an Ecuadorian woodwind band at our wedding. "Finally a wedding band that doesn't play 'Unforgettable.'" Give me a little credit. "Unforgettable" won't be played at my wedding no matter who the band is. I'm more concerned with getting some classic seventies disco. But Anita's delight went beyond music. "You know, Ecuadorian men are really sexy. Great skin. I'm definitely going to want an introduction."

Sure. What better reason to hire a wedding band than to procure dates for your friends?

Mandy, on the other hand, was horrified by the idea. "Those men in the subway? Playing at your *wedding*? This is a disaster! Do they even have waltzes in Ecuador? You can't do this! Their music doesn't have downbeats!"[30]

But what can I do? The music was the one thing Stephen really cared about. I'm making all the other decisions. Shouldn't he at least make this one? No matter how completely stupid it is?

february 22nd

I called our photographer to arrange for a meeting. I wanted him to come see the church and my parents' house and talk with us about portraits. After all, doesn't he need to assess the lighting conditions?

Yes. But not now. It seems that winter is low-season for brutal crimes and fires, which means to a freelance newspaper photographer that times are tough. He's got to stay

---

[30] A musical impossibility? Who knows. But why quibble?

glued to his police scanner in case something good—
BAD—comes up. He'll get back to us in the spring.

february 23rd

S tephen is planning to sue the city for his pothole injury.
After spending the last six years attending law school
and failing the bar exam three times, Larry's finally a bona
fide personal injury attorney. He has big plans to advertise
his services on buses and public-access cable. *This* is the
source of Stephen's decision to sue.

According to Larry, Stephen has a solid case: a wretched
pothole, a police report, eyewitnesses—and thirty-six staples in his head.

Luckily Larry's graciously volunteered to represent
Stephen free of charge. It's his *wedding present* to us.

Cheap bastard.

Meanwhile, Katrina's decided that it'll cost $500 to re-
design my dress, and even then she can only promise that it
will be "okay."

Five hundred dollars for a dress that's "okay"? That's
obscene. But what could I do? I *have* to wear this dress. It's
my familial cross to bear. Besides, $500 is still cheaper than
a new dress and I can use the extra money to rent a tent for
the reception.

I gave Katrina my blessing. Cut the thing to shreds. My
check's in the mail.

february 25th

I spoke with Lucy last night. I filled her in on my latest disasters. She advised me to follow my heart, but I think it's too late to elope.

february 28th

I knew I couldn't afford a big-time caterer. And I knew that none of the city caterers would travel upstate for a $10,000 wedding. So I acted responsibly. I aimed low.

Apparently not low enough.

Karry, of Karry's Kitchen, a nice little caterer located two towns over from my folks, took one look at my budget, then packed up her display book. "I'm afraid there's no way I can do dinner for ninety in your price range."

I was mortified. Ticked off. Alarmed. "Well, do you have any suggestions? Is there anyone else I should call?"

"Yes. Chef Boyardee and Little Debbie."

Nice. Real nice.

With such monetary realities in mind, Stephen and I have decided to honeymoon in South Carolina. This way we don't need to worry about passports, visas, or shots. And we can actually afford to sleep in a hotel instead of the backseat of our rental car. Besides, Stephen's got this incredibly romantic notion about the beach. "It's so warm and relaxing. How could you not want to go there? Unless, of course, you've seen *Jaws*."

Oh, and for the record, I've officially decided to take Stephen's last name.

march 2nd

After picking up my wedding ring from Lancaster's I spent the entire night strutting around my apartment with it on my finger. Imagine me, Ms. Costume Jewelry That Comes on Little Plastic Squares from the Twirling Display Racks at Macy's, all decked out with a gold band and an emerald ring. Sure, I've got nothing on those Indian brides who wear so much gold it looks like lamé, but I do feel special. Like a princess. Or a syndicated talk-show host.

I'm well aware of all the antiquated reasons why married women are decorated in precious metals and stones. To display their husband's wealth, to ensure them monetary compensation for their soiled purity should their fiancé/husband suddenly dump them, to publicize their husband's ownership of them, and, lastly, to highlight their worth—like giving a prized pig the biggest pen.

But screw it. My husband's not wealthy. We paid for our rings with *our* money. My "purity" was soiled long before we met. And the only thing about me that Stephen possesses is my love.

And if this is about highlighting my worth, then forget the rings. Bust out my crown and scepter, because I'm a damn good person with good intentions—most of the time. But for now I'm putting my wedding ring back into its box. I once heard that wearing your ring before the ceremony is bad luck, and I've got enough to worry about without some hex hanging over my head for *Bytes Infinitum*.

march 3rd

Anita came over last night to watch bad TV. During a commercial break I told her I was changing my name to Amy Sarah Stewart. I expected her to rant. To accuse me of being a sellout, a Stepford Wife, a Mandy.

Instead she dissolved into hysterics.

ANITA
That's priceless! Your new initials will be A.S.S.!

Maybe I won't take Stephen's last name.

march 4th

I've called eight caterers and none of them will do our wedding. Between date conflicts, budget restrictions, and outright disinterest, I've come up empty-handed.

For all its billions of chapters, *BB* never once mentions how to handle being turned down by everyone you ask. I guess the answer is obvious. Forge on. Grin and bear it.

No wonder Prudence smiles so much.

march 6th

Not being able to sleep has given me plenty of time for reflection. I spent all last night thinking about the first time Stephen and I met at our friend James's party. Who would've guessed that almost two years later we'd be getting married. How bizarre. If you had told me back then, I would've said you were crazy. But here we are.

And what if I hadn't gone to the party? What if I hadn't met Stephen? What if I hadn't heard the warm, embracing laugh that won my heart?

I'd probably be dating a sociopath. A freeloader. A white-collar criminal. Or (D), All of the above. But never again. I won't ever date another man. I'll never have a romantic dinner with anyone else. I will never see another man naked. I will never have sex with another man. Stephen is the only man I will ever date, see naked, have sex and eat with for the rest of my life. For the remainder of my mortal existence I will be exclusively with Stephen.

Is that humanly possible? Am I genetically capable of this? Sure, Stephen's great, but is he THE ONE?

march 7th

The more I look at Prudence the more convinced I am that she's trying to tell me something.

march 8th

To comfort myself from the painful realization that my wedding dress will undoubtedly have a frontier theme, I decided to shop for shoes. Again.

Having gone to all the department stores, bridal boutiques, and specialty shops I could think of, I finally braved the Bridal Building in Queens.

To my mind the Bridal Building is where dreams go to die. It's filled with wholesalers and a handful of retailers who make a living off bridal misfortunes. What's that, you say you've got almost no money? Fear not. People without the ability to utter complete sentences will sell you the cheapest, tackiest, most grotesque wedding accessories that child laborers in Malaysia, Taiwan, and the Dominican Republic can make. And in an effort not to discriminate, there's a healthy showing of products manufactured domestically by preteens in Mississippi and the Bronx.

Needless to say, I brought my *own* nylon peds. The last thing I need is some crusty foot fungus—international or domestic.

The Bridal Building is truly bad to the bone. The architect must have been a sadist, because there are virtually no windows. Just like in casinos on the Vegas strip, your internal clock is set by the buzz of fluorescent lights. Is it day or night outside? Who the hell knows. You're stuck in the land of stale, recycled air and permanent noon. But unlike the lush, albeit tacky decor of Vegas, the Bridal Building is stark and clinical. Its hallways of cheap Formica and yellowed linoleum floors lead you to an endless number of unmarked doors—like an old medical building with unlicensed doctors lurking around every corner. Is this periodontistry or organ donation?

I spent hours wandering into single-room stores filled with progressively less attractive merchandise. Plastic bridal bouquets, fuchsia garter belts, and cubic zirconia engagement rings with adjustable bands. On an up note, I did see wedding dresses uglier than my own, but there was no time to gloat. I have three months and fourteen days to find wedding shoes.

So I forged on through rows of stiletto-heeled white pumps and bubble-gum-pink sling-backs adorned with tiny plastic angels. I saw open-toed mules with fur appliqué and white sandals with long leather laces that tied all the way up your thigh. If it hadn't been *my* wedding I would have laughed. But it was. So I was just about to cry when I happened to catch sight of some rhinestone hair combs in Mrs. Cho's Bridal Accessory Shoppe.

I made my way to the cabinet. Was that really an attractive object in the bastion of all that is cheap and flammable? Yes! The hair combs were darling—and could be used to highlight a fabulous hairstyle without causing radio-wave disturbances, like Prudence's massive headpiece. Suddenly my mind was racing. I'd never considered wearing anything other than fresh flowers in my hair.[31] But these hair combs were so delicate, so sparkly, so special. Just the thing to add a touch of class to my cowgirl bridal ensemble.

But as I took the comb from the display cabinet and brought it to my head, Mrs. Cho—a diminutive Korean woman with a piercing voice—shouted, "No! Fa kids."

ME
Excuse me?

MRS. CHO
Not fa adults. Too little. It's fa children.

ME
Sure. But couldn't a grown-up wear these hair
combs if she wanted to?

MRS. CHO
It's not hair comb. It's tiara. Like princess. Fa little
kid princess. You too old.

And tearing it from my hand, she swiftly returned it to the display case.

Since when do hair accessories have age limits?

---

[31] A veil was too old-fashioned, not to mention virginal, for this Big City gal. Besides, if everything goes right you only get married once, so who's got time for modesty?

march 9th—3 A.M.

I once saw a news report about a woman who went insane from sleep deprivation. Not nutty, or irritable, or cranky, but full-out INSANE from lack of sleep. For anyone who's remotely skeptical, let me tell you now—

Oh yeah, it could happen. *Just keep me in your crosshairs.*

Every night I get a bit closer—sleep-deprivation *extremis*. And Stephen's certainly no help, with his damn "little" snores and the way he throws his arm across my lungs. Even if he doesn't sever my oxygen supply with his bony elbow I'm sure to go deaf from those foghorn snores. Deviated septum, my ass!

How can *this* be the man I'm going to spend the rest of my life with? *What the hell am I thinking?!!*

I must be insane. I can't be insane.

I'm too well dressed!

Maybe I should bail. Maybe that's what Prudence has been trying to tell me.

march 10th

It's been several weeks since I heard from Gram. Nothing but silence. Silence isn't good. Silence means something bad is brewing. Now as I lie awake at night, I'm waiting for the other shoe to fall.

march 11th

I'm screwed. I need to edit an exposé on sanitation disposal, reassign an article on computer-related joint diseases, and come up with a complete list of summer story ideas for the June issue, by *tomorrow*. Sure, I could have done these things yesterday. Or last week. But no. I've been running around with my head cut off looking for a caterer and a florist and a loophole in my medical plan that will qualify me for mental-health benefits!

All this because of a wedding that I'm no longer certain I should be having.

march 12th

Stephen is refusing to sleep over anymore. He says I make him nervous. How could I possibly make him nervous? I'm the one doing everything, so it's not like I'm asking him to participate beyond his one task of finding a band, which he's doing slowly and poorly and I'm beginning to worry he won't complete until two weeks before the wedding. So let's be real. I'm the one who's got an unrelenting list of things to do, not to mention finding a pair of wedding shoes!

And how difficult can it be to find shoes? I'm not asking for a miracle. Just something classy, comfy, and affordable that I can walk in without breaking my neck, and he says I'm making *him* nervous? *Oh, please.*

Let him try being a BRIDE!

Official THINGS TO DO List

~~1. Choose wedding date~~
~~2. Tell boss wedding date~~
~~3. Vacation time for honeymoon~~
~~4. Decide on honeymoon~~
~~5. Get minister~~
~~6. Choose reception venue~~
~~7. Make guest list~~
~~8. Choose maid of honor~~
~~9. Choose best man~~
10. Register for gifts
~~11. Arrange for engagement party~~
~~12. Buy engagement ring~~
~~13. Buy wedding rings~~
~~14. Choose wedding dress~~
15. Choose maid of honor dress
16. Order wedding cake
17. Hire caterer
18. Hire band for reception
19. Order flowers for ceremony
20. Buy shoes
21. Plan rehearsal dinner
22. Invites to rehearsal dinner
23. Hire musicians for ceremony
~~24. Decide on dress code~~
25. Get marriage license
~~26. Hire videographer~~

27. Hire photographer
28. Order table flowers
29. Order bouquets
30. Order boutonnieres for men
31. Order nosegays for women
32. Order invitations
33. Decide on wine selection
34. Postage for invitations
35. Choose hairstyle and makeup
36. Buy gifts for attendants
37. Buy thank-you notes
38. Announce wedding in newspaper
39. Buy headpiece
40. Buy traveler's checks for honeymoon
41. Apply for visas
42. Get shots and vaccinations
43. Order tent if necessary
44. Order chairs/tables if necessary
45. Make budget
46. Divide expenses
47. Make table-seating charts
48. Choose bridesmaid dress
49. Decide on menu
50. Decide on hors d'oeuvres
51. Decide on dinner-service style
52. Decide on staff-guest ratio
53. Decide seated or buffet
54. Reserve vegetarian meals
55. Reserve band/photographer/videographer meals
56. Make photo list
57. Choose hotel for wedding night

58. Hire limo for church-reception transport
59. Buy guest book for reception
60. Find hotel for out-of-towners
61. Decide on liquor selection
62. Hire bartenders
63. Verify wheelchair accessibility
64. Choose processional music
65. Choose recessional music
66. Choose cocktail music
67. Choose reception music
68. Choose ceremony readings
69. Prepare birdseed instead of rice
70. Schedule manicure/pedicure/wax

march 13th—1:37 A.M.

Just when I thought things couldn't get any more complicated, overwhelming, or confusing . . .

I HAVE A SEX DREAM ABOUT MY CONGA-
DRUM-PLAYING, EXCEEDINGLY HANDSOME,
EX-BOYFRIEND RICK!

In exactly three months and nine days I'm committing to
be with Stephen for the rest of my natural life, and here I
am dreaming about Rick playing my bare bottom like a
conga drum of love *while riding a Ferris wheel at Coney Island*?!

march 13th

I am totally freaked by my Rick sex dream. After he played
my bare bottom he played the rest of me. For *hours*.
Really well.

I don't know what to do. I have to talk to someone about this, but who can I tell? I feel so dirty and guilty and ugh! I can't stop calling Stephen.

ME

Hi, honey. It's me. I love you. I love you so much. I really, really do.

STEPHEN

Is something wrong?

ME

No! Why would you say that? How could anything ever be wrong between us?

STEPHEN

I didn't necessarily mean between us.

ME

Oh. Well, nothing's wrong.

STEPHEN

Then why have you called me thirteen times today?

ME

No reason. I just want you to know I love you. Very much. More than any other man in the entire world.

STEPHEN

Is it "that" time of the month?

ME

No!

STEPHEN

Then tell me what's going on. If our marriage is going to work we'll have to learn to communicate. Clearly something's bothering you.

ME
Ah—

STEPHEN
Wait a minute. I know what this is about.

ME
You do?!

STEPHEN
This is about sleeping arrangements, isn't it?

ME
Ohmygod! It's meaningless. I swear!

STEPHEN
Amy, relax. If I'd known that my not sleeping over
would upset you this much, I never would have
done it.

ME
Huh?

STEPHEN
I just wanted a few nights of solid sleep without you
tossing and turning every twenty minutes. But forget
it. It's not worth putting you through all this agony.

ME
Ooh. Yeah. The agony.

STEPHEN
I'll just start sleeping over again.

ME
Great. Wait. No! I'm still having trouble sleeping.
Let's wait until I figure things out.

march 14th

What am I going to do? The last thing I want is to have sex dreams about other guys while I'm in bed with Stephen.

Ewwwee.

After months of insomnia and praying for sleep I'm now terrified to close my eyes lest some silken ex-lover suddenly appears. What if these dreams never stop? Do Stephen and I sleep separately for the rest of our lives? Do I buy twin beds? That means new sheets. Sheets are expensive!

march 15th

Last night it was Jonas. The abstract-expressionist. He was working with oils and I was his canvas. He didn't stop working until he got it right. *Really* right. And to think I was upset by those dreams where I forgot to invite my mother to the wedding. Those were Disney productions compared to these EXTRAVAGANZAS OF THE FLESH!

Needless to say, Barry was the last person I wanted to see when I arrived at the office. "Are your articles ready? The Division meeting's in less than ten minutes and we still have to distribute your proofs."

I couldn't take it. "Bite me, Barry! Just bite me!" The entire office went silent. Even Barry was speechless.

I think it's time to seek help.

march 16th

I'm calling Mandy and Anita. Somewhere between yin and yang there must be a voice of reason. Or at least knowledge of how to procure strong pharmaceutical drugs without a prescription.

march 17th

I convened an emergency meeting at Frutto di Sole.

ME
There's something important I need to talk about.
But first you have to swear that you won't repeat a
word of this conversation.

MANDY
Sounds exciting. Is that why you've
gone incognito?

ME
What?

MANDY
Your outfit. The quiet black suit, the silk scarf
wrapped around your neck, the dark sunglasses.
Hello! Amy, we're indoors.

ANITA
You don't like it? I think it's sexy. Very
Sophia Loren.[32]

---

[32] Sophia Loren? Sure, she's stunning and classy, but she's like 110 now. At least cut me a break and stay in my century. Isabelle Adjani, anyone?

ME

That's great. Now will you both shut up and swear
to secrecy so I can get on with it?[33]

ANITA

I swear.

MANDY

So do I.

ME

This means total secrecy. No telling your hairdresser
or coworkers, no matter how much they plead. And
under no circumstances may you ever mention this
to your significant other.

MANDY

I assume you're referring to Jon.[34]

ME

Yes.

MANDY

And exactly what do you have against Jon?

ME

Nothing.[35] It's just a formality. Now swear.

MANDY

I swear. But this better be good.

---

33 Does everyone have friends like this? Here I am with two of my closest friends
and they're more interested in my "look" than my state of mind. If a friend of
yours showed up to a restaurant dressed like a spy, wouldn't you be more concerned about her mental health than whether or not it's a viable fashion alternative? Can't anyone see I'm dyin' here?!

34 Well, duh.

35 Nothing we can talk about.

I hunched down and lowered my voice. You never know who could be listening.

ME

I've been having sex dreams about old boyfriends.

MANDY

That's horrible!

ANITA

Are you kidding? That's great!

ME

Anita, I'm getting married in three months. I'm not supposed to be having sex dreams about other men. What am I going to do?

ANITA

You're going to sleep as much as humanly possible. Just because you're getting married doesn't mean you shut your mind off. And these dreams don't mean you don't love Stephen. After all, haven't you agreed to subjugate your entire existence to him on June 22nd?

MANDY

Oh, please. Amy's right to be worried. It's a dangerous thing when a woman dreams about having sex in a sauna with a man other than her husband.

ME

Who said anything about a sauna?

MANDY

Oh . . . Well, I was just illustrating what type of sex dream a person *might* have were she dreaming on a fairly regular basis about adulterous encounters.

ME

I see.

ANITA

I can't believe you guys are being so puritanical
about this.

MANDY

It's not puritanical. It's practical. You can't fully give
yourself to one man when you're dreaming about
another.

ANITA

But dreams are harmless. Besides, maybe those
dreams weren't really about sex. Maybe they were
a symbolic gesture. A way of saying good-bye to
past lovers.

MANDY

I never thought about that![36]

ME

Terrific. But how many times do I have to say
good-bye?

march 18th—3 A.M.

I had another sex dream. About *JON*.
And I was *into* it. Now, in addition to being unfaithful,
I'm desperate!
Yuck!

---

[36] Why does she sound so relieved?

march 18th

My first dress fitting with Katrina. She's straightened and cropped the sleeves to a three-quarter length, which has eliminated all traces of *Godspell*.

But I still look like Nellie Olsen after a nasty tumble down a well.

Katrina kept shaking her head mournfully as if the situation were terminal. You'd think for $500 she'd have a better bedside manner.

I'm finally beginning to understand why the Moonies opt for massive group weddings. No caterer, no band, no bridesmaids. And in a group of a thousand brides, who's going to notice your dress?

march 20th

My day was going so well. I'd only had a brief sex dream about my eleventh-grade boyfriend, Denny, found a florist, and gotten a compliment on my June story ideas from Mr. Spaulding. Then Barry opened his mouth. "So what type of invitations are you sending out? Modern or traditional?"

The kind that doesn't have your name on it, *Barry*. Poor moron. Like getting rid of me is going to be that easy. *One day she got married, and Poof! She was gone.* I wish he'd give it a rest.

"I really haven't thought about it."

"You mean you haven't ordered them?"

"Nope."

"But you're getting married in three months and two days.[37] When my friend Denise got married she ordered

---

[37] Not that he's counting.

her invitations months in advance. And F.Y.I.—they were stunning. Dusty rose, thirty-two-thousand linen-bond paper printed with apple-red ink and tissue inserts. I'd be happy to get the printer's name and number if you'd like."

Great. And how about pushing me into oncoming traffic while you're at it. "Thanks but no thanks, Barry. I'll be fine."

Or will I? Maybe Barry was onto something.[38]

I immediately called Mandy, who flipped out. "What do you mean you haven't ordered your invitations? Didn't you read Chapter Thirty-four of *Beautiful Bride*?"

"I started to skim around Thirty-one."

"This is your wedding! You can't skim. There's no skimming in matrimony!"

I was a basket case for the rest of the day. What had I done? Here I thought the scales of bridal calamity had finally balanced out. Maybe all wasn't great, but at least it was placid. And now this.

I ran home after work and turned to Chapter Thirty-four. The more I read the quicker my pulse raced. According to *BB*, invitations must be sent out approximately six weeks before the wedding: not so far in advance that people forget, but early enough for them to clear their schedule. Add to that an average of two months to print invitations, make the necessary corrections, address and mail them. Six weeks plus two months. At this rate, my wedding invitations have to be ordered *last* week!

The apocalypse must be near—because Barry was right.

---

[38] Quick! Someone smack me. Next I'll be saying Jon's a Rhodes scholar.

march 21st

Panicked about our invitation dilemma, I decided to call Stephen at work. It was only 5 P.M. but he'd been working since seven in the morning and I could tell he was tired and distracted. So it was no surprise when instead of offering some advice he lamely suggested I ask my mother for help.

Pass the buck much, *Stevie*?

march 21st—10:30 P.M.

Although I'd been civil to Stephen during our earlier phone call I felt bad about all the hostile things I'd said in my head. After all, he's been working like a dog. Of course he's distracted. I decided to call him at home and tell him how much I love him. Between his late nights at the office, my being overwhelmed with wedding details, and our current separate sleeping arrangements, we'd barely seen each other this month.

But Stephen wasn't home. So I called his office.

After six rings he finally answered the phone. But before I could say "hello" I heard Louise giggling in the background. It was almost midnight and they'd been in that office together since 7 A.M. What the hell was she *giggling* about?

Unable to come up with an acceptable answer, I hung up.

march 22nd—1 A.M.

I can't get Louise's damn giggling out of my head. She was too pleased. Like a kid sneaking an extra slice of cake when no one was looking.

Well, it better not be *my* cake that Louise is munching on!

Wait a minute! How can I even think this way? Stephen and I are about to get married. Shouldn't I trust him implicitly?

march 22nd—2 A.M.

MANDY
I can't believe you're calling me at two in
the morning.

ME
If it makes you feel any better, I called Anita first
but she hung up on me.

MANDY
Actually that makes this even more annoying.

ME
Sorry, but it's an emergency.

MANDY
No, it's not. You heard some woman giggling.
They've been working for a thousand hours. She
was probably just giddy from exhaustion. Like me.
Tee-hee, tee-hee, tee-hee. See? I'm giddy from
exhaustion too.

ME

Come on, Mandy. What if my sex dreams have
driven Stephen away?

MANDY

Did you tell him about them?

ME

Of course not. But what if he *sensed* them?

MANDY

Listen to me, Amy. Men sense almost nothing. It's
their best and worst trait. Now go to bed. I'll tell you
when it's time to worry.

march 22nd

Against my better judgment I took Mandy's advice.
Twice. First, I decided not to worry about Stephen
and Louise. Although I did ask him to start sleeping over
again. And for the record, he was very pleased.

Second, I went to Mandy's printers.

Berington Stationers is located just around the corner
from Tiffany's. It's filled with "sales associates" seated in
Louis the Schmooey chairs behind Louis the Schmooey
desks. Each desktop is oddly devoid of any office supplies,
save a single pad of linen paper embossed with the store's
name. The sales associates, all of whom are women, wear
conservative blue dresses and a single strand of pearls.

The woman I dealt with was so uptight and brittle I was
afraid she'd snap in two. Ms. Handel must have sensed
I wasn't the typical Berington customer, because during
our five-minute conversation she mentioned six times that
Berington uses only the highest quality paper and engraving,

both of which are quite "precious." Read: expensive. Or more likely: overpriced.

Disgusted by her wealthier-than-thou attitude, and horrified to discover that her attempts to shame me were in fact working, I thoughtfully shook my head and sighed. "I'll have my driver bring my secretary over tomorrow morning. She'll give you the necessary details and choose the paper." Uncertain as to how to reply, Ms. Handel cagily asked for my name and phone number—ostensibly to schedule an appointment for the following day.

I happily complied. "Miss Astrid Rockefeller, 555-5633."

My one regret upon leaving Berington Stationer's was that I wouldn't see Ms. Handel's face when she called the Leather Fetishists Chat Line.[39]

march 23rd—1:45 A.M.

A nthony the inventor. I'd forgotten how good he looked wet.

march 23rd

S tephen may actually have a case against the city.
According to Larry, the pothole Stephen tripped on is six months overdue for repair. It's a clear example of municipal negligence. They're filing a complaint next week.

Terrific. Now he'll never deal with the band issue.

---

[39] Yes, I have the Leather Fetishists Chat Line number committed to memory. It has something to do with a college dorm room, day-old pizza, and the guy who delivered it—but that's all I'll ever admit to.

march 24th

I can't stop thinking about that rhinestone comb at the Bridal Building. It would look great alongside Lucy's enamel barrette. Except I'll have to find some twelve-year-old to buy it for me. How nuts is that? It's like some cosmic payback for all those high school years I spent convincing adults to buy me beer.

march 25th

After briefly deciding to use my free time to make my own wedding invitations with a computer, I remembered that I have no free time. So I went to Bunny's Printing Emporium in Chinatown. I chose Bunny's based on her well-worded advertisement in the Yellow Pages — "Nice, Speedy, Cheap." Located between a dumpling house and a porn shop, Bunny's was about as far from Berington Stationers as you could get. Anywhere from sixty to seventy-five years old, Bunny herself stood behind the counter, dressed in a nylon jogging suit. Her overflowing ashtray and the garbage can filled with Budweiser empties revealed that she smoked almost as much as she drank.

Stranded on a deserted island without food, Bunny would have Ms. Handel for lunch, then pick her teeth clean with the remains.

After listening to Bunny's tale about how her printing shop was there "long before the Chinks came to town," I explained my desperate situation. It turns out that in addition to being racist Bunny is also fully knowledgeable about her industry. Willing to inform and ready to haggle, Bunny provided me with a quick education about wedding invitations, which boils down to:

Colored paper, illustrated designs, special enclosures, calligraphy, and engraving all cost more.

I settled on a medium weight, cream-colored paper, thermal printing, and standard R.S.V.P. enclosures. I personally would address the envelopes, using my laser printer at work. On Bunny's advice the invitation's distinctive touch would come from its clever wording. As Bunny reminded me, "Talk is cheap."

march 26th

Stephen's grandparents sent me a present. Although the gesture was incredibly thoughtful I suspect Mrs. Brockton hasn't bonded with my decision to keep my maiden name. The present was a throw pillow with the name "Mrs. Stephen Stewart" embroidered on both sides.

Now I don't have a new identity. I have *no* identity.

march 29th

I asked Anita to use her twelve-year-old niece, Molly, as a front and buy the hair comb from Mrs. Cho at the Bridal Building.

Sure, it would mean Anita taking the train out to Queens. But she's my best friend. I'd do it for her. And Molly lives in Queens. So it really could be viewed as a nice family outing for the two of them.

Besides, I *NEED* that hair comb.

After I begged and pleaded she finally gave me a half-hearted "yes." Which was fine, since she also gave me a handful of sleeping pills that she'd pirated from the health editor at *Teen Flair*.

march 30th

Anita's sleeping pills knocked me out cold. Not a sex dream in sight. Unfortunately they also left me groggy and gullible.

When my mother asked how the wedding plans were going—Why wasn't the florist coming to see the site? Why wasn't the caterer coming to see the kitchen?—I actually answered her. *Honestly.* I told her I was having trouble finding a caterer. That our florist was dragging his feet. But that I did have a photographer and as soon as he got a break from chasing fires, knifings, and shoot-outs he'd surely stop by to say hi.

She offered to help.

I may have been overly medicated, but I wasn't stupid. I know her offer was well-intentioned, but the best-laid plans . . . I could just see it: I let her help with some small task and before I know it she's wiping everyone's nose, handing out multiplication flash cards, and ordering ninety hot lunches from the school cafeteria. With value and size as her main objectives, TASTE is destined to be overlooked.

Despite Stephen's insistence that it might be a good idea, I politely declined.

march 31st

Stephen was panicked because the computer program he's been working on was almost complete when they found a flaw in it. His company's future is depending on the success of this program. If the program fails or isn't released by early September he's out of a job. So I understand that he's under a lot of pressure.

But does that mean we have to get PLAID dishes?

No joke. There we were, standing in the middle of Bloomingdale's trying to register for wedding gifts, and Stephen decides he wants the plaid dishes. Plaid. Like that damn couch isn't enough for him. He wants to see plaid at every meal for the rest of our lives, because you know we're keeping these dishes until the day we die. They're BONE CHINA, for Christ's sake. We'll never spend the money on another set.

It was our first real fight since the engagement. He refused to budge and I refused to give in. We were at a complete impasse. And then it hit me—How can we get married if we can't even agree on a china pattern?

So I broke down in tears.

april 1st

Prudence doesn't want to get married. That's what her expression's all about. Trapped against her will in *BB*'s glossy cover, Prudence is straining to warn me, "Don't do it, Amy. You can still turn back!"

april 2nd—2 A.M.

If I burn my hateful "Things To Do" list, will it wash away my woes?

Official THINGS TO DO List

~~1. Choose wedding date~~
~~2. Tell boss wedding date~~
~~3. Vacation time for honeymoon~~
~~4. Decide on honeymoon~~
~~5. Get minister~~
~~6. Choose reception venue~~
~~7. Make guest list~~
~~8. Choose maid of honor~~
~~9. Choose best man~~
10. Register for gifts
~~11. Arrange for engagement party~~
~~12. Buy engagement ring~~
~~13. Buy wedding rings~~
~~14. Buy wedding dress~~
15. Choose maid of honor dress
16. Order wedding cake
17. Hire caterer
18. Hire band for reception
19. Order flowers for ceremony
20. Buy shoes
21. Plan rehearsal dinner
22. Invites to rehearsal dinner
23. Hire musicians for ceremony
~~24. Decide on dress code~~
25. Get marriage license
~~26. Hire videographer~~

27. Hire photographer

28. Order table flowers

29. Order bouquets

30. Order boutonnieres for men

31. Order nosegays for women

32. Order invitations

33. Decide on wine selection

34. Postage for invitations

35. Choose hairstyle and makeup

36. Buy gifts for attendants

37. Buy thank-you notes

38. Announce wedding in newspaper

39. Buy headpiece

40. Buy traveler's checks for honeymoon

41. Apply for visas

42. Get shots and vaccinations

43. Order tent if necessary

44. Order chairs/tables if necessary

45. Make budget

46. Divide expenses

47. Make table-seating charts

48. Choose bridesmaid dress

49. Decide on menu

50. Decide on hors d'oeuvres

51. Decide on dinner-service style

52. Decide on staff-guest ratio

53. Decide seated or buffet

54. Reserve vegetarian meals

55. Reserve band/photographer/videographer meals

56. Make photo list

57. Choose hotel for wedding night

58. Hire limo for church-reception transport
59. Buy guest book for reception
60. Find hotel for out-of-towners
61. Decide on liquor selection
62. Hire bartenders
63. Verify wheelchair accessibility
64. Choose processional music
65. Choose recessional music
66. Choose cocktail music
67. Choose reception music
68. Choose ceremony readings
69. Prepare birdseed instead of rice
70. Schedule manicure/pedicure/wax

april 2nd

My second fitting with Katrina. It took every ounce of strength not to burst into tears. The dress was five inches too long and three inches too tight in the hips.

I can't believe I'm paying for this.

Meanwhile, Backstabbing Barry has begun to work overtime on a regular basis. Needless to say, he's taking pains to publicize this fact. I can only guess he's doing it to make me look bad. But since he seems to accomplish less work in sixty hours than I do in forty-five, I'm not going to worry.

Too much.

Does anyone know when Martha Stewart's *Weddings* magazine comes out?

I don't know how it happened. One minute everything was fine, sort of, then suddenly things were spinning out of control and—

But I should start at the beginning.

Due to some bizarre cosmic alignment Stephen left work early enough to join me at the florist's. It was during this visit that the florist finally decided to mention that the tropical flowers I want for the wedding, the very flowers we'd been discussing for the last three weeks, would have to be specially shipped from the Pacific. At a cost so astronomical I swear I thought he was calculating in yen.

I was furious. Why had we wasted all this time talking about tropical flowers if they were going to cost more than a new kidney? I immediately threw a fit.

It was around here that Stephen decided to pay some attention. Gently putting his hand on my shoulder, Stephen, my knight in shining armor, my hero, looked that idiot florist straight in the eye and said, "Would you please excuse us a minute."

Huh?

And before I could express my disbelief, he was dragging me out of the store, "Amy, you've got to relax. You're acting like a complete lunatic because lotus blossoms are indigenous to the Pacific."

"It's ginger blossoms, *not* lotus blossoms. Now, what's your point?"

"My point is that it's a reality that precedes your birth and will far outlast your lifetime. So who cares? It's just a bunch of flowers."

Just a bunch of flowers? How dare he be so cavalier about all the energy and time I'd spent trying to create a moving and memorable wedding on an anorexic budget while he's been sitting in front of a souped-up television monitor scratching his ass with a programming manual.

"Gee, Stephen. Let's think—who cares? Hmmm . . . That's a toughie, but wait, I think I know the answer . . . *I* CARE!"[40]

It was around here that I noticed people on the sidewalk edging away from us. Like we might be dangerous, or even worse, contagious. In a matter of seconds we'd become that bickering couple you hurry past on the street and feel really sorry for. Then you feel really happy it's not you. Except now it was *me*. My day had come.

"You're right, Amy. I understand that you care. And that's real touching—"

Wait! Is that sarcasm I hear sneaking into this heartfelt reply?

"But it's not that big a deal. We'll get something else. Something cheaper. Now relax. You're starting to sound like Mandy."

"What's that supposed to mean?"

"You know exactly what it means. Mandy went nuts over that crazy wedding of hers."

(Here's where it got really good.)

"The flowers, the carriage, the cake . . ." Then with the world's most pathetic expression of sorrow, he shook his head. "Poor Jon."

Poor *JON*!

"Are you kidding me? That loser would be lucky to get bitch-slapped by someone as great as Mandy. That she actually *married* him is fucking unbelievable. You can't possibly take his side."

---

[40] And let's be real—so does he, the Big Faker. He may not care about the flowers, but trust me, he's got *his* issues. Or have we forgotten who whined about not wanting Father MacKenzie because he was "creepy." And who insisted on no finger foods. And who made us *reschedule our entire wedding* in order to accommodate the National Basketball Association!

"This isn't about sides, Amy. It's about perspective. And you've completely lost yours. First the bridal registry. Now these flowers . . . I didn't think I was marrying someone like this."

STOP. EVERYTHING.

What the hell did that mean? It suddenly occurred to me that I hadn't heard Stephen's warm, embracing laugh in a VERY long time.

"Is that a threat?"

"Don't be ridiculous."

"Well, it sounded like a threat. Like maybe if you'd known I was someone like *this*, you wouldn't have proposed."

"That's not what I meant."

"Then why'd you say it? You could have said, 'Gee, I think Skipper is a nice name for a dog.' Or, 'Wow, the vegetarian lasagna is delish!' But no. You *chose* to say you didn't think you were marrying someone like *this*!"

"You know what? You're right. I said it and I meant it! You're running around screaming about lotus blossoms—"

"Ginger blossoms!"

"Whatever! It might as well be daisies! I like daisies. But did you ever ask me what I like? No! Instead you're being a total pain in the ass, which is really disappointing, not to mention a *gigantic* turnoff!"

"Oh yeah? Well, the hell with you!"

And I stormed away. Never once looking back. That was five hours ago. And I still haven't heard a word from Stephen.

I don't think we're getting married anymore.

april 4th—1 A.M.

What am I going to do? How am I going to tell my parents? My friends? *Barry?*

I've already called in sick for work tomorrow. I left a message on Kate's voice mail. There's just no way I can face the world. There's no way I can get out of this bed.

I am completely numb.

Part of me wants to call Stephen, part of me wants him to call me, and part of me never wants to speak to him again. I don't know what to do. What to think. What to feel.

All I do know is that every time I look at my emerald engagement ring, I cry.

april 4th

My apartment has never seemed so hollow. With the exception of an occasional car horn or squeaky bus brake from the street below, my apartment is as silent and still as a tomb. As if it's been sealed off from the rest of the world. Forgotten. I feel forgotten.

I wish the phone would ring.

To remind myself that I'm still alive I've decided to keep a steady stream of food entering my body. Except that after four boxes of Kraft macaroni and cheese, the only thing I can taste is doubt. Am I relieved or completely devastated?

If I thought planning a wedding was tough, I can't imagine how difficult it is to unplan one.

I finally called Anita around noon. Except she's out of town on a business trip—some profile of a thirteen-year-old boy who recorded a top-ten single in his uncle's root cellar—and won't be back until tomorrow. So I called Mandy. Because I really needed a hug.

Within the hour Mandy stormed my apartment brandishing a basket filled with comfort food and self-help tapes, determined to put Humpty-Dumpty back together again.

MANDY
Ohmygod!

Wrapping her arms around me, she embraced me like a soldier returning from war. I sank into her embrace.

ME
Thanks for coming over.

MANDY
Of course I came over. You need me. Besides, my
two o'clock showing got canceled. Now,
how *are* you?

ME
I think I'm numb.

Mandy glanced with disapproval at the mountain of Kraft mac and cheese boxes littering my floor.

MANDY
No wonder. Now tell me what happened.

Well, it all started when Stephen accused me of being like you. . . .

ME
I don't know. First we were talking about flowers,
then he was talking about my behavior, and then
I was storming off.

Mandy popped a self-help CD into my stereo. Suddenly some woman with clogged nasal passages was bleating in

syncopated rhythms over a tambourine track. I climbed
back into bed.

                            MANDY
        I don't understand. I thought things were going so
        well—you ordered those invitations, didn't you?

                             ME
        Yes. In only five weeks I'll have 120 invitations to a
        wedding that's not happening. I've got a lifelong
                    supply of scrap paper.

                            MANDY
        Don't be ridiculous. This is just a bump in the road.
                    Things will smooth out.

Then she looked at me. Panic in her eyes.

                            MANDY
        Please tell me you haven't told anyone about this.

                             ME
            I left a message for Anita, but that's it.

                            MANDY
        Thank goodness. The last thing you want is to hear
        this story repeated at some cocktail party next
        year. . . . Which makes me think. We should
        definitely remind Anita to keep her trap shut.
                    Now really, how *are* you?

                             ME
            I'm mad. I'm sad. I'm relieved. . . .

Mandy removed two spoons and a pint of reduced-fat Ben &
Jerry's ice cream from her goody basket and climbed into
bed with me.

MANDY

Here, have some ice cream.

I obeyed.

ME

I'm serious, Mandy. It's like I can't think straight.
And when I do, I just get so angry! You had to hear
him. He couldn't give a damn about all the work I've
done for this wedding.

MANDY

Men are so spoiled. They want things their way, but
they don't want to work for it and they certainly
don't want to hear the gory details.

ME

Exactly!

Mandy yanked the ice cream away from me.

MANDY

Don't hog.

I had forgotten that I was still eating it.

ME

Honestly, I'm beginning to see how this could
all be for the best.

MANDY

If by "best" you mean a surefire way to grow old
alone, then yes, breaking up with Stephen is
a grand idea.

ME

He said I was a turnoff!

MANDY

Heat of the moment, inflamed passions . . .
Isn't he part Greek?

ME

No.

MANDY

Well, anyway, you're very emotional right now. You
and Stephen just had a little tiff. You love him. He
loves you. That's all that matters.

ME

Mandy, you're not listening. It wasn't a little tiff.
He called me a *pain in the ass*. We had a huge,
make-a-scene-in-broad-daylight blowout.

MANDY

You argued in *public*?

Mandy shivered.

ME

Yes! I'm telling you, it's over. The whole thing
is finished!

I couldn't help myself, I was crying again. Mandy wrapped
her arms around me.

MANDY

Nothing's finished. I've got a plan that will fix
everything. First we put a new outgoing message
on your answering machine. You'll sound happy
and peppy like someone who's having a lot of casual
sex. That way if Stephen calls, he'll panic and
apologize immediately. But if he doesn't call I'll

get Jon to call him about some silly computer question. Jon will get the scoop and report back to us and . . .

Comforted by hugs and plied with reduced-fat dairy products, I continued to listen as Mandy outlined her calculated plan to reunite me with Stephen. And though I was uncertain it would work, and even more uncertain that I wanted it to work, it did occur to me that Mandy had missed her calling. She really should have gone into the military.

MANDY
Don't worry. We'll have you walking down that aisle if it kills me.

april 4th—10 p.m.

After spending the entire day in my apartment I was overwhelmed by the need to see people. To make contact with the outside world. To breathe the semipolluted air of car exhaust and dry-cleaning fumes. So I threw a long coat over my sweats and went to the newsstand. Just because my life had ground to a halt didn't mean the rest of the world had.

Even at 10 P.M. the streets were well populated. And everywhere I looked I saw men. Men with women, men with men, men by themselves. Men leaving restaurants, going to bars, walking their dogs, talking to themselves, and scratching their balls. That's when it occurred to me that I could flirt with these men. That as a single woman I could introduce myself, chat them up, and even bring them home.[41] The hell with Stephen. Let's see if any of these fine young gentlemen thought I was a *turnoff*.

So when I caught the newsstand guy checking me out I stood tall and proud—shoulders back, boobs forward—until I remembered that I hadn't showered today and that perhaps he wasn't so much enamored with my looks as he was disgusted by the oily clump of hair matted to my scalp. Or my face, which was bloated from sobs and high-sodium snack foods. And just as my boobs were falling back and my shoulders were slumping forward, I noticed the display of bridal magazines behind the counter.

I bought *People* and called it a night.

april 5th

I took another sick day from work. And to be honest, I really do feel sick. I may have lost Stephen, but between the fine folks at Kraft and Mandy's goody basket, I've eaten his weight in foodstuff. Unlike those thin girls who get depressed and can't eat, I'm biologically driven to drown my sorrows in cheese dip.

And for the record, I've officially forgone bathing for forty-eight hours. A fact that did not escape Anita when she came to my apartment—straight from the airport.

ANITA
Filthy really isn't a good look for you.

ME
It's part of my angry phase—I'm the anti-bride.
Thanks for coming.

---

[41] Not that I've ever brought a complete stranger home. (At least not since college.) After all, they could be psychotics with hacksaw fantasies or cross-dressers who look better in lingerie than I do.

She gave me a hug.

ANITA

I knew you couldn't have one of those normal,
repressed weddings. I knew you'd delve
into hysterics.

ME

I didn't delve. If anything, it was only a dabble. And
it was wholly justified. He said I was *a pain in the ass*.

Anita laughed.

ME

What are you laughing about?

ANITA

Nothing.

Opening her suitcase, Anita removed an 8 x 10 glossy of
Bobby Flax—the thirteen-year-old whose root-cellar record-
ing was burning up the pop charts.

ANITA

Here. I thought this would cheer you up.

Bobby had scribbled "Love Ya, Babe" in red ink.

ANITA

I know it's not a solution to your immediate problem.
But in four years he'll be at his sexual peak. And
those braces are coming off next summer.

Anita poured us some cheap white wine she found in my refrigerator. I climbed back into bed.

ANITA

So, do you want to talk about it?

ME

It's pretty simple. I was struggling, as usual, to plan
our wedding and he was entirely unhelpful and
unappreciative and unsympathetic. And then he said
he didn't realize he was marrying someone like "this"
and that I was a *turnoff*!

ANITA

Harsh! What'd you do?

ME

I told him to go to hell, then I came back here and
began my crusade of food and filth.

ANITA

Very mature.

ME

Thank you.

Anita sipped her wine. It was clear she was trying to find a
way to say something that I wouldn't want to hear. After
two false starts, she finally got it out.

ANITA

Look, I don't mean to sound unsympathetic. And
I certainly don't like seeing you so upset. But
on an intellectual level, as well as a personal level,
I've always felt that matrimony was a losing
proposition. Anything that involves monogamy is
unnatural. We're not supposed to be with one
person forever. Even most married people aren't
with one person forever.

I thought of Bianca Sheppard. And Donald Trump. And my cousin Paul who'd had a "mistress" for six years before anyone found out. Yes, Anita was definitely onto something. And it wasn't necessarily a bad thing. It was simply a reality. People had urges. Why deny them? Just look at my sex dreams. Besides, I never wanted to get married. I never wanted to be a wife. I just wanted to love someone for longer than a calendar year.

ME
Maybe you're right. Maybe canceling this wedding
is the best thing that could happen to me. Stephen's
a wonderful guy, but do I really want to spend
eternity with him? Especially now that I've gotten
a glimpse of the future—me doing all the work, all
the planning, and him sitting back and criticizing
and . . . ohmygod!

Unable to sit still, I jumped up and grabbed Anita by the shoulders.

ME
What was I thinking?! I don't want to be *married*!

ANITA
Like I've always said, marriage is a societal ill.

ME
No wonder I've felt so miserable! I've been ill!

It was as if I'd suddenly been released from some horrible burden and I could finally see sun peeking through the clouds. It was hope. It was freedom. It was my life reclaimed!

ANITA
Not to mention a total farce.

ME
You're absolutely right!

ANITA
I know. Now get the hell out of this bed and make up with your fiancé.

ME
What?!

ANITA
You heard me. Shake a leg. You can't get married without some sucker to say "I do."

ME
But you just said marriage is a societal ill. You said it was a farce!

ANITA
It is. But I've never seen you so happy as when you're with Stephen. So for you, I'm thinking maybe marriage won't be so pathetic.
Maybe.

ME
So you think I *should* get married?

Anita averted her eyes and mumbled,

ANITA
Yeah. Just don't tell anyone. Especially that troll Jon.

I clutched her tightly to my bosom.

LAURA WOLF

ME

Thank God! Because I *really* want to marry him!

And before you could say "Hello, Sybil," I was sobbing again.

ME

I miss him so much! I miss his tilted smile, and his laugh, and—

ANITA

I know, I know. You miss his smile, his laugh, his knobby knees—

ME

You think his knees are knobby?

ANITA

Forget I said it.

I continued to cry.

ME

I wanna get married!

Anita poured herself another glass of wine.

ANITA

Before you launch into your "I Love Stephen" show tunes, there's something I need to say. He's a fool for calling you a turnoff, and he's got no business complaining about all the work you've done, but as far as his not helping goes— that's your fault.

Excuse me, but when did the Tough Love seminar start?

ANITA
You told him it'd be okay if he did nothing. You're
an enabler.

I was so shocked that I stopped crying.

Could I really be an *enabler*? It was like discovering I
was tone-deaf. Or had really bad breath. If you hadn't
cringed the minute I opened my mouth, I never would have
known.

But what if Anita was right? Lord knows she's right
about Stephen being an idiot. Maybe I am responsible for
this mess. And all for what? A wedding? Well, like Anita
says, you can't have a wedding without some sucker to say
"I do."

But where's my sucker?!!!

ANITA
Now please, mellow out. It's just a wedding. You can
always have another one.

april 5th—11:30 P.M.

What have I been thinking?! My fiancé's petrified
about losing his job and I pick fights with him about
dishware and flowers. I abuse my position of authority and
turn my secretary into a serf. I forget to call my favorite
relative despite the fact that she's got chronic health problems. I resent my mother for saddling me with the world's
ugliest wedding dress. And my own grandmother hates me.
Stephen's right! I have become a pain in the ass!

Who still hasn't found wedding shoes!

I swore I'd never let my wedding get the best of me.
New Year's resolutions #s 4, 5, and 10. But suddenly here

I am. My nerves are shot, I haven't slept in months, and I've got the onset of back acne. Yick. Somewhere along the line I became what I've always hated –

A BRIDE!

So despite Anita's pleas, now is not the time for me to "mellow out." Now's the time for me to tell Stephen how incredibly sorry I am for totally losing perspective, for being a pain in the ass, for enabling his bad behavior, and for jeopardizing the very thing that means the most to me—my love for him! Or more accurately—his love for me.

From now on I keep my priorities straight and my head screwed on properly. I'm getting a clue. And buying a vowel. "A 'u' please, Vanna." For *u*nder control.

The hell with tropical flowers and unique presentations. Daisies, carnations, and bud vases for all!

But first, I need to get my fiancé back.

april 6th

I spent all night trying to figure out how to reconcile with Stephen—assuming he even wanted to, which looked unlikely, since our last exchange ended with me telling him to go to hell.

But I had to try. Our Flower Shop Fallout had driven home how much I love him. Yes, he was insensitive, and yes, he was unappreciative, but for that I had to assume part of the blame.[42] For in Stephen's immortal words, I had become a real "pain in the ass."

And yet I couldn't bring myself to pick up the phone. I was just too scared. What if he hung up? Or told me that it was over? It felt so odd—less than a week earlier this was

---

[42] A fractional part—say, between one-fourth and one-third.

someone to whom I could tell anything, and now I was literally too nervous to call him. So I decided to take a less direct approach.

One that involved neither face-to-face contact nor linguistic interaction. In fact, the crux of my plan was rooted in his total absence.

At eleven o'clock in the morning, when I was certain he'd be at work, I went to Stephen's apartment. Using my key I let myself in, and hoping to convey the depth of my affection, put a vase full of daisies on top of his big-screen TV.

After all, hadn't he vehemently declared his appreciation for daisies?

But in the middle of this heartfelt, conciliatory gesture I realized that unlike my apartment, which was littered with the remains of my bingeing bacchanal, Stephen's apartment was positively tidy. Sure, men grieve in a different way, more machismo than melancholy, but a close inspection revealed that the garbage was void of sob-filled tissues, and stacks of our relationship mementos—amassed for grieving purposes—were nowhere to be found. It was like we'd never fought. And like I'd never existed.

Stephen had already moved on.

Faced with the obvious, I locked the apartment and slid the key under the door.

I walked home. Over thirty-six blocks in the freezing cold, chiding myself for being so careless with something so precious. I had sabotaged my own happiness. Even Mandy could do nothing to save it. By the time I was opening my own apartment door I was too exhausted to cry.

Or so I thought . . .

Until I saw that my entire living room was filled with ginger blossoms. While I was putting daisies in Stephen's living room, he—assuming I was at my office—was filling my living room with ginger blossoms.

It was like "The Gift of the Magi."

Seconds later the phone rang. It was Stephen calling from his apartment. Daisies in his hand. I didn't know where to start, so I just spewed. "The flowers are beautiful and you were right I have become a pain in the ass but I've been so overwhelmed and everything just seemed so important and I'm so sorry and—"

"No, I'm the one who's sorry. I love you so much. You've been terrific about handling all the wedding arrangements and I've been a complete dolt. I've been so wrapped up with work that I haven't stopped to thank you. I never should have complained and I promise that I'll deal with the wedding band, and Amy—you're the biggest turn-on in the entire world."

Now, *that's* what a girl likes to hear.

april 6th—8 P.M.

Considering my own emotional roller coaster, I feel like I should personally apologize to all the brides whom I mocked or ridiculed about their wedding hysteria.

But time's tight. And that could take all week. So I left an apology on Mandy's answering machine. She can be symbolic of everyone I taunted. Besides, I mocked her the most. Whether she's aware of it or not.

I called Lucy today. Resolution #6—Call Lucy twice a month—has bitten the dust hard. It's been over six weeks. I know she doesn't hold it against me, she's far too gracious. But I hold it against myself. Especially since a new problem concerning her sugar levels has landed her in the hospital twice since our last conversation. I tell myself that I don't have enough time to call her. But that's a lie. The truth is, I don't make the time.

As usual, Lucy was far more interested in hearing about my life than talking about her own. Aware that for Lucy, as a housebound woman obsessed with tabloid news, I often function like an issue of *The National Enquirer,* I did my best to recount the highs and lows of my life—including the infamous Flower Shop Fallout—with as much dramatic flair as possible.

I was alarmed by how little embellishment was needed.

Round two at the bridal registry.

This time we had a hearty meal beforehand and wore sensible shoes. As for the plaid dishes, we compromised and decided to skip china altogether. Instead we're registering for two sets of casual tableware. This way, if a piece breaks, we can afford to replace it.

As for the rest of the registry, we made sure only to ask for things we'd really use. Have you noticed that every married couple has either a pasta machine or bread maker stuffed in the back of their kitchen cabinet? Used only once, if at all. And the cappuccino maker. Oh, *please.* Do you really see yourself slaving away over steamed milk when a cup of freshly brewed Colombian takes less than three minutes? Not to mention the fact that those cappuccino makers have about 1,005 parts, which need to be individually dismantled and cleaned after each use.

But most important, we registered for gifts in *every* price range. When Bianca Sheppard got married the third time, she registered at Tiffany's. The cheapest thing on her registry was a $125 sterling silver lemonade stirrer. I'm not kidding. I couldn't afford to eat out for the next month. And I haven't had lemonade since.

april 10th

I couldn't wait to tell Mandy the great news.

ME
Great news! Stephen just told me that the
Ecuadorian woodwind band is already booked on
June 22nd!

MANDY
I know.

ME
What do you mean you know?

MANDY
They'll be playing at my cousin Whitney's birthday
party in the Hamptons. You can thank me later.

Wow. Sometimes Mandy's *really* scary.

april 11th

Stephen must have told his mother that I was having difficulty finding a caterer, because Mrs. Stewart called me at 7:15 A.M. to offer some assistance. She recommended Betsy's Banquets. I thanked her for her help, and meant it sincerely until she mentioned that Betsy's Banquets caters for the Upstate Kennel Association. I've seen Mrs. Stewart feed Chuffy right off her plate too many times not to wonder if Betsy feeds the dogs or their owners. Or both.

Don't get me wrong. I've got nothing against dogs. Heck, I saw *Benji* six times. But that doesn't mean I want to eat his food.

april 12th

And people say I'm paranoid.

Last night Stephen and I went upstate for dinner. The purpose of the evening was for us to bond as a family and to review some issues regarding the wedding reception.

It was also the first time I'd seen Gram since her unfortunate dental incident with my Sacher torte.

But the minute we arrived Gram was headed for the door with bingo chips in one hand and a wad of singles in the other. When I reminded her that the whole evening was designed to enable Stephen to get to know the family, she just laughed. "Oh, sweetheart. I don't need to be here for that. Besides, disappointment's a hard thing to witness."

Excuse me?

Then as she exited the house I distinctly heard her whisper in Stephen's ear, "Too bad you didn't marry up. Maybe next time."

Stephen just laughed. He says every family's got a char-

acter and that Gram is ours. That's a real embracing, non-judgmental way of looking at things and it certainly makes me more comfortable about the idea of introducing him to my uncle Rudy, who believes excessive belching to be a sign of appreciation. But what Stephen doesn't seem to understand is that Gram's no character. She's sharp as a tack.

That's not goofy talk she's spouting, it's venom.

april 13th

The Wedding Cake. The culinary representation of our nuptial love.

It had better be REALLY good.

Wedding cakes from caterers tend to look great but taste like cardboard. The caterers are assuming that by the end of the festivities your eyesight will be sharp but your taste buds will be catatonic from heavy drinking. In a perfect world I'd ask some gifted relative to bake us a towering tour de force of strawberry shortcake. But alas. My family specializes in Moist 'N Easy. The kind you microwave, not bake.

So I called Bianca Sheppard. The cakes have been delicious at every one of her weddings. Moist, creamy, and beautiful. Bianca says she gets all her wedding cakes from Piece-A Cake down in Little Italy. And unlike her wedding dress recommendations, she swears Piece-A Cake is reasonably priced.

Let's hope so. Otherwise it's my dear friend Sara Lee.

april 14th

We had an interoffice meeting today about the "Faces in the City" issue. *My* issue.

In front of the entire staff I reviewed the progress we've made with our ten "Faces." I discussed the focus of each profile and what our writers had come up with thus far. That Face #5, Ingrid Narez, an infamous performance artist from Spanish Harlem, had insisted on doing most of her interviews wearing an eyepiece and no shirt was of particular interest to everyone.

After my formal presentation I took suggestions for the issue's sidebars. Kate proposed a survey about employee satisfaction with bosses. On a scale of one to ten, 10 would be "highly satisfied" and 1 was "hoping for terminal illness." Everyone laughed. Barry laughed the loudest.

Nice. Real nice. Besides, she *could* have been referring to him.

april 15th

Finally we're getting something accomplished!

Lucy called with the name of the niece of a friend of hers in Wisconsin who is married to a caterer in upstate New York. Confusing? Yes. But at least it works in my favor. Jeb is a graduate of the American Culinary Arts School and he's willing to work within our budget.

All hail Lucy!

april 16th

Mrs. Stewart has invited me to join Kimberly and her next weekend at the annual Kennel Club Invitational. Chuffy's showing in the "Open Bitch" category. Whatever that means.

Reasons to go:
Nice to bond with future mother-in-law.

Reasons NOT to go:
Afraid to bond with future mother-in-law.
Don't like Kimberly.
Don't like dogs *that* much.

Reasons why I HAVE to go:
Mother-in-law will never forgive me if I say no.

What do you wear to a dog show?

april 17th

I went upstate today to meet with Jeb the caterer. His house is like a glorified log cabin tucked deep in the woods, so I expected he'd be a Grizzly Adams type. But no. He's this middle-aged white guy with dreadlocks. Standing in his huge commercial kitchen, he was busy slicing raw onions into a salad for a local horticulture club. His eyes were so bloodshot he could barely see, but he cut straight to the chase.

"Here's the 411, Amy. No way we're doing lobster risotto and pumpkin bisque for ninety people with your budget. End of story. But I appreciate your not wanting to go the traditional route of chicken, beef medallions, et cetera. So my suggestion is to go ethnic. Mix things up. Do some couscous, stewed vegetables, seared fruits, then throw a little lamb in there to sate everyone's carnal needs. I know that your group isn't accustomed to feasting on nuts and berries, but these things are cheap. Besides, it'll enable you to put your money into some top-quality lamb. It'll *seem* expensive, but it won't be. We'll craft a visual presentation so sensual it'll look like Manet on a plate.

My mom, Mrs. Stewart, and Mandy are going to hate this guy. I gave him a deposit on the spot.

april 18th

Mr. and Mrs. Stewart are struggling to establish a vaguely civil relationship for the sake of their children. How thoughtful. Unfortunately they've decided to use our wedding as Part One of the peace process.

Their first point of agreement in a year and a half: They will jointly host (read: pay for) our rehearsal dinner the night before the wedding. Mrs. Stewart will select the restaurant. Mr. Stewart will split the cost.

Their second point of agreement in a year and a half: Stephen's brother, Tom, can't be a guest at the wedding. He must be a groomsman.

Stephen is furious. I'm incredulous. Tom is delighted. He's already called Stephen twice to say he won't wear a cummerbund.

Tom, Mitch, and Larry. It's like having the Three Stooges at our wedding. So why pay for live entertainment—when I can just shoot myself instead?

april 19th

Now that Tom's a groomsman, I need another brides-maid. I thought about asking Kathy or Paula, but I just kept coming back to Anita. It's simply the right thing to do—whether she knows it or not.

So after forty-five minutes of begging her to see things from my perspective, and ultimately invoking her poetic endorsement of my marriage to Stephen[43], Anita finally agreed, "Well if I'm going to be at the circus, I might as well be one of the clowns."

Ain't love grand?

april 20th

My third fitting with Katrina. It's barely two months away from the most important fashion day of my life and I still look like I should be birthing livestock rather than getting married.

Every time she asks how the "retooling" is going, I just want to scream.

As God is my witness I'm going to bury this dress the minute my wedding is over.

Meanwhile Mandy wants to know if I've chosen the bridesmaids' dresses. She's worried about having enough time to properly accessorize.

The bride won't have shoes, but the maid of honor will have a stunning handbag.

Since I can barely dress myself for this event I've de-cided to relinquish all issues concerning bridesmaids' dresses to Mandy. I don't even care if she, Nicole, and

---

[43] "Maybe it won't be so pathetic."

Anita wear the same style. Let them choose something they like and will wear again. As long as it's ankle length and sleeveless I'll be happy.

That should please Anita. She's got fabulous upper arms.

april 21st

I finally got a chance to call Piece-A Cake. They scheduled a tasting for June 6th. Stephen's promised to come with me. Since I view the cake as a symbol of our union, it needs to be something we both like. But since I'm allergic to hazelnuts (I break out in hives) and mocha gives him migraines (it reminds him of a particularly stressful childhood vacation his family took in Zurich), we've got to be careful. Luckily we both like strawberry.

april 22nd

The Kennel Club Invitational was today. Who knew dogs used hairspray? Chuffy herself wore more Aqua Net than all the geriatric women of south Florida. Sure she was sticky, but she looked good.

And when's the last time you heard a bunch of well-dressed people say things like "She's a delightful bitch." Can't remember? Well, welcome to Thousand Pines Country Club in upstate New York! Sure they allow blacks and Jews, but half-breed mutts without pedigree? Forget it. The local pound's down the road.

The fact is, these pooches are worth more than I am. It's humbling. Not to mention educational. Among the many things I learned today:

- If the ship were sinking and Mrs. Stewart could save only one family member, she'd choose Chuffy.
- Kimberly has an unrelenting obsession with expensive jewelry. Particularly that which now belongs to me.
- Never wear open-toe shoes to a dog show.

april 23rd

Bianca Sheppard's getting married again. Who knew she was even dating? I called Mandy the minute I got the invitation. Apparently Bianca met George Carson a few weeks ago at the dermatologist's office. She had heat rash. He had eczema. Love was a foregone conclusion.

And who knows? Maybe the fifth time's a charm. I hope so—for George's sake.

They're getting married here in the city in the Markson Hotel ballroom (where I happen to know the basic venue charge starts at $12,000). And even though it's just two weeks before our wedding, I think we'll go anyway. By that point I'll be thrilled to think about a wedding other than my own.

april 24th

It's been more than three weeks since my last sex dream. At this rate I'll be off Anita's sleeping meds any day now.

And though I'm enormously relieved, it's also begun to strike me as a bit depressing that getting married means denying yourself the right to such pleasures. Maybe Anita's right. Maybe these dreams are harmless. After all, I am marrying Stephen. What greater commitment could I offer another human being? Does dreaming of lustful sex with someone else take anything away from that? Do I love Stephen any less? Of course not. And I bet Stephen would agree. After all, he's free to have sex dreams too if he wants. It wouldn't bother me a bit. Unless, of course, he was dreaming about Louise. I mean, come on, she's built like friggin' Barbie. But it doesn't matter. Stephen wouldn't have sex dreams. Sure he likes sex. A lot, actually. But he's not the type to dream about it.

Is he?

april 25th

The shit has officially hit the fan.

I got a phone call at 1:30 this afternoon from George Harriman of Harriman Carpets, one of the "Faces in the City" profiles. He'd been sitting at the Park Avenue Café for over an hour waiting for me to show up to a lunch meeting that I didn't even know was scheduled. He was understandably ticked off. I apologized profusely for the mix-up, promised to reschedule with his secretary, then stormed out of my office and gave Kate a scolding that she'd never forget. I reminded her that Mr. Harriman's profile was a focal point of the issue, that Mr. Harriman's time was incredibly valuable, as he's on the board of directors for over twelve different charitable organizations, was the regional spokesperson for the Urban Children's League, and ran one of the biggest carpet companies in the country. Then I told her the next time she wanted to forget to inform me about a meeting she should choose someone less important.

That's when Kate stood up and informed *me* that she

had told me about the meeting, that it was written in my appointment book, and that she had included it on to-day's itinerary—a copy of which was sitting on top of my desk.

I looked at my appointment book. She was absolutely right. The meeting was right there. The whole thing was my fault. And everyone in the office knew it.

april 26th—2 A.M.

I can't sleep.

I keep thinking about that girl in my freshman litera-ture class. The one who married the guy with chronic dan-druff. She was so desperate to marry and there were hundreds of guys to choose from—wealthy, handsome, pre-med, pre-law, well-groomed. But she chose the one with de-cent tennis skills and dandruff.

I used to think it was an act of desperation, but now I think maybe it was love.

april 26th

I broke down today in the office bathroom. Tears of appre-ciation all over the place.

Because things aren't good. They're *great*.

When all this fighting, negotiating, and planning is over I am going to spend the rest of my life with the world's most incredible man. Someone who may not be perfect but who understands me, accepts my faults, loves my strengths, and keeps me smiling no matter how many foolish ideas he has about our wedding band.

I don't ever want another wet and wild sex dream again. Not about Rick or Anthony or Jon or Denny or Jonas or Tim or Dylan.

All I want is Stephen. My wonderfully boring Stephen!

Overwhelmed by emotion, I decided to call Stephen's office and share my love. Louise answered his phone. Apparently Stephen had stepped away from his desk. After offering to take a message she mentioned how sorry she was that the Ecuadorian woodwind band had fallen through. It seems she's a fan.

But if the band plays in the subway station near Stephen's house and Louise lives all the way across town, how does she know what they sound like?

Breathe. I must remember to breathe.

And then I called Anita.

ME
This is a warning. Louise is a sign. I've been
inconsiderate, self-centered, and I enjoyed my sex
dreams. I'm being punished.

ANITA
By whom?

ME
By God!

ANITA
God? I thought you were an agnostic.

ME
I am. I was. Maybe I'm reconsidering.

ANITA
Don't tell me you found God while planning your
wedding. Where was she? Hiding in the
flatware department?

ME

I'm being serious, Anita.

ANITA

That's what worries me. Look, this is why I didn't want you to get married. It's turning you into an idiot. Besides, assuming there is a God, don't you think she'd be more merciful than to pit one woman against another?

ME

You've got a point.

ANITA

That's the first intelligent thing you've said in months. Now remember, if you start hearing strange voices, it's not God—it's your Inner Bride. So unless she's telling you to serve premium liquors at your reception, silence her immediately. She's *insane*.

april 27th

The good news and the bad news.

The good news: I went upstate tonight to sample the menu Jeb is proposing for our wedding reception. Lamb with almonds and currants, couscous, and glazed yams . . . It was fabulous! As is Jeb, who continues to be the most pleasant, easygoing man, despite his ongoing battle with hay fever. I may not be having a fancy New York City wedding in some elegant ballroom, but you can be damn sure the food will be KICK-ASS. No beef medallions for this gal.

The bad news: On the way back to the train station I stopped in the mall to buy a twelve-pack of nylons. A man was taking a leak against the side of the building. It was Reverend MacKenzie.

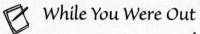 *While You Were Out*

4/29 11:05 A.M.

From: Your Wedding Photographer

Message: Has a last-minute double suicide to photograph. Needs to reschedule this afternoon's meeting about portraits.

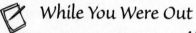 *While You Were Out*

4/29 11:06 A.M.

From: Kate

Message: Your voice mail box is too full to accept messages. Please empty it IMMEDIATELY.

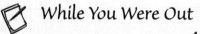 *While You Were Out*

4/29 11:15 A.M.

From: Mandy

Message: Has chosen an ankle-length sleeveless dress made of Asian nubby silk in an elegant cherub pink with a hint of silver for the bridesmaids. Will this coordinate with your tablecloths?

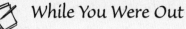

While You Were Out

4/29 11:25 A.M.

From: Julie Browning

Message: Anne Von Trier wants a guarantee that her profile will be ahead of James Royce's. Can she do that?

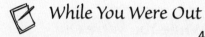

While You Were Out

4/29 11:35 A.M.

From: Anita

Message: What the hell is "Asian nubby silk in an elegant cherub pink with a hint of silver" and why does she have to wear it?

While You Were Out

4/29 11:43 A.M.

From: Jeb the caterer

Message: Has forgotten how many people he's supposed to be feeding at your wedding.

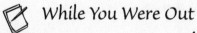

While You Were Out

4/29 11:45 A.M.

From: Mr. Spaulding

Message: Bring the article drafts for the June issue to the 12:30 meeting.

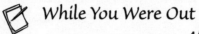 ### While You Were Out

4/29 11:49 A.M.

From: Mandy

Message: Please inform Anita that verbal abuse is an inappropriate mode of communication among civilized human beings. Especially since cherub pink will help to offset her sallow undertones.

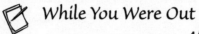 ### While You Were Out

4/29 12:04 P.M.

From: Anita

Message: The entire concept of bridesmaids and bridesmaids' dresses is hateful and barbaric. Could she tend bar instead?

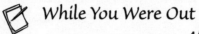 ### While You Were Out

4/29 12:15 P.M.

From: Stephen

Message: Has to work late again. Don't wait up.

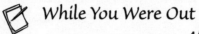 ### While You Were Out

4/29 12:25 P.M.

From: Rick

Message: "Long time no see." Back in town. Has a conga-drum gig at the China Club tonight. Wants to catch up.

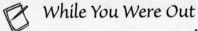 **While You Were Out**

4/29 12:35 P.M.

From: Mr. Spaulding

Message: They're waiting for you in the 12:30 meeting.

 While You Were Out

4/29 12:48 P.M.

From: Kate

Message: Payroll doesn't have my check. You never signed my time sheet. My rent is due TOMORROW.

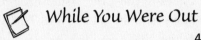 **While You Were Out**

4/29 12:53 P.M.

From: Mr. Spaulding

Message: Where are you?

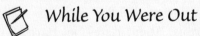 **While You Were Out**

4/29 1:05 P.M.

From: Mr. Spaulding

Message: Wants to see you in his office immediately.

 While You Were Out

4/29 1:06 P.M.

From: Macy's Linen Department

Message: Your grandmother-in-law has purchased monogrammed towels for you. The store needs to

confirm the spelling of your name. Is it "Stewart" or "Stuart"?

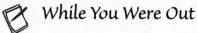 **While You Were Out**

4/29 1:06 P.M.

From: Kate

Message: I quit.

april 30th

Mr. Spaulding called me into his office to discuss my ability to see my "Faces in the City" issue through to completion. Perhaps *Barry* should take over. The weasel! I adamantly assured him that wouldn't be necessary. He's giving me one more—read: LAST—chance.

Meanwhile, Kate has really gone. Poof! Like a cloud of angry smoke. She requested her final paycheck and COBRA medical extension. She even took her Backstreet Boys screen saver. Barry is livid.

And I feel horrible. About Kate. Not Barry. My life has become this huge mass of scary—that spews. I'd run from me too, if I could. But I can't.

april 30th—10 P.M.

If a man who is prone to spontaneous gestures suddenly proposes marriage, what are the chances that he really means it? Sure, he planned my proposal. Sort of. But it's not like he ever mentioned marriage before that.

april 30th—10:30 P.M.

MANDY
Well at least this time you had the decency to have your panic attack *before* my bedtime.

ME
I'm serious, Mandy. Do you think he regrets proposing?

MANDY
Did he actually go with you to register for sheets?

ME
Yes.

MANDY
Then what greater sign of commitment do you expect from a man? Now, relax. There's no reason to worry.

may 2nd

The first step in solving a problem is admitting you have one: I can't plan this wedding alone.

There, I said it. Ugly but true—I need HELP.

I'd ask Stephen but he's too consumed with his computer program. He can barely get dressed in the morning let alone help plan a wedding reception. As for the band he's supposed to hire . . . I figure we'll be firing up my dad's 8-track and poppin' in some Pat Boone.

Then there's Mandy, who despite her pledge of fealty has basically retreated into the matrimonial black hole with Jon.

It's time for desperate measures.

may 3rd

I asked my mother for help.

I chose five specific tasks for her to handle. Things I can't possibly do and she can't possibly screw up. I feel better already. It was the best decision I've ever made. And she was delighted.

Who knows, maybe it was a mistake not to ask for her help from the start.

I'm such an idiot.

may 4th

Nicole called this evening. She wanted to talk. (Okay.) She wanted to come over right away. (Curious.) Alone. (Ding Ding Ding!) That's when I knew something was wrong. The last time my sister came over to my apartment alone was four years ago, when I got stuck in a bustier that I bought on a whim. It was the kind that slips over your head. Getting it on was a quiet struggle, but as I fought to get out of it the metal stays caught my hair and left me naked from the waist up with my arms trapped above my head and the bustier wrapped around my face. Dialing the telephone necessitated a whole new yoga position. And since unlocking the door was physically impossible, I called Nicole, who had an extra set of my keys. It was that or my dad, and there simply wasn't enough therapy in the world that could have enabled us to recover from that experience.

But tonight as I waited for Nicole it occurred to me that perhaps she was attempting some type of pre-wedding sisterly bonding. The kind of thing Jane Austen characters did. But when she walked through the door I knew something was wrong. She looked anxious and tired. Like she hadn't slept in weeks.

> ME
> Are you all right?

> NICOLE
> Yes and no. I need to talk to you about something. Something important.

As she sat down on the sofa Nicole took a cigarette out of her purse. My sister hasn't smoked since she was twenty-one and Chet made quitting a condition of their marriage. She glanced around the apartment and chuckled.

> NICOLE
> Hey, do you remember the time I came over here to rescue you from that crazy push-up bra—

> ME
> Yeah, yeah. It was a bustier and that's not why you came here. Now, what's going on?

> NICOLE
> Chet and I are splitting up.

It was like someone punched me in the stomach, then banged my head against the wall. I don't remember sitting down but suddenly I was.

> ME
> Are you kidding me?

> NICOLE
> No. It's real and it's final.

> ME
> What happened?!

NICOLE

A lot of things. It's been coming for a while.

ME

I had no idea.

NICOLE

We didn't advertise.

ME

But I mean, there's got to be a reason . . . oh God, is
there someone else?

Nicole looked at me in shock.

NICOLE

How did you know that?

ME

Sonofabitch! I always suspected Chet was too good
to be true. Under that Perfect Man façade was a
dirtbag having an affair with some tramp!

NICOLE

Actually, I'm the dirtbag having the affair.

ME

Excuse me?

NICOLE

I said I'm the one who's having the affair. And
Pablo's no tramp.

ME

Who the hell is Pablo?

NICOLE

Pablo's the guy I've been seeing for the
last six months.

ME
Six months!!!!

NICOLE
I know how it sounds. But it's for the best. Chet and
I haven't been happy for a while.

Nicole spent the next two hours telling me how her marriage was a mistake from the beginning. How she and Chet were so used to being together after all those years in college and how they were so afraid of the uncertainty that their post-college future held that they married out of fear and complacency. The first year was fine, but after that things just got bad. They simply weren't happy. And while Chet was willing to spend the rest of his life in denial, Nicole wasn't. She wanted to be happy. She wanted a chance to find her true self.

As I listened to Nicole's story, and wondered how some guy named Pablo who works for the cable company could help my sister find her true self, I began to feel increasingly sick. I know it sounds selfish—my sister and her husband get divorced and *I* have a nervous breakdown. But I couldn't help it. I'd always considered their relationship to be the gold standard for a healthy marriage. One where the participants were blissfully in love and whose inner workings seemed harmonious. I thought if I was really lucky I could have a marriage like hers. Now I learn that the ideal to which I aspired didn't really exist. What does that mean for me?

Nicole stood up to go.

NICOLE
Thanks for listening.

Hey, if I couldn't be there to support her wedding, I might as well be there to support her divorce.

NICOLE
I guess I just wanted to practice on you before
telling Mom and Dad. I know they're going to be
devastated. I just hope they remember that it's my
happiness that counts most.

Yeah, right. That's what I was hoping for, and look what
happened there—value, size, and frontier wedding attire.

ME
Of course they care most about your happiness.
We all do.

NICOLE
Oh, and thanks for giving me the courage to
end my marriage.

ME
Why me?

NICOLE
It was listening to your wedding plans that made me
realize I had to leave Chet.

Excuse me, *WHAT?!*
But it was too late. She was already out the door.

may 5th

CHET AND NICOLE ARE DIVORCING.

CHET AND NICOLE ARE DIVORCING.

CHET AND NICOLE ARE DIVORCING.

may 6th—2 A.M.

Just when I'd gotten used to the idea of me being married, Chet and Nicole are breaking up. It's like the whole world's flipped inside-out.

Or maybe things have been backward from the start. Maybe it's Nicole who's not the marrying kind.

may 6th

I went down to Chinatown and picked up the invitations from Bunny. It was the first really hot day we've had this year and Bunny's shop hasn't got air-conditioning. One would think the case of Budweiser chilling in a Styrofoam cooler by the cash register would help Bunny beat the heat. But no. To relieve her discomfort, and add to everyone else's, seventy-something Bunny was wearing hot pants and a halter top. It wasn't pretty.

But the invitations are. Crisp, clean, and pristine, they're beautiful.

As I turned to exit the shop Bunny hacked up some smoker's phlegm and offered a nugget of wisdom. "Listen, kid, marriage can be great or it can stink. My first two were disasters. But the third was a keeper. We had twenty-six terrific years, right up to the minute he kicked from liver failure. And if I hadn't spent those five years in court fighting over his bodily remains with the *other* wife he'd been hiding up in Buffalo, my memories of him would be nothing but sweet."

Yes, Bunny. Love *is* a battlefield.

Robert and Theresa Thomas

and

Ms. Abigail Brockton Stewart

and

Mr. James W. Stewart

Joyfully Invite You to Share
in the Celebration as Their Children

Amy Sarah Thomas

and

Stephen Richard Stewart

Tie the Knot of Matrimonial Delight
on June 22nd
2 P.M. in the Afternoon
at the United Presbyterian Church
in Hopbrook, NY
Dinner Reception to Follow, Chez Thomas
R.S.V.P.   Festive Attire

may 7th

My parents are refusing to discuss Nicole's divorce. Something along the lines of if they ignore it, it will go away. Fat chance. I've been trying that with Gram since Christmas.

On another unfortunate note, Human Resources still hasn't found a replacement for Kate, and Barry won't stop grousing about it. Loudly. Especially when Mr. Spaulding's within earshot. Our temps have ranged from English-as-a-Second-Language students to unemployed street performers. How a street performer can be out of work is beyond me. But suffice it to say that not one of them has known Microsoft Office or where to buy a decent pair of wedding shoes.

That's right, I asked.

may 8th

While Stephen and Mitch went to hear potential wedding bands at a Long Island club, Paula and Kathy came to my apartment to help prepare the invitations. I'd already had my temp address the envelopes on the laser printer at work, but we still had to stuff the envelopes (invites, protective tissue paper, response cards) and stamp them. We were doing fine until I noticed that Kathy had started to slip. Her once neatly aligned stamps were suddenly slapped haphazardly on envelopes. Some listed to the left, others sloped to the right.

How much skill is required to stamp an envelope? I immediately reassigned tasks.

We were done by midnight. After a crazed scramble back in March, the invitations were now under control. A hundred and twenty beautiful invitations would be mailed out six weeks prior to my wedding. Eat your heart out, *BB*.

may 9th

Having completed her five designated wedding tasks, my mother decided to take the bull by the horns. Shooting straight from the hip, it was "tough love" all over the place.

My menu is too outlandish. My floor plan has no "flow." My floral design is poorly conceived. And my caterer is a *pothead*?!

"Come on, Amy. You honestly didn't know? Why do you think his eyes are always bloodshot?"

"I don't know. Onions, hay fever, a high pollen count?"

"Try a quarter ounce of reefer a day. Trust me. I teach public school. I know these things."

Reefer, food, flowers, flow. Whatever. Just handle it. I hereby abdicate my throne.

may 10th

Things are starting to come together. The July issue of *Round-Up* is falling into place with an extensive six-page article on hot trends in municipal playgrounds. My "Faces in the City" issue is on schedule, with four of the ten profiles already completed. And my wedding is now officially a Terry Thomas Production.

Welcome back, life.

may 11th

Stephen hired a band for our wedding. *Diggie's Delight* will be headlining at the Thomas-Stewart reception. Though they favor classic rock songs, their repertoire ranges from classical to jazz instrumentals, they own their own sound system, and for an extra fifty bucks they'll provide the ceremony music.

Sold.

may 12th

Mrs. Stewart and Chuffy joined us at United Presbyterian for our second meeting with Reverend MacKenzie. We reviewed the basic structure of the ceremony and the wording of the vows.

Afterward, Mrs. Stewart reminisced about United Presbyterian—the moving Christmas pageants, the invaluable Sunday school lessons—then broke down in tears about her life ravaged by divorce, a world that no longer appreciates heavy brocades, and her preliminary stages of menopause. As Stephen comforted his mother the only thing I could think of was Reverend MacKenzie whizzing in broad daylight, and how NOT to shake his hand.

On the train ride home, as Stephen and I cuddled in our seat, he happened to mention that Louise has canceled her wedding. Something about cold feet.

MANDY
Okay, Amy. It's time to worry.

may 13th

D ue to insufficient postage, all 120 invitations have been returned. My elegant invitations are now covered in hefty black RETURN TO SENDER stamps.

Can this be anything but an ugly omen?

may 14th

M y newest temp is a musical theater aficionado named Fabrizio. Although he's a fairly good secretary, he can't seem to work without singing Sondheim. As much as this annoys me, it drives Barry absolutely nuts.

Barry hates Sondheim. He's more the Andrew Lloyd Webber type. Think *Evita*.

So it was with mixed feelings that I interrupted Fabrizio's snappy rendition of "I Feel Pretty" to send him down to Bunny's to get 120 new envelopes. When he returned I had him print the addresses and restuff all the invitations. I was about to have him mail them when I reconsidered. I'm already one week behind *BB*'s schedule, so there's no room for error. I personally went to the twenty-four-hour post office and mailed them myself.

Afterward, Mandy came to my apartment to show me

the bridesmaid dresses. Ankle length, sleeveless, and a stunning shade of rosy-pink, the dresses are classy and sophisticated. Everything that my wedding gown should be but ISN'T.

What the hell's the point of having a wedding if the bridesmaids look better than the bride? This event is supposed to be about *me*. I'm the center of attention. I should be the best-looking, or at least the best-dressed, woman in the room.

But what can I do? It's certainly not like I can say that to anyone. They'd think I was the most egoistic person on the planet. And maybe I am. But that's okay.

I'm the damn bride!

Meanwhile, I can't help but worry that the man I'm about to marry is having an affair with his genetically perfect female coworker. On a rational level I know Stephen is good, honest, and faithful. But he's still *human*. And anyone who watches daytime television knows that every man with proper urological functions has been unfaithful at some point in his life. Hell, if it weren't for infidelity and evil twins, soap operas would cease to exist.

And while Anita says my Inner Bride is insane, Mandy is convinced that no one gets cold feet and cancels their wedding unless they've met someone else. I'm just praying that someone else isn't Stephen.

Is there a nonconfrontational way to ask your fiancé if he's nailing his coworker?

may 15th

Turns out Nicole's paramour, Pablo, is the guy who comes to your house and hooks up your cable. Stephen suggested that if you can't beat them, understand them, or condone their actions, the least you can do is get free cable. I think he's onto something.

New York Electric Works
"We keep the energy flowing"

Dear Valued Customer,

Please be informed that your check to New York Electric Works in the amount of $45.19 has been returned unpaid. If you do not pay the entire amount due by the above date a 19 percent interest rate will be assessed on your balance. Additionally, as per our company policy, a $15 returned check fee has been assessed on your account.

Sincerely,
Narda Mingala
Account Representative

may 16th

This is great. Here I am throwing a $10,000 party, but I can't pay my damn electric bill!

may 17th

We're Jewish.

may 18th

At first I thought it was some old show tune. The forgotten "We're Jewish" medley from *Fiddler*. But no. As Mrs. Stewart, Stephen, and I sat around the living room merrily telling my folks about the beautiful United Presbyterian Church, I could sense that all this joy was really making Gram mad.

So I wasn't too concerned when she suddenly stood up and clutched her heart. I figured this was just the most recent in her string of attention-stealing ploys. The old Heart Attack routine: clutch your heart, hold your breath, and get that "faraway look" in your eyes. Standard summer-stock fare.

I am so naïve.

Heart attacks are for amateurs. Gram is a world-class pro. "We're Jewish!"

Excuse me?

"No church. No minister. It's an insult. It's a *shandeh*!"

A *shandeh*? Since when did Gram start honing up on her Yiddish? From the corner of my eye I saw Mrs. Stewart clutch Chuffy tightly to her bosom, no doubt wondering what the hell a *shandeh* was.

Mom struggled to reason with Gram. But Gram just shook her head. Her parents were conservative Jews. They had a Judaica store in New Jersey, for which she used to make ceramic dreidels. But my grandfather was Protestant so she didn't mention it. After they were married she moved to upstate New York and raised her family in a Christian home. She didn't want to inconvenience anyone. Until NOW.

It seems thirty-five days prior to my wedding is the most convenient time to mention that my family is intimately linked to thousands of years of religious history and turbulent social events. That my people are strewn from New York to Jerusalem. That we are the Chosen.

Well, that's just swell. Had it been any other point in time I would have been interested to hear all about it. But not NOW. Not when I'm getting ready to tie the knot in a Presbyterian church under the eyes of friends, family, and Reverend MacKenzie.

"What do you mean 'no church'? It's a done deal. We've reserved the date. Mailed the invitations. Had premarital counseling with the minister!"

My mother tried to calm me, to contain the situation, to make sense of those years spent painting Easter eggs. "Mother, please. Are you *certain* you're Jewish?"

"Of course I'm certain. What do you think? Jews are stupid? Don't forget, this makes all of you Jewish too."

With enough of her own domestic problems to last a lifetime, Mrs. Stewart slipped Chuffy into her handbag and politely said her good-byes. Two minutes later she was gone. Like a rat from a sinking ship.

How dare Gram turn my wedding into a sinking ship! I was furious. My parents were speechless. And Gram was on her way to bingo — but not before declaring me an anti-Semite and hip-checking my college graduation photo to the floor.

The upside? Stephen finally agrees that Gram's a lunatic.

may 19th

Chapter Thirty-nine of *BB* suggests that couples alleviate stress by taking minivacations prior to their wedding. Where can we go on $23.50?

may 20th

My family is still stunned by Gram's outburst concerning our Jewish roots. Considering how much energy we're already expending to plan my wedding, and to deny Nicole's divorce, it's a miracle we're not running to some clinic, begging for sedatives.

Thankfully, my mother, who for the first twenty-four hours was leaning toward official conversion for the entire family, has eased up on the issue. She's come to her senses and agreed that my wedding should go ahead as planned— whether or not Gram chooses to attend. I suspect this has something to do with her realization that as an observant, kosher Jew she'd need to wash two sets of dishes and forgo bacon.

Meanwhile, Mandy insists I resolve the Stephen/Louise issue A.S.A.P. "How can you, in good faith, enter into a life-long union with someone who may be cheating on you? A happy marriage is based on trust."

She's right.

So we've decided to go behind Stephen's back and spend next Wednesday spying on him.

may 21st

We got our first R.S.V.P. for the wedding today. It was so exciting to see that familiar cream-colored envelope sitting in the mailbox.

And I can't tell you how pleased I was to learn that Hans Lindstrom will be attending my wedding.

may 23rd

More R.S.V.P.s. People are actually coming to my parents' house festively attired on June 22nd.

Now I *have* to get married!

may 24th

I'd been trying to reach Anita for the past week. I know she's been busy; certainly every time I call her office she's either in a meeting or on an important call. But for Christ's sake, it's *Teen Flair*. How important can it be? Have the Hanson boys cut their hair? Has cherry-flavored lip gloss been linked to weight gain?

Doesn't she realize that my wedding is twenty-nine days away and I still don't have my beautiful rhinestone hair comb? Had she even remembered her promise to take her niece Molly to the Bridal Building and buy it for me? Sure, Lucy's blue enamel barrette was beautiful, but that hair comb was the finishing touch!

I kept trying.

ME

Hi, it's Amy Thomas calling again. Is Ms. Jensen available?

ANITA'S SECRETARY

No, I'm afraid Ms. Jensen is in the ladies' room.

ME

Again? That's the fifth time today.

ANITA'S SECRETARY

Yes, well, I'm afraid Ms. Jensen is suffering from a urinary tract infection.

Wait a minute . . . *a urinary tract infection?* Anita was avoiding me just like I'd avoided Mandy![44]

And who could blame her? I've called her ten times a day panicked about Stephen and Louise, complained incessantly about my dress, and even cried once or twice or seventeen times over my nonexistent shoes.

Anita's secretary must have sensed my sudden horror, because she put me on hold. Moments later Anita answered the phone.

ANITA

Hi, Amy. What's going on?

ME

Look, I know you've been avoiding me and
I'm sorry that I've called you ten times
today—

ANITA

Sixteen.

ME

Whatever. Just tell me if you and Molly went and
got my hair comb.

ANITA

Yes, we went. No, we didn't get the comb.

ME

Why not?

ANITA

Because it's not a hair comb, Amy.
It's a tiara.

---

44 Except her secretary was obviously more of a "team player" than Kate ever was. Kate absolutely refused to use the UTI excuse.

ME

Come on, Anita. You know how important that comb is to me, and you didn't buy it because Mrs. Cho thinks it's for kids?

ANITA

It *is* for kids. It's what prepubescent girls wear in those pervy child beauty pageants.

ME

But it's an integral part of my hairstyle!

ANITA

And you're a thirty-year-old woman obsessing on some toddler's Taiwanese tiara. Now calm down. I'll call you later.

First of all, it's Korean, not Taiwanese. Second, how the hell am I supposed to "calm down"?

Single people just don't get it.

may 25th

I no longer need to go undercover with Mandy in an effort to assess my fiancé's fidelity.

The truth is OUT.

I dropped by Stephen's office. Unannounced. Just a friendly "in the neighborhood, thought I'd say hello" visit. But no sooner did I push the elevator button than the doors opened wide, and off stepped Louise—with her tongue jammed down the throat of a HUNKY, SIX-FOOT-TALL BLOND WITH THE BODY OF AN ADONIS! *Nothing* at all like Stephen!

may 25th—11:30 P.M.

The fact that I so easily lost faith in Stephen's love is frightening. Nicole, the Stewarts, and Bianca Sheppard-Douglas-Izzard-Santos-Rabinowitz are all proof of the fragility of marriage.

But true love should be hard as a rock.

It's something I see between the Brocktons, my parents, and though Stephen would kill me if he heard me say this, I also see it with his father and Misty. Love is strong, binding, and brave. It rises to the top—even if it is unpopular.

I know our love is strong. I really do. But I've got to remember that nothing survives without faith.

may 26th

We got our first official wedding gift today.

Stephen and I are now the proud, joint owners of a shiny seven-speed blender with an adjustable base.

may 27th

It's amazing how much progress has been made since my mother ascended to the wedding-planner throne.

Chairs, tables, table linens, a tent, and the dance floor have all been rented. Bartenders have been hired. The floral design has been reconceived and orders have been placed. The menu has been revised.[45] And the wine has been purchased. All in just two weeks. Asking my mother

---

45 After weeks of negotiation, Jeb finally agreed to serve chicken breast if my mother promised to stop pressuring him about entering drug rehab.

to help was the smartest decision I've made since deciding to marry Stephen.

And work's back on track too. Since I'll be honeymooning until mid-July, D-day on the proofs for my "Faces" issue is set at the second week of June. To make sure I meet that deadline I've instituted a new rule—no wedding-related phone calls at the office. And this time I'm sticking to it. Be it the florist or the bandleader, leave a message on my machine at home. And if it's an emergency call, my mother. I've purchased a pager for her, which has convinced her fourth-grade students that she's dealing drugs on the side. They are thoroughly delighted.

But that's not to say that things at work are calm. On the contrary, tensions are running high. Barry spent the morning short-tempered and muttering as Fabrizio serenaded us with a medley from *Gypsy*. Somewhere around the chorus of "Everything's Coming Up Roses," Barry snapped.

"Dammit, Fabrizio, Sondheim's a wordy lightweight with no passion!" Fabrizio gasped. Then shrieked, "Andrew Lloyd Webber's a hack and a plagiarist!"

I was expecting fisticuffs.

But as much as Barry despises Sondheim, he knows Fabrizio's the best temp we've had since Kate's departure. So he directed the remainder of his frustration at me.

"You! This is all your fault. Kate didn't sing Sondheim! Kate didn't even know who Sondheim is! Now, for Christ's sake, would you hurry up and get married? YOU'RE KILLING ME HERE!"

My pleasure, Barry, except I still don't have shoes!

LY EVIL AND ENDLESS
Official ∧ THINGS TO DO List

1. ~~Choose wedding date~~
2. ~~Tell boss wedding date~~
3. ~~Vacation time for honeymoon~~
4. ~~Decide on honeymoon~~
5. ~~Get minister~~
6. ~~Choose reception venue~~
7. ~~Make guest list~~
8. ~~Choose maid of honor~~
9. ~~Choose best man~~
10. ~~Register for gifts~~
11. ~~Arrange for engagement party~~
12. ~~Buy engagement ring~~
13. ~~Buy wedding rings~~
14. ~~Buy wedding dress~~
15. ~~Choose maid of honor dress~~
16. Order wedding cake
17. ~~Hire caterer~~
18. ~~Hire band for reception~~
19. ~~Order flowers for ceremony~~
20. Buy shoes
21. ~~Plan rehearsal dinner~~
22. ~~Invites to rehearsal dinner~~
23. ~~Hire musicians for ceremony~~
24. ~~Decide on dress code~~
25. Get marriage license

26. Hire videographer
27. Hire photographer
28. Order table flowers
29. Order bouquets
30. Order boutonnieres for men
31. Order nosegays for women
32. Order invitations
33. Decide on wine selection
34. Postage for invitations
35. Choose hairstyle and makeup
36. Buy gifts for attendants
37. Buy thank-you notes
38. Announce wedding in newspaper
39. Buy headpiece
40. Buy traveler's checks for honeymoon
41. Apply for visas
42. Get shots and vaccinations
43. Order tent if necessary
44. Order chairs/tables if necessary
45. Make budget
46. Divide expenses
47. Make table-seating charts
48. Choose bridesmaid dress
49. Decide on menu
50. Decide on hors d'oeuvres
51. Decide on dinner-service style
52. Decide on staff-guest ratio
53. Decide seated or buffet
54. Reserve vegetarian meals
55. Reserve band/photographer/videographer meals
56. Make photo list

57. Choose hotel for wedding night
58. Hire limo for church-reception transport
59. Buy guest book for reception
60. Find hotel for out-of-towners
61. Decide on liquor selection
62. ~~Hire bartenders~~
63. Verify wheelchair accessibility
64. ~~Choose processional music~~
65. ~~Choose recessional music~~
66. ~~Choose cocktail music~~
67. ~~Choose reception music~~
68. ~~Choose ceremony readings~~
69. Prepare birdseed instead of rice
70. Schedule manicure/pedicure/wax

may 28th

It was an act of desperation, but I have less than FOUR WEEKS. Can you really blame me for going to Manfield Blossom—one of the most expensive shoe stores in the entire world?

Let ye not be the first to cast a stone lest ye be in possession of a fabulous pair of wedding shoes!

The store, located just off Fifth Avenue's rarefied shopping district, looks like a fancy gift box. It's tiny and immaculate and filled with wildly expensive merchandise. Shoes for thousands of dollars. Handbags for the annual cost of an entire family of migrant laborers. You know you can't afford to shop there just by looking at it. So I dressed up for the occasion. Not to celebrate my folly but to avoid detection. The last thing I wanted was to set off some snotty salesperson's riffraff meter. Just let me shop in peace and quietly check out the price tags, without any hassle or humiliation.

And there they were. My wedding shoes. A pair of lovely cream-colored Mary Janes with a Holly Golightly twist—rich satin, a sturdy heel, and an understated square buckle.

One problem. They were *$400*.

Quick! If I cancel the bridesmaids' bouquets and the band plays for three hours instead of four can I afford it? Yes! Minutes later a saleswoman dressed in skintight designer clothing was slipping the shoe of my dreams onto my foot—

Or was she?

My toes were in but the top of my foot wasn't. The saleswoman was pushing the heel. I was pulling the strap. But the shoe refused to surrender. It wanted nothing to do with my foot. Then, adding insult to insult, the saleswoman looked up and said, "Your feet are too fleshy for our shoes."

Too fleshy?! What? Like they should go on a diet? Be shipped to fat camp for the summer? Walk off a couple pounds? Is it my fault Manfield Blossom's shoes are designed for anorexics with bony feet who can afford to pay exorbitant prices because they don't spend money on food?

So much for avoiding detection.

may 29th

It's official. I'm having an afternoon reception with a chicken buffet, New York state wine, and tap water. When I reminded my mother that some people don't eat chicken she just scoffed. "It's a wedding reception, not an airplane ride. We don't need a *selection*." She's right. Screw 'em. No lobster risotto, French wines, or lamb. Value and size. Thanks, Mom. It'll go great with my dress.

At least my bridesmaids will look good.

may 30th

Houston, we have a problem! Chapter Nineteen of *BB* clearly states that 25 percent of invitees will decline. We already have eighty-five acceptances and only two declines, with thirty-three still outstanding! What's wrong with these people? Don't they have anything else to do with their lives? Don't they know we've only budgeted for ninety?!

To make matters worse, Stephen's brother, Tom, is suddenly refusing to wear a tuxedo. He needs to be "special." Oh, he's special all right. How about a straitjacket and a muzzle?

Meanwhile we've got to go to Bianca's wedding next weekend. I would have completely forgotten about it if Mandy hadn't asked if we wanted to split a gift with her and Jon. She says that etiquette declares it unnecessary to send gifts for a fifth wedding, but she felt badly sending nothing. Since I can barely afford to keep my utilities on, I think I'll just wait for wedding Number Six.

june 1st

Barry has managed to convince Mr. Spaulding to reschedule the "Faces in the City" advertisers meeting from June 18th to Friday, June 21st. Something about "better timing." For everyone but me.

Creep.

Barry knows that my rehearsal dinner is upstate that Friday night. He knows that I was intending to take the day off, to spend it with my parents, preparing for one of the biggest days of my life. But the advertisers meeting is crucial to the "Faces" issue. To *my* "Faces" issue. It would be totally irresponsible of me not to be there. And there's no way in hell I'm letting Barry take my place.

Weasel.

So there's only one thing to do. When Stephen goes upstate on Friday morning to help his parents with the rehearsal dinner, I'll have him bring all my wedding things. This way I can take the train straight from the advertisers meeting to the dinner.

Work, dinner, wedding, clothes . . . I can do it. I can do it.

june 2nd

With Louise's help, Stephen has successfully delivered his computer program. Yippee!!![46]

The whole office finished the day with a case of champagne and a sigh of relief. They have a new product to release in September, the business will stay afloat, and Stephen still has a job. He's so happy!

And totally relaxed. He actually asked if there was anything he could do to help with the wedding.

There are barely three weeks left—Is he kidding me?!

---

[46] And *Yippee!* for the lovely and talented Louise, who has moved in with Sten, the sexy Swede she was groping in the elevator.

june 3rd

Capitalizing on Stephen's free time, we went to City Hall to get our marriage license. Luckily in New York State you don't need a blood test. Just a ballpoint pen, valid identification, and some cash will send you on your way to legal matrimony.

Welcome to the practical side of marriage.

Although the marriage office was dingy and cramped, anticipation filled the air. Stephen and I were among fifty couples all waiting to profess their undying love for each other—to the government. That's right. Tell the Census Bureau, the tax man, and my congresswoman that we're in love, dammit!

You could almost hear the office clerks thinking, "Fools. You'll be back. And next time, bring correct change." But even the bureaucratic indifference to affairs of the heart couldn't dampen our spirits. Every couple was holding hands and grinning.

And when the clerk asked what my name would be after marriage, I proudly became Amy Thomas-Stewart. Legally able to call myself Amy Thomas or Amy Stewart, I was still, most important, me.

june 4th

The floodgates have opened and the presents are pouring in. According to Chapter Forty-two of *BB*, guests have a year after the wedding to send a gift, but already my apartment's teeming with cardboard boxes and Styrofoam pellets. It's almost enough to make me forget how much this event's costing us.

Almost.

* * *

Dear Mr. and Mrs. Kendilinski,

We greatly apreciate the blender you sent us for our wedding. It will undoubtedly aid in our culinary adventures.

Sincerely,
Amy and Stephen

* * *

Dear Cousin Jane,

We greatly apreciate the iron you sent us for our wedding. As neither Stephen nor I possess any skill in this area, we are hopeful that your gift will assist us. I was, however, sorry to learn that you will be unable to attend our wedding. Perhaps we can get together sometime after our honeymoon.

Warmest regards,
Amy and Stephen

* * *

Dear Mr. Munson,

We greatly apreciate the Aboriginal death mask you sent us for our wedding. My future father-in-law informs me that you spend much of your free time in Papua, New Guinea, so we delight in knowing the authenticity of such a unique gift. Certainly I have never seen anything like it. It will be a lovely addition to our new home.

Sincerely,
Amy and Stephen

june 5th

Our cake tasting is tomorrow at Piece-A Cake but Mr. Spaulding has scheduled a 5:30 P.M. staff meeting and Stephen's got a court appearance for his pothole debacle.

Surprise, surprise. It looks like my mother will have to decide.

june 6th

My mother has informed me that our wedding cake is going to be mocha with a hazelnut filling covered in yellow frosting and white sugar flowers. Hazelnuts and mocha.

I hope our guests enjoy eating our wedding cake, since we can't without me swelling like a blowfish and Stephen passing out from excruciating cranial pain.

june 7th

While I'm thrilled to be on a first-name basis with my UPS delivery person, receiving these wedding gifts is beginning to raise all sorts of unexpected feelings in me. Guilt, annoyance, resentment, shame . . .

After all, a lot of people made big sacrifices to send us such nice things. Not everyone's rolling in it like Mandy and Jon. And I don't want our marriage to nickel and dime those I love. Lucy actually sent us the serving platter from our dish set. That cost fifty dollars, and she's on a fixed income!

Then there are our parents' friends, people we've never

met. Complete strangers at our wedding for forty bucks a head. So is it any surprise that I get annoyed when they send cheap gifts like a set of dish towels? Of course not. But after getting annoyed I begin to feel ashamed. Ashamed for judging the worthiness of complete strangers solely on the monetary value of their gifts. That's *really* gross.

But not as bad as the fools who send us gifts that weren't on our registry. How smug are people who decide they know what you want better than you do? Especially if they've never met you. It's one thing if someone happens to know your taste. But the complete stranger who sends you a hand-carved clock shaped like a cow that moos on the hour? These things aren't cheap. Nor are they returnable. I hate that.

Then you're faced with the decision of whether to keep a gift you hate just in case the person who gave it to you happens to come to your house. Who's got that kind of storage space? Forget it. Stephen and I have already decided that if we don't like it, we're exchanging it for something we need. And if we can't exchange it we're giving it to charity. Let the less fortunate listen to that damn mooing cow.

But of course I'll be sending everyone a thank-you note regardless of what they give us. And I do mean "I," because Stephen's chicken scrawl is so illegible people often mistake it for Arabic. It's long and laborious, this process of writing thank-you notes. I've already written thirty-eight, which means I've had to devise thirty-eight different ways to say thank you and still sound sincere. But that's all right, because I really am thankful.

Dear Jerry and Mimi,

We greatly apreciate the bowl you sent us for our wedding. Seldom have I seen so many brilliant colors on a single object. What an original selection. It will be beautiful on our coffee table.

Warmest regards,
Amy and Stephen

❁   ❁   ❁

Dear Nancy,

We greatly apreciate the mosaic bowl you sent us for our wedding. It reminds me so much of the Roman antiquities I adore. What an original selection. It will be beautiful on our coffee table.

Warmest regards,
Amy and Stephen

❁   ❁   ❁

Dear Katrina,

How thoughtful you were to send us a wedding present. We greatly apreciate the copper bowl. While both modern and colonial, it will make a lovely centerpiece for our coffee table. What an original selection.

Sincerely,
Amy and Stephen

june 8th

I'm going to kill Bianca Sheppard! It took me two months to find "Sweet Sugar Kisses"—a song that's regal, moving, and romantic without being hackneyed like "Here Comes the Bride." And Bianca stole it! I'm certain I mentioned it to her when we spoke about wedding cakes in April. I mean, *please*. What are the chances of someone you know using an obscure B-side jazz instrumental as their processional music? Now all those people who come to my wedding who also went to Bianca's will think Stephen and I stole it from her. It was ours, dammit! It was ours!!!

june 9th

Sure I've got seven decorative bowls, five saucers, two teacups, an iron, a blender, and an Aboriginal death mask, but I still don't have wedding shoes!

june 10th

I picked up my dress from Katrina today. She said she felt badly about taking my money since the dress is still just "okay." Nice. Real nice. That's my WEDDING DRESS you're talking about, lady!

But considering the speed with which she pocketed my check, she couldn't have felt that bad. At least it fits well. And while it may not be perfect, it certainly is unique.

That's got to count for something, right?

Nicole stopped by my apartment while I was trying it on. She was on her way to some dance club with Pablo and wanted to borrow the bustier that she so mercilessly

 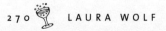

mocked four years ago. It seems that Pablo's turned June Cleaver into a city-loving club rat. It beats Mr. Coffee.

She took one look at my dress and shook her head. "You're actually going to wear that?"

"Yes, I'm going to wear it. It was Mom's."

Nicole lit a cigarette as she riffled through my closet. "I know. She begged me to wear it when I got married, but I refused. I can't believe you said yes."

Excuse me — WHAT?!

My mother offered this dress to Nicole *first*? What about sentimental gestures? And our big, emotional moment?!

I am the world's biggest sucker, with the world's ugliest wedding dress.

❋   ❋   ❋

Dear Suzy,

We greatly apreciate the framed reproduction of Poussin's *Rape of the Sabine Women* that you gave us for our wedding. I am always amazed by how vividly the Baroque painters were able to capture the pain and misery of the human condition. Thank you so much for thinking of us.

Warmest regards,
Amy and Stephen

❋   ❋   ❋

Dear Mr. Lindstrom,

We greatly apreciate the set of salad and dessert plates you gave us for our wedding. They will undoubtedly enhance our dining experience for years to come.

We look forward to meeting you at the reception, as my mother-in-law speaks very highly of you.

Warmest regards,
Amy and Stephen

❖   ❖   ❖

Dear Anita,

Stephen greatly apreciates the year's supply of edible underwear that you gave us for our wedding. He's always been a fan of dessert.

Love,
Amy

june 11th

I just got our wedding gift from Mandy and Jon. It's an orange enamel stock pot, and I just know it's a reject from their wedding. It's not from our registry, it's not their taste, and it's certainly not ours. Mandy knows we registered for stainless steel. It's in a nondescript box without any store name, so I can't return it or check to see that they actually bought it.

The thing just screams *RE-GIFT, RE-GIFT, RE-GIFT!*

It'd be one thing if they couldn't afford to buy us a gift, but they're the most affluent friends we have. And to think Stephen and I spent all that money on their damn fluted crystal vase. I feel like I should mail a thank-you note to the *original* sender.

june 12th

After two hours of deliberation the jury has found in Stephen's favor. They are awarding him $100 for each of his thirty-six stitches. That's $3,600! I almost wish he'd had forty!

Who knew Stephen cracking his head on the ground was a stroke of such luck!

This is a godsend. We need this money *so* badly. And to think, we owe it all to Larry. And the best part is that since he agreed to represent Stephen for free—as a wedding present to us—we actually owe him nothing!!!

june 13th

As soon as I'm back from my honeymoon, assuming I survive this wedding, I'm suing *Beautiful Bride* for everything they've got. Seventy-five percent acceptance rate, my ass! We've got 115 people coming! That's 95.8333 percent! There goes that "extra" money from Stephen's lawsuit.

So much for solvency.

june 14th

Having been actively involved in the wedding planning process for a mere twelve days, Stephen has officially begun to worry—the rehearsal dinner, Misty's relatives, his tuxedo, his brother Tom's refusal to wear a tuxedo, Larry's prospective toast, the cake . . . blah, blah, blah. Amateur.

Meanwhile a stray cat crossed the sidewalk in front of me today. I was fairly certain that it was dark brown, but it *could* have been black. I'm not usually the finger-crossing, salt-tossing type of superstitious person, but it's EIGHT days before one of the biggest events of my life. Not to mention the fact that the proofs for my "Faces" issue are due tomorrow. So who could blame me for chasing the cat down the block, across the street, through an alley, and into a Dumpster just to make absolutely positively certain that it was dark brown?

june 15th

Lucy's doctors are concerned that travel will exacerbate her circulatory problems.

She can't come to the wedding.

I've been crying all day. What's the point of having a wedding if Lucy can't be there to share it with me? It's been her unfaltering support that has gotten me through these past few months.

My 115-person wedding suddenly feels very lonely.

june 16th

Anita called and invited me to dinner at Snap Dragon—a Chinese restaurant in SoHo. I assumed she wanted to apologize for callously refusing to buy my hair comb. But Snap Dragon's carnival atmosphere of music and booze hardly suited my mood. After all, hair combs, wedding dresses, and obnoxious Tom were meaningless in the face of Lucy's absence. But Anita insisted and I reluctantly agreed.

Thank goodness, because it turned out to be my wedding shower. Anita-style! Snap Dragon's back room was filled with my girlfriends—Mandy, Paula, Kathy, Jenny, Suzy . . . even Nicole was there. And for the next four hours we ate, drank, laughed, reminisced, yelled at the top of our lungs, stood on tables, and made a total spectacle of ourselves.

It was one of the most incredible evenings of my entire life.

Here were all of my girlfriends joyfully celebrating not only my wedding but our years of friendship. Humorous stories were shared. Humiliating tales were told. And then there were the gifts: lingerie, sex toys, a *Dustbuster*? Paula gave me a salon gift certificate for two. Nicole returned a doll she'd spent our entire childhood denying she'd stolen. And Anita, forever impressed with Gram's moxie, gave me a book, *How to Make a Jewish Home*.

Later in the evening, as a man dressed like a firefighter strutted across tabletops stripping down to a leather G-string, Mandy quietly whispered in my ear, "By the way, have your sex dreams stopped?"

"Yeah, pretty much."

Mandy smiled. "That's good to hear." Pouring herself another glass of wine, she absently looked around the room. "So what did you do? Use a book? A shrink?"

"No, the dreams just stopped on their own. Why?"

"No reason."

Mandy never says anything for no reason. And I was acutely aware that she was changing the topic when she asked if I'd purchased wedding shoes. But I told her my humiliating fat feet/Manfield Blossom story anyway. She just shook her head. "You really don't want to find wedding shoes."

Is she kidding?! "Of course I do. I'm getting married in *six* days."

"Exactly. And if you find wedding shoes you'll have

nothing left to worry about *except* the fact that you're getting married in six days. Those shoes are just a scapegoat for your wedding anxiety. Trust me. I did it too. Except my scapegoat was those damn Holland tulips."

But before I could marvel at my own powers of deception, Nicole sat down next to me and lit a cigarette. "Hey, sorry to interrupt, but I've got a favor to ask. Since Chet's obviously not coming to the wedding, I'd like to bring Pablo."

Great. "First off, smoking's bad for your health. Second, don't you think it's a bit premature to be inviting Pablo to family events? Mom and Dad are going to be really upset."

"True, but it's your wedding, so they can't make a scene."

That's what she thinks. But how could I say no? After all, if she's willing to celebrate my wedding as her own marriage falls apart, the least I could do is allow her a date.

june 17th

As a politically correct gesture Stephen came to my apartment after his bachelor party last night. At three in the morning he stumbled in, drunk out of his mind, slurring his words, and stinking of cigars.

Oh, yeah. He was wearing a Viking helmet.

It was hysterical. After professing his love and slobbering all over me, he passed out partially clothed.

I took some Polaroids for posterity.

As soon as I got to work I called Mandy to compare notes. Had Jon also returned home wearing a Viking helmet? Mandy didn't know. She'd been in the shower when Jon returned home at 7 *A.M.* "What do you think they did until seven in the morning?"

I don't even want to know. "Played some pool. Ate breakfast." Yeah, right.

june 18th—1:35 A.M.

I've shredded my "Things To Do" list. I now understand that *Beautiful Bride* and Prudence, with her flawless skin and million-dollar dress, are agents of the devil. Who else would promote the following:

#47. Make table-seating charts
If my guests can find their cars in the mall parking lot, then they'll have no trouble finding an empty chair in my parents' backyard.

#52. Decide on staff-guest ratio
How's 1 to 115? Rest assured that my guests have all been to the salad bar at Wendy's. They'll be able to serve themselves just fine.

And my personal favorite:

#58. Hire limo for church-reception transport
Limousines and the Thomas family. It's like cooking truffles with Pam. How ridiculous.

Face it. My "Things To Do" list is simple: find shoes.

june 18th

Anita called to confirm the plans for my rehearsal dinner.

ANITA

Oh, there's one more thing. It's not a big deal, but I
think I should mention it.

I thought she was going to harass me some more about the
hair comb. But I was wrong.

ANITA

In the thank-you note you sent me, you misspelled
the word "appreciate."

ME

What are you talking about?
A-p-r-e-c-i-a-t-e.

ANITA

No, it's a double "p."

ME

Are you certain? I mean, like you absolutely verified
it with a dictionary AND a secondary source?

ANITA

Yes, Merriam-Webster's and my higher-than-
average IQ. But don't sweat it. Just spell it correctly
in the rest of your thank-you notes.

What "rest" of my thank-you notes? I've already sent out
seventy-six with the line "We greatly apreciate your gift. . . ."
Every one of our wedding guests must think I'm a complete
moron!

ME

Are you certain that one "p" isn't some alternate
British spelling?

june 19th

I used Paula's gift certificate and went to the salon after work. I'm sure she assumed that I'd take Mandy with me, but I took my mother instead. After getting a haircut and a massage, we had our toenails painted matching shades of red.

This was the first time since we started to plan this wedding that my mother and I spent quiet time together. For the last ten months our meetings had been consumed with hysterical family members and the crazed minutiae of a "Things To Do" list.

But here we were, three days from the wedding, still breathing. It was a miracle. A miracle my mother had worked incredibly hard to bring to fruition. Without her, I might have had a decent wedding dress, but I probably wouldn't have had a wedding. Terry Thomas had delivered with flying colors for her firstborn. Sure, she did it without the fanfare and emotional fervor I had hoped for, but as I was finally beginning to realize, that didn't diminish her sincerity.

So as our toenails dried a heartfelt shade of red, I told my mother how much I loved her, then thanked her for all her help.

Reclining in her pedicure chair, aglow with post-massage bliss, my mother put her hand over mine. "I know you think Nicole is some sort of family favorite. But it's not true. My guarded enthusiasm for your wedding had everything to do with how much I love you. When your sister first decided to get married, I was thrilled. I felt it was the natural conclusion to what had already been a long and happy relationship. And because of that I threw all my energy into her wedding, never once stopping to consider if it was a sound idea. Then as time passed and I saw how her marriage was evolving, I began to reconsider. I began to wonder if it had been a mistake. It had nothing to do with Chet. I've always felt that Chet is an extremely decent human being. It's just that they were so young, and they'd really never dated anyone else. And since I never took the time to think about these issues before they wed, I've spent the last five years praying that they'd done the right thing. Except now that they're divorcing, I know they didn't. And I can't help but blame myself. Yes, it was Nicole's decision, but I'm the mother. I should have taken better care of my baby. Because that's what mothers do. And that's why I was cautious about your marriage. It wasn't because I'm indifferent to you. It's because I love you."

Me too, Mom. I love you too.

june 20th

After trying on every white shoe in the city of New York, I returned to the Kenneth Cole store two blocks from my house and bought the same white satin sling-backs I tried on ten months ago. They're simple, they're classic, and they're affordable. If only I'd bought them ten months ago, I could have saved myself a ton of anxiety. But Mandy's probably right. If I hadn't agonized over my shoes I would have found something else to agonize about.

One thing's for sure—I'm NEVER taking them off.

TO: Backstabbing Barry
FROM: Amy Thomas-Stewart
MESSAGE: Kiss my ass!

I was *magnificent* at the advertisers meeting. Featuring statements peppered with salacious details—the performance artist who delights in nudity, the reclusive novelist with the mysterious past—I eloquently discussed our ten profiles and held everyone's attention from start to finish.

That's right, fellas, throw your advertising dollars our way, because this issue's gonna sell out!

And when the meeting was over Mr. Spaulding personally presented me with a wedding present from the magazine: a crystal picture frame from Tiffany's. I was speechless and touched.[47] I almost felt sorry that I'd decided not to invite any of my coworkers to the wedding.

Racing to catch my train upstate, my arms filled with a change of clothes, shoes, and makeup, I felt like I was floating. I'd impressed the advertisers, pleased my boss, received a picture frame, and in less than twenty-four hours would be marrying a wonderful guy.

But before leaving the office I called Human Resources and specifically requested that Fabrizio, the Sondheim fanatic and Barry's least favorite temp, be hired on a permanent basis. I considered it a wedding gift to myself.

Because I'd been unable to take the day off from work, the church rehearsal for my wedding took place without me. It seems that Gram magnanimously stood in for the

---

47 Actually, I was speechless and touched and mindful of the fact that it would require a trip to Tiffany's in order to exchange. It's really too fancy for us, and besides, we could REALLY use the cash.

bride. Analysis anyone? But according to Nicole the event took place without a hitch—except for Tom bickering with Mitch and Larry about which one of them was the Best Man. Tom's insistence that blood relations came before friends was countered with the announcement that Stephen didn't even like Tom. My mother finally solved the dilemma with a round of "I'm Thinking of a Number." Larry won. I'm certain it was rigged.

The rehearsal dinner was held at the Mayflower Grill. Only a thirty-minute drive from my parents' house, no one in my family had ever been there. Romantic and cozy, the restaurant was filled with heavy brocades. Mrs. Stewart herself had been the design consultant. And while the menu featured traditional American food, I sincerely doubt that the Pilgrims ever paid $7.50 for an à la carte order of yams.

The entire wedding party and both our immediate families were at the dinner. That included April, Stephen's videographer cousin, who although still dressed exclusively in black had painted her fingernails blue for the occasion. And to my surprise, Gram was also in attendance. Clearly unwilling to miss a good meal, she commanded court from a distant corner, where it was reported she was nursing a sudden bronchial infection. Every toast mysteriously provoked a round of wheezing, followed by a meek apology for the interruption.

I know everyone raved about the meal but I can't remember what I ate. In fact, I was so consumed with excitement that I barely noticed the little things. Like the fact that someone had foolishly placed Mrs. Stewart within smacking distance of Misty, and that Jon complained about the wine being too dry.[48] The entire evening just seemed magi-

---

[48] Proving once again that Jon is undeniably a horse's ass.

cal. Even my mother's toast, which started with "We never thought Amy was the marrying kind . . ." and ended with "She was just waiting for the right man to come along."

Amen.

Stephen and I stayed side by side for the entire evening. I think seeing our families assembled like this, with our wedding party present and the clock ticking down, really drove home the fact that by tomorrow afternoon we'd be married. That the months of preparation, anxiety, fights, and excitement were all coming together. Not next month. Not next week. But tomorrow afternoon—despite the fact that our photographer never managed to see our site or check the lighting conditions. But it was too late to worry. We both knew that whatever was going to happen would happen. There was nothing we could do except hold each other's hand.

This is the last night I'll go to sleep a single woman. And before climbing into the bottom bunk of my childhood bed, I called Lucy and told her how much I love her.

july 5th

South Carolina was fabulous. Beaches, sun, and absolutely nothing to worry about. We woke up when we wanted, ate where we wanted, and wore what we wanted. Pure pleasure and love.

Which is the way it should be. Actually, it's the way the wedding should have been too. But it wasn't—exactly.

The night before the wedding a huge storm appeared from nowhere at 2 A.M. Despite our pricey tent, the 12 tables, 115 chairs, 3 serving stations, and the dance floor all went flying. All the work that my family, my bridesmaids, and Jeb had done that afternoon was lost. And to make matters worse, the wind was accompanied by rain, so everything that was originally white became black and muddy. My parents and I dragged everything inside,[49] then watched in disbelief as the beige living room carpet, which had been shampooed the week before, turned a foul shade of gray.

Annoyed with the mess and her hysterical bride-to-be daughter, my mom chose that moment to scold my father for not getting a haircut for the wedding. She ranted about how he looked like a hillbilly who'd been raised in the woods.[50] And though my father protested that he'd been too busy retiling the downstairs bathroom to get to the barber, my mother would have none of it. At 3:26 A.M. she was cutting his hair with the kitchen shears as he sat on the closed toilet seat in his pajamas and a raincoat. By 3:30 A.M. he'd gone from a middle-aged hillbilly to a Cub Scout. An angry Cub Scout.

Unable to stand another moment, I went to bed. This wedding had gone from my hands to my mother's and now into fate's. If the rain didn't stop there was no way to fit a band, the dance floor, a buffet dinner, and 115 people inside my parents 1800-square-foot house. Needless to say, I cried myself to sleep.

I woke up the next morning comforted by the sight of my childhood bedroom. Sure, it's been converted into a den with a La-Z-Boy chair and a color television, but my bunk bed remains, as does my Shaun Cassidy poster on the wall. For a moment I imagined putting on my clogs and overalls and running to catch the school bus outside Jamie

---

[49] Gram conveniently slept through the entire ordeal.
[50] Which was an exaggeration. He looked more like a middle-aged hippie in search of a Byrds concert.

Mitchell's house. Then it occurred to me that the light coming through the window was *sun*.

I jumped up and looked outside. The chairs, dance floor, and serving stations had all been cleaned and restored. The tables were covered in linens and bud vases. Beautiful paper lanterns gracefully dangled from the trees. And some guys in low-riding jeans were bent over assembling a stage for the band. It was my wedding day. I looked in the mirror and smiled. Then noticed my first gray hair—a reminder of what a long, hard road it had been.[51]

Mandy arrived a few minutes later with a light breakfast in hand. I opted to skip the meal. For the first time in my life I was indifferent to food. Besides, Mandy's foot was tapping. We had less than ten minutes to get to the hairdresser's, where we'd meet Anita and Nicole. Then the four of us would return to the house, change our clothes, and head over to the church to meet my family, Reverend Mackenzie, the guests, and, God willing, Stephen. Mandy had the whole thing planned out. She even borrowed her father's brand-new Mercedes for the occasion—an "S Class."

Since my town's not known for its upscale salons, my bridesmaids and I had to settle for appointments at *Glamorous Lady*, a local beauty shop that's been coiffing my mother's locks for the last fifteen years. And since she still has hair, I figured, how bad could they be? Besides, we're simple women. No high-voltage electrical appliances would be required for our appointments.

Unfortunately, "glamorous" is a subjective term.

An hour later I was seated under a thermal-nuclear dryer hood, bearing the load of fifty-six rollers, struggling to comprehend how my beautician, Abigail, could possibly

---

[51] Not one to dwell, I yanked it out immediately. From the root.

think a case full of curlers would in any way replicate the Gwyneth Paltrow hairstyle depicted in the magazine clipping I'd given her.

Meanwhile, Nicole, who'd resigned herself to looking like Annette Funicello in *Beach Blanket Bingo*, was desperately shielding herself from the geriatric assistant who was bombing her with Aqua Net. To her credit, Anita refused to allow anyone to touch her. After washing, towel-drying, and brushing her own hair, she used the remaining time to sniff my dryer hood for signs of singeing. And Mandy, who was supervising her beautician with an iron fist, finally lost her cool when the frustrated beautician resorted to subterfuge and tried to secretly slather Mandy's up-do with a floral-scented mousse. I'm not sure who slapped whom first.

Having officially destroyed my mother's long-standing relationship with the Glamorous Lady salon, my bridal party and I raced home. Nicole looked like she was wearing a helmet, Mandy smelled like cheap hand soap, and I, fifty-six curlers later, could have done dinner theater as Shirley Temple. Anita just shook her head and said, "I told you so" as she desperately pulled a wet comb through my curls.

According to Mandy's schedule we had exactly fifty-five minutes to make me look like a bride, then an hour to get to the church. After a frantic search for an AWOL shoe, Nicole steamed my wedding dress, Anita pinned yellow roses in my hair, and Mandy did my makeup: "Daytime Elegant, for the subtle yet photogenic effect." I then proceeded to rip three pairs of pantyhose without ever getting them above my knees.[52] With one eye on the clock and the

---

[52] God bless the veritable bridal emergency kit that Mandy had loaded into the trunk of her father's car. Although I'm still not sure what that double-stick tape was for.

other on our last pair of hose, a frustrated Mandy sat me on her lap and *put my pantyhose on for me.*

By one o'clock three stunning bridesmaids and one not-so-shabby rodeo bride were speeding toward the church in a borrowed Mercedes.

By 1:05 I was physically ill.

According to Anita, I looked washed out. According to Nicole, I looked like death. Nice. As Mandy casually cited nerves and stepped on the gas, beads of perspiration clustered in my cleavage and I began to shake. It occurred to me that I hadn't eaten all day.

Mandy was hysterical. "How could you not eat? I brought you breakfast! It was perfectly balanced for protein, carbohydrates, and fat!"

Anita clutched her head. "Would you just shut up and find some food."

"She's getting married in less than an hour. Where am I supposed to go? Arby's?!"

Just then Nicole's Girl Scout survival skills kicked in. "Look! There's a 7-Eleven on the next corner." They don't give proficiency badges to just anyone.

Too panicked to argue, Mandy floored her father's Mercedes into the 7-Eleven parking lot. As Anita bolted from the car Mandy yelled after her, "Only white food! There's no way I'm letting her stain that horrible dress. Now hurry up!"

Without looking back, Anita flipped Mandy the bird and raced into the store. Through the plate-glass window we watched customers stare with incredulity as the woman in stiletto heels and a sleeveless, ankle-length dress made of Asian nubby silk in an elegant cherub pink with a hint of silver sped past the porn aisle and rounded the Slurpee dispenser.

Minutes later Anita returned to the car with a bag of

popcorn, vanilla ice cream, and a loaf of Wonder bread. The Wonder bread was on the house—a wedding gift from the day manager, Rajit. Ravenously stuffing popcorn into my mouth, I began to feel my shakes disappeared and my color returned. Mandy flipped the key in the ignition. We had less than twenty minutes to make the thirty-minute trip to the church. There was only one problem. The car wouldn't start. Mr. Alexander's $90,000 S Class engine was dead.

Mandy banged on the steering wheel. "I'm going to sue those bastards at Mercedes-Benz! Then I'm going to kill the guy who sold this piece of junk to my father. And I'm going to shoot his mechanic and . . ."

As Mandy planned her hit list Anita ran to the pay phone to call a cab. Nicole looked at me, knowing full well that our town has three taxicabs, only one of which worked on Saturday. "Jeez, you'd think this wedding was cursed or something."

Nice. Real nice.

The clock was ticking. My wedding was starting in less than twenty minutes, and I was stuck in a 7-Eleven parking lot with popcorn kernels wedged in my gums and vanilla ice cream melting on my dress. It was a disaster too large to comprehend. After an agonizing year spent planning my wedding, could it really end like this?

Was this what the wedding-shoe search, the venue hunt, the Barry fights, the Kate debacle, the band crisis, the Louise scare, the dress disaster, the invitation rush, the pastor pursuit, and the near-collapse of my relationship with Stephen had all been for?

And just as I began to lose my mind, HE appeared.

Like a knight in shining armor, Rajit—7-Eleven Day Manager Supreme—stood at my window with a look of

genuine concern on his face. "Are you having trouble with the car?"

It was all Mandy needed. "Those bastards at Mercedes stuck us with a lemon and—"

Rajit calmly raised his hand. "I understand. If you want, I will leave the stock boy in charge and give you a ride to your church. My car is parked in back."

We were never so happy to see a 1987 Mazda Miata in our lives. As my three stunning bridesmaids wedged themselves into the nonexistent backseat, I sat alongside Rajit as he broke speed limits through four towns to arrive at United Presbyterian Church in record time. We were eight minutes late for the ceremony.

While my mother frantically accosted me, and my bridesmaids dragged our bags into the church, I begged Rajit to come in for the ceremony. But he refused. Someone had to mind the frankfurter wheel. And before you could say "Big Gulp to go," he was gone.

Seconds later I was hustled into the church foyer, bombarded with mood-altering substances—a Valium from Mandy and a shot of Jagermeister from Anita. Already anesthetized by euphoria and fear, I refused both. So Nicole took them. Then off I went with something old (my mother's dress), something new (my shoes), something borrowed (Mandy's ruby earrings), and something blue (Lucy's barrette). I felt like I was dreaming. Even my horrible dress didn't seem so horrible anymore.[53] And the yellow roses that Anita pinned in my hair looked beautiful. Probably better than that comb would have, since truth be told, it really was a toddler's tiara. But I'll never admit that to Anita. Or Mrs. Cho. How *embarrassing*.

---

[53] Although I suppose the final verdict won't be in until I see the wedding photos.

As I moved down the aisle, flanked on either side by my parents,[54] the members of Diggity Dog treated us to a moving interpretation of "Greensleeves."

And from there on it's a blur.

I remember that instead of a tuxedo Tom was wearing a blue sharkskin suit,[55] that my parents were crying,[56] that Gram had positioned herself at the center of the front pew, and that some skinny guy was running around taking photos of me. It was our infamous photographer whom we'd never met.

Before you knew it I was telling Reverend MacKenzie that "I do" and Stephen was flashing his beautiful tilted smile while slipping a wedding band onto my sticky vanilla ice-cream finger.

At the reception Diggity Dog played everything from classical music to funk. And upon the bride's request they played a kick-ass version of "Brick House."

While our guests enjoyed themselves Stephen and I spent most of the afternoon shaking our guests' hands and thanking people for coming. Yes, it was overwhelming, but it did give us a chance to meet Pablo, who was surprisingly nice—and nothing like Chet. He's witty, gregarious, and four years younger than Nicole. He's also generous. We're getting free HBO as our wedding gift.

We also got to meet our photographer, finally. Thankfully he was festively attired, professional, and sober. Al-

---

[54] It seemed right that we should take this walk together. For while it may be a tradition for fathers to walk their daughters down the aisle, it's a reality that the majority of mothers spend every moment prior to that day worrying about report cards, doing laundry, and breaking their backs to ensure that their daughters grow up with common sense.

[55] Which actually made it easy for us to tell the photographer which guy *not* to take any photos of.

[56] Not just because Nicole invited Pablo.

though he did take his photos with an abundance of urgency, as if he were dodging a sniper's bullets.

As for the food, our chicken buffet was delicious and the cake was divine. Or so I'm told. Stoned out of his mind, Jeb had three slices.

I think Mitch and Larry were also stoned, or maybe just drunk, because after striking out with all the single women in their twenties they hit on April, who despite her Goth attitude and quasifeminist beliefs found them fascinating. Ah, to be nineteen again. Maybe she was the one who was drunk. Needless to say, Larry and Mitch are prominently featured throughout our wedding video, as is the classic moment of Anita hip-checking Stephen's sister, Kim, across the dance floor.

Apparently there were several classic moments I wasn't aware of. Gram discovering Reverend MacKenzie peeing behind my parents' garage, someone slipping a glass of New York chardonnay into Chuffy's water bowl, and my former boss, Suzy Parker, the "mad weeper," meeting Hans Lindstrom. According to Mrs. Stewart, they've been dating ever since.

And Mrs. Stewart didn't do too poorly herself. She danced for hours, exchanged family anecdotes with my parents, and by the end of the reception had agreed to go on a singles' cruise with my cousin Lydia. Love was in the air.

But when the time came for my bouquet toss, it was the Repeat Offender herself, the current Mrs. Bianca Carson, who caught it. You should have seen the look of horror on Mr. Carson's face. That's when I knew it was time to call it a night.

Stephen and I piled into Pablo's car with Nicole and headed for our bridal room at a local bed-and-breakfast. Imagine our surprise when Pablo drove past the B & B and got on the highway. It turned out that Mr. Stewart had booked us a suite at a luxury mountain resort located twenty miles away. It was an incredibly magnanimous gesture—and it was all Misty's idea. Who knew?

The next afternoon we were on a plane to South Carolina for much-needed rest. Days on the beach. And nights under a cloudless sky that extended forever.

We also took a moment to write a few postcards:

A Note of Thanks—to Rajit, who abandoned his convenience-store duties to help a total stranger in her hour of need.

A Note of Apology—to Kate, who endured far more than she should have, and who, after witnessing countless scenes of wedding hysteria, has enough blackmail material to ruin me.[57]

And finally . . .

A Note of Reconciliation—to Gram, who despite her recent antics is still the only relative I have who reads *Round-Up*.

Before returning home, Stephen and I took a few extra days and went to Wisconsin to surprise Lucy. She was so shocked that she started to cry. Then I started to cry. And when Stephen began to well up with tears, despite the fact that he'd never met her, we all started to laugh. Although there was no way to re-create our Grand America adventure from twenty years earlier, we did ride the Ferris wheel at the local state fair.

And now we're home. I can't wait to get back to work on my "Faces" issue. I've got all sorts of ideas for the layout. But the BEST news is that Barry has quit his job at *Round-Up*. He's become the stage manager for a regional tour of

---

[57] A gift of two Backstreet Boys concert tickets, along with backstage passes (courtesy of a connection at *Teen Flair* magazine), to follow.

Sondheim's *A Little Night Music*—starring Fabrizio! Apparently, in my absence the two got better acquainted, and during walks in the park and drinks at the bar around the corner had a meeting of the minds. And then some. Their tour leaves for Baltimore in August. Until then they're enjoying the summer at Fabrizio's house in Elizabeth, New Jersey.

Now, *that's* a wedding present.

Speaking of which, I still have tons of thank-you notes to write. People to whom I need to express my a-p-p-r-e-c-i-a-t-i-o-n. I also need to recycle all the packing papers, boxes, and Styrofoam pellets that came with every gift; start looking for our new apartment; check the photographer's proofs; choose our photos; buy photo albums; pay all the wedding bills; return Mandy's earrings; get my wedding dress to the cleaners and have it hermetically sealed for posterity. . . . You never know, maybe the Frontier theme will be cool by the time my kids get married.

As for *Beautiful Bride,* I gave it to Anita, along with a note warning her to take Prudence and all her rules in stride. I never got a chance to read the last twelve chapters, but I figure maybe someday Anita will. I know she says she's not interested in getting married, and that's just fine. But you never know. After all, that's what I used to say.

Yet here I am. A wedding-day survivor.

There are so many emotional moments prior to a wedding. Some are euphoric, some are devastating. Peaks and valleys. Just like the rest of life. But without a doubt I'd say it was worth it. Sure, I thought I could rise above the hysteria and have a hassle-free wedding. Instead I failed. Miserably. But in failing I didn't necessarily lose. In fact, I won—I married someone I truly love.

The funny thing is that although we place so much energy and importance on our wedding day, it isn't the biggest day of our life. The biggest day of your life is every day thereafter. Because it's not the pledge to love someone that matters, but the act of fulfilling that pledge that is most important.

In other words, it's only just begun.